The Cannon Family
James & Esther Cannon
Reese and Rose Cannon (Sandy and Randy)
James "Jay" Cannon, Jr.
Leela and Nicolas Hendrick (Sara)

Joseph and Sabrina Cannon
Dr. Karl and Cassi Rogers (Karlton and Mariah Lewis-Rogers)

Discover the amazing heritage of the Cannon Family as we journey through a typical family...dealing with everyday struggles, problems, love, and unwavering faith.

Pastor Cannon Series
Pastor's Daughter – Leela
Pastor's Daughter II – Cassi
Pastor's Son – Reese
Pastor's Son II - Jay

Pastor's Son II
Jay

Pastor Cannon Series – Vol. 4

Rai Lindsay-Wallace

First Blessed Press print edition published in 2020
Reprinted 2022

Book cover designed by Same Rijn/Knox Designs

Book Edited by Andreaedits4_U

Book Format by baqir3795 (Fiverr)

Photo Credit: Kent Wallace

ISBN: 978-1-7328993-5-3

Printed in the United States of America

Dedication

I dedicated this book, especially to my cousin Terrance F. Cannon. Your recent departure (9/5/21) from earth and entrance into heaven, has left us all with a hole in our hearts, but we rejoice that one day we shall see you again. I know you're laughing in heaven.

I dedicate this fourth book in Pastor Cannon Series to the Cannon Family. Though this book is fiction, the Cannon name is my heritage. My grandparents, Nathaniel and Leila Mae Cannon, taught me a lot about endurance, prayer, faith, love, hope, longsuffering, and the value of family.

To my loving, supportive, affectionate, faithful, greatest man alive – my forever Sweetie Pie, Kent. We just keep getting better and better, together.

To my family – Kent, Maurice, Ashley, Karlton, Grace, Kayla, Lauren, Briana, Mariah, Lamad, and Omari – I love you all beyond words!

To my Lindsay family – all of you – I love you!

To Christopher, Natalya, Aniyah, and Breyona – my adopted family!

Acknowledgment

I first would like to acknowledge: my Papa, Father God; Jesus Christ, my Lord, and Savior; the Holy Spirit, my faithful companion. There is no "me" without "You"! I'll keep on writing as long as You keep on inspiring! Because of YOU, I can put messages of the heart on paper for others to read and find messages of love, hope, forgiveness, and healing.

To my GHH family – all of you – I love you more than I can express. This year has been a trying year. Together, we have fought and won!

To all my family, friends, and reader fans, I dedicate this book to you. You have supported my dream of writing without fail. I appreciate you all and love you even more. Keep praying for me as I pray for you!

Contents

"The righteous perish, and no one takes it to heart; the devout are taken away, and no one understands that the righteous are taken away to be spared from evil. 2 Those who walk uprightly enter into peace; they find rest as they lie in death." (Isaiah 57:1-2).

Prologue

2007

"Nine more months with us, Sgt. James Cannon, Jr.," Lt. John Hoggin said as they walked the area, checking the grounds with other soldiers. "The army is sure going to miss the likes of you. You're an excellent soldier. I am retiring in six months myself, so I understand why you are not reenlisting."

"Yes, twelve years is plenty of time. The war has been brutal, especially this year. After being deported two times already and possibly going a third, I've sort of lost myself and my faith. I need to rediscover my spiritual identity if that makes sense." James, known as Jay to family and friends, stated.

"It does. Sometimes, out here, we not only lose our sense of humanity, but we lose ourselves. I'm looking forward to returning and getting to know my family again. I've been married twenty-five years, and we've been apart so much in the past seven years, I sometimes feel like I'm separated and not married," Lt. John Hoggin nervously chuckled. "I have four children, all married with children. I hardly know my grans. The youngest Joshua, just turning two, doesn't even know me. During short visits, it's like I'm a stranger in my own home. Yes, it's time to retire. I have a lot of catching up to do with my family."

"Yes. After my last visit, Christmastime, I have been homesick. Both my siblings, Reese and Leela, are married with families. I think settling down and possibly starting a family are the missing pieces of the puzzle in my life. Of course, I need to find myself first. I'll be good to nobody with how messed up I am now."

"You messed up?" the Lieutenant laughed. "You're about the sanest person here. Without your faith and you encouraging all the soldiers here, regularly, truly, we would have all lost our minds by now. You've been a blessing to us, Sgt. Cannon, and I, for one, am going to miss your spiritual guidance and encouragement."

"Thanks, Lt. Hoggin. It's my duty to share the Gospel, but lately, I feel like I'm faking it. After all that I have seen and done, I feel like a hypocrite. My faith is shaken. God seems so far off, almost like a distant memory. I can't seem to see or feel Him anymore."

"Unfortunately, I know what you mean," Lt. John sighed heavily.

The two walked in silence, both in deep thought. "Going home will help me rebuild my life, my relationship with the Lord, and with my family."

"I feel the same way. I am looking forward to going home, and…" a piercing sound shattered their surroundings. Random gunfire exploded near the barracks. Dust clouded the scene. Sounds of chaos shattered the silence. Darkness blanketed the atmosphere. Everything happened so fast.

One minute, Jay was talking with his superior, the next, both their lives had halted. Jay checked himself over. Seemingly, there was no repercussion, no blood, no injury, just soreness from hitting the ground. Then, he looked over and saw the Lieutenant, blood spilling through his crisp uniform. He had been shot in the chest area, and his right arm shredded like paper. There was blood everywhere.

Looking around, Jay's stomach churned. "Sweet Jesus, not again! Not the Lieutenant," Jay moaned. He knew without even checking that Lt. John Hoggin was no longer in the land of the living. Another casualty of war!

"Why Lord? Just six more months…six lousy months…and John would be home with his family. Why couldn't You just have spared his life for six more miserable months? Why?"

Jay looked around. Soldiers were now surrounding him, along with the medical profession and a host of superior-ranking officers. Jay was sickened at heart. Another tragedy. Another life is gone too soon—another nail in the coffin of his feeble faith.

Always calm before the storm! Why can't there just be peace in the valley?

I'm in the storm with you. I am in the valley with you. I'm in the darkness with you. I'm in the warzone with you. That's why you're still alive.

But not John.

But you are. No one can tell God what to do or accuse Him of doing evil.

—Well, I'm tired of the storms! Where are You? Have You forgotten about us over here? Have You closed Your eyes while the enemy keeps attacking Your people, Your children? Lieutenant John Hoggin was a believer. I led Him to You. For what? So, he could die over here and go to heaven while his wife waited for his return? Why? Why? Why?

Jay was angry. God had spared his life, but that wasn't enough. Even long after they removed the Lieutenant's lifeless body, all Jay could see was Lt. John's shredded arm and all that blood. His hope of returning home was crushed – just like him.

Chapter 1

2007

"**P**reacher man, why *you* always giving people false hope? Telling them that things are going to get better when we are in the middle of a war. Many have already died, and hope died with them. Still, how many more of us will die or suffer from some horrendous injury? Worst yet, we could be captured by the enemy and tortured to death." Lewis initiated the conversation at the lunch table.

Jay had met Lewis Trevino in his second year in the army. Lewis was not a Believer, but he had a giving and honest heart – a servant heart, like Jay. Lewis was the military clown, always cracking jokes and pulling pranks. Albeit Jay and Lewis were opposite, from two different worlds, there was an instant connection between them. Lewis was real, nothing phony about him. What you see is what you get, and Jay appreciated that about him.

"As long as there is life, there is hope. Rather here on earth or in heaven." Jay smiled, always up for the challenge. Usually, the two friends steered away from religious discussions. Though Lewis didn't believe, Jay faithfully prayed that God would open up the door for him to share Jesus Christ with his friend one day. Perhaps today was the day, even though Jay felt as far from God as he could possibly be. "Death doesn't necessarily mean the end. For some of us, it means a life of unlimited happiness. No pain, no suffering, no dying, and no war."

"That's hocus-pocus. Who knows this for sure? Who knows if there really is a God?"

"I do."

"And how? Don't say that nonsense about faith and stuff. That's just wishful thinking to me."

"My belief in God is based on my faith in His existence." Jay remained steadfast.

"How can you believe in something you can't see?" Lewis shook his head.

"Just like I believe in the air that I breathe. I can't see it, but I know it's there, and I need it to live. Likewise, I need the Lord."

"That's different."

"Not really. You're trying to understand with human reasoning if God exists. So, I'm relating the natural to the spiritual."

"It's kind of hard to believe in a God that supposedly has All-power in His hands, and yet, so many evil things are happening everywhere. Look at what happened to Lt. Hoggin. He was a great man! About to retire and be with his family! He believed in Your God, and Your God couldn't even spare his life!" Though they had seen many deaths, the Lieutenant's tragic demise had rattled everyone's cages. No one felt secure or hopeful that they would make it out of this dreadful war. "Until I see God for myself, then I don't know if He exists. I have to see Him to believe!"

"You sound like Doubting Thomas."

"Who?" The Bible was foreign to Lewis.

"Hold on," swiftly Jay took his NT out of his pocket and began reading John 20:24-29.

"Doubting Thomas understood how crazy all this religion stuff sounds."

"Religion, yes. Jesus, no. It's not about religion, but a relationship. One day, my friend all will see Jesus is real – just like Thomas."

Every knee will bow, and every tongue will confess that Jesus is Lord.

Noticeably, there was an unusual friendship between the soldiers. Though Lewis was a hard nut to crack, for most people, Jay saw Lewis' tender side. Throughout the years, Lewis loosened up to Jay, unmasking his true identity. Although Lewis counted himself as an agnostic, Jay's lifestyle earned him much respect from the *seemingly* complicated soldier. Jay didn't just preach it; he lived it. That is up until lately, being that Jay felt like the biggest phony ever.

One thing Lewis never did was talk about his family. Jay figured he was a loner, estranged from his family for some reason. Lewis never received any mail or packages until Jay asked his mother, Esther, to send a birthday gift to Lewis because he had no one else in his life. Esther and several of the mothers in the church started sending Lewis cards and care packages every other month from that time on. No one knew just how that touched Lewis.

However, three months before being deported to Iraq, Lewis opened up to Jay about his life. It could be because death hovered over them like smoke from an unquenchable inferno. None of them knew whether or not today was going to be their last.

Reservedly, Lewis spoke openly of his harrowing family history and why he enlisted in the army to escape his abusive home after graduating from high school. Growing up, Lewis witnessed his dad regularly physically abusing his mother and other siblings. He was the youngest boy of six siblings, five boys and one girl, the youngest of them all. I know one of my brothers isn't living, not sure about the rest of them.

"My father was a militant. His father was a Vietnam veteran. He became his father, a guiding force for abuse. My father ruled his home with an iron fist and a rod. He didn't believe you were thoroughly punished until he saw some blood or a bruise. My older brothers protected me until I was old enough to fend for myself. All my brothers left home before I graduated, and I haven't heard or seen from any of them. I don't know if they are even alive."

"That's terrible," Jay felt terrible for his friend. For Lewis to share his life story with him, cost the soldier a lot – his pride and privacy, two of which mattered a great deal to Lewis.

"My oldest brother nearly killed my father before he left home. Dad had hit Rodcrick one too many times. Roderick took my dad's rifle and beat him mercilessly. Dad was hospitalized for nearly a month. Roderick was on the run from the police for a year before they caught him. He served four years in jail. While my father was in the hospital, our home was peaceful for the first time in our lives.

It was too short-lived." Lewis exhaled, reflecting before speaking again.

"Most of my brothers have served time in jail. Terrance, a year older than me, went to jail for distributing drugs to a minor. And Frank went to jail for stealing, I think, but he killed himself after serving only a month."

"Military was your escape...from home and jail," Jay surmised.

"Yes. I didn't want to end up like my brothers, who sadly turned out to be just like the vicious father we all hated."

"What about your younger sister?"

"Isabella," Lewis said the name with such passion. "She wasn't punched around and physically beaten like us." The truth hurt as Lewis choked out his response, disturbingly, remembering the horrendous abuse of his baby sister. "Instead, dad molested her. He raped her...his *own* child."

"He was a sick man." Jay had never hated anyone, but if there was a man to hate, at that moment, it was Lewis' father. *Lord, have mercy on his wayward soul.* "Is he still alive?"

"No. My brother Damien shot him with the same rifle Roderick used to beat him with. Damien came home one day and found him...him...you know...with my sister." The memory still was a fresh wound, which hurt gravely. Lewis fought to keep his emotions in submission. The conflict was more brutal than the war itself. "He's still in prison as far as I know."

Jay just shook his head, feeling his friend's inward struggles. "And your mother?"

"Autopsy said heart attack. But dad killed her." Cynically he replied. "Years and years of abuse had taken a toll on her. Plus, when they took Isabella from us – she was never the same."

"Sorry to hear that."

"She was a Christian," he whispered. Jay barely heard the acknowledgment. "She taught us the Bible growing up. After years and years of living in *"hell,"* I couldn't believe in a God who would allow my sweet mother to be abused like that. I couldn't serve a God that allowed a man to torment an innocent woman to death, literally. A God who closed His eyes while Isabella, sweet Isabella, was being molested by her father."

"I know it doesn't make sense to you now, but God cared deeply about your mother and…"

"Stop!" Lewis shouted. "No need to try and convince me that He cared. *Because* He didn't. Actions speak so much louder than any words. His action was to do nothing though He could. Now that's cruel."

Lord, help me show him, You.

"Lewis, man, I just hate that your childhood sucked!"

Lewis chuckled. "Sucked is right!"

"What happened to your sister?"

"I tried to find Isabella but couldn't. Over the years, I just gave up. I'm grateful that she was taken from my family. Maybe she found a better life. That's the one thing I'd like to know before I die. That Isabella is alright."

"You're not about to die!" Jay was concerned about Lewis' increasingly "giving-up" attitude, more so after Lt. Hoggin's death.

"You don't know that," Lewis looked his friend in the eye. "None of us know that."

Jay remained silent. It was futile to argue with the truth. "I'll add Isabella to my prayers."

"Suit yourself." Lewis shrugged. "I just wish I could find out if she's okay and if she's alive and happy. Izzy was such a pretty girl." He reached into his pocket and pulled out the worn-out photograph.

"She was just twelve then." Lewis handed Jay the photo. "We're six years a part. Even then, Isabella looked sad."

"She looks like you, just prettier." Typical, always trying to find the positive in such adverse situations. "She looks like an angel."

"Outwardly," Lewis replied. "Inwardly, ugliness abided, even at a young age. Izzy carried so much anger inside of her. Bitterness for life. She had a halo of melancholy shadowing her every footstep. There was only one thing that made her eyes light up."

Jay was intrigued, "What?"

"Dancing." The memory took Lewis back to a pleasant time in his life. "She was a natural. Her body was so limber that she could bend and flex and move like a swan."

"Sounds like my sister, Leela."

"I wonder if she is still dancing?"

"I know a private investigator back at my home church, Herman. Do you mind if I ask him to do me this personal favor of trying to find her?"

Lewis' eyes seemed hopeful. "I've tried, but perhaps he'll have better luck."

"It's not luck," Jay corrected. "My friend Herman depends on a Higher Power."

"Whatever, man," Lewis slightly smiled, admiring Jay's firm conviction, even if he disagreed with his beliefs. Jay was solid, never wavering or waffling in his faith.

Only if Lewis could see Jay's heart. Jay's faith had been tossing like the sea, up and down, to and *fro* – doubleminded.

Nevertheless, a door had opened for Jay to help his friend, not just find his sister, but hopefully find Jesus Christ.

"Hey Herman," Jay called his old friend. "I have a potential client for you."

"Who?"

"Me."

"What now? What is missing now?" Herman laughed. "It's not another lost puppy mission, is it?"

"Not this time," Jay chuckled. "It's a girl…lady," Jay went on to explain, filling in as much of the blanks as possible, based on the sketchy information Lewis had shared with him previously.

"Sounds like a challenge," Herman loved a challenge. That's why he got into the investigating business in the first place. After being a cop for seven years, dissatisfaction with the job fueled his desire to make a difference. Herman realized that there was more to just arresting folks and putting them behind bars. He wanted to help the victims, help people find criminals, lost children, cheating spouses, etc. Anything to bring peace to a person's heart. "So, is it pro bono, or are you paying me for my hard labor?"

"I'm paying. How much?"

"I'll send you a bill," Herman replied. "What about this war business? Are you fighting on the front line?"

"War is all around us, friend. It's a trying time right now, Herman. Keep us all lifted in prayer. So many innocent people are losing their lives."

"I know you can't say much, but man…is it worth it? We're fighting for this foreign country when our nation is in a mess. Just don't make sense."

"Just keep praying. Regardless, we're at war, and it doesn't look like it's going to end anytime soon."

"Your dad says your time in the army is about up. I know you're glad about that."

"Yes, I am. Until then, I'll have to do what the government requires of me. God will protect me. Besides, everyone is fighting in some fashion or another. Maybe not on the front lines, but we're all in this war together and feeling the casualties just the same."

Herman remained silent momentarily. "Life is hard, but our God is still good."

"All the time. Thanks for helping with finding Isabella. I believe that this is the link needed to bring my friend Lewis back to Christ."

"Always the rescuer."

"It's my greatest duty," Jay responded with pride. "I'll be waiting for your call. This means a lot to my friend…a great deal."

"I'll make this a priority. In the meantime, look for my bill in the mail," Herman teased. "There may be a war going on, but momma still got to eat."

"How is Fran? I don't know how she's put up with you this long."

"My wife knows she's got a good thing."

"Take care."

"You stay safe." Herman was suddenly serious. "We are all praying for you."

"Thanks. God bless you and your family." Jay closed his out-of-date flip phone, his mind suddenly reflecting on the war. Many of the soldiers he had counseled were already fighting, and many had already lost their lives. For the past year, Jay had been given the duty of relaying the news to loved ones whose son, daughter, wife, or husband had been a casualty of war. This was sometimes harder than the war itself. The only advantage, Jay usually could visit home for a few days.

Chapter 2

"It's time," Lewis grimly looked to his friend, "Our number is up. We're gearing up to fight again."

Jay nodded, dreading the inevitable. This wasn't his first time, but Jay was hopeful that this would be his last – not unto death, but an end to his military assignment. Several of his military buddies were right dead smack in the middle of the fighting.

"Are you scared?" Lewis inquired.

"No. Maybe apprehensive, but not afraid. What about you?"

"I *ain't gonna* lie, man. I'm shaking in my boots. We don't have a clue about what's *gonna* happen. Look at all the soldiers who have died before us. Gone just like that!" Lewis snapped his fingers. "I'm not ready to die. I have a whole lot of living to do."

Nope, you're not ready to die. Not until you know Jesus. "That is where we differ. I've lived a good life, and if I die while fighting in this war, I know I'll have a better life in eternity. That's why I don't fear."

"No sermon, Preacher Man! Not today. I can't bear another damnation sermon."

"That's not me, brother, and you know it. I only speak of love and life."

"Have you called home yet?" Intentionally, Lewis changed the subject.

"Yes. My parents are shaken a bit, but we prayed." His mom Esther cried, while his dad encouraged Jay through affirmations in the Bible and prayer. By the time Jay hung up the phone, his faith was somewhat renewed, and he had inner peace. "My life is in God's hands."

"Well, I guess, I'm on my own," Lewis shrugged. "No family to call."

I wish Herman would find out something before we head out. "We still got about a month. A lot could happen between then and now.

"Since your time of serving is almost up, you probably won't have to go fight at all."

"Lieutenant said I'm going." Jay hesitated. "Lewis, you're not on your own. You *got* me."

"That I do!" Lewis patted Jay on the back.

"We have a week off, why don't you come home with me for a visit with my parents."

"I'll think on it." Usually, that meant no. Lewis was a loner and didn't like being around many people, especially other people's families. It only magnified his messed-up, lonely life. He would have to witness firsthand all the things, the love, and attention he had missed out on with his dysfunctional family.

"I hope you'll come. Mom wants to meet you."

"I'll think on it," Lewis repeated. "Let's go grab a bite to eat. I'm starving."

That was Lewis' way of closing the chapter on the subject. "I could use a bite to eat myself." Jay dropped the conversation.

"I found her," Herman called later that night.

"Praise Jesus!" he repeatedly shouted. "I knew you would. Where is she?"

"You're not going to believe this. Isabella lives in Williamsburg County, forty-five miles from here."

"What?!" Jay sat down. "You're kidding, right?"

"No, man. Isabella is a waitress at a bar."

Jay could tell his friend was holding back. "What else?"

"She's lived a rough life, man. She…she…looks like a street girl. She has pink hair, piercings everywhere, black lips and eyes, gothic looking. She's a mess. Drug addict, I'm sure."

"My goodness." Jay wasn't prepared for this. He didn't know how he was going to tell Lewis about his sister. "Are you sure it's the same girl?"

"Isabella Arielle Trevino," Herman opened the file. "She's been in several foster homes and been arrested for drugs, stealing, and petty crimes. It looks like she even lived on the streets for a while. She stays in and out of this home in an awful area with about four other people, from what I can tell. They all look like druggies."

"Wow!" Jay ran his fingers through his military haircut out of habit.

"I have the address. Didn't you say you were coming home? I could arrange a meeting."

"I'm not sure what to do now. I guess I owe it to my friend to tell him about her. We both are being sent to fight. Maybe he could help her before he leaves."

"So, I take it you're bringing him home with you." Herman chortled. "Bringing home another lost puppy…only this isn't a puppy…but he's lost just the same, right?"

"Just the same," his voice was melancholy. "I was hoping this reunion with his sister would be the key to his heart softening. Now, I'm not so sure."

"You never know." Herman surmised. "God works in amazing ways. Who knows what He's up to? All we need to do now is trust Him with Lewis and Isabella. He'll do the rest."

"You're right. Thanks, Herman. You're the best! Can you send information via email? Hopefully, I can retrieve them. The service isn't so good here. Did you get a picture?"

"Several pictures of her and some of her friends—the place she works and where she lives. They are not so pretty, my friend."

"Just send them to me."

"Sure thing. Give me your email address again."

Jay relayed the information to him. "Oh, by the way, when will I get the bill for your services."

"This one is on the house," Herman spoke earnestly. "I have a feeling that God orchestrated this, and I like planting seeds on good soil. I'll wait on the harvest for this payment. Keep in touch, friend."

"Certainly. Bless you." Jay hung up the phone and dropped to his knees. Though lately, it felt like his prayers had been bouncing on the wall like a rubber ball. Not able to perforate the throne room of God, Jay knew that the only thing that would help in this situation was prayer. A door to Lewis' heart, albeit it was made of a fortified steel frame, was there. However, it wasn't going to be easy to penetrate or pry open.

God, touch Lewis' heart. Soften it. I'm putting this situation in Your hands.

Cast your cares on Me.

"Hey man," Lewis greeted Jay at the door the next day. Lewis had stayed out the previous night. "What's up. I was just about to go drinking with some of the guys. I would have asked you to join us, but I know this religion thing would only interfere with our fun."

"It's not religion. It's Jesus!" Jay modified. "Can we talk a minute?"

"Sure. The guys will wait."

After sitting down, Jay handed his friend the folder containing information about his sister. Previously, he had printed what Herman had sent him.

"What's this?" Lewis was suspicious.

"I found your sister?"

"Really?" His voice rang with hope. "I can't believe it!" Fleetly, Lewis opened the folder. "I just can't…" his words caught in his throat as he began reading the file and held up a picture of his sister. Lewis was floored.

Jay watched his friend closely. Usually, his facial expressions were blank and unemotional, but suddenly it was as if the rock-solid wall had cracked. One teardrop seeped through his eyelid, but Lewis refused to let another fall. Lewis wouldn't cry— Never! His dad trained him and his siblings not to cry, not to show weakness. However, inwardly his soul wept. Lewis' worst nightmare had come true. Again, he glanced at the photo of his long-lost sister. Lewis didn't recognize her. Isabella was a stranger, hiding behind a mask of pain. Darkness was everywhere, in her eyes, in her countenance – darkness and emptiness.

"It's worse than I could have imagined," Lewis finally spoke. "How could this be?" Lewis looked to his friend for answers. "How?"

"I'm sorry." Jay pitied his friend. "I don't know, but at least you've found her. Maybe you can help her."

"How? I'm about to go to a war I don't want to fight in. I may never see her."

"If you go home with me, you can. Your sister lives forty-five minutes from my hometown. You have to try. Isabella needs you, and you need her."

"She was in six foster homes. A foster parent molested her. She ran away at least three times and was homeless. Look at her!" he handed Jay the picture. "She's a freak. My beautiful sister is a freak!"

Jay stared at the picture for the first time. Remembering the photo of her at the age of twelve, which Lewis carried in his wallet, the resemblance was like night and day. Isabella had grown up *hard* and fast. Though she appeared much older, Isabella was only twenty-two. She still had a young soul. However, life had aged her outwardly. Jay beheld pain in her eyes in the close-up photo, similar to his friend Lewis' eyes.

"I guess you're coming home with me," Jay stated.

"I guess so," Lewis rubbed his eyes. "I *got* to see Izzy before combat."

"I'll make the arrangements."

Chapter 3

Sitting around the family table with his parents, Jay realized just how much he missed family time with those he loved. Looking over at his friend, he could see how uncomfortable Lewis was with all this display of genuine love at the table. He just wasn't used to feeling so wanted and accepted.

Lewis spoke very little, speaking only when asked a question, and he kept his head lowered, avoiding eye contact. Pastor James discerned immediately that Lewis was a troubled soul; thus, he silently prayed for him. All Jay's mother, Esther, wanted to do was smother him with her love, as if Lewis was her *own* hurting child. She felt his need for nurturing and pampering. Esther wanted her love to spill over into every dry place in his heart. Several times, Esther reached over and squeezed Lewis' hand and gave him one of her warmest, sweetest smiles. Only, Lewis felt too uneasy about receiving her sweetness. All of this attention unnerved him.

Jay would have to spend as much quality time with his family before deployment while keeping Lewis company. Every night since they had come home, he and Lewis had ventured to the bar where Isabella had worked. Regrettably, Isabella wasn't there. The boss said she didn't call or anything. "It's not like Bell," the boss nicknamed her, "she's one of the ones I can count on." Lewis hated the name Bell, the pet name his father had given to Isabella.

On the third day home, Jay drove Lewis to the address Herman gave them every day, but she was never there. The street address was that of an abandoned shack. The place was unlivable, the roof half off, the place boarded up, and patched up. The government should have condemned it. No one should ever have to live like that. Lewis was sick to his stomach at the thought of his baby sister living in such a *dump*.

Lewis was discouraged. Jay felt helpless to help his friend. On the fourth day of their visit, Jay and Lewis went back to the bar. Lewis had several alcoholic drinks before Jay cautioned him to stop.

"Leave me alone!" Lewis shouted. "I'm a grown man!"

"We didn't come here to drink, but you're wasted!" Jay remained calm. "What if your sister walks in?"

"So what? She's used to people like me," his words slurred. "Now, you, on the other hand, would probably scare her away. Look at you! Dressed in a suit in a bar like you're going to a church service." Lewis scoffed, the liquor speaking through him. "You need to loosen up!"

"And you need to quiet down," Jay said through clenched teeth. "People are staring."

"*Let'em* stare!" Lewis shouted louder. "I don't care! I'm about to be killed in this war. That's right. *Me* and my partner are being deported soon! You'll probably never see our faces again!"

"Be quiet!" Jay grabbed his friend's arm. "You're embarrassing me."

"And you're getting on my…" Lewis stopped, caught off guard as he looked over Jay's shoulder. There she was, a ghost from his past entered the barroom doors. "Izzy!" Lewis called her by her nickname. "Izzy!"

She looked at him with disbelief. Isabella stood frozen as he called her again. She hadn't heard that name in years. She couldn't get her legs to move toward the man, who looked exactly like her brother Lewis. *It is Lewis! Oh my goodness! It can't be!*

Lewis covered the distance between his sister and himself in seconds. "Oh, Izzy!" he hugged her close to his chest. Time couldn't erase the love Lewis felt at that moment for his sister. Distance hadn't. Nothing could. Isabella meant everything to him.

"I can't believe it's you, Lewis." Her eyes misted, leaving footprints of black streaks from her heavy eyeliner. "How did you find me?"

"Long story." Lewis looked her over, from the top of her head to the sole of her feet. His sister looked like a hot mess. There was no other way to see it. She looked like a prostitute, wearing black skintight pants, a red strapless, see-through tank top, and a red polka-dot bandanna tied around her pink and blue matted hair. She had an atrocious amount of makeup, charcoal-lined eyes, and black lips. Yes, a gothic mess!

"What happened to you?" Lewis couldn't help but ask. The photograph, which the private investigator gave them, hadn't prepared him for the Isabella that stood before him.

"Life." Isabella shrugged her shoulders.

"Come sit down. Let me introduce you to my best friend." Lewis literally pulled his sister over to the table where Jay sat earnestly watching the both of them.

"I'd rather not." Suddenly, Isabella felt wary. One thing for sure, she didn't trust men! Not to mention her brother, who had gone AWOL ten years ago.

"Oh, come on. Jay won't bite. He's a harmless mouse." Lewis chuckled. "Oh, it's so good to see you, Izzy! So good!"

Isabella sat between the two men. The room was dark, Jay couldn't get a good look at her. However, it was evident that Isabella wasn't too happy to be in his company. She looked like a scared rabbit about to hop right on out, at the first chance.

Lewis talked nonstop. He constantly rattled on and on when he was happy. Albeit, he was somewhat intoxicated, seeing his sister had sobered Lewis up a bit.

"We have so much to catch up on in two days."

"Two days." Isabella was unhappily surprised.

"Yeah, we have to go back Sunday."

"Go back where?"

"To Iraq!" Lewis yelled. "Bloody war!"

"But...but...we've..."

"I know," Lewis held her hand affectionately. "We've just found each other."

Jay sensed their longing hearts. The siblings needed each other like they needed air. There was a deep bond of which distance and time couldn't separate…even after all these years.

"Lewis, I noticed a hotel not too far from here. How about I take you two there. It will give you both a chance to catch up on things and talk all night, and the next two days if you like." Jay recommended.

"Sounds good to me." Lewis was grateful for his friend. No matter how bad he treated Jay or what he said to Jay, he knew his friend had his back and vice-versa.

"What *you* think, Izzy? You got time for your, brother?"

"Yes," she lowered her eyes, trying not to cry in front of this strange man who made her nervous. Everything was hitting her at once. Seeing Lewis brought happiness, but it was overwhelming. She fretted over reconnecting with her brother, who would be leaving in two days… maybe forever this time.

"Oh, I forgot, my friends!" Isabella turned around to see where they were, but they were nowhere to be found.

"They left." Jay spoke, "Shortly after you sat down."

"Oh," Isabella was surprised and hurt. She didn't know why they left, but she felt she wouldn't be seeing them anytime soon, which worried her. She didn't know where she'd sleep after her brother left. Since the authorities boarded up her rundown home, Isabella had been sleeping from pillar to post and even in abandoned cars.

"Don't worry, Izzy," Lewis knew his sister, even after all this time. When she worried, she always bit her lip, which she was presently gnawing on. "I'm here now."

Isabella smiled, then nervously glanced over at Jay. Something about him stirred unusual feelings within.

"But you'll have to excuse me for a moment," Lewis suddenly felt sick. "Got to go to the men's room. I'll be right back. Look after her," Lewis ordered his friend.

"I won't let her out of my sight," Jay grinned.

"You better not!" Lewis shoved his friend and trotted off.

"He's so happy he found you," Jay cut through the tension. "I haven't seen him this happy since – ever!"

Isabella lowered her head and said nothing, still biting her lip. She didn't trust this stranger.

"So, you work here?"

"Sometimes."

"It seems to be a lively place."

She said nothing.

"Would you like something to drink?" Jay detected her uneasiness. "I could get you something."

"A Pepsi," she answered, looking up at him momentarily. In an instant, their eyes locked. Jay detected something familiar in her eyes. It was the same look he saw in Lewis' eyes – fear, mistrust, and loneliness.

Jay was drawn to her large green eyes…like he was drawn to Lewis the first time he saw him. He felt as if he had been hypnotized and couldn't think for himself.

"A Pepsi," she repeated nervously. *Are his eyes really yellowish? How strange, and yet so…so magnetic. Hush! He's in a different league. Look at the way he's dressed. Weird. Square.*

"Oh…I'm sorry," Jay stammered badly. He sought the waiter, getting her attention to come over.

"Hi Bell," the waiter recognized her fellow worker. "It's good to see you again. When are you coming back?"

"I don't know." Shamefaced, Isabella looked away.

"*Sho'* miss *ya gal*," the waiter smacked her lips. "Customers have *been* asking about you. You know the streets ain't no good for you!"

"I know," sheepishly, Isabella smiled.

After receiving the two Pepsis, Jay was relieved when he saw his friend walking toward them. Being near Isabella made Jay slightly comfortable, which he couldn't understand why. Isabella had rattled him. Why was this peculiar woman affecting him?

Isabella reminded him of a lost, sickly puppy. One that he had rescued many times when he volunteered with the fire department before joining the army. Jay had rescued countless helpless puppies from either a fire – from going into a sewage drain – escaping a car, and sadly, from abuse. Isabella was so lost, sickly, and hurting. Deep down, Jay wanted to rescue her and to save her, just like her brother. Still, Jay couldn't understand why she was pulling on his heartstrings so, but she was, and Isabella didn't even know it.

As he watched the interaction between the siblings, Jay thought of his own – Reese and Leela. They meant so much to him. Yes, they had their rivalry moments growing up, but Jay would give his right arm to help them in any way. Jay couldn't imagine his life without either of them. Yes, he understood the brotherly bond that Lewis felt for Isabella.

Lewis saw his sister through the lens of love. Looking beyond all the gothic makeup, outlandish clothing, pink and blue hair, and those awful black *cat* eyes and black lips, Lewis beheld such sadness. Underneath the camouflage, somewhere in there, Lewis saw the little sister he had left behind, and he loved her.

Later, checking into the hotel, Lewis walked Jay to the car while Isabella took a shower.

"She is pitiful, man! I can't believe that's my *Lil sis*! Lewis sighed. "She probably hadn't showered in days…weeks! "

"She needs you," Jay put his hand on his friend's shoulder and eyed him, "more than ever."

"I don't know what to do for her."

"Just love her," quickly Jay answered. "Love may not erase all the bad stuff, but it's the best cure for a broken heart."

"Sure, hope so," Lewis mumbled, "because I got enough love for the both of us."

"Good."

"I guess I'll see you Sunday."

"I'll pick you up around five. Call me if you need anything before then. They're plenty of restaurants around here and a shopping mall within walking distance. You may want to buy her some clothes. Do you need any money?"

"No, I'm fine." Suddenly, Lewis was in deep thought. "I wonder where she's staying or if she'll have a place to stay when I leave?"

"From the looks of it, probably not. And did you see how quick her friends, or whatever they were, just left your sister? She seemed worried."

"I can probably pay for a month for her to stay here and then send Izzy some money."

"Take it slow. Isabella may not want to stay here. Remember, she's been on her own. It may be hard for her to let someone else take care of her."

"Yeah! We *got* a lot of talking to do." Lewis appeared lighter, less weighted down since coming to Lincoln. "But I'm sure glad I found her. I owe you a lot, Jay." He turned away, endeavoring to compose himself. "I'm sorry for the harsh words earlier...you know I didn't' mean it."

"Not even worth mentioning." Jay earnestly replied.

"I guess...*your*...*your* God...gets the credit for this lost and found case."

"Yes. Although He used my friend Herman to find Isabella, it is God who gets all the glory."

"I'll have to thank Him, personally." Lewis winked, then walked away.

"Praise You, Jesus!" Jay whispered. "Miracles happen every day!"

Chapter 4

In the interim, Jay spent most of the following two days with his parents. It was so good to be home. They lavished him with so much attention. Yet, he wondered about his father. He looked so tired and so old. Had he really aged that much since the last time Jay saw him?

Jay asked his mother if his father had been overworking in the church and her only response was, "Of course. You know your daddy. His door is opened to all. He never stops. He's always running to and *fro* like a chicken with its head cut off. Visiting the shut-in, going to the hospital, elderly homes, and last week we had two funerals."

"Dad is not as young as he used to be. He needs to slow down. Share some of the responsibilities with his assistant pastor or ministerial staff," Jay cautioned.

"Slow down!" Esther laughed. "Not possible. James can't sit still for one moment."

"He looks so tired, Mom," Jay repeated worriedly. "When is the last time he had a physical checkup?"

"I'm not sure," Esther thought hard. "I'll have to make one for him. He's probably overdue for sure. *Shoot*, we both are!"

The conversation was dropped. Jay occupied most of the afternoon at the church with his father. The two prayed together, discussed Sunday's sermon, and shared a nice father-son lunch. It was just like old times.

"You seem better," James stated. "I was concerned about you during Christmas. You looked as if you had lost your joy."

"It's been rough, Dad, I'll admit. I'm trying to find my way back…back to believing again."

"Never stop believing, Jay! No matter how bad it gets. No matter how many bad things you have seen and experienced, you must be steadfast, immovable, always abounding in the work of the Lord, knowing that your labor…what you're doing for the Kingdom is not in vain. God has and never will forsake you, son. Remember, His ways are higher than our ways. His thoughts are higher than our thoughts. Therefore, we have to trust that He has our best interest at heart, no matter what it looks like, no matter what it feels like, and no matter what it seems like," James paused, then quoted a familiar passage in Job. "Shall we indeed accept good from God, and shall we not accept adversity? We're going to go through bad times, as well as good. It shouldn't stop us from believing."

"I know you're right, Dad. Just keep praying for me."

"Always, son." James knew now that he would have to pray even more.

That evening Jay went out with Janice, his old girlfriend. The twosome dated in high school and a little before he joined the army. Jay and Janice were crowned prom king and prom queen their senior year. Everyone expected them to marry, including their parents. However, at the age of nineteen, Jay joined the army. Subtly, he broke it off with Janice. He didn't think it was fair for Janice to wait for him, especially when he wasn't ready for marriage, and she was. Secondly, Jay always felt that something had been missing between them.

Nevertheless, Janice remained single. During Jay's brief visits home, Janice gladly made herself available to him. She was internally hoping that Jay would rekindle their relationship. Everybody in the church knew that Janice was saving herself for Jay – everybody but Jay. That's why Janice wrote him faithfully and sent care packages to Jay for twelve years.

After going to the movies, Jay and Janice enjoyed a quiet dinner at a local restaurant. Familiar faces surrounded them. People kept coming over, glad to see the two of them still together. Surely, tongues would be wagging when Jay left town.

"I forgot what it was like to be home," Jay grinned. "Small towns with big gossipers. Everybody knows everybody, and everybody tells everything!"

"Yes. The minute you got off the plane, everybody knew you were home." Janice giggled. "You're a celebrity here."

"Fame by association. I'm the son of the infamous Pastor James Cannon," Jay replied without any emotion one way or the other. "My dad is the true *celebrity*."

"You all are." Janice corrected. "The Cannon name is so well known and respected here."

"Okay, enough about the Cannons. How are you doing, Janice? You're beautiful as ever," Jay sincerely complimented. That was one thing that drew Jay to Janice, her flawless natural beauty. She was perfect, sometimes too perfect. Yet, it was her sincere faith that moved Jay to ask her to be his girl when he was just seventeen years of age.

Her face turned three shades red. "Thank you, Jay. You're still so thoughtful." Janice looked intensely at him, wanting him to know she was so happy to be in his presence.

Jay read more in her eyes than he cared to acknowledge. "Still working at National Bank?" He cleared his throat nervously.

"Yes. I've been promoted as a Manager," she informed proudly.

"That's wonderful! You deserve it. You've always been such a hard worker. Are you still directing the adult choir?"

"Absolutely." Janice had been the choir director for the last three years. "The choir has grown so. We now have three different adult choirs."

"Dad said the membership of Word Alive Fellowship has nearly doubled in the last two years."

"It's true." Janice took a sip of her soda.

An awkward silence followed. "Who is the lucky fellow? Mom said you were seeing someone."

"Nothing serious." Flatly, Janice answered, hating that his mother had mentioned anything about her love life. "Marty Trapp and I are just friends. You remember, Marty? He graduated with us."

"Swell guy. I've always liked him." Jay eased into the conversation. "I think you two make a lovely couple."

He might as well have stuck a pin in her and sucked out all the life in her. Janice felt hopeless for his affection. It wasn't Marty she wanted. She wanted Jay. After all these years, Janice still loved him.

"I think we make a lovely couple," boldly Janice retorted, treading on thin ice.

Jay was speechless. He couldn't think of one good thing to say at the moment.

"You must know that I have cared for you all these years. I've never stopped caring for you. My letters revealed my affection, didn't they?" Boldly, Janice reached across the table and affectionately caressed his hand. "There has always been something special between us. It's beyond friendship, don't you agree?"

More like sisterly! "Yes…but…"

"Do you remember our first kiss?"

Jay nodded. This wasn't going the way he had hoped it would. Far from it!

"It was in the haunted house at the fair. I was so scared. I started screaming. You tried to make me stop, but I wouldn't. You pulled me, but my legs wouldn't move. I kept crying and screaming, and then you kissed me."

"I couldn't think of anything else to do to shut you up." Jay laughed.

"It worked."

"I guess it did," Jay looked away.

"That was the very night I lost my heart to you," Janice spoke softly. "And I never got it back."

Jay was dumbfounded. All he expected tonight was a friendly movie and dinner with an old friend. Sure, they dated on and off for several years, but nothing serious. At least not on his part. Besides, hadn't she been serious about another guy in church before. *Oh, but he's married!*

"Say something," Janice prodded.

"I don't know what to say," Jay cleared his throat again, running his hand through his stubby hair. "I mean…a lot has changed since we seriously dated. We're not the same people, especially me. I'm a mess. War has messed me up, and I'm about to go again."

"But my feelings are the same. Actually, that's not true. My feelings for you have intensified. Every time you come home, we get together and spend quality time together. When you're away, we write, and we call each other whenever it's possible. Those special things drew me closer to you. We may not say the words, but I'm always thinking about it. I love you, James Cannon," she confessed, "with all of my heart. I'm not getting any younger, and neither are you. I've been putting my life on hold in hopes of you finally realizing how much you care for me. I want to marry and have children. Now that you're going to fight in the war, I figured I have to be honest with you. If you feel nothing more for me than friendship…then Jay…I can't keep seeing you…not like this…not anymore. I love you too much for just friendship."

"But…I didn't ask you to wait on me. I made it perfectly clear not to wait on me. My future is uncertain right now. This is not the time to be making significant choices." Jay found his voice again, frustrated that Janice was putting all of this on him now, knowing he'd be deported soon. "As I said, I have changed, Janice. I'm not the same guy you knew. A lot has happened. I've lost a lot of my friends through the war. I've seen things that have caused my heart to become stony in places. I can't sleep throughout the night without horrible dreams. I just cannot think about a serious relationship. It's not fair to you."

Her eyes watered. "It's not the deployment, Jay. It's me. Just say it, Jay. Be honest." Janice insisted on knowing the truth. "I'm not a baby. I'm a grown woman. I can handle it."

"I need time." Jay gazed at Janice, who was near tears. She was still so beautiful. Janice fit the mold of a husband's dreams. She was intelligent, self-confident, and independent. Yet, Janice was humble and always putting others above herself. She loved the Lord and served Him faithfully. But something was missing – Jay didn't love her like a man should love a woman in a committed relationship.

There just isn't any spark! Maybe that's fairytale stuff. But mom and dad have sparks flying all the time, even now. This morning they were kissing in the kitchen and looking all gooey-eyed at the table at one another. There's got to be more.

"How much time?"

"I'm not sure," Jay honestly replied.

"When do you leave for Iraq?"

"Two weeks."

"Then, in two weeks, I expect an answer before you leave."

The rest of the meal was spent in silence. The ride home was quiet as well. Boundaries were crossed, and there was no turning back. One way or the other, Janice had thrown the fishing pole, hoping to catch Jay. Time would tell whether Janice caught the fish of her dreams or came up empty-handed.

Jay walked Janice to her condominium door. "I had a good time, Jay. I'm sorry that I loaded so much on you, but life is too short."

"No problem," he forced a smile. "I'm glad you were honest. I think you are a wonderful woman, Janice. You mean a great deal to me, and…"

Brazenly, Janice silenced him with a kiss. First, the kiss was timid and uncertain. Both were testing the waters. The kiss deepened as Jay willfully kissed her back. He wrapped his arms around her waist as Janice encircled his neck with her arms. It felt sort of right. It had been a while since he had kissed a woman. As a matter of fact, Janice was the last one….and his first one, as well.

It was Janice who pulled away, feeling rather good. She had anticipated kissing Jay for some time now. "Call me before you leave."

"I'm leaving Sunday at 5:00 a.m. You'll still be in sleepy land."

"It doesn't matter," Janice reached up and caressed his cheek. "I'll gladly be awakened by you…anytime."

"Okay." Jay stared at her briefly, searching his heart to find something more. Jay wasn't sure if what he was feeling at the moment was lust or love? Either way, he needed to put space between them for now. "Goodnight, Janice."

"Goodnight, Jay."

Jay drove home, confused as ever. *What in the world! How in the world did all this happen? Janice wants more. She wants marriage. She's sweet I do care for her – but marriage? Love?*

True, everyone was expecting him to marry a hometown girl, specifically Janice. Though Jay never pledged his heart to her, he knew she cared deeply for him. Perhaps, over the years, he had taken advantage of her faithful friendship. Janice was the spitting image of a pastor's wife, like his mother. She worked in the church, giving of herself and time toward the kingdom of God. Jay couldn't shake the fact that something was missing! Or was it just Jay and all the war and stuff he had to deal with? Perhaps the war was clouding his sight to see what was really in front of him – Janice's love.

Chapter 5

On the airplane, Lewis couldn't stop talking about his sister. In two days, he discovered the trauma that Isabella had endured during their ten years of separation. It was even more gruesome than the information Herman had reported in the file.

No wonder Isabella Trevino appeared so hard on the outside and lived such a vicarious, promiscuous lifestyle. She was bitter and broken. Her parents had let her down. Her siblings had let her down. Foster care had let her down. The church had let her down. Life had let her down. Was there any reason to look up?

"She's working at the bar again. It's not a great place to work, but it'll put food on her table. The Boss looks out for her as best he can. I had a long talk with him, letting him know if anything isn't kosher with Izzy for him to call me at any time. At least she'll have a nice room to stay in for a month."

"And then what?"

"I'll pay for another month and another until Izzy can get on her feet."

"What about drugs? Didn't you say she uses?"

"She's not addicted, I don't think. I think Izzy just does it because of the group she hangs out with. I'm not sure. She was mysterious about a lot of things. She figures she's been independent this long, no need for me trying to tell her how to live her life now. I get it."

"I know you want to help your sister, but are you sure she can handle it? Sending her money may not be wise. Will she use it for the hotel or other things…like drugs? I mean, she's been in jail, and she…"

"She's my sister!" Lewis brusquely defended. "I wasn't there to help Izzy before, but I am now. There is no way I'm going to abandon her now! I want her off the streets! She doesn't deserve the lousy hand that has been dealt to her. Izzy deserves better."

Jay understood his friend's motivation. "Maybe my father can help her find a better job. He's got connections. Did she graduate from high school?"

"Yes." Lewis hated leaving his sister behind. He wanted to protect her. "She even went to a trade school for accounting. Izzy has always been good with math. She had to drop out because she couldn't afford it. I encouraged her to go back. I told her I would help pay for it."

"That would be a good start."

"Man, you wouldn't have recognized her without the Halloween face on," Lewis leaned back in the airplane seat, closing his eyes, envisioning his sister. "She was beautiful again. Innocent. Like the Izzy I knew. She was shy, sweet, and funny. She laughed and laughed. It was as if she didn't even recognize her *own* sound of laughter. I could tell it had been a long time since she's truly laughed." Lewis suddenly became quiet. "I hate leaving her behind."

"I know it's hard. Knowing Isabella is alive and for now, taken care of should ease the burden. Plus, you'll keep in touch."

"What if…" The thought nearly choked the life out of him as Lewis' eyes popped open in fright. "What if I don't come back?"

"Don't say that!" Jay demanded. "We're both coming back!"

"I hear you," Lewis wasn't convinced. "She needs me."

"Yes, she does, and you need her," Jay added. "Everything will work out."

"I sure hope so," Lewis closed his eyes again, drifting off into a peaceful sleep with his sister on his mind.

Subconsciously, both thoughts were occupied with people in Lincoln, SC. Lewis dreamed of Isabella, while Jay's thoughts were of Janice and the conversation he had with his father after dropping Janice off.

"If you don't love Janice, son, let her go," Jay's father urged. "Janice has been pining over you too many years already. It's time you stop dipping in and out of her life and decide if you intend on marrying Janice or not. Stop, leading her on."

"Leading her on," Jay felt wrongly accused. "I'm not leading Janice on, Dad. I told her not to wait on me."

"Yes, you told Janice with your lips, but every time you come home, you contact her and spend quality time with her. You sit by her in church. You act like you're in a relationship. You're a grown man, thirty-two to be exact – stop playing games. Someone is bound to get hurt, and I don't want it to be Janice. Esther adores her, and so does Leela. She's a good woman with a great heart. You could do a lot worse, you know."

"I will not be pressured, Dad," frustration crept into his tone. "We're friends. Beyond that, I just don't know!"

"Too friendly for friends, son." Pastor James sat down across the kitchen table from Jay and handed him the platter of homemade cookies. "I'm not pushing you into anything, Jay. But I've seen how Janice desires more. It's the same look I used to see in Nicolas for your sister. Janice loves you. The question is, do you love her?" Pastor James scooted his chair back. "Pray about it, Jay. Pray really hard."

Shaking off the memory, instinctively, Jay envisioned those piercing, frightened eyes of Isabella, which moved him. She was an unusual being. He'd never been acquainted with someone so gothic before. Yet, Jay knew it was all a façade. *I wonder what she looks like without all the black clothes and makeup. Lewis said she was beautiful, but he would say that.* Still, something about Isabella intrigued him. Yes, she had a hard life, and automatically Jay desired to help her – just like he wanted to help all wounded soldiers. Isabella was definitely wounded.

Nevertheless, there was an instant connection between them. *That's all! I want to help Isabella because of Lewis!*

Will I see Isabella again? Does it even matter?

Will she keep the room in the hotel?

After Lewis' deportation, will Isabella go back to the street-life? Go back to living like a harlot?

37

The notion made Jay queasy. He didn't want Isabella to go back to the streets. Yet, what power did he have to stop her? What power did her brother have to change her life? Like a lightbulb coming on, Jay realized one thing. *We have no power. Only God has the power!*

Subsequently, Jay began to pray for God to protect her. To heal her! To deliver her from the streets. To save Isabella, adopting her into His Heavenly family. Fervently, Jay prayed as if it was a matter of life and death. Little did he know, in time, it would be. It was! Decisively, Jay determined to always pray for Isabella. The lady with the pink and blue-matted hair had touched his very soul.

Why can't I think of Janice like this? Why doesn't she touch me in places that have been unmoved for so long?

It is so strange that Isabella has stirred my heart with something familiar – hope!

Chapter 6

The sound of the war cry was deafening. The endless echoes of tremendous destruction alarmed the soldiers. There was no way to drown it out, conceal it, or ignore it. It was fierce and never-ending. Fighting in a war had to be the closest thing to *hell* on earth. It just had to be! It was perpetual torture, causing fear to just sneak up on you and stay there unwanted and unmoved. Innocent bloodshed. Young and old alike, falling by the wayside. Killing for a cause, and yet, wasn't killing sinful? Kill or be killed! Defend your country. However, taking a life was still taking a life. Physically, mentally, and spiritually the war was taking a toll on everyone. It was an all-consuming fire of invisible flames, unseen but felt. Unseen but heard. Unseen, but inhaled. Unseen, but spreading like cancer to every part of the physical body and the nations.

Like gentle lambs being led to the slaughter…all these devoted soldiers, friends, fathers, and army brothers were being led, not knowing what was ahead, doing their patriotic duty to defend and fight for their country. It was an honor and a privilege. However, it was also a sacrifice.

Four months Jay had been in Iraq; it was only supposed to be three for him and then return home. Hopefully, it would be soon. Like the others, Jay felt the oppressive hands of war grip his entire being with dread and, at times, fear. Though he didn't fear death itself, at times, his body trembled with the thought of how he might die. Witnessing the senseless, *torturesome* death of his fellow soldiers wasn't something one could just dismiss or forget.

Cries of panic could be heard everywhere – of terror, not peace. War was horrible! Tragic! No one really wins! Loved ones lose. Families lose. Communities lose. Soldiers lose. The loss of human life is tragic, no matter what side or what country. It affects nameless, countless people. War is incurable, many injuries beyond healing—no remedy for your soul, no magical potion to heal the heart, which had been damaged.

In the middle of wartime, amid the fighting, the truth can appear perverted, and evil reigns. Nevertheless, Jay knew the truth. Truth always reigns! Even in wartime, God had equipped Jay to speak the Word of life to the soldiers that were dying, physically and spiritually. God used him to snatch many from the gates of hell. Though Jay prayed for healing, the soul was frequently healed, while the body returned to the dust from which it came. War, like a roaring lion seeking whom it may devour, unfortunately, found its victims. Jay witnessed many good men die for a cause they believed in. Was he willing to die so that others may live?

Frankly, some days it was hard to believe. Especially on days when Jay saw, firsthand, limbs blown off, heads severely wounded, leaving faces unrecognizable, numerous innocent lives. Innocent children were killed by a car bomb, IED, or gunshots. All of this tested Jay's faith, for sure.

One day seemed like a month and one month seemed like a thousand years. Time held no meaning in war. Through all of it, Jay strived to believe that God had a reason for him being here. A reason for him standing in the gap for so many soldiers, even when his own life was at stake.

"It's tragic," Lewis said one night, as they nestled down to find a little sleep, hopefully. It had been a long day. Two more of their fellow soldiers had died, heroes. "Will this war ever end?"

"It's brutal," Jay agreed.

"I'm sore all over. I'm tired of this!" Lewis complained. He was frustrated. Not just over the war, but more so about his sister. He hadn't heard from her. He'd written to her several times since being in Iraq; she didn't respond. Though mail was slow coming and going, he still should have received something by now. Lewis even had Herman, Jay's friend, look for her again, but seemingly Isabella had disappeared again. "If it weren't for my sister, I'd probably take a bullet to my head and end this mess."

"Don't say that!" Jay sat straight up in his bunk. "You're talking crazy. We're all tired, but we can't give up."

"Why? It's not worth it. All these innocent young boys are dying. Shoot, I'm thirty, and people in their early twenties are dying. It's pointless."

"Still, you can't go around talking like that." Jay snapped. He, too, was frustrated. "I won't have it!"

"What's ailing you?" Lewis was surprised by his friend's outburst.

"You! That's what!" Jay reclined back on the bumpy, hard mattress. "I don't want to lose another friend, especially not my best friend," his tone was laced with emotions. "To something so selfish as suicide."

Lewis closed his eyes, thinking about his friend. Jay was family. He loved Jay. Though he never spoke the words aloud, Lewis loved him. Honestly, he didn't want to lose Jay either. "I feel you, man," he finally stated. "Likewise."

"Isaac was ten feet away from us today when the vehicle drove over an IED and blew up. He was coming to get us. It could...could...have...been us."

"I was thinking the same thing," Lewis confessed painfully. "I don't want to go out like that, Jay. My body parts all over the place. It just doesn't seem right."

"I'm worried about you," Jay melancholy acknowledged.

"Don't! We all *got* to die. I just don't want to die that way."

"That's not why I'm worried," Jay hesitated. "You're a brother to me, Lewis. If we both die tomorrow, I'd want to see you again in heaven. To think that I'd never see you again after this life breaks my heart." Jay's voice cracked with emotion. "I don't fear my death...I fear yours."

Lewis pondered his friend's statement but remained silent.

"You need Jesus, Lewis. If you die right now, you're going to hell. You think this is bad...hell is eternal torture. I'm not trying to scare you to Jesus. I'm just loving you to Him," he paused. "You're looking for peace. The only peace you'll ever find is in

Jesus. Lewis, you've had it hard. You were abused as a kid. You lost your mother tragically. Your sister was abused and molested and now you have no idea where and what Isabella is doing. You're consumed with bitterness and anger, and unforgiveness. But where has all that gotten you? What can you do to help your sister? The only One, who can help Isabella or you, is the Lord. You need Him." Jay's soul pleaded. "You need Jesus."

"I want peace." Lewis felt something strange drawing him this time. Thus, he felt something odd on his face. Lewis reached up and touched his skin. It was wet – wet with tears. Tears of old. Lewis hadn't cried in a long time. Not even when he saw his sister, his eyes moistened, but Lewis held his tears at bay. Now, the water flowed from his soul. The water of pain. The water of regret. The water of hope. There was something powerful about this moment. Lewis felt something more extraordinary tugging at every string of his heart. A Presence of love saturated the atmosphere.

Jay got out of his bed and knelt beside his friend, endeavoring not to awaken the other soldiers. But it was too late. Though the soldiers' eyes were closed, their ears were wide open.

"Kneel with me," Jay whispered.

Willingly, Lewis obliged. Only Lewis wasn't the only one kneeling. Every man in the bunk knelt.

Oh God, I know why You sent me. I'm here as an Ambassador to lead Your children back home to You. I surrender to the call. Use me!

Jay led the men into a simple yet profound prayer of salvation. Each soldier believed from his heart and confessed with their mouths that Jesus was the Son of God and asked Him to come into their hearts. Also, they prayed for His protection and God's divine will to be done in their lives. In a moment, things had changed for them all. Jesus was now the Captain of their Army...their personal Lord and Savior. Directly, they were connected by the precious blood of Jesus. Twenty-five Soldiers now in the True Army of the Lord!

Afterward, Jay began singing *"Amazing Grace"* as the other men joined in. His vocalizing wasn't great, but God's anointing made Jay's voice sound like angels. Peace abided in the atmosphere. Joy filled their hearts. And Love knitted each man together. No matter what…the soldiers would remember this night—a night when Jesus came into their hearts to live forever.

As everyone returned to their beds, Jay lingered by his friend's side.

"I've found peace." Lewis swiftly confessed. "I can't explain it. But no matter what happens to me, I'll be alright. But Jay, you must promise me one thing."

"Anything."

"I want my sister to know this peace. I want Izzy to know **our** God. If something happens to me and you live to tell about it, make sure you look after Isabella. Just like you didn't give up on me, don't give up on her until she knows Jesus." Both of them were shedding silent tears. "Just like you, I don't fear my death…I fear hers. I want to see her again."

"You have my word. I promise." Jay embraced his friend. They held onto each other as if they would never do so again.

"I love you, Jay," Lewis whispered for the first time.

"I love you, Lewis."

Chapter 7

Eight days later, Jay's life came to a temporary standstill. He and Lewis were walking, patrolling their assigned area, near the makeshift hospital. Lewis was still chatting, talking about something he read in the Bible. He was so excited, so zealous about the Word of God. Like a sponge, Lewis was soaking it up, cherishing his newfound relationship with Jesus and His Word.

"Peter was my kind of guy. He got off the boat and walked on water to Jesus while his homies stayed back, wondering who in the world was that walking on water. Peter was bold and daring! Willing to walk on water, getting his feet wet, instead of staying in the boat like the others."

"Yeah, you and Peter are a lot alike." Jay laughed, so glad his friend had come to the knowledge of Jesus. It was so good to see his eyes light up. Sadness shadowed his every move. Today his crystal green eyes told a happy story. Lewis was a changed man.

"Just like when he chopped the man's ear off. He was standing up for Jesus. Peter loved Jesus. He wasn't' going to let just anybody come in and mess with Jesus." Lewis babbled. "That's how I feel, man. As long as I'm living, I'll stand up for Jesus."

"Amen."

"And I'll stand up for you," Lewis was serious. "I'll always have your back, Jay."

"Thanks. And, I'll always have yours."

"I don't know why I waited so long. I've never known such peace. It's amazing! I spent my whole life angry. Mad at the world! Mad at a dead man. What a waste."

"But look at you now!"

"Yeah, look at me," Lewis' smile was broad and genuine. "I'm happy. Right smack in the middle of a war, I'm happy. Who would've thought…" Lewis' words trailed off as he bolted away, like a leopard, running toward…toward…a little girl.

"Get down!" Lewis shouted to the girl, aware of the danger lurking. "Get down!"

Jay looked over and saw snipers aiming their guns at them, but a little girl was innocently caught in the middle.

Where did she come from? Jay was perplexed. *I didn't see her before.*

Everything moved in slow motion at that moment, and yet it was rapid, in real-time. Jay watched as his friend went down, using his body to shield the innocent little foreign girl. Lewis took the bullet, snatching the child's life from death. Then another shot and another. In horror, Jay watched as his friend seemingly lifeless body slumped over the girl.

The sounds of machine guns blasted in Jay's ear. Both sides were fighting, but Jay was numbed. Suddenly, it was a bloody battle. All he wanted to do was get to his friend. Crawling toward Lewis, Jay didn't even think he would make it. Bullets were flying all around him. It was so close. So strong. So real. He heard his heart pound like drums; his lips quivered, and suddenly fear crept into his bones, and his leg trembled, like jelly. Jay cringed like a frightened child between two bullies…death and eternity. It was silent. *Lewis? Lewis?* His mind called, but his mouth was muted.

Lord, why are You silent while the wicked swallow up the righteous? Why do you tolerate their treacherous deeds?

His best friend was a wounded soldier, fallen at the hands of the enemy. No, Lewis wasn't dead! *Thank You, Lord!* Lewis' head slowly turned toward Jay as others crowded the area, running after the snipers.

With all of his strength, Jay fought to get up. He felt wetness dripping down the right side of his face. It was red hot. Blood. His own blood. He'd been shot too. Suddenly, Jay felt it. It was coming from his ear. A head wound, perhaps. And then he tried to lift his arm, but it hurt too badly. His right leg was burning. Somehow, someway, Jay mustered the strength to crawl to his friend, who was hanging onto life by a single thread.

It took some time before Jay's body cooperated with his brain. It seemed like an eternity before Jay reached his friend. Jay knew it was bad, very bad. With the help of another, Jay lifted Lewis from the frightened little girl. Unharmed, she looked with shock at the injured soldier who had saved her life and to Jay, whose amber eyes she had never seen on anyone. Then, she ran away like a terrified animal. She was afraid of everyone!

Jay watched the little girl as she became a distant shadow. His friend had saved her life. Lewis Trevino, a hero! *My best friend is a true hero!*

"Bury me in Lincoln, SC, your hometown," Lewis coughed out his last will and testament.

"Don't you dare die on me, now!" Jay pleaded. "Shhh, save your strength."

"No need," Lewis continued, "I see the light. It's the brightest light!" Lewis' countenance shone like the sun. "The whitest robe you ever want to see."

Tears clouded Jay's vision as he beheld Lewis' transformation. He wasn't in any pain, though he should have been in excruciating pangs.

"Don't forget your promise," Lewis whispered, "Izzy. Tell her about Jesus. Tell her I'm waiting for her."

"I promise," Jay wasn't sure he heard him, tears streaming down his face as his heart broke into about a thousand pieces.

His friend's hand went limp; his soul was ready as Lewis batted his eyes, trying to find the strength to open them again. "Look after Izzy. She's all alone. Don't leave her. Stay with her until she knows the Lord. Then, she will not be alone."

"I promise," Jay repeated with conviction.

"I love you, Jay. God used you to save my life."

"I love you so much." Emotionally Jay was wrought. *This is a Jonathan and David moment*, Jay thought to himself.

"Here," Lewis struggled to retrieve the photo from his pocket and handed it to Jay. The picture when Isabella was just twelve years of age; his last sweet memory of her before she was taken away from him. "Under my bunk is a safety box with legal papers. Combination is my birthday. I don't...don't," he struggled to finish. "Give her the money in my bank account. I left it to you, but please give it to Izzy." Lewis struggled to breathe. "As Jesus said to John, you look after Isabella now. Love her as I love her."

"I will."

"I never thought I'd see angels," Lewis looked up again, and then to his friend, he uttered, "Preach Jay for Jesus. Till we meet again," Lewis uttered his last words.

Jay ached all over, but the fleshly pains could not compare to his broken heart. His body refused to hold him up any longer. Sinking to the ground, Jay groaned like a mortally wounded human. At that very moment, his anger was fierce. Something inside perished. *God, You take, and You take, and You take. When will You give again?* His best friend had gone and left him. Yet, Jay had the blessed assurance that one day they would meet again. However, now Jay couldn't find solace in knowing. He loved Lewis more than any earthly man. He was his authentic friend. Lewis was his brother.

Speedily, Jay discovered the extent of his injuries as he blanked out, bleeding to death. He had lost a lot of blood from the gunshot wounds in his right arm and right thigh. Thankfully, the bullet entered and exited his arm. However, it stayed lodged in his thigh area, in the bone. It was too dangerous to move it. Another bullet was somewhere in his head, from the shot that went through Jay's right ear. At the makeshift hospital, he underwent a grueling surgery. No surgery could save his permanent ear loss. From now on, Jay would be deaf in his right ear. The bullet missed his brain. Another miracle. However, it did cause some injury and hemorrhaging. Jay survived the surgery, though it was touch-and-go a few times. After surgery, Jay was put in an induced coma. The physical injuries would never equate to Jay's internal wounds. Wounds that only the Father could truly see and heal.

Jay stayed at the hospital for two months. Jay hung between death and life. A battle for his soul and spirit and flesh. Partly, Jay yearned to be with Lewis, Lt. John Hoggin, and all the other soldiers who had risked their lives to fight for their country. The Pastor's son was tired, too weary to battle for his life. But he wasn't alone. Jesus was making intercession for him. His parents were standing in the gap for him. Christian soldiers were holding vigil for him. His hometown church had a twenty-four-seven prayer chain going.

Though it was touch-and-go several times, on foreign soil, Jay pulled through. God wasn't through with Jay yet. Though Jay had awakened from his coma, he was still very much dead inside. Jay felt as if he was in *hades*, suffering, and death surrounding him. He could see blood gushing like a dam, bursting all around. He could still hear the howling sounds of screams that one could never forget. Broken bodies were wounded from every place imaginable—dying at all ages. It was horrific—permanent visions engraved in his heart and spirit. Nothing could silence the wretched sounds of war. Nothing could silence the bullet that took his beloved Lewis away from him.

Yet, it was time for Jay to go home!

Before being a civilian, Jay was going home with one last duty to take Lewis home to Lincoln to be officially buried. It was a promise he was grateful to keep. Now, for the other promise. To find Isabella, take care of her, and lead her to Jesus – that was a mountain he wasn't sure he could climb, but for Lewis' sake, Jay would try.

Home! Jay's hand balled into a fist, wanting to strike out at anyone…anything. His heart was paralyzed by tragedy and grief. He had left home a whole man, but Jay was returning, half a man. He was ripped to pieces by this cruel war! Sorrow had taken a foothold in his soul without permission.

Jay had been scarred for life. Witnessing his best friend's brutal death was the last button needed to push Jay into severe depression. He grieved for his friend.

I'm taking you home, Lewis. I'll do everything in my power to find Isabella, Izzy as you call her. It's going to take a miracle. You better be watching out for me. I'm going to need some help convincing her that she needs Jesus. You were a tough nut to crack, but Isabella…I do believe I've got my hands full with her.

Blustery irrational dangers of the enemies tossed like great waves in his mind. Jay felt its stormy rains beat upon his heart, flooding his inner peace, leaving its footprints of turmoil.

Home! I'm not sure that it's really home anymore!

Chapter 8

Upon his arrival home, Jay's mom insisted he go straight to bed. He was still frail. His head felt like a ton of bricks were pressing on it, giving him a perpetual migraine. Plus, with his right ear permanently deaf, his right arm in a sling, and a permanent limp in his right leg, Jay felt crippled all over. He suffered physically, mentally, and mostly spiritually. Jay was grateful for his mother's love, but Esther was hovering way too much. He needed his space and solitude, neither of which she was willing to give him. Understandably, Esther had nearly lost her son to war.

Lewis stayed on his mind. Jay envisioned the scene of his death over and over again. The little girl he protected would never know her hero's name. Reaching over the side of his bed, Jay retrieved Lewis' military dog tags. He wanted to give them to Isabella, but Herman still hadn't located her again. There was so much to do and so little time to do it. Jay felt pressed to keep his promise to Lewis.

James and Esther Cannon made all the arrangements to have a small funeral service for Lewis in three days. With no family and no relatives to contact, it seemed deplorable for such a great soldier not to have numerous people pay their last respects to this unsung hero.

Replacing the dog tags on the nightstand, Jay fumbled in his wallet with one hand to retrieve the photo he retrieved from the safety box Lewis had stored many memories, letters, and information. His eyes were wet with agony. It was a photograph of Lewis and Isabella taken at the hotel. Lewis was smiling so big. He was happy. It was so obvious that he adored his baby sister. Isabella still had on all black, but there was a glimmer of hope in her pale green eyes. Jay was thankful that his friend's latter days were filled with happiness due to his commitment to Christ and reunion with his sister.

Oh, how he loved Lewis. Lewis made Jay become a better Christian. He challenged Jay's beliefs, causing Jay to study more and know Christ more for himself. Though privately, Jay wrestled with his faith, Jay never let it hinder him from sharing the Word with others. No doubt Lewis had impacted Jay's life, and indeed he would miss his friend until the day Jay departed his natural life.

Isabella and Lewis looked a lot alike. Her large crystal green eyes lined with black as her head rested on her brother's shoulder. Her pink hair was somewhat tamed and hung, cleanly straight and long. Their Hispanic features from their mother's side and their African American heritage from the father's side made a lovely artistic combination.

Oh God, help me to find Isabella. Help me to keep my promise to Lewis, finding her and leading her to You. She needs You!

And you need her!

Where did that come from? Jay's forehead crinkled

"Why the frown?" Pastor James entered his son's room.

"Just thinking," Jay looked at his father. "I must find Lewis' sister. She doesn't know he's…he's…"

"Herman will find her," James assured. "How are you feeling? Do you still have a monstrous headache?"

"Yes."

"In the Name of Jesus Christ, I command this tormenting headache to go! Loose him now!" Pastor James laid his hand on the top of Jay's head, speaking with authority. "Be healed and set free now in Jesus' name, amen. What about your right ear?"

"It's there. I just can't hear out of it. *At least* I can still hear out of the left ear."

"God spared your life, son," Pastor James always found the positive to concentrate on. "Surely, it could have been a lot worse."

"Like Lewis," Jay swallowed. There wasn't a minute in the day when he didn't think about Lewis.

"Lewis is home with Jesus. This is not our home. We are all heaven-bound."

I sure would like to join him. Jay felt sorry for himself.

"I'm sure glad you're home." Pastor James slid the chair from the desk over to Jay's bedside and sat. "I'm glad you're out of the military for good, son. This war is terrible on everybody."

"My life has changed, Dad," Jay professed. "I'm not the same man I was before the war. I don't know if I even like myself anymore. The war made me hard, callous, and less sensitive to…life in general." Jay lingered, giving thought to how much he wanted to share with his father. The father and son always had such an open, honest relationship. "I saw terrible things…things that I can't get out of my mind or my heart."

"I can't imagine your pain and what you saw. I can't comprehend going through what you and the other soldiers had to endure. All I know is that God brought you back. He kept you alive for a reason. He was with you then, and He is with you now. You'll have to rediscover yourself and your identity through Jesus Christ. You have to heal here," James put his hand over Jay's chest. "The Lord draws nigh to the brokenhearted and to those whose spirits are crushed. You're brokenhearted and crushed, and God is ever so near you. All you have to do is call Him, and He'll answer." Wisely, Pastor James counseled, perceiving his son's inner struggles.

"One night Dad and an amazing thing happened. A fear like I've never known restrained me tightly as if a noose was around my neck. I was lying in the bunk. I knew death was coming…not for me…but Lewis," Jay inhaled and exhaled several times before going on. "I feared I'd never see him again, and I told him. That night Lewis gave his heart to Christ. But that wasn't the most amazing thing Dad. All the other men in the barrack knelt and asked Jesus to come into their hearts—twenty-five soldiers. Not one man in the barrack wasn't saved. God used me to lead all those men to Him."

"You've been chosen, James Cannon, Jr.," the pastor called him by his given name during serious discussions. "Called while you were in your mother's womb—to impact the lives of others. You're a pastor's son. The one to follow after me."

"Dad, I'm not so sure about that now." Jay shook his head. "God can't use me like this. I'm a mess. My faith has been shattered. I saw too much! Heard too many bitter cries of death and hatred."

"If God can use me, most definitely He can use you." Pastor James pressed his son's hand. "He'll heal your heart. He'll ease the pain of your memories. He'll give you the strength to go on. In the meantime, you rest. Don't worry about anything. Reese is coming over today, and he'll check with Herman to see if there is anything we can do to find Isabella before Friday."

"Lewis mentioned the names of his brothers. I think he had four. One was in prison for killing his father; I think his name was Damien. Another brother's name was Roderick. I can't remember the other two. According to Lewis, they all served time in jail before."

"How sad," James shook his head. "They've all suffered a great deal."

"Maybe Herman can find them as well. I feel I owe it to Lewis. I know one of the brothers committed suicide."

"We'll work on it. Now you rest." James headed for the door. "Oh, Janice called. She'll probably come by tonight. Are you up for it?"

Truthfully, he wasn't, but Jay felt he owed it to her. Still to this day, he hadn't given Janice an answer. So much had happened. Jay knew what he had to do. No need to put it off any longer.

"Yes. I'll see her."

"Good. She's such a sweet lady." Pastor James added his two-cent worth. He was a big fan of their relationship.

Oh, God. I can't think straight. I know what dad wants and what mom wants, but it's not what I want.

Again, Jay glanced at the photo of his friend and sister. Lingering, he stared at Isabella. She fascinated him. Her eyes magnetized him. Jay drifted off to sleep with her on his mind. Isabella invaded his dreams. It had been a long time since he had a peaceful dream...nothing tragic...no bombs, no IEDs, no causalities of war...no death. Just serenity, like soft clouds, Isabella consumed his subconscious.

54

"Oh, Darling!" Janice hurried to Jay's bedside. "Thank God, you're alright. I was so worried about you. I thought that I had lost you forever. Oh, can you hear me?" she fretted. "Is it your left ear or your right ear?

"I can hear you just fine," Jay smiled. "It's my right ear."

"I'm so glad you're home. So glad you're alive. Your mother said your head hurts badly. I'm here to help take care of you. Is there anything I can do?"

"Nah, just prayer."

"I haven't stopped praying," she ran her fingers through his hair. "Your mom told me that bullet fragments shattered in your right leg, and some are still there. It sounds so painful."

"Yes."

"Shot in the ear," she sighed loudly. "You could have been killed. God's grace saved you."

"Yes."

"I just can't imagine," Janice bent over and hugged him. "I just can't imagine."

"I'm alright." Jay felt uncomfortable with her nearness. So many things were left unresolved with them.

"I am sorry about your friend." Janice sat on the side of his bed. "I'm sure it's very hard on you."

"I miss Lewis more than anything. We were so close in such a short time. It was as if I had known him all my life."

"The choir is going to sing at the memorial for him."

"I'm glad. I was hoping Reese would sing '*Amazing Grace.*'

"Oh, that would be lovely," Janice's voice soared. "I love hearing him sing it."

The remembrance of the entire barrack singing '*Amazing Grace*' after the salvation prayer brought tears to Jay's eyes. He could almost hear the sound of triumph in the room, Lewis singing louder than them all. Even off-key, it was the most glorious sound to Jay's ears.

Tenderly, Janice wiped the tears from his eyes, caressing her hands against his face. "I'm here, Jay. Please let me help you through this crisis."

Jay put his hand over hers. "Thanks for being here, Janice. I need…need…"

"Shhhh, " Janice put her finger to his mouth. "I understand. I'm so glad you need me. It feels good to be needed." Janice brushed a soft kiss on his lips. "You rest, and I'll be back tomorrow. Is there anything I can bring you?"

"Chocolate," he grinned. "Any kind will do."

"Chocolate it is!" Janice kissed him again. "I'm so glad you're back for good, Jay. *Now maybe we can pick up from where we left off.*

Chapter 9

Sitting on the front row, a few days later with family and friends, Jay's heart, already broken, crumbled to even more tiny pieces as he listened to his father perform the heartfelt eulogy for Lewis Trevino.

"Psalms 116 declares, **'Precious in the sight of the Lord is the death of His saints.'** Death is painful to us, while precious to the Lord. Why? Because He longs to have His children with Him." James began.

Gratefully, many church veterans came to support the unsung hero, one they had never met but was sure to meet in heaven. Disappointed that none of Lewis' blood relatives were located yet, Jay felt he had let his best friend down.

Herman even left notices, letters, and messages for Isabella, but nothing resulted in his effort. Three of Lewis' brothers were deceased, while the eldest Damien was serving life in prison.

Esther felt her son's inner struggle as she held his hand tightly in hers. Physically, Jay was still hurting, but the mother fretted over Jay's emotional scars. He was so withdrawn and so sad all the time. His once glowing yellowish-brown eyes were now dull with grief and despair.

Succeeding the heartfelt eulogy, in which Pastor James offered hope and encouragement, Reese stood on the platform and sang *'Amazing Grace.'*

The words of the song comforted Jay as he drank the soothing sounds of his brother's anointed voice. With each stroke of the guitar, peace poured into Jay's being. Every note, every chord, every beat of the soft drums in the background ministered a healing balm to Jay's raw soul. Silently, Jay wept unashamedly.

Behind him sat Janice. Affectionately, she leaned forward and pressed her hand against his shoulder. Jay turned to show his appreciation. For a moment, Jay thought he saw someone in the back of the church. He blinked several times to clear his blurred eyesight but sighed when he realized no one was there.

My mind is playing tricks on me. I wish it were Isabella. Oh, how I wish! I tried Lewis; I really did! Jay turned and faced the front again.

Reese returned to his seat, beckoning his brother to get up for remarks. "Do you need help?" Reese recognized that his brother was still physically weak, with a noticeable limp, and obviously, his head was still throbbing.

"I'm fine, Reese," Jay stood. "Excellent job. Lewis would have enjoyed hearing you."

"I believe he did. He's here. Don't ask me how I know it, but I just feel it…here." Reese touched his heart.

"Me too," a fat teardrop descended upon the side of Jay's right eye, where several scars settled. "Thanks."

Jay slowly limped his way to the podium, a place where he once felt comfortable before. Now, he felt awkward. If only his head would stop pounding. *Lord, give me the strength.* Although Jay didn't think he could proceed with giving final remarks to his friend, duty called for it. Looking at the audience, Jay knew he was a blessed man. Though his family barely knew Lewis, they came to support the one they loved. Reese sat with Rose by his side on the front pew and the twins next to her; Leela, Nicolas, and their energetic, year-old daughter, Sara, named after Nicolas' belated mother. Janice and her parents were there. Veterans from the church and countless church members came out to support the Cannon Family. When one hurts, they all hurt.

Once again, Jay caught a glimpse of a shadow standing outside the closed church doors, slightly visible through the glass at the top of the doors. *Could it be?* Jay looked again, but the shadow was gone. Jay cleared his throat and began his remarks.

"Lewis Trevino was and will always be my best friend. He taught me more about friendship, integrity, and honesty in the last seven years than any human I know. When I met Lewis, he had a massive chip on his shoulder. He was angry at the world, and anyone who came in contact with him knew it. Yet, Lewis had this inner confidence that I've only witnessed in one man, and that is my father, Pastor James Cannon. Lewis knew who he was and didn't try to be anyone different.

"Though at first, he wanted nothing to do with what he called "religion" and "religious nuts," somehow we clicked. We connected in an unusual way. I know God brought us together. Sort of like Jonathan and David, in the Bible. We were kindred spirits, intertwined by the hands of God." Jay sniffed, lowering his head for a moment. "Lewis was such a wise man, educated by experience and what he called the *Hard Knock Life*. With all my heart, I miss him, already and I long to see him again. I'm so glad he knew Jesus. I'm so thankful God used me to witness to him our blessed Savior. After his salvation, Lewis was so happy and excited. He cherished his relationship with Jesus Christ. Now, Lewis had a Heavenly Father who was always there for him, a Big Brother Jesus, who prayed for him faithfully, and a Friend in the Holy Spirit, who never let him down. Lewis finally has the perfect family. If Lewis were here now, there is one thing I think he would want me to say to you all, 'Live for Jesus, and He will live for you. Laugh often and love everybody always,'" Jay smiled. "Then he would welcome you into God's big family and say something like this: 'There is always room for one more. Come and join my happy family. Everybody is welcomed.'"

In closing, Jay bowed his hand, then looked up, and saluted his friend in heaven. "Til we meet again!"

The church's gravesite was right around the corner. It began to drizzle, reminding Jay how even death brings about a renewal of life, restoring the grass, plants for food, and replenishing the earth to flourish. Burying his friend was the hardest thing he had ever experienced. Even his wounds couldn't equate. The burial was short and sweet.

Leaving the gravesite in the funeral home's limo, Jay took one last glance, looking behind him, and nearly froze as he thought for sure this time that someone was standing at the grave.

"The service was wonderful," Janice interrupted his focus, slightly turning him to her. "Your remarks were so heartfelt. Lewis would have been proud." If Lewis' death taught him anything, it was to be true to yourself and others around you.

"Thank you." Jay offered a friendly smile. Turning back to the gravesite, he sighed. No one was there. Jay felt that he was leaving a piece of himself behind. He was thankful that Reese rode in the limo with him. He didn't want to be alone with Janice and his parents. Speculation mixed with presumption would leave the town gossiping for days.

Death is never satisfied, only fueled by the fire of grief and sorrow. Truly Jay was grieving, yet it was more than the grief that was pricking his bleeding soul. He had a twofold promise to keep to his friend. One was done, but the other bothered him. How was he going to find Isabella? How would she handle the news that her brother had died and been buried already?

While Jay's family ate and fellowshipped in the dining room with their guests, Jay rested on his bed, lying in darkness, a prisoner suffering in past chains. He had a terrible headache that refused to go away. Even the prescribed medicine didn't dull it. The day's happening was too overwhelming for him.

Oh, if I could just have one more day with Lewis. The tears rolled from his eyes. *One more day.*

Till we meet again, the promise of Lewis came to mind.

"Till we meet again," Jay whispered.

As Jesus said to John, you look after Isabella now. Love her as I love her. Jay remembered Lewis' heartfelt appeal

"I will."

His mind journeyed to Isabella. Her name was melodious. He could only envision how she looked like Lewis described her temporary change without all the 'war paint.' In the photo of the two of them, Isabella was still gothic-looking. Inwardly, Jay wondered if she went back to dressing in her dark, spooky attire. Were her eyes still painted with black charcoal? Is her hair still pink and blue, and wild? Her clothes still the wardrobe of a rock star or worse?

She's so opposite of Janice. Jay pictured the two ladies in the same room. Janice, ten years older than Isabella, was mature and refined. In contrast, Isabella was girlish and earthy. Yet, in the bar, Isabella appeared older than Janice.

I won't let you down, Lewis. I made a promise, and I intend on keeping it. I'll find Isabella, and I'll show her Christ. I promise.

Jay drifted off to sleep.

Chapter 10

month later, Jay was endeavoring to move on with his life.
Still suffering severe headaches and right leg throbbing most
of the day, Jay pressed on, anyhow. No longer bothered by his
hearing loss in the right ear, Jay was just grateful that he could still
hear. As long as someone didn't speak to him from his right side,
Jay could hear clearly.

If only he could go to sleep at night and sleep in peace. In
his dreams, he was taunted by the war. Without permission, the
painful memory of his best friend's death haunted him. The sounds,
the bombs, the gunshots, and even the silence tortured him during
his slumber. Would he ever be able to shake off the horrifying
memories of the war and what it did to him and others?

Jay was working more with his father in the church office,
keeping up with the church records and the ministry's business side.
Although, he knew that his father was endeavoring to ease him back
into ministering subtly. Jay had missed working with his father.
Their times together were precious. The days were filled with silent
worship. Jay learned so much from his father. It wasn't so much
what he said but what he did. Pastor James taught by demonstration;
his life spoke volumes. Doing and not just saying and living out what
he preached—being a doer and not just a hearer. He was an epistle,
known and read by all men.

Pastor James was a man of substance. Jay figured that if he could become half the man his dad was, he'd exceed most men. Jay found himself slightly concerned about his dad. The sixty-one-year-old *legend* appeared rather tired and exhausted at times, nearly out of breath. Pastor James never complained. The telephone rang all day with requests to talk with the pastor, soliciting counseling, prayers, answers, encouragement, and sometimes just a listening ear. Frequently, his doors were open to counsel married couples. Visits to the hospital were made regularly. Every Tuesday and Thursday at eleven, Jay accompanied his father to two local prisons. One for women and the other for men.

James never stopped going. No wonder Pastor James looked tired. HE WAS TIRED! People were draining him mentally, physically, and spiritually. The demands of the church were too much for one man. Though he had four other ministers, Minister Daniel, Evangelist Diane, Youth Minister Nicolas Hendrick, and Minister Thomas, an elderly, and only retired man, who was failing in his health, they were all busy working full-time jobs, supporting their families, and traveling to smaller ministries, in the rural areas where Pastor James had started storefront churches and in-house ministry for people who couldn't travel far.

"You need to slow down, Dad." Jay cautioned one day. "I'm thirty-two, and I'm tired of just following in your footsteps. When was the last time you and mom took a vacation?"

"We're working on it," James answered. "We were going on a cruise to Jamaica, but that's when my brother Joseph had a heart attack last year. You remember?"

"Yes, I do, and I remember momma saying, the doctors ordered Uncle Joseph to start relaxing and taking some time off," Jay spoke with concern. "Seems like you need to do the same."

"Now that you're here, I was thinking of taking Fridays off. So, I wouldn't be here but on Tuesday, Wednesday and Thursday. I could use a break."

"That's a good idea. I think I can handle it. Of course, I know that church folks probably wouldn't want to talk to me, but I'll fill in as best I can."

"You'll be great." James patted his son on the shoulder. "Look how you handled Mother Nelson. She came in here ranting and raving about Sister Faye sitting in her front seat for the past two

Sundays. You calmly explained how bad Sister Faye's eyesight had been and that she couldn't see from the back anymore. Then you suggested, 'Why don't you sit right next to her. She'd appreciate your presence. Besides, what difference does it really matter where we sit, just as long as we're in the House of the Lord. He's everywhere.' It was the way you said it that caused her to leave here smiling."

"Mother Nelson has always been a pistol, but she's got a good heart."

"See, that's what I'm talking about," James recognized his son's humble characteristics. "You always find the good in everyone, even the ones who are pistols."

"I've learned from the best."

"So have I," James pointed upward. "How's your head?"

"Still feeling pressure. Some days are worse than others." Jay was learning to live with the headaches, a reminder of the war he had left behind. "Perhaps this is my thorn," Jay reasoned.

"The devil is a liar! The word says by His stripes you are healed. Therefore, you were healed and will always be healed of migraines and whatever else the enemy tries to give you. You just got to give it back, son! Submit. Resist. And he will flee. Work the word. It works only if you work it. Ponder that."

"I hear you, Dad."

"Doer, not just a hearer. Anyhow enough preaching. When do you go back to the doctor?"

"Next Friday," Jay answered. "But it shouldn't take long, and your secretary will be here if an emergency comes up. I still want you to take Fridays off."

"Next Friday, I can't. I have a lot to do. Several appointments I've already scheduled and intend on keeping." It was settled, Pastor James would be there Friday. "We'll see about the next week. Right now, I have a few things to look over before going home."

Jay was thankful that his parents' home was within walking distance. He hadn't bought a car yet but planned on looking around very soon. "I'll walk home."

"I don't think that's a good idea, with your head hurting and your leg still in pain. Let's go. I can do this another time." Pastor James locked up his drawer and grabbed his keys. Once again settled, they were both going home in Pastor James' car. There was no need for Jay to protest.

"I need to get a car," Jay mumbled under his breath. "And soon!" With that in mind, Jay texted Reese

What are you doing after work?

Nothing. You got something in mind?

Yes. I need to go car shopping.

Cool. I'll pick you up after work. Around 6:30p.m.

See you then.

Jay and Reese went to several car lots before Jay found the car he just had to have. Usually not the flashy type, Jay highly favored a beige convertible four-seater Lexus.

"It's more than I plan on paying for a car, but it's sweet!" Jay admired the car. *Lewis sure would love this car.*

"Sweet it is!" Reese agreed. "If you don't get it, I will."

"I'm sure Rose would have something to say about that."

"Oh, Rose," Reese chortled. "I forgot I'm not my own man anymore. Got to check with the *wifey* first."

"You don't think I'm crazy, do you? It is expensive." Jay was cautious. "Maybe I should look around some more. Get something more practical and a lot cheaper."

"What's more practical than this? It's a four-seater, even though it's sporty. When your bachelor days are over, this still will work." Reese was very persuasive. "Life is short. What's that you said your friend would say…Live life to the fullest. Well, if this *ain't* the fullest, what is?"

"It's only material, Reese." Jay logically responded. "I can't take it to heaven."

"No, but it will sure feel like you're riding on the pearly streets paved in gold."

"You're crazy." Jay laughed. "Really crazy. I miss hanging with you."

"Me too," Reese became serious. "It's like old times. I'm glad you're home."

"Me too," Jay closed the car door. "Let's go purchase my new car."

"Hallelujah!" Reese hollered joyfully. "You really have changed. The *old* Jay would have never bought this car."

"You're right," Jay shook his head. "I'm becoming too much like you – *fly by the seat of my pants kind of guy.*"

The brothers laughed. It was so good for them to reunite, even under the terrible circumstances that brought Jay to this point in his life.

Saturday evening, Jay took Janice out for a joyride in his new car, with the hood down. After riding around for about an hour, the two ate dinner on the outskirts of town at a barbecue place. It was a good day. Janice was elated to be with Jay. He was sending out all the signals of commitment and affirmation of their relationship

Jay had purposed tonight to tell Janice that he was ready for a committed relationship. After all the hinting and implying coming from his parents, Jay believed that he could make it work. He could learn to love Janice like she deserved to be loved. He needed to settle down and start a family of his own.

Even though Janice never bought it up again, Jay felt hangdog for not stepping up to the plate and hitting a home run with the girl who had pined over him for years. It was time. Time to commit himself to someone. After all, his dad depended on him more and more in the ministry. Soon, his dad would want even more of him. As of now, Jay wasn't ready. Helping his dad at the church was a *whole other* ballgame than actually preaching. Many, many years on down the road, after his life had leveled out a little and Jay didn't feel so messed up inside, maybe his dad could pass the mantle onto him. *Maybe!*

Jay figured he needed a wife. Someone to fit in the pastor's wife mold. He couldn't think of anyone more fitting than Janice. She was perfect! Perhaps, by marrying Janice, he could at least consider returning to ministering the Gospel.

Lewis would say I'm settling.
Mom would say I'm coming to my senses.
Dad would say, do the right thing.
But what do you say?

I say...Tonight, I'm taking the first step toward a long future of commitment and marriage. It would make his family happy, for sure. Janice would be happy. But what about Jay?

War took so much from me. Janice can give me companionship.

Jay had even secretly purchased the ring to prove it. Whether or not he gave it to Janice tonight, time would tell.

"You don't seem to be in much pain tonight," Janice commented. "Is your headache gone?"

"I've taken quite a few pills to counter it." Jay looked at her closely. "I didn't want anything to hinder this night with you."

Janice felt all gushy inside. The way Jay looked at her, she knew what was coming next. *Thank You, Lord!*

"Janice," he reached for her hand, "I have been thinking a lot about us and..."

It's her! Jay lost his train of thought as he saw someone who looked like Lewis' sister walk past the restaurant.

He leaped out of the chair, his leg now throbbing, but that didn't matter.

"Jay!" With bewilderment, Janice called after him.

"I'll be right back," he turned to her. "Just stay here. I'll explain when I return." Jay fled out the door, trying to catch up with the lady who looked just like Isabella, but this time with purple and blue hair.

He ran down the street, limping and hopping, thinking he saw Isabella way ahead of him. Then he caught the back of her, but she wasn't alone. She was with a man. He was a big man, triple in size to her petite frame.

That can't be Isabella! He trailed the two, watching them as they turned into a sleazy motel around the corner. The young lady opened the door and let the man enter. As the door closed, Jay's heart finally decelerated.

Was that Isabella? She looked like the girl I saw in the bar. Only her hair is purple and blue and not pink and blue. Dark shoddy clothes! If only I could have gotten a good look at her. Now what? I'll come back. Maybe I'll drop Janice off and come back and see if the guy leaves. Yes! That's what I'll do.

What about Janice? And the commitment? Marriage?

I'll deal with that tomorrow. Tonight isn't the right time. Jay's mind reeled over seeing the girl who had to be Isabella. *No need to rush! We have time!*

Let patience have its perfect work, and then, in the end, you will be found lacking nothing!

When Jay returned to Janice, she could tell that things had changed. His entire demeanor had changed. His mind was occupied with the lady he told her about – Lewis' sister. Inwardly, Janice found herself jealous. There appeared to be something more than the fact that Jay might have found Lewis' sister. Something else displayed in his yellowish-brown eyes that alarmed her – a spark of expectation!

When Jay dropped Janice off, he seemed distant and eager to leave.

"After church, can you come over for dinner?" Janice felt desperate for his attention, like a flower without water.

"No. I better eat with the family. I wouldn't want to disappoint my mother. Family dinner is still the highlight of her week. Reese and Leela's families are coming over."

Janice hoped he would invite her, but he didn't.

"I'll call you, though." Jay pecked her on the cheek. "Have a goodnight's sleep. See you in church." Jay trotted off like a schoolboy with a limp.

He waved, got into his car, drove off, and headed back to the motel.

Chapter 11

Jay parked his Lexus several rows from the room he thought Isabella was in. For hours he sat there. Seemingly, the guy would stay the night unless he had already left, which Jay doubted.

What kind of life does she live? Is this her boyfriend? Or is it her meal ticket for the week? Jay remembered Lewis telling him on the airplane that when Isabella couldn't make ends meet, prostitution was her solution.

Engaged in promiscuity, offering her body to anyone who passed by or showed interest to support her life was mind-boggling to Jay. It seemed that there was some other way to survive. This was entirely a distinct world of sin and shame, which Jay had only heard about, read about, even talked about, but never experienced. Jay recalled the explicit details Lewis had told him about Isabella.

"From her lips, Isabella said that nothing could satisfy her insatiable appetite to be loved. She was looking for a man to make her feel wanted and needed. She wanted a man's affection, just like she had always wanted her father's love. However, he abused her...in the worse way. He treated her sinfully; therefore, she was only following in his footsteps. Even her foster parents abused her love, especially the men. People had always let her down, even her mother when she was living. Isabella loathed the thought of being like her mother. A Christian, taking all that crap from a man. Her

mom said her dad was weak-willed and that prayer was the only thing that could help him. Prayer! Isabella laughed when she said it. Hadn't her mother prayed enough? Countless unanswered prayers. God wasn't present but absent in their lives. Endeavoring to be nothing like her parents, especially her father, Isabella purposed that a man would have to pay her for her love – for sex! Never would she give it for free and let another man take from her what her dad had stolen years ago without restitution."

The conversation made Jay feel sorry for Isabella. She wanted to be loved, but she was going about it the wrong way to receive it. Love wasn't something you buy; it was something you gave without expecting anything in return. Love was selfless.

Jay sat upward when the motel door finally opened. The big guy came barging out the door, leaving the door open. He was running like a criminal, skedaddling from a crime scene.

Something is wrong! Jay waited for the guy to get totally out of sight. His heart was pounding like drums in his chest. Suddenly, Jay heard the familiar distinct war cry rambling in his ears. Yet, this wasn't war, or was it?

Jumping out of the car, Jay cautiously walked toward the motel room, constantly looking around him for fear that the big guy would come back. He felt as if he was back in Iraq, danger lurking all around him, like a thief in the night – to take something from him – even his own life. As Jay came near, he heard someone moaning and groaning. His heart stopped beating for a moment as he pushed the door, opening it further.

A woman was lying motionless on the bed.

"Are you alright?" Guardedly, Jay drew nearer.

Instantly, Isabella screamed! A scream that caused Jay's heart to palpitate irregularly. She thought the abuser had returned. "Get out!" Isabella leaped up, tossing her shoe at him. "Who are you? I'll scream rape if you don't leave!" Though she was in severe pain, Isabella would do everything in her power to defend herself. Frightened, her knees knocked together, rattling an unusual sound.

"Hold up!" Jay raised his hand. "Isabella...Izzy!"

She stared at him in disbelief. No one called her Izzy but...Lewis. The man seemed familiar to her. Still, Isabella didn't trust him. After all, he was a man, and evil lingered in the heart of every man. She feared him, and Jay knew it.

"Who are you?" Isabella yelled again.

With his hands held up, like he was being arrested or something, Jay responded, "Jay. I'm Lewis' friend. I met you at the bar, remember?"

She took a good look at him—*the handsome man with the yellowish-brown eyes.*

Face to face with a prostitute, Jay was floored, yet pity consumed him. It was grossly evident that the big, burly man had taken advantage of Isabella, abusing her physically. Painted eyes of charcoal black lined like owl eyes, the right eye was blue-black from being punched. Her painted lips of scarlet were swollen and bleeding, and her cheek was dark purplish with an imprint of some kind, possibly a ring imprint. Her ears were lined with several earrings on each ear. Her blue and purple hair was all over the place, totally in disarray. Black streaks from crying made Isabella's makeup appear clownish. She was a *hot mess*...borrowing the former words of his beloved friend, Lewis.

"Are you alright? Do you need to go to the hospital?"

"For what?" Isabella scoffed. "This *ain't* nothing." She pointed to her face, though she kept her hand to her stomach. Apparently, she had been hit there as well. "Why are you here? Is Lewis with you?" Isabella panicked, not wanting her brother to see her like this. She had tried to stay off the streets, but she couldn't afford it. After she didn't receive any more money from her brother, Isabella was on her own again, and working at the bar just didn't pay the bills or feed her other habits.

Jay felt sick. How was he going to tell Isabella about her brother? Though he knew she was doing her best to show no signs of pain or weakness, Jay knew she was hurting, physically and emotionally. "No."

"Then, where is he?"

"Perhaps we should see about you first," nervously he replied. Jay just wanted to tend to her wounds. Observing Isabella's lips still bleeding, he just wanted to take care of her.

"Forget about me!" Isabella yelled at him. "Where is Lewis?" For some reason, she ran to the door and looked outside. No one was in sight. Her heart sank to the floor when she turned around and saw grief in his eyes.

"I'm...I'm...s-o-r-r-y..." Jay couldn't get the rest out.

73

Lethargically, Isabella understood as she stood before him, half-dressed; her feet were suddenly frozen to the floor. Pain gripped her like a woman in labor. She couldn't scream anymore. Everything came to a halt at that very moment. Time stood still. Her heart thundered crazily, though the silence was booming. The deep, dark pain she was suffering was almost too much for her to bear.

Suddenly, the lights went out! Everything was dark and black! Isabella fainted.

Jay alertly perceived that her legs were not going to hold her up much longer. Rushing to her side, just in time, Jay caught Isabella and scooped her into his arms, and held her like a baby needing to be comforted by her mother. She was light as a feather. Looking down at her, Jay knew that he could never just walk away and leave Isabella. Not just because he promised Lewis, but in an instant, an unforeseen, invisible force had linked them together. Jay knew that without a shadow of a doubt, it had to be God.

Leisurely, Isabella's eyes opened, staring up at him. She fought to keep her tears at bay. There was an inward struggle going on. Like her brother, they didn't cry. They were taught not to cry or show signs of weakness, like their mother. Yet, her heart ached, desiring a release and a relief!

"It's okay. Cry if you want. It'll make you feel better," Jay encouraged, still holding her. "Just let go."

A sob caught in her throat, but she wouldn't let it out. Though her world was torn apart and she had no other family near, Isabella had to be strong. She had to keep her composure. After all, life would go on. The bad things would keep happening, and she would keep enduring.

Abruptly Isabella leaped out of his arms and sat on the bed.

"Life stinks! It has nothing to offer you but hardship and much trouble. I curse the day I was born. Why did I have to be born?" Isabella spewed out her disdain for life. "Lewis was stupid to fight in a foolish &#%!@ war that cared nothing about him?! I hate life! I hate YOUR GOD – even though I don't believe YOUR GOD exists! You're like every other man – &#%!@ useless!

"Where was YOUR GOD when my brother was being killed?" Isabella looked directly at Jay, such hatred displaying in her eyes, but she was speaking low now, on the right side of Jay. "If there is a God, then why does He allow so much pain?"

"Excuse me," Jay turned to her, but he hadn't heard clearly what she was saying. Deafness in his right ear could be such a hindrance at times.

She looked at him.

"I'm sorry. I know you're talking, but I'm deaf in my right ear. A war injury."

"You lost your hearing. My brother lost his life." Isabella sighed like a wounded animal. "I'm assuming Lewis has already been buried."

Jay nodded.

Isabella stared at him for some time before speaking. "Thanks for telling me about Lewis." Hastily Isabella stood, desiring just to be alone. "Please leave!"

The last thing Jay wanted to do was to leave. Isabella needed help, even if she didn't know it. Black and blue all over, visible scars and bruises, still bleeding, Isabella was in no shape to be by herself. *Perhaps that big guy broke her ribs or something.*

"Let me get some ice for that lip of yours…and your jaw," purposely, Jay ignored her, brushed right past her, and headed to the small kitchen area.

"Get out!" Isabella repeated. "Who do you think you are?" She bolted in front of him, slamming the empty freezer. "This is a motel! I don't have ice!"

"I'll go get some," swiftly Jay headed for the door. "I'll be right back. Please don't leave, and please let me in when I return. I have so much to tell you about your brother," Jay hoped just by mentioning Lewis she would accept his help. "Anything else I can get you?"

Confused, she shook her head and watched the strange man excited. His gentle tone calmed her, somehow. Yes, Isabella longed to hear about her brother. Anything! Once the door closed, Isabella plopped on the bed and wept for her brother. She couldn't hold back the tears. Anguish lay on her chest like heavyweights. Isabella felt so all alone. No one would see or hear her tears, but her – and God.

Oh, Lewis! How could you leave me? How could you leave me? Now I have no one.

Shortly afterward, Jay returned, knocking only once before realizing the door was unlocked. "You really should lock the doors," he said as he entered. He stopped dead in his tracks, beholding her red eyes.

"You should go home now," she sniffed. "I don't need your help."

"This isn't the safest motel. That guy could come back."

"Maybe tomorrow, but not tonight," Isabella said nonchalantly. "He *got* what he wanted tonight."

Jay looked appalled. He'd never met a lady like Isabella. Some would find it hard to call her a lady, but Jay was different. He saw beyond the camouflage. He saw the mask which hid her true self. Hopefully, God would use him to help her discover her identity, just like He'd used him to help Lewis.

"Sit up, please," Jay asked nicely.

Annoyed, Isabella obeyed, wincing in pain.

"I think you have some internal damage." Jay surmised, witnessing her pain, as he put this icepack to her jawline. "Perhaps, your ribcage is…"

"Don't play doctor on me," Isabella snapped. "I'll be fine in a few days."

Tenderly, Jay cleaned up the blood on her face and lips. "I think you need stitches on your lip."

"It'll be fine. This isn't my first rodeo with a busted lip!"

"What a shame. To desecrate such beautiful lips," the words just rolled off his lips, shocking both Jay and Isabella.

Isabella jerked away! "I'm not your girl! If you want something from me, you'll pay for it just like all of the rest of the guys. No freebies here!"

"Hold up." Jay chuckled, genuinely amused that she had thought of him in that way. *Maybe I should be flattered!*

"Oh, you think it's funny!" Isabella exploded. "You think you're too good for me. I have you know I have doctors for clients. Lawyers. Professional people. Not all of my customers are like Big Tim, but Big Tim pays the same money."

"I…I wasn't saying that. I'm sure you're worth…" his foot was in his mouth for sure now. "I mean…Why? Why do you sell your soul for money?"

"It's not my soul I'm selling, holy man. It's my body!"

"But why?"

"A girl's *gotta* eat and live."

"Why not go back to school and finish up your accounting degree. Lewis said you were always so smart and loved math."

"Too late for all that." Isabella grimaced. "I am who I am, and if you don't like it, you can leave!"

"I apologize if I offended you."

"You can't offend me! I could care less what you think about me! Listen, I'm tired. I just want to go to sleep. Unless you want to sleep with me?" Isabella goaded, not seriously, but just enough to rustle his proper feathers.

"Perhaps, I'll come back tomorrow," Jay swiftly felt uncomfortable. After all, here he was, a godly man in a motel room with a prostitute. What would others think? Forget that she was Lewis' sister. It still didn't seem right. "Maybe we can talk…at the park…or something…"

"Nah, forget it!" Isabella wanted to stay as far away from Jay as possible. He was making her feel uneasy in her own skin. No man had the right to do that to her anymore.

"I'm tired, too. I have church in the morning," Jay insisted. "You've obviously, had a rough day. So, let's just talk tomorrow," he repeated.

"No!"

"You have to…"

"I don't have to do anything!"

"For Lewis' sake," Jay spoke tenderly. "He gave me something to give to you, and…there's so much I have to tell you."

She weighed her options. Isabella had nothing tangible from her brothers, and if Jay had something, she wanted it even if it cost her being in his presence again. "Okay, tomorrow at three. I have clients to attend to later. I'll meet you at the park around the corner. Don't be late or I'll leave. And don't come back here ever again. You're bad for my business."

"No problem." Jay walked to the door.

"When did he die?"

"December 17th." Jay turned and looked at her, waiting for her to say something else. But she didn't. "Goodnight."

Isabella closed the door, went back to her bed, and wept.

"I have nobody!" her heart moaned.

Chapter 12

Sunday morning, Jay woke up discombobulated. There was an unusual feeling of uneasiness and excitement within him, each emotion struggling for control. Partly, with strange anticipation, Jay knew he would be seeing Isabella today, after church service. Though obviously, the two ran in different circles, something about Lewis' sister left him spellbound. Maybe it was because Isabella was a lost soul. She needed help. It was a Cannon's trait to help those who couldn't help themselves. Plus, his promise to Lewis – he would take care of Isabella. It was his duty!

Still, something else was tugging at him. Subtly, fear engulfed him. There was an overpowering foreboding in the atmosphere. Jay felt it.

Oh God, what is it?

Pray!

The inner voice was strong and demanding.

Pray!

Jay dropped to his knees and began fervently praying. Why the urgency in prayer? Who was it that needed divine intervention? Who was in trouble? He had an inkling that he was interceding for Isabella. *Lord, what is happening?*

Jay had felt the same foreboding about Lewis' dying without knowing Jesus. *Oh God, don't let Isabella die without knowing You.*

I must show her the way. I promised Lewis. God have mercy on Isabella. Save her. Deliver her. Protect her. Please, God, watch over her. I promised Lewis. Help me keep my promise!

Pray!

Whomever it is, they shall not die but live and declare the Lord.

Jay felt desperate. Jay had to release this burden. It was much too great for him to bear. *Into Your hands, I commit Isabella. I can't save her. Only You can. I submit my father, mother, sister, brother, and their families into Your hands.*

The worship service was filled with an abundance of joy. There was such a sweet anointing in the atmosphere, just what Jay needed – a refreshing! A revival in his spirit. Restoration of the mind and soul. The praise team ushered the congregation into the holies of holies.

Jay read the Scriptures and lead the morning prayer. Since returning home, Jay was gradually growing spiritually, and it felt good. The empty hole in his heart was being filled with love again. The hatred that war placed in his heart was somewhat surrendering to love, covering a multitude of sins. At times, it still gnawed at him, but Jay pushed it back with prayer and praise. That's what his earthly father had taught him. Something that Jay forgot during wartime. The grief of losing overrode the goodness of God's protection over him.

Intentionally, Jay was finding his way back to God. However, he still wasn't ready to step into his father's shoes of preaching the Gospel just yet. Jay was still uncertain if he would ever be prepared for that. Since he had changed, maybe his calling had changed too.

The gifts and calling of God are without repentance.

As Jay took his seat in the pulpit, among the other ministers, Pastor James whispered in his son's ear, "Good job. I'm so proud of you."

Jay looked at his father, and abruptly fear seized him. His father looked ill. He was sweating. "Are you alright?"

"Excellent," Pastor James confessed. "The joy of the Lord is my strength."

Was I interceding for Dad and not Isabella? Lord, what are You trying to tell me?

Be still and know that I am God.

"We must open up our hearts to one another. We must love our fellow man. Regardless, of who they are and what they are doing or what they have done," Pastor James preached with utter conviction and authority.

"Jesus said to the Pharisees...the Christian men and women pointing their fingers at the sinner woman....*'he, without sin, cast the first stone.'* None of them could, for we all have sinned. We all have fallen short of His glory. We have all missed the mark. We have all strayed to the left instead of the right pathway. Many have walked on Broad Street instead of Narrow Street. At one point or another, we all have had skeletons in our closets. Yet, our Lord has been mindful of us and merciful toward each one of us. Thus, Jesus looked around and said to the woman. *'Where are your accusers?'* She said, *'they are gone.'* Then He said woman, *'your sins are forgiven go and sin no more.'*" Pastor James paused, letting it soak in. "*Go and sin no more.* Shouldn't we be as forgiving...seeing how we all have sinned? None of us are perfect, and yet we are looking for perfect people. Then when they don't live up to our expectations, we cut them loose. We point fingers at them. We lift up our high and mighty heads as if we are better than them. Well, I'm here to say to you...you without sin, cast the first stone. If you're perfect, then go ahead and beat your fellow man down. Go ahead and judge the adulterous woman. The murderer. The homeless. And even the prostitute. Do you know why she is like she is? Have you taken the time to ask?"

Jay's heart pounded in his ears. The prostitute...*Isabella has been raped and abused. Her lifestyle now is a product of her childhood. Forgive me for judging her. Oh God, help me help her!*

"We do not know why the adulterous woman was the way she was. Perhaps the woman was abused, mistreated, abandoned, or just looking for someone to love her and fill the empty void in her life." Pastor James continued preaching. "We must take the time to ask questions and not rashly judge. We say it's wrong, and that's that! Well, Jesus knew her sin was wrong, but He cared about her. He's a compassionate Savior, and He didn't want her to die in her sins. He didn't give up on her. He didn't just toss her aside. He didn't allow them to continue to humiliate her and harass her. What about you? Who are you giving up on today? Your child? Your parents? Your friends? Your husband? Or perhaps it's a stranger? Who are you condemning with your harsh words? We mustn't, Saints. They need Jesus, and we are the guiding light that leads them to Him. God hates sin, but He loves the sinner? What about you?"

Every Word pierced Jay with conviction. It was his obligation to love others despite their sin, like Isabella. He had to love her back to Christ. Love her even if she behaved unlovable. Lewis expected that of him. His heavenly Father expected it of him. Jay looked down at his watch. It was 12:30. Soon he'd meet up with Isabella. His heart raced at the prospect of seeing the wild lady again. Isabella had pricked his tender heart.

He looked in the congregation, and his eyes landed on Janice, who was staring back at him. She gave him a friendly smile, batting her eyes as if to flirt. Jay returned the gesture.

Why can't I love her as she loves me? The thought nearly paralyzed him. The truth hit Jay as if he had just rammed into a brick wall, head-on. *I'm not in love with Janice, and I never will be. Then how in the world could I consider marriage?*

"We must..." James firmly spoke, suddenly grabbing his chest and falling to the floor.

"Dad!" Jay sprang to his feet. "Dad!"

The next thing Jay and the family knew was that they were all heading to the hospital. In a matter of seconds, everything had changed. Esther rode to the hospital in the ambulance with her husband. It was evident to all that Pastor James had suffered a heart attack. Upon his arrival at the hospital, Pastor James was rushed into surgery. There was no time to waste. Confirmed by the medical professionals, Pastor James had suffered a heart attack.

In the waiting area, Jay and his family stayed in constant prayer. Everyone was troubled, especially Esther. Jay looked around at the people whom he loved so dearly. Reese was comforted by Rose. Reese had endured much, and now he was happier than ever. Sandy and Randy, now five, going on fifty, loved their new mother, Rose. Reese envied them. His sister Leela was comforted by her husband, Nicolas. They were indeed a happy family. Leela, now a mother of a year-old, feisty daughter, Sara, had overcome many obstacles. Jay witnessed the identical love of his parents in both

Reese and Leela's marriages. His heart ached to know the feeling of having a helpmate to lean on. How often had he seen his parents lean on one another, support each other, and just love each other through the good and the bad times? Witnessing it with his siblings, Jay felt lonelier than ever.

He glanced at his watch, which revealed three-thirty. He sighed. *Isabella is gone for sure now, and she said not to come looking for her if I didn't come on time. Oh God, give me a second chance with her.*

Fret not and be of good courage.

Jay looked up and beheld Janice and her parents. Esther went to her friends while Janice moved in Jay's direction.

"How is Pastor James," Janice embraced Jay.

"We haven't heard anything else," Jay answered, still feeling lonely.

"Pastor James will pull through. He's a fighter." Janice inspired. "As you mentioned to me previously, he has been overdoing it, working so hard."

Jay nodded.

"Can I get you anything?" Janice was always the thoughtful one.

"No thanks."

They sat in silence for a while before Janice boldly put her arm around him, pulling him closer to him.

Jay smiled and analyzed her. Janice wanted so much more from him. More than Jay was able to give, and he knew that now. That was the tragedy of it all. He'd given Janice hope only to dash her dreams to smithereens later. It made him feel low-down.

Lord, bless Janice with a helpmate who deserves her!

Meanwhile, Isabella had waited almost an hour for Jay because she desperately wanted whatever her brother had left her. Anything from Lewis would be irreplaceable. Feeling lesser and lower than human, Isabella yearned to take the lifeline that Jay had offered her – a piece of her brother – a glimmer of light in such darkness.

Frustrated and furious, Isabella finally gave up hope of Jay showing up. *Just like every man in my life – a no-show! Useless!*

Liars! Undependable! Jay is no different! I should have never gotten my hopes up! Never!

Fool me once! But he won't fool me twice! Isabella left, vowing not to give Jay another thought. Just like Lewis, he was dead to her!

Several hours later, the Cannon family was informed that Pastor James had survived the surgery and was taken to ICU. Though it was still early, Pastor James' prognosis was good. Everyone hugged each other and gave thanks to God for taking care of Pastor James. At this time, the hospital waiting area was filled with church members. Also, his brother Joseph, his wife Sabrina, their daughter Cassi, also first cousin to Jay, Leela, and Reese, and her husband, Karl were there. Cassi and Karl's children Karlton, their toddler son, and daughter Mariah, now twelve years old, were staying with their neighbor.

That night Joseph and Sabrina stayed with Esther. Cassi and Karl stayed with Leela and Nicolas. Reese and Rose stayed in his old room with the twins, Sandy and Randy. Reese wanted to be close to his mother. Jay went to his bedroom, alone.

Father God, I want a wife. I don't want to be alone anymore. I know that Janice is not the woman to fill those shoes. But, who have You chosen for me?

Knock. Knock. Reese entered his brother's room. "Would you like some company?"

"Not really," Jay laughed. "We're a little too old for sleepovers, *Lil* bro."

"Hush!" Reese plopped on the king-size bed. "My bed is crowded. Four people in one bed *is* a bit too much."

"I guess you can crash with me tonight."

"Boy, what a day," Reese sighed. "I can't believe dad had a heart attack."

"He's been looking rundown lately. He's overdoing it at the church. He's being pulled in so many directions. What good is it to have ministers and not delegate some of the responsibility? Isn't that what Jethro said to his son-in-law Moses? He said you will surely wear yourself out."

"Jay, he's tried that," Reese replied. "But they don't follow through. Like, dad, they are older, except for Nicolas, and I think tired. I believe that's why you're here."

"I admit, preaching is the last thing I wanted to do when I returned, but now, I'll do whatever it takes to relieve dad of some of the load. He has to replenish his strength and take time out for himself. I'm glad I'm back to help out at the church. It's a lot for one person to handle such a large congregation. Also, dad needs to hire more staff, I think."

"You know, dad," Reese smirked. "He wants to keep it in the family. I think he wants me and Leela to work on staff, but I have other dreams. I love teaching music and the band, and Leela loves teaching dance. Nicholas is on the staff, but his job keeps him from being there a lot."

"Mom works part-time, but still, it's not enough. All the other ministers, including Nicolas, are swamped with their own jobs, family, or in the retirement stages." Jay added. "We have to make dad see that he needs more people. I'm sure others are called into the ministry, too."

"Good luck!" Reese turned over. "I'm going to sleep. I want to be at the hospital early."

"I guess we all do," Jay turned the other way. "Goodnight."

"You and Janice looked good tonight," Reese noted. "It's about time you give her that ring you got hidden in your nightstand."

"How did you know?" Jay turned over to face his brother.

"Mom. She knows everything."

"She's been snooping in my drawer?"

"No. I think she was cleaning your room, the phone rang, and she needed a pencil. So, she looked inside your drawer...and there it was, a diamond ring. At least that is what Leela told Rose."

"Mom never said a word," Jay turned back over.

"And she never will."

"I'm not marrying, Janice," Jay candidly admitted to his brother. "She's great. Good to talk to. Loves the Lord, but I am not in love with her."

Reese sat upward and looked his brother directly in the eyes. "You either love someone, or you don't. You cannot make your heart do what it's not meant to do. If only I would have listened to my heart screaming, I would have never married Genesis. The first time I saw Rose, I knew she was the one. I didn't know it was love, but I just couldn't stop thinking about her. She made me want to do right, be right, and live right. I can't explain it, but when the right woman comes along, you'll know. She makes you want to be a better man."

Jay thought about his brother's wisdom for a while before saying anything. "Love compliments you."

"Absolutely!"

"Wow." Jay admonished. "And I always thought you were the slow one."

"Oh yeah!" Reese hit his brother with the pillow. "Well, I beat you at discovering true love."

Jay returned the pillow with a smack on his head. "Okay, you're one up on me!"

"Nope, three! I got Rose, Sandy, and Randy!"

"Hush up!"

Chapter 13

By the following evening, Pastor James was looking better. He was still in ICU for observation, but Pastor James' vital signs and overall health had improved significantly to his doctors' astonishment. Prayer works.

Though many people came to the hospital, only family could visit with Pastor James. An abundance of flowers and cards were sent to the hospital for the pastor. Reese and Jay were constantly taking flowers home. Though Pastor James didn't have a hospital room yet, there was no way that a hospital room could contain all the flowers being sent.

When Pastor James was, at last, moved to a private hospital room, his brother had a heart-to-heart with him. "You can't do it all, brother." Joseph cautioned his brother to change the way he was doing things at the church. "You know that I have been where you are. The unending pace that you are treading will kill you if you don't slow down. Doing a good thing doesn't mean it's the right thing. God places people in our lives to help us fulfill our purpose on earth. However, it's up to us to utilize them. We must pour ourselves out like drink offerings to others so that they can maximize their gifts. How will they, if we don't let go of some of our extra duties?"

"Like what?"

"Like counselors. Use the ministers you already have and train new ministers. Send them to classes. You don't have to counsel every single person. Also, delegate others to visit the hospital and prisons. You can't do it all. You remember how Moses had to delegate. Let your leaders handle the small cases and bring only the serious cases to you. Start there. Don't spend all your time at the church. Work from home, away from the building we call church. When people see your car at the church, it compels them to stop by even when they don't need to. Set business hours, and that's that."

"So many changes."

"It's necessary. You're not a small church anymore. The congregation is too big for just you."

"You're right." Pastor James understood he had to make some significant changes when he returned.

"Why don't you let Nicolas preach more often? You say he's an excellent youth minister."

"He is," James consented, "but he's so busy at work. Besides, he's more comfortable with the youth ministry and not necessarily the adult ministry."

"Jay is back. Let Jay preach for the next few Sundays. He's ready." Joseph believed what he was saying.

"I'm not sure. Jay has been through so much. He keeps everything bottled up inside. He was so broken when he first came, but I do see the light shining in his eyes again. He doesn't want to be pushed. When he first came home, Jay said he wasn't ready."

"That's a good sign." Joseph laughed. "We're never ready. We just have to be willing."

"You're right."

"As I have aged and matured in the ministry, I preach three Sundays and allow my assistant pastor to preach or other ministers to preach fourth Sunday. It allows me to be ministered to and for them to grow spiritually."

"I'll pray about this and then talk to Jay."

"Good. God has much more work for you to do, and you can't do it fully if your body is worn out, brother."

Pastor James was discharged from the hospital on Friday. That evening Jay had finally had some time alone with his father. With

88

his father's crisis abating, everyone was relieved and didn't hover on the patriarch as much. Jay missed their private time at the office.

"Minister Daniel is still out of town. Minister Thomas is sick, and well, Nicolas is over the youth ministry. I don't want him to neglect that part of the church ministry. I need for you to preach Sunday."

"I'm not ready, Dad." Jay cringed at the thought.

"You're ready," James affirmed. "I've prayed about this, and I feel settled in my spirit that this is what God wants. God used you to minister to His children during wartime, and now He has sent you here to do the same. We're in spiritual warfare, son. Who better to tell it than someone who has lived it."

"I'm a wreck, Dad. I'm better than I was, but I'm still shipwrecked and battle-scarred. I'm walking on eggshells all the time, sure that an invisible bomb is about to explode, or a bullet is about to come shooting at me. I'm always looking over my shoulder. I'm forever trembling with anxiety. I cannot close my eyes and get a good night's sleep without horrific dreams invading my sleep. I'm just not ready, Dad. How can I minister to others about faith…when I'm not so certain where I stand with faith?"

"No excuse is good enough with God. Moses wasn't ready to lead the people out of Egypt. He had many excuses, and yet, God called Him to do it. Moses wasn't perfect. He was a murderer, but God had a message for him to share with others," James reassured. "Just as I believe you have been called to share a message with the church. I need you, Jay. God needs you."

Silent tears flowed as Jay listened to his father, the man he looked up to and always wanted to be like him. Yet, now Jay figured he'd never be like him…not with fear consuming him.

"It's never too late to be what you've been called to be. A journey of a thousand miles begins with a single step. You were born to preach, Jay. I remember all the times when I was preparing my sermon notes and reading aloud; you would sit by listening. I would preach for an hour, and you'd be clapping and jumping up and down with your sister until Leela got tired and fell asleep. You were my best audience then. It became a habit. And the times I was working at the church, I'd ask Esther to bring you over so you could listen to me practice my sermon. You never grew tired of it. All through middle school and high school, you would sit and listen to my sermons before anybody ever heard me minister any of them." James paused. "I was training you then and didn't even know it."

"That was so long ago, Dad. A lot has happened since then."

"Experience is the best guide in reaching others. Good experiences and bad experiences help us become better teachers of God's word. How can you tell somebody about healing if you've never really been sick? How can you relate to the tragedies of death if you've never seen anyone die? Or talk about a storm if you've never been in one yourself. Your pain can be another's gain."

"Dad, can I think on this, some? Maybe Uncle Joseph can send one of his ministers for Sunday."

"Maybe," James pacified. "Pray about it, son."

"I will," Jay got up. "You rest, now."

"I love you, Jay."

"I love you too, Dad. So glad you're feeling better."

Instead of going back to his room, Jay decided to go for a drive. He was too restless to sit still. He thought of calling Janice, but it wasn't fair of him to keep using her for his own good. He had to let her find her Boaz.

While driving, he picked up his cell phone to call Reese but hung it back up. Reese had his own family, which made him feel all the more lonesome. Suddenly, Jay found himself driving toward Williamsburg, heading to the motel where he had last seen Isabella. With all that was going on with his father, Jay had yet to reach out to her again. He knew that she was probably mad at him for standing him up, which he couldn't help because of his father. *But she doesn't know that. She probably won't open the door.*

As fate would have it, the moment he pulled his car into the parking lot, Jay saw her. Isabella was about to open the door to the motel, alone. Quickly, he jumped out of his car and ran to her.

"Isabella!"

She turned and saw him. Quickly, Isabella put the key in the lock and rushed inside, slamming the door behind her.

Jay knocked on the door several times. "Please open up, Isabella. I need to talk to you."

"You had your chance! Go away before I call the cops."

"Please, listen. I couldn't help it! My father had a heart attack that Sunday."

Isabella said nothing, still not opening the door.

"Please, Isabella," Jay called her name with sweetness.

Her name never sounded so good before. It startled her. "Go away."

"Please, Isabella, I need...I...need...to talk to you," Jay begged. He needed her more than she needed him right now. The awareness of this revelation significantly alarmed him.

Slowly the door opened. "Aren't you afraid to be alone with me? I could tarnish your good name?"

Jay stood at the door for a moment, the weight of her words pressing on him. After all, he was expected to fill in his father's shoes. He was a pastor's son, about to preach the gospel, too. "Uh, can we go to the park?"

"No. I'm tired." Isabella looked Jay over from head to toe. *Besides, he ain't dress for no park. It looks like he's just coming from church or work.* His gorgeous eyes beckoned her to let him in, but she wouldn't surrender.

"Please," Jay wanted to do what was right.

"No!" Isabella slammed the door. Jay was pulling at her heart, and she didn't like it. He'd either meet her on her terms or nothing at all. Deep down, Isabella wanted to go to the park with him, but what for? He wasn't her type. She didn't want any connections with good...and he obviously was a good man.

"When can I see you? I need to talk to you...about your...brother."

"Just go home."

"Please, Isabella."

Silence.

More silence.

"I'm tired. Meet me at the park tomorrow around noon. You better show up or don't ever contact me again."

"I'll be there, and I'll bring lunch. I promise I'll leave you alone after that..." *if you don't want to see me again.*

"Bye!"

Returning to his car, Jay felt hopeful and anxious. He had something to look forward to, which was rare.

Why do I feel so helpless around her? She makes me crazy, and I don't know why!

Chapter 14

Saturday, Jay awakened feeling as if he hadn't slept at all. He had tossed and turned all night and broke out in a sweat, soaking his body thoroughly. Between dreams about the war, soldier friends dying, and him standing in the pulpit, unable to say one word – Jay felt exhausted.

Discontented, Jay concluded there was absolutely no way he was ministering on Sunday. He didn't want to let his dad down, especially now, but he wouldn't be a fake! Listlessly, Jay called his Uncle Joseph, against his father's wishes. He just wasn't ready yet. His heart was still raw from the war. He didn't blame God as much anymore, but Jay's relationship with God wasn't where it needed to be. He'd seen too much and just couldn't shake the negative perspective he had about everything, including his beliefs. Absolutely, Jay believed in God and His omnipotent power. However, seemingly the door had been closed on his prayers being heard and answered. Countless times, Jay prayed for healing, safety, deliverance, mercy, protection, to live and not to die for his fellow soldiers. Yet, many died tragically or came back half a person, in many ways. Why did God allow it? Knowing He never sleeps or slumbers, possibly God blinked too long when it came to answering Jay's prayers.

"Uncle Joseph," he began, "dad is pushing me to step into his shoes." Jay ran his fingers through his hair. "I'm just not ready."

"None of us are really ready," Joseph replied. "Not in our strength, but in His strength, we can do all things. *'Not by might, nor by power, but by my Spirit says the Lord,'*" Joseph quoted the familiar scripture in the book of Zechariah. "Your father is doing only what He feels God wants. Right now, my brother James needs you more than you know it."

"Well, I'm not ready," Jay repeated firmly. "I know it's short notice, but can you possibly send one of your ministers for Sunday?"

Mulling it over, Joseph was caught between a rock and a hard place. He didn't want to come between father and son. However, the Gospel had to be preached. "I'll be there."

"Thank you, Uncle Joseph."

"I need to see my brother anyway. I think Sabrina and I both will come."

"I appreciate it. I know my parents will be glad to see you both after my dad gets over being mad at me."

"I'll be praying for you, Jay. It's never easy doing what God has called us to do. Nevertheless, we all have to step out of the boat sometimes and just get our feet wet. Don't be like the eleven who stayed in the boat. Be like Peter, walk on water."

Jay didn't respond.

"You've been through a lot, no doubt." Joseph went on. "God brought you back here for a reason. He saved you and preserved you for such a time as this."

Jay listened to his uncle, sounding so much like his father. "I know, Uncle Joseph. Thank you for coming Sunday. I'll let dad know right away."

Needless to say, Pastor James wasn't too happy that his son retreated from answering his request. Nor was he glad that he called Joseph. Albeit, Joseph had others to minister at his church. Still, he knew that his brother, like him, didn't like to be away from church on Sundays. Ultimately, James had to put his son, Jay, in God's hands. There was no better place to be.

Impatiently Jay watched the clock unhurriedly tick by. He couldn't understand his anticipation of seeing Isabella. Certainly, duty called for him to help Isabella and to keep his promise to Lewis. Still, Jay found himself excited about having lunch with the eccentric young lady. She intrigued him. Underneath all the gothic look, Jay assumed that there was a kind, loving soul who just wanted to be cared for and loved. To uncover the mask and find the bona fide, Isabella thrilled Jay. If only she would allow him such fortune.

Just before noon, as Jay was about to leave for his lunch date with Isabella, he received an unexpected visitor.

"Janice is at the door," Esther entered his room.

"Not now," Jay was frustrated, tying his new Nike tennis shoes. He hadn't owned a pair in years. Jay couldn't remember the last time he wore jeans, a sweatshirt, and tennis shoes, but the occasion seemed to call for it. "I have to meet someone."

"Who?" Esther's eyes arched with concern. The fact that her son was dressed so unusually casual, more like Reese, alerted her. "Are you seeing someone else? If so, you can't string Janice on like that. She's a nice girl."

"I'm not seeing anyone, Mom." Jay stood up. "If you must know, I'm keeping a promise to Lewis."

"What promise?"

"I found his sister again."

"I see," Esther wasn't convinced. Her son had a look of hope in his eyes, something she hadn't seen in a long time.

"No, you don't see, Mom." Jay cautioned. "Don't go reading anything in this. Isabella…"

"Isabella," Esther repeated.

"Isabella is quite different from… Well, she's from a different world. I promised Lewis that I would help her find her way to Jesus."

"Sounds just like your daddy. Just be careful," inwardly, she fretted over Jay. "Oh, and what about Janice?"

"We're just…"

"Friends," Esther completed his familiar phrase. "Well, it's time you make that clear to her."

"I will, Mom," Jay kissed her on the forehead. "I must go, now," he bypassed his mother and trotted down the stairs, where Janice was waiting.

"Hi, Jay! Wow, you look handsome in a sweatshirt and jeans. It's been a long time since I've seen you dressed so casually! I'm impressed."

"Time for a change." Jay shrugged his shoulders.

"I know you weren't expecting me, but I wanted to surprise you with a picnic." Janice jumped in. "I have everything in the car. All I need is you."

"Um…uh…" Jay cleared his throat, "I'm sorry, but I have another appointment which I have to hurry to, or I'll be late."

"An appointment on Saturday, dressed in jeans," Janice wasn't buying it. Although Jay never lied to her before, something smelt a little fishy.

"I'll tell you more about it later," Jay practically pushed Janice out the door with him. He didn't want to be late for his appointment with Isabella, fearing he'd lose his chance of ever talking to her again.

"Wait!" Janice halted, refusing to budge another step. "What's going on, Jay? Who are you going to see?"

"Janice, I am not trying to hurt you, but I must go."

"Jay, I have gone out of my way to plan this day for us, and…" she was near tears.

"Well, you should have relayed that to me." Jay eyed her, feeling her pain. "But, this is very important."

"And so is this!"

"How about I come over tonight, and we'll have a picnic on the floor, by the fire?"

"It's not cold enough for a fire."

"Okay, forget the fire," Jay was impatient. "I'll just come over, and we can talk then."

Janice felt torn. She wanted to be mad, but she also wanted to be with Jay. "You promised to tell me all about this important appointment tonight."

"Yes, I promise." Jay opened her car door. "See you tonight. I'll call before coming over."

"See you tonight. Don't be too late." Janice blew him a kiss.

Oh Lord, I need Your help on this one! Jay dashed to his car and hurried to the park.

Jay nervously sat on the worn-out park bench centered in the middle of the park. He was ten minutes late. *I pray that Isabella hasn't already come and gone!* He was anxious as if this was his first blind date. Only there was nothing blind about this date. Jay knew what to expect. A feisty, spunky, yet troubled young lady, which secretly thrilled him.

On the way, he picked up a variety of sandwiches from the deli nearby. Uncertain of her preference, he selected several kinds, along with potato salad, chips, iced tea, and bottled water. For dessert, he purchased several homemade cookies. Strangely, Jay wanted to please her, not just with lunch, but with a simple picnic. He endeavored to overindulge Isabella with kindness since she had been treated so shoddily by most men and people in general.

He unsuspectingly borrowed a tablecloth from his mother, along with plastic utensils and tableware. In the center of the picnic table, he put a fresh tulip arrangement, which he bought at the flower station next to the deli shop.

Lewis, I think you'd be proud of me. Hopefully, your sister will feel the same way.

After waiting about twenty minutes, Jay had just about deduced that Isabella wasn't coming and started putting up the tableware.

"Hi," shyly Isabella came from behind, taken aback by the picnic display. *Wonder what he's expecting in return.*

"Hi, Isabella!!" Loudly, he exclaimed, delighted to see her. He stood and greeted her, unsure whether to shake her hand, hug her, or just smile. Jay settled for smiling.

"All this for me," timidly Isabella sat down, observing Jay's laidback attire. She figured he'd be dressed as if he was going to church again. "I thought we were just going to talk about my brother." *What is he up to?*

"Of course," Jay wanted to ease her mind. "I thought while we talk, we could share a small picnic lunch."

"Small," she repeated, observing the feast spread out before her as if she were someone special.

"Well, uh..." Jay chuckled, taking a seat from across the picnic table, "I didn't know if you like tuna salad, chicken salad, ham, or turkey or grilled chicken subs. So, I purchased all, thinking what we don't eat now, you can enjoy it later."

No, he didn't! No one ever cared what I liked or didn't like. "Thank you," Isabella lowered her head.

"Would you like iced tea or bottled water?" Jay was ready to serve her.

"Tea," she answered. "So, what did you want to tell me about my brother?"

"How about we eat first and then talk later." Jay started, still slightly nervous. "Here are the plates." When Isabella reached for a plate, their hands touched, which was electrifying to both of them. The brief yet potent contact sent her heart racing and thumping like a beaver pecking a tree.

Eating in silence, the two felt awkwardly uncomfortable. Isabella ate, not looking up once, while Jay ate but couldn't keep his eyes off her. Today, her hair was purple, with red highlights. Her pale green eyes were aloof and impenetrable. Isabella appeared all hard on the outside, yet Jay discerned that inwardly she was tender. Intrigued, Jay aspired to get to know this tender side of hers.

"Lewis said when you were younger, you loved to dance," Jay spoke, shattering the wall of silence between them.

"Yes. I loved dancing," her voice was almost chipper, as her eyes temporarily lit up.

"Do you still dance?"

"No."

"My sister owns a dance studio. Perhaps you can join a class or something there."

"Don't dance anymore," Isabella spoke with finality.

Why does she wear the war paint? Why does she cover her beauty with such ugliness? Maybe she doesn't want others to see her true self? Perhaps she is masking her pain through makeup. If only...

"How did Lewis die?" Isabella blurted the question that had plagued her since Jay's disclosure of his death.

"Oh..." Jay put down his sandwich, his appetite completely gone now. Concisely but candidly, Jay relayed Lewis' heroic efforts to save a little girl, which ultimately cost him his life. "I've never known a human to actually lay down his life for someone, in this present day, until I went to Iraq. I only knew one Man, and that's Jesus. I saw it with my own eyes in Lewis' courageous actions. I'll never forget what Lewis did."

"Did the girl live?"

"Yes."

"My brother was a hero," Isabella finally looked him in the eye, tears slowly ebbing down her face. "He was always my hero." When I was young, he was always protecting me and looking out for me."

Jay watched the pain shadow her countenances. As her tears fell silently, black streaks lined the sides of her cheeks. Her war paint left its marks all over her face. Jay wanted to reach over and wipe the stains away but feared he would scare her to stop talking. Instead, he handed her his handkerchief.

"He took many beatings for me," she continued. "When I was taken from my home, the only person I missed was Lewis. I…I…loved him so," Isabella couldn't stifle the anguish any longer. Unexpectedly, Isabella wailed like a wounded animal.

In an instance, Jay was beside her, holding her in his arms. Isabella buried her head in his chest and wept for some time, overcome with grief. She wept for her brother. She wept for his tragic death. She wept for her past life of pain and sorrow. She wept for the nameless little girl whose life he saved. She wept to find relief if that were at all possible.

Holding her, Jay inadvertently stepped into his friend's shoes. To be her protector. Her watchman. Her guardian. Her friend. Her comforter. And even her family. Jay didn't want Isabella ever to suffer alone, again. Though Lewis couldn't be there, he tried to assume her brother's caretaker role.

Abruptly, Isabella pulled away and scooted off the other side of the park bench. She wiped her face with Jay's hankie as best she could, realizing that her face was a mess. The evidence of black stains covered the previous white hankie Jay gave her. Embarrassed, Isabella didn't want to face him now as she slipped the damaged hankie into her pocket.

"Where is he buried?"

"He wanted to be buried in Lincoln. I looked for you but couldn't find you or any… living relatives…"

She turned in horror. "Any?" her eyes moistened again.

"I'm sorry. Only Damien is alive, but he's…still in prison," Jay's heart ripped into pieces at the obvious trauma this was causing Isabella.

"Oh my!" she covered her face with her hands, "I never thought that we would all die such pathetic lives. All except Lewis. He made something out of his life," she sniffed. "He died a hero."

Cautiously, Jay eased near to her and rested his hand on her shoulder. "Lewis died in peace, the peace that only comes from Jesus. He was the happiest I'd ever seen him. Your brother told me he was happy and wanted you to be happy."

Slowly, Isabella looked at him. "He was happy."

"Truly," Jay answered.

"How? Why? He didn't look so happy when he came to see me?"

"He wasn't," Jay replied solemnly. Jay told of Lewis' and the other soldiers' conversion in the barracks in the sincerest and softest tone. Isabella stood still, hands still covering her face as she listened. When Jay finished, Isabella released her hands and stared as if to see if he was for real.

"I'll never believe!" her words were abrasive. "My mother believed, and she died. Lewis believed, and he died. What good did their believing in God do them?"

"They are together now," was Jay's first response, "and one day, they hope to see you so that you can spend eternity with them."

"It'll never happen."

"Why do you try to pretend to be so hard? So uncaring?"

"Don't try to make out *like* you know me!" she lashed back. "Because you don't! You don't know anything about me."

"I know that you wear all that hideous makeup to cover up any sign of beauty because you feel so ugly inside."

"How dare you!" His careless words had pierced her vulnerable heart. Instinctively, she tossed his handkerchief at Jay. She wanted nothing from him. As surely as sparks fly upward, Isabella knew his words were accurate. Yet, she couldn't own up to it. She turned from him and started walking away.

Jay followed Isabella.

Her footsteps halted in place when she came to a small stream. She stood still in silence, beholding its quiet beauty. Jay stood beside her.

"This is a lovely place," he replied delicately.

She remained quiet, thinking over all the things Jay said about her brother. She was happy that he had finally found peace.

She wondered if it were truly possible to know such peace since all her life she only knew of turmoil. Was it possible for someone like her to have that kind of serenity? After all, she had lived a horrible life and done some awful things! Would God want her?

"I'm sorry for what I said," Jay was remorseful.

"No need," she shrugged.

Reaching into his pocket, Jay retrieved Lewis' military dog tags. "Lewis would have wanted you to have these."

Finally, she turned and looked at Jay's hands. Isabella took them, clenching them tightly. These were her brothers. She would always hold them sacred to the heart.

"And this," Jay handed her Lewis 'safety box. Inside was an old watch, the photo that they had taken together the last time the siblings saw each other, several other pictures of Lewis in his soldier uniform, a photo of his mother, her twelve-year-old photo, and ten thousand dollars left over from the insurance policy which Lewis made Jay the beneficiary.

Jay watched her as she caressed her brother's pictures, staring at them with love in her eyes. He saw such softness, not the hard-shell she only let most people see. She lingered on the picture of Lewis with his arm wrapped around Jay's shoulder. Then she counted the money, gasping as she counted out ten thousand dollars.

"Lewis wanted you to go back to school. Now maybe you can."

"I can't believe Lewis left me money."

"Please keep it safe," Jay warned. "It should go in the bank first thing Monday, if at all possible."

"Don't tell me what to do!" Isabella snapped.

"I'm sorry. I didn't mean to…."

"No, I'm sorry," Isabella felt bad for snapping at the man who was being so kind to her. After all, he was Lewis' best friend. He had shown her brother kindness, and now he was doing the same for her. "I'll do right by my brother."

"I know you will." Jay smiled. "And there is one more thing Lewis wanted you to have." Jay handed her a small Bible that he had given to Lewis.

"I don't want it." Isabella shook her head.

"But I promised Lewis I would give it to you."

"I don't need a Bible. I'll never read it. But…I'll take it because Lewis asked you to give it to me."

"He's marked some scriptures that changed his life."

"I won't read it," Isabella repeated more firmly than before.

"Isabella," Jay called her name so sweetly. "I know that you and Lewis had experienced such tragedy and heartaches that I don't take lightly. Lewis shared a great deal with me, but the peace that your brother had before he died can also be yours. A peace that makes the past bearable and fills it with blessed hope."

"Stop preaching to me. I don't care about all that. I'm happy that Lewis found what you call peace and Jesus, but I'm way worse than Lewis. I'm unsavable."

"We all were at one time. The Bible tells of many seemingly unsavable people; yet, Jesus came for those kinds of people."

"Lewis didn't tell you everything about me because he didn't know the half of what I've become."

"But God does, and He still loves you."

"No one can love me," Isabella scoffed. "I don't even love me."

"God loves you. Lewis loved you, dearly," *and I…* he cut the thought right off…

"Anyhow, I better be going." Isabella quickly turned and headed back to the picnic area.

Oh God, help me reach her. What now?

Believe in Me! Believe in her!

Once at the table, she busied herself by helping him repack the plates and things.

"Keep the food," Jay beseeched her kindly, "I don't need it."

"Thanks." Isabella kept moving her hands. With the task finished, she felt awkward and at a loss for words. "Thank you for everything. Goodbye."

The final word cut him deep within. He couldn't imagine not seeing Isabella again, which confused Jay. Isabella stood before him a mess, with her colorful hair, face smudged with blackness, clothes or should he say lack of clothes, Isabella was so unattractive at first glance. Yet, Jay saw something beyond the natural eye. He saw a little girl trapped in an adult body of a painful past. He knew that deep down, Isabella was beautiful. Jay longed to help her discover her true beauty…her true self.

"Would you like to see your brother's grave?"

She hadn't thought to ask him about it. "Yes."

"We can go now."

"I can't." Isabella quickly rejected. "I have other plans. I must hurry now, or I'll be late."

There were no other plans. Isabella just wanted to be alone. She needed time to grieve alone. Time to just savor her brother's love, musing over his pictures. She missed him. She ached for Lewis, and Isabella didn't want Jay to see her so vulnerable. He'd already seen her weakness as she wept before him. Like all men, Isabella assumed he'd take advantage of her in her time of weakness. Though Jay appeared different from anybody else she knew, Isabella didn't trust her instincts right now. She was too close to breaking to trust anything.

Jay was disappointed but endeavored not to show it. "What about tomorrow? I have to attend church, but maybe about five or six in the evening?"

"That will be fine."

"Should I pick you up at the motel?"

"I reckon," Isabella walked away. "Thanks for the food," she turned and looked at him one final time.

"You're welcome," Jay beamed. "See you tomorrow."

He watched her until he could no longer make out her body. For no reason at all, he felt optimistic. Isabella hadn't completely closed the door. Jay vowed that he wouldn't give up on her just like he didn't give up on Lewis.

She's a tough nut to crack, Father, even more, challenging than Lewis. I feel helpless, but I know You are my Helper.

I'll never leave you or forsake you. I'm with you!

Chapter 15

That night Jay sat on the floor with Janice attempting to enjoy a picnic dinner, but his thoughts were elsewhere. All he could do was think about Isabella. *Is she with someone else? Did her other plans include a man? Will she continue to live this lifestyle even after receiving the money from her brother?*

"Earth to Jay, earth to Jay," Janice snapped her fingers in his face.

"Oh, I apologize," Jay felt as if he had been caught in the act of adultery. Although he wasn't married to either woman and had not overstepped the boundaries of intimacy, he still felt busted.

"Hope you were thinking of me," Janice leaned closer, resting her head on his shoulder.

Jay just smiled.

"So tell me about your appointment."

Here it goes. Jay felt apprehensive, but he was a man of his word. "You know how much I miss Lewis," he began. "You remember me telling you that Lewis had a sister, and he wanted me to help her."

"Help her," Janice sat up, looking directly at him. "Help her with what?"

"It's a long story, Janice." Jay didn't feel much like sharing Isabella's personal story with Janice. It didn't seem right. "Let's just say that she's been through a lot. She's a lost sheep, needing to find the True Shepherd."

"Oh, I see," peculiarly, Janice felt threatened by the stranger. "And well, did you help her?"

"It's not that simple." Feeling uncomfortable, Jay stood up. "She's suffered a great deal. It's going to take some time."

"You mean you're going to be spending more time with her?" Janice stood up and faced him. She was about to confront her future. Possibly the thing she feared the most was about to come true.

"I have to."

"How old is she?"

"I think she's in her early twenties, not sure. She looks much older because of the hard life she has lived."

"What's her name?"

"Isabella."

Just the way he said her name, Janice knew there was much more to this woman. "So, where does that leave us?"

Here it really goes! "Janice," Jay took her hands in his, "you know I care a great deal for you. You've been very patient with me, but...but...I just don't...think...that we can go beyond friendship." *There! Oh God, I feel so bad...and relieved at the same time.*

Janice dropped his hands immediately, matching her heart, which had fallen. The time had come for the truth to show up. Unfortunately, it wasn't the truth she had wanted to hear. *How could he do this to me?* "I don't understand," her eyes watered. "The other night, I thought...I thought you were going to propose to me."

"Propose?" he didn't suspect she knew.

"Well...after you left that night, I was so upset, and well, I called your mother to see if you had made it home, and your mother said, 'congratulations!'"

Oh no! She didn't!

"She was only trying to make me feel better. Then, she told me about the ring she found in your drawer."

"I can't believe my mother is being a busybody. She had no right."

"She didn't mean to." Janice defended. "And you shouldn't be mad at her. Anyhow, what about the ring? Were you going to propose to me that night?"

"I…uh…yes…maybe," Jay grudgingly admitted, running his fingers through his hair. "But…"

"You saw that girl and went after her," the memory frequently haunted Janice.

"It's not like that, Janice. Isabella has nothing to do with it. It's just…something is missing between us. We've been friends for so long. I just can't get my heart to go beyond friendship."

"I had such hope, and now my hope is gone." Janice crumbled to the floor in a heap of tears. Her world was shattered.

Jay fell to his knees to comfort her. "I'm sorry, Janice. I thought I could marry you and learn to love you like you deserve to be loved. I've been trying to tell you this, tell everybody, but nobody seems to listen or understand. The war changed me, Janice. Look at me!"

Reluctantly, she obliged.

"My hearing is not the only thing missing," he explained, "my heart is missing. I've lost my heart for life! I question my faith all the time. I don't know who I am anymore. How can I marry anyone when I don't know my own identity. It's not fair to you or me."

"Do you love me?" Janice had to know. "Because if you do, I'll wait for you to discover who you are again. Jay, I'll wait for you."

"You've been waiting too long for me, Janice. It's not right. I don't want you to wait anymore. Go on with your life. You deserve better."

"Do you love me?"

"I will always love you, Janice," Jay answered truthfully. *Just not the way you deserve to be loved.*

"Then, that's all I needed to know. I'll wait for you," Janice stood up, resolved.

"No." Jay nearly shouted. "You can't. I don't want you," the harsh truth rolled off his lips.

"You don't want me," the words felt like a *stun gun* just pierced her heart, shocking it out of rhythm.

"Janice," Jay felt trapped like in the war, "I am not going to marry you. Not today. Not tomorrow. Not ever."

Silent tears flowed freely as Janice shook all over. "Finally, the truth. Though it hurts, I can deal with the truth."

"I'm sorry," Jay struggled with his emotions as tears pricked his eyes. He loved Janice, like a sister. She meant so much to him. Her letters kept him going during the war. Her prayers helped sustain him. Just knowing that he could talk to Janice comforted Jay on many lonely nights. "I wish things could be different."

"Things are different," Janice stated matter-of-factly. "We'll never go back to the way things used to be. I will survive this, and I will move on."

"Forgive me, Janice."

"Forgiven," she replied honestly. "Goodnight, Jay, and Goodbye."

"Goodbye." Jay left. He felt hurt for causing her pain, but deep down, there was a sense of relief. He knew that he had done the right thing.

God, please comfort Janice and send her the right man who will love her unconditionally.

Returning home, Jay felt drained. In times like these, he would talk to his father, pick his brain, and seek spiritual guidance, but not tonight. Jay knew that he had disappointed his father about preaching the next day, and he didn't have the heart to talk to him right now, especially not about his personal life.

Unable to sleep, Jay got out of bed and went to the kitchen searching for his mother's homemade double chocolate brownies. That was the cure for his aching heart. Chocolate was pretty much a weakness of all the Cannons and the antidote to making them feel better.

Thinking he'd be alone, Jay discovered his mother in the kitchen drinking milk and eating a chocolate brownie. Chocolate was definitely Esther's weakness. Her waistline was beginning to reveal it.

"Can't sleep either?" she asked.

"Nope."

"Join me." Esther got up and fixed Jay a glass of milk and retrieved a saucer for the brownie.

"How is dad?"

"Health-wise, he's improving." Choosing her words carefully, Esther answered.

"I know he's disappointed in me."

"Not in you. He just wants you to walk in your purpose."

"I will."

"He knows the war has changed you, Jay," Esther launched her lecture. "We all know it. Losing people to the war is difficult, especially when it was so obvious how connected you and Lewis were."

"Oh, Mom, I miss Lewis so. I never thought I would miss anyone like this." Jay confided. "I've lost several friends and good men in the army. But, Lewis was different. He was a great guy. He taught me a lot about life. I was knowledgeable in books and spiritual things, but Lewis taught me many things I was clueless about. He was streetwise smart. Together, we complimented each other well, as friends."

"I'm glad you had such a friend in the army. God knew your need then and sent you Lewis so you wouldn't be so lonely."

"It's more than that. Lewis made me a better Christian, Mom. He expected me to live what I preached, even when my faith was faint. If I said something, Lewis wanted me to prove it to him in the Bible. He just didn't take my word for it." Jay chuckled. "I felt that God was training and testing me, through Lewis. Lewis had me under a microscope, seeing the real me. I know that sounds strange, but it's true."

"Not strange at all," Esther understood all too well. "That's what your dad said about me. He said when he met me that I looked straight through him as if God was using my eyes to see the real James."

"Really?"

"Really."

"Wow!" Jay bit a chunk out of the large brownie. "I'd expect that much from you. You're such a godly woman with a heart of pure gold."

"Maybe now, but not then."

"Huh?"

"When I met your father in college, he had rescued me from one of my many male callers."

"You're kidding." Jay nearly strangled on his brownie. He had never heard a bad word spoken about his mother. Yet, now he heard from the horse's mouth that she wasn't such an innocent filly.

"No, I'm not. While your dad walked around with books in his hands, I walked around with a male holding mine. Always a man around me."

"Mom!"

"Don't mom me. I'm not the same woman I used to be." Esther eyeballed him. "God used your father to change me."

Isabella. Suddenly she popped into his head.

"Anyhow, one night at a frat party, your dad came. He never went to parties, but later, he told me God had orchestrated his footsteps to the party. I was dancing with a guy, and the guy started getting way too touchy-feely. I left him on the dance floor and went outside for some fresh air. The guy followed me outside and wouldn't leave me alone. He became more aggressive, and I screamed. My scream came to your father's ears, and he punched that guy so hard that the guy had to be rushed to the hospital. Your dad knocked him plum unconscious."

"Dad?!" Jay just couldn't imagine his dad hitting anyone.

"Yes, your dad. He didn't even know me, but he defended my honor. What little of it I had back then." Esther giggled.

"My goodness, Mom. You make it out like you were some kind of...of..." Jay couldn't even say the word.

"Slut," Esther finished his thought. "I wasn't a slut in the sense of the word sleeping around, but I misled men back then. I would date one, and then another, and sometimes two or three at the same time. I was really out there, confused and full of myself."

Jay was shocked. All he could picture was his mother being a saint all of her life.

"But why were you like that?" Jay gulped his milk down, leaving the glass squeaky clean. His throat was so dry and parched from this conversation with his mother.

"I just wanted the attention." Esther went on to expound a little more, never really talking about her life before James to her children. "You see, it was just me, my mother, your aunt Grace, and Grandpa Reese, your great grandfather. I loved him dearly. After he died, I was lonely for a father figure...a man in my life. I never knew my father. He left when I was four. My mother worked hard, saving up money for me to go to college. When I got there, I had never known such freedom, especially not around boys. I didn't want to get close to anyone, but I enjoyed the attention. Everyone I got close to left me. My mom gave me three daddies, not legally, but they all left me. So, I associated men with pulling up stakes and leaving me high and dry."

"And dad?"

"He was too religious for me, at first. James was always telling me what was right and not right. So, I started challenging his faith. I'd make him tell me why? Show it to me in the Bible. He said he never studied the Bible so much until he met me," again Esther giggled.

"Like Lewis."

"Like Lewis." Esther acknowledged. "With all the questions I was asking, and all the answers he was giving, I found myself hungry for more of James' Bible and religion. I started going to church with him and spending time with him. His family didn't like me initially. They thought I was too worldly for him, but I guess I grew on them."

"Oh, Mom, what an awesome testimony." Jay loved and respected his mother even more for sharing this with him.

"Like your dad told his parents, *'he couldn't help who his heart loved.'* No more than you can, Jay."

"Huh?"

"I have known for some time now that you don't truly love, Janice. Not the way your father and I love each other. Your father and I both wanted you to love Janice. I guess we've pushed our feelings onto you, causing undue stress. It's just that Janice is such a sweet Christian woman."

"She is," Jay agreed. "I tried, Mom. I fervently tried to love her."

"Love is not something you try, Jay," Esther rectified. "It's something you do…involuntarily, without thought."

"I can't marry her, Mom," Jay spoke truthfully.

"Did you tell Janice?"

"Yes."

"How did she take it?"

Jay started to mention the ring to her, but rubbing his mother's nose in her overstepping boundaries just didn't seem right now. "She took it better than I thought. She said she would survive this and that we could not go back to the way we used to be. Friendship is out."

"That's understandable." Esther watched her son closely. "And, how are you?"

"I feel relieved, Mom. Feeling as if I had to marry her out of obligation was a burden too heavy for me to carry anymore. It was dragging me down, making me depressed even more."

"I'm glad you both were honest. Now Janice can go on with her life and you, with yours. Is there someone else who your heart pines for?"

Jay wondered if his mother already knew the answer. "No, not really."

Knowing her son, Esther probed further, "Lewis' sister?"

"Her name is Isabella." Jay opened the door slightly. "We're opposites. She's...she has purple hair." Jay laughed. "Red, blue or orange hair."

"Purple hair," Esther's forehead wrinkled in worry. "Blue hair." She couldn't get past the colorful hair to say anything else.

"Well, it was pink when I first met her."

"Pink!" Esther covered her mouth with her hands. "What in the world!"

"My sentiments exactly." Jay got up, intending to go back to bed. "Don't worry, Mom. There won't be a shotgun wedding. And I won't dye my hair purple."

"James Cannon, Jr., you get right back here!" She called after him, but he kept going. "James!"

"Goodnight, Mom!"

Lord, pink...purple...hair!

Chapter 16

$\mathcal{J}$ay sat uncomfortably in the church pews as he listened to his Uncle Joseph's sermon. The Word was stepping all on his toes. Joseph's title alone, *No Excuses*, hit home with Jay. He preached about Moses being called to lead the people out of Egypt. Moses had many excuses, but not one of them negated God's purpose for his life.

"Hey, you want to switch shoes," Reese leaned over and whispered in his brother's ear after church. "I know your feet are hurting. Uncle Joseph was walking all over your shoes."

"Hush up!" Jay whispered back. "Look who's talking. You've been running from being the Minster of Music for years. Janice is doing what you ought to be doing."

"Ouch!" Reese played. "I think I better keep on my own shoes because you just hammered a nail in my foot."

"Better your foot than your small puny head."

"Now, look who's talking." Reese playfully shoved his big brother. "If that *ain't* the pot calling the kettle black."

"Hi Reese," Janice interrupted the playful banter she witnessed so often between the brothers. "Jay," Janice acknowledged him coolly.

"Hello Janice," Jay chimed in. "You look lovely today."

"Thanks," she refused to look into those mesmerizing yellowish-brown eyes of his fearing that it would draw her into its clutches. "Reese, has Rose already gone home?"

"Yes," Reese answered, wondering about the sudden tension. "She's helping mother with dinner today."

"Please tell her to give me a call later." Janice turned to walk away.

"Wait." Jay gently grabbed her arm.

"I'll leave you two alone," Reese wanted to bow out gracefully.

"That's not necessary," Jay needed his brother to stay. "Janice, I really…"

"Don't!" Janice's loud outburst caused others to look. She was somewhat embarrassed as she took a step back. "There is nothing for us to say. As a matter of fact, when Pastor James is better, I am going to talk to him about resigning from my position at the church. Under the circumstances, I don't think…I can…" Janice couldn't finish as she dashed off.

"What in the world is going on, Jay?" Reese hated witnessing Janice's pain. He had grown to care for her as a very dear friend and faithful director of music.

"Well, I guess you may need my shoes, after all." Jay patted his brother on the back. "Seems like we'll need a Minister of Music after all."

At the Cannons' dinner table, everyone assembled as usual. Leela and her family. Reese and his family. And, of course, Jay alone. The discussion jumped from subject to subject, lingering on the subject of Janice and her forthcoming resignation from the ministry.

"I can't believe she's just going to leave like that." Pastor James was hurt, having no idea this was about to happen. "Is she being guided by her emotions or by the Spirit? We just can't all run out on what God has called us to do because it's uncomfortable." Pastor James then looked at Jay. "Moses didn't like going to Pharaoh, and yet, it was his God-given assignment that made him do it, in spite of his personal feelings."

"You and Uncle Joseph must have talked about the message," Reese looked up from his plate at his brother, whose eyes were no longer yellowish but reddish and fiery.

"We talked, but nothing was said about his sermon."

"Well, Joseph preached the same thing," Esther announced. "It was a good message."

"I was hoping Joseph would come for dinner, but Cassi's baby boy is sick. He wanted to hurry home and check on him."

"We'll keep little Karlton in our prayers," Esther stated.

"God will take us out of our comfort zone." Pastor James jumped back to the earlier subject. "It's not good to be comfortable too long because you can easily become complacent. Stagnant. Not moving and not growing."

"Aright, Dad," Leela interrupted. "You're getting all riled up. We've already had one sermon today; now is not the time for another one." Always the outspoken one.

"You had a sermon," Pastor James teased. "I haven't."

"Dad!" Leela sighed.

In agreement, little Sara squealed. Everybody laughed.

"See, even Sara doesn't want to hear another message from her Pa-pa," Leela winked at her dad.

"Alright, Sara, you better mind your manners," Pastor James winked at his granddaughter. "Don't be acting like your momma already."

"Honey," Esther spoke with her eyes. "Let's just leave Janice in God's hands."

"You're right." Pastor James looked at his son. "Are you certain that God is satisfied with your decision not to marry Janice?"

"A hundred percent."

"Okay, then, as my smart wife said, we'll leave this in God's hands." Pastor James smiled at his son. "Well, Reese, I guess you better be praying about the Music ministry. It looks like we need a Minister of Music more quickly than you thought."

Just like that, the tides had turned, and now the spotlight was on Reese.

"He can do it," Rose admonished, always her husband's number one fan.

"It's about time." Leela laughed at her brother.

If looks could kill, Leela would be eight feet under with the look Reese gave her.

"What about you?" Reese winked at his sister.

"Well…"

"Okay, enough, you two." Esther knew where her children were going with the conversation.

Around five o'clock, Jay excused himself from the family before they convened in the den to watch a movie.

"Be careful," Esther knew where her son was going. Though she had given Jay and this new girl to the Lord, she still fretted whether Jay was being steered in the right direction…by the Lord or subtly by the enemy, using this strange girl, Isabella.

"Always," Jay winked at his mother and left.

His heart fluttered as Jay neared the motel. Again, he felt both anxiety and enthusiasm. He wanted to see Isabella! Why? It didn't make sense. Lewis had called her a freak when he saw her picture for the first time because she was so weird-looking. Yet, Jay knew it was all superficial – a camouflage to hide her hidden troubles.

He knocked on the door several times, but no one answered. Jay assumed that she wasn't there and had stood him up. The mentation rocked his usually calm world. Knocking a few more times, Jay decided it was useless. Returning to his car, Jay heard the sweetest sound stop him in his tracks.

"Where are you going, preacher man in that sporty car?"

The sound of her voice fascinated him. Jay turned with the biggest grin on his face, flabbergasted. He couldn't believe his eyes at the vision that stood before him. Walking toward him was the loveliest creature God had ever created – the authentic Isabella. There was no war paint, no gothic colors around the eyes or mouth. Isabella's face was flawless, with only a hint of makeup and a soft pink lipstick. There were only streaks of a blondish color in her natural chestnut hair, which was long and hanging freely down her back. No pink, purple, red, or blue color in her hair. Now ever so close to each other, Jay was even more surprised not to see numerous earrings in her ears or even the hoop earring in her nose. Isabella only wore simple studs. No punk rock clothes, only a black pair of slacks, a grey knit shirt, and black flats. She looked every bit of eighteen, though she was twenty-two. Some of her innocence had been unveiled.

"Wow!" Jay couldn't contain himself as their eyes locked for a long time. Isabella was breathtaking! "Isabella."

"The one and only!"

"My goodness, where is all the...color?" he purposely looked at her hair.

"In my bathroom," Isabella laughed. "Don't get used to it. I have my orange dye waiting for my return. I just thought this was fitting for my brother. It's how he last saw me, before...well, you know." Isabella lowered her eyes bashfully. She could feel his eyes on her.

"Lewis would be pleased." Jay, at last, spoke through his hoarse voice. "Isabella, you are beautiful."

She drank in his words like spring rain on a hot summer day. "Thank you."

"Shall we go?" Jay rushed to the other side and opened her car door.

"Chivalry hmm...thought it was passé."

"You haven't heard my dad's sermon about that." Jay closed her car door. "Dad says that men should always show chivalry toward a woman. It's the unwritten rule of the Bible. Not written but implied."

"Sounds like your dad is a wise man."

"Very," Jay smiled at her, then cranked up the car. The forty-minute drive to the gravesite was pleasant. Albeit Jay did most of the talking, he enjoyed hearing her laugh. Isabella's eyes twinkled when she laughed. Jay never imagined that the evening would be so refreshing.

Yet the gathering was bittersweet, as Jay parked his car at the cemetery. Opening her door, he took Isabella's hand to help her out. Her hand trembled in his. Jay's heart languished at that very moment.

"Do you want to go alone?"

She shook her head, unable to speak now.

Still holding her hand, Jay guided her to her brother's grave.

Inwardly, Isabella admired the tombstone, which read: *A True Hero – One who laid down his life for a stranger.*

"It captures the essence of who he will always be to me, my hero," she sniffed.

"A hero indeed," Jay squeezed her hand.

She knelt, pulling Jay with her, not willing to release his hand. Isabella needed him. He gave her strength at a time when she needed it the most.

"Oh, Lewis. I miss you so. I never stopped loving you. I never stopped needing you. Now...now I have no one."

"I'm here," Jay whispered, wanting to comfort her. "You're not alone."

Isabella turned and looked into his mesmerizing eyes and then suddenly released his hand.

His hand felt cold, like ice. Her warmth was gone.

Tenderly, with the same hand, she reached up and touched his cheek, ever so gently. Then her hand gently touched his right ear, tracing the scar left by surgery. Isabella said not a word, but her watery eyes, matching his, spoke oracles.

"Thank you for being so kind to my brother and me." She smiled at him. It was a radiant smile, and a warm hug all rolled up into one. "I can never repay you for helping my brother," she sniffed more. Her silent tears became an outburst of deep suffering.

"Your brother helped me to become the man I am today."

Isabella gazed at him a long time, seemingly forever, and yet it was only a few moments. "You're a good man, Jay. I know that now."

Every ounce of his fiber wanted just to wrap his arms around this fragile woman and shield her from any more pain. Jay desired to reach over and run his fingers through her wavy hair. To caress her cheeks with his hands. And to...to...claim her soft, pink lips as his own.

Get a grip!

Sensing his desires, Isabella turned away and looked at the tombstone. It seemed that she was praying as she closed her eyes. All too soon, Isabella gathered her strength and stood up. "I'm ready."

Jay looked at the grave one more time and started walking toward his car. He thought to retake her hand but perceived her sudden coolness.

"Have you eaten?" Jay didn't want this evening to end just yet.

"I'm not hungry."

"What about some dessert? I know of this little café not far from here that advertises any kind of homemade cakes, pies, cookies, brownies, and one-hundred percent pure chocolate candies."

"I take it you're a chocoholic."

"Guilty!" Jay grinned, showing his pearly whites. "All of us, Cannons are!"

Isabella couldn't deny that Jay was such a handsome guy. So clean-cut and neat. His eyes sparkled. His lips were perfect. His teeth were straight and white. A tall body frame and muscular physique complimented him. Even with a slight limp, and a few visible battle scars, Jay was alluringly attractive. It scared Isabella that her heart was doing flips over him, her stomach completely in knots in his presence. Isabella knew it would never work. He was a pastor's son, and she was the daughter of a monster!

"What you say about having some chocolate with me?"

"No thanks." The atmosphere was becoming chillier inside the car than outside.

"Come on," Jay insisted, helplessly stargazing at Isabella. Considering his right ear, Jay was so conscious that he might miss something precious she'd say. "I promise I won't bite. Just dessert, nothing else."

Torn, Isabella couldn't resist. "Okay."

"Good." Jay's heart lifted.

"Can I ask you something?"

"Anything!"

"Your ear? Does it bother you that you can't hear out of it? Does not hearing in one ear handicap you in any way?"

"Not really. I mean, if someone is talking on my right side, I can't hear a thing. Usually, I can adjust my position when someone is talking to me like I'm doing now. The left ear seems to be sharper than ever."

"And your limp?" she couldn't help but notice it.

Jay thought a minute before he replied. "I hate the limp, but I still have my legs. Many of my retired army buddies are missing limbs. I'm blessed," Jay shrugged.

"I'm glad you didn't die," she said quietly.

Her honesty startled Jay, while at the same time giving him such peace. "Me too." *I came back for you!* Another startling realization.

An awkward silence followed.

"You have the most unique color eyes I've ever seen," later Isabella replied nervously. "Yellow and brown. It's amazing."

"A Cannon trait. A few of us men on my mother's side inherited it. My grandpa Reese, actually my mother's grandfather, inherited amber eyes, yellowish-brown eyes from his dad, and on down the line. My brother, Reese, has the same color eyes."

Uneasy, Isabella turned and peered outside the passenger window, thinking about how amazing this man was affecting her. In such a short time, Isabella was feeling something mysterious for him. Jay made her want to be a better person. Just like Lewis. The truth is, Isabella not only cleaned up for Lewis, but she also did it for Jay as well.

"Your eyes are unique as well. They appear the lightest color green, but almost crystal, clear like."

"Unfortunately, I was the only one of the Trevino clan who inherited our daddy's wicked eyes. We called them the eyes of the transparent Monster."

"Well, there is nothing monstrous or wicked about your eyes," Jay differed. "They are lovely…just like you."

Her heart did another flip. *I need to get out of here. This is not good for me. It's all an illusion. Too good to be true. I can't let my guard down around him. It's dangerous!*

"Here we are." Jay parked in front of the café. "Let's try it out!"

Isabella admired Jay's boyish look. He was so happy. Once again, he took her hand in his after he opened her car door.

"My lady, let's indulge ourselves in hopefully the finest chocolate in the Universe."

"Thank you, Sir. My pleasure." Isabella played along.

"No, the pleasures all mine," Jay winked.

Another flip! *Heart, I hope you can take all this flattery.*

After purchasing a mixture of chocolate candy, for Isabella, Jay bought a bag of chocolate-covered pecans and a specialty bag of chocolate bells with caramel on the insides. Definitely, these would be his favorite chocolates forever.

"Why don't we sit and have a cup of cappuccino?"

"I'm tired. I have a big day tomorrow." Isabella said more than she meant to.

"Do tell?" Jay playfully shoved her.

"I'm going to Southland Tech tomorrow."

"Wonderful!" Jay beamed at the news.

"It's nothing. I'm just updating my records and taking a test of some kind."

"It's a great start." Jay opened her car door. "Lewis would be so proud of you."

That was her motivation. Somehow, Isabella would make him proud. Even if he wasn't here to see it, somehow, Isabella hoped that he would know it, even up there in heaven.

He turned the car ignition and looked over at her, and said, "Isabella, I'm proud of you…very proud of you."

Her heart swelled up with overwhelming joy. Here was a man who barely knew her, and yet Jay was proud of her. "Thank you."

Chapter 17

*J*ay didn't want his precious time with Isabella to end. He hadn't felt so free in such a long time. He enjoyed every part of the evening, including the painful time at the cemetery. For it was there the two shared a common bond. They both loved Lewis; his death brought them closer together.

Escorting Isabella to the motel door, Jay searched for something to say to keep the conversation going. "Will you stay at this motel much longer?"

"No."

"Where will you go?"

"I've been checking out a few places," Isabella answered vaguely, unsure if she wanted Jay to know her whereabouts.

"Maybe I can help."

"No thanks."

"Can I see you again?"

"What for?"

"I just want to see you."

"What for?" Isabella put her key in the lock, purposely avoiding eye contact.

Tenderly, Jay turned her around, and touched her chin, tilting it upward, forcing Isabella to look at him. "I just want to see you again."

"But why?" Isabella's insides quivered, her knees went weak, and her heart was beating out of control.

"I like spending time with you. I enjoy your company. Did you enjoy mine?"

She nodded.

"Well," Jay couldn't explain the urge to taste her lips. He longed just to touch her. He had never experienced such a craving before for anyone – not even Janice. He had to get his flesh under control.

Isabella sensed that Jay wanted to kiss her every bit as much as she wanted him to. However, fear gripped her tightly. He was a man. They all had a motive. They all wanted something from her.

"Well, I like you, Isabella. Not just because you're Lewis' sister, but because... you're you. I think we could become good friends."

"What about the pink-haired or the blue-haired me? What about the lady with black eyes and weird clothes? What you see tonight, this is not me, Jay." Isabella pointed to her clothes. "What you saw yesterday, that was me."

"That's not you, Isabella. That's a frightened woman, trying to conceal her fears. Trying to hide behind a mask. Someone trying to cover her pain."

"Don't get all psychological on me. I'm not your patient, and you're not the *shrink* coming to rescue me from a life of gloom and doom."

"That's not why I am here."

"I don't believe you. Maybe it's because you feel you owe my brother. You don't owe him, and you don't owe me. I'm not a charity case. I have taken care of myself all my life, and I don't need you or anyone else to do it now." Isabella deliberately contended with Jay, wanting him to leave her alone...for good.

"Isabella, you're a sweet woman who has endured much suffering. This is both the truth and a fact. But what is even more truthful and more factual is that you deserve better. Lewis wanted a better life, and I believe deep down, you want it too."

"And you think you can give me better?" Isabella raised her nose at him.

"I think you can give it to yourself...with help." *With God!*

Isabella lowered her head. Everything was happening so fast. She wasn't used to the good things being offered to her without a price. "I'm unworthy of your friendship."

"It is I who is unworthy." Jay tilted her head upward again. This time not allowing time or fear to come between them. Jay gave into the desire to kiss her. He lowered his head, and their lips met for a fleeting moment. It was a delicate peck on the lips, soft and sweet.

She was enamored by the gentle touch of his lips to hers. For a split-second, Isabella felt like a little schoolgirl, not a care in the world. Then abruptly, like a bolt of lightning, Isabella pushed away. Stunned. Scared. Stupefied.

"That should have never happened," Isabella trembled, her voice quivering. "You're sneaky. You caught me off guard. I was vulnerable."

"I...uh...am sorry," Jay ran his fingers through his hair. Her accusatory indictments threw him for a loop. Here he thought that Isabella liked it, but she was calling him sneaky. Startlingly, Jay felt like a scumbag.

"You're right about that! You're Sorry for sure!" Isabella was mad, swiftly opening her door. "Please just leave me alone. Forget me, as I'll forget you." She slammed the door, hoping he'd think she was some *nut job*, and stay far from her as possible. Privately, Isabella didn't think she could withstand if he came near her again. She'd lose herself. *And is that a bad thing?*

Jay stood there, dumbfounded, in a daze.

"If you need me, Isabella..." Jay spoke through the door.

"I don't need you!" she fired back. "I don't need anyone."

"If you do, call me at any time." Jay slipped his card under the door. "Anytime, Isabella."

Isabella said nothing. Jay reluctantly went to his car, still baffled by the way the evening ended.

What in the world just happened?

Patience. Let patience have its perfect work.

Listening to his car pull away, Isabella threw herself on the bed and cried, pounding her pillow!

Why? Why did Jay have to come into my life and make me want more? I was settling for a life of hardness, and here he comes in, looking all good, smelling all good, talking all good...and making me feel all good! It's not real. Jay will try to change me and discover I'm not worth it! He'll see the real Isabella, the dirty, no-good for nothing Isabella – the tramp Isabella and leave me...just like everybody else!

Man looks on the outer appearance, but God looks at the heart...

What? Isabella sat up, wiping her eyes. Her mother had quoted that so many times when she was younger.

"Oh, momma, I miss you so! I need you now, more than ever. Lewis is with you...please, please tell him I miss him too." The sincere heartfelt utterance sprang forth from her heart and out of her mouth.

I will never leave you or forsake you.

What? Another scripture her mother quoted faithfully. Isabella could feel her mother's presence. Instantly Isabella called back from memory, one night, just before her mother died. Her mother was brushing her hair singing '*Amazing Grace.*' Then her mother put the brush down and said with the utmost love...

"*When my father and my mother forsake me, then the Lord will take care of me. That's in Psalms 27:10. Remember that my sweet Isabella. One day I won't be here anymore, but God will always be with you...to take care of you. He will never leave you or forsake you. Don't turn away from Him. Love Him and serve Him. I know you've had a hard life, but all things are working together for your good. You may not see it now. But one day, you will. And I'll be looking down from heaven, smiling and rejoicing because you're happy. I have prayed to my God to send you a godly man, one who truly loves the Lord and one who will love you with all of his heart. Isabella, you were created to be a pastor's wife. I knew that on the day you were born.*"

"Really, Momma? Like your momma?"

"Yes, like Nana."

"*I wish I knew her.*" Isabella's grandmother had died before she was born, thrusting her mother to grow up fast and marry young.

"*Me too. Remember what I am saying to you today, Isabella. You are a pastor's wife.*"

"*Okay, Momma.*"

The memory brought fresh tears but also a sense of peace. Isabella hadn't remembered that conversation until that very moment.

Mom knew then that she was going to be with the Lord forever. She was preparing me. Oh, Mom, I can never be a pastor's wife now. Not after the life, I have lived. Perhaps...

How fragile is life? How delicate is happiness? How sensitive is one's heart's desire? All like a passing breeze, here one minute and gone the next.

Jay was feeling sorry for himself as he lay on the bed, unable to sleep. He felt so out of control. At least in the army, he didn't have to think so much about what to do. Everything was set for him. Here on civilian territory, Jay overthought things. He was not in control like he was in the war. Like a puppet, military life controlled him. They told him what to do, where to go, when to go, how to go, and so forth. Decisions were already made.

Now, Jay had to make his own decisions, put on his big-boy britches, and make manly decisions. Decisions whether to walk in purpose or not. To preach like his father? To work within the ministry continuously, or to find a *so-called* real job? He had a business degree. Perhaps it was time to use it.

He just made a difficult decision about Janice ending their friendship. Now, decisions about Isabella Trevino. Was there a chance for them to be friends or more? Would she fit into his conservative lifestyle? How did Isabella fit the mold of a pastor's wife?

Slow your roll! Jay cautioned himself.

Oh God, what now? Where do I go from here? I promised Lewis that I would look out for her. I messed up. I crossed the line with her tonight. She'll probably never see me again.

Are you doing this for Lewis or yourself?

Jay mulled the question over before truthfully answering. *Both!*

Do you believe in Me?

Yes, of course.

Do you believe that I am here for you to help you?

Yes, of course.

Do you believe that I have called you to share my Word, in and out of the pulpit?

Jay hesitated, realizing that he must answer truthfully.

Yes.

Take a step into your destiny, and I'll walk with you. I will go before. I will be your rear guard. I will be in you, always.

Yes, Father.

Share Me with Isabella.

I want to, but how?

Love her to Me!

Momentarily, Jay dropped to his knees, seeking God's revelation and instruction. *Show me how Lord!*

Chapter 18

It had been a long week for Jay. While his father recuperated at home, Jay was busy at church, overseeing the ministry. So much hinged on him making the right choices. Not wanting to worry his father, Jay fervently prayed for direction. He wanted to rely on the other ministers and leadership, but apparently, his father had taken on the entire church's load. Unfortunately, they were not dependable, which was unacceptable. Running a church was hard work, and it required a team. The Body of Christ is made up of many members, each with their callings. From the least of these to the greatest of these, everyone had a role to play. Everyone was needed. After walking in his father's shoes, Jay appreciated his father even more so. Pastor James made it look so easy. However, Jay discovered looks could be quite deceiving. This was a hard job, but as his father always said, "It was the most rewarding thing he had ever done."

The counseling part came the easiest for Jay, but it was also the most draining. It required a good listening ear, patience, honesty, thorough spiritual knowledge, and sensitivity to the spirit. Jay was thankful for the educational training in chaplaincy in the army, which equipped him in helping the hurting. While serving in the army, Jay had much practice counseling his fellow soldiers. Many came to him for advice and spiritual guidance. He learned to listen for the things not directly being said. Unearth the root cause of the problem, and many times those were the things on the surface, but the things hidden.

This week alone, Jay had counseled four couples. The Joneses were contemplating divorce. Infidelity was involved. It was hard for the spouse to let go of accusing and blaming, although they wanted to work their marriage out. Another couple, the Adams, was young and very naïve. They just didn't understand the reality of marriage and the hard work that it took to make it work. The Odell's weren't speaking. They were living as roommates. Last but certainly not least, Jay counseled the couple, which pulled on his heartstrings.

Tammy and Chance Peterson. They were young but wise for their age. They had been married for three years…three grueling years of trials. Before marrying Tammy, Chance was a *thug*, a hardened criminal. He had been incarcerated for four years for stabbing a man after robbing his home. It was in prison that Chance gave his life to the Lord.

In fact, Pastor James and his church ministered at the prison one Sunday evening. Chance usually didn't attend service, but something was tugging on him to come and see what they were talking about. Chance sat in the room, taking in the powerful message about God's mercy and love, and Chance found himself walking to the altar with tears streaming down his face. Pastor James prayed for him, and Chance accepted Jesus into his heart. He had never been the same since.

After getting out of prison, Chance found a job at a local warehouse. It was there he met Tammy, who worked in the office. They talked often and shared their lunch breaks reading the Bible. It was a beauty and the beast romance, for sure. Chance and Tammy fell in love and married.

Tammy's parents, whom Jay knew well, were against the marriage. The ideal man for their daughter to marry wasn't a man with tattoos all over his body, nor a man who served time in jail for trying to kill a man to feed his drug habit.

Though Chance was now transformed, Tammy's parents still didn't accept him. As a result, Tammy was often caught in the middle. Notwithstanding, Chance's past life of crime repeatedly infringed upon the couple's present lives.

Chance had done so many people wrong when he was on the streets. Frequently past criminals interrupted their lives, breaking into their homes, sending threatening mail, calling at all times of the night, and making threats to kill Tammy or Chance.

During this counseling session, Tammy had just received a call from one of Chance's old homeboys saying if her husband didn't come up with the five thousand he owed by Sunday night, he was going to hurt her dearly.

"I'm afraid, Pastor Jay. I know I shouldn't walk in fear, but…but…I can't help it."

It felt strange hearing someone call him Pastor anything, but for some reason, though Jay requested to be called just Jay, both Tammy and Chance kept adding the title Pastor.

"I'm leaving!" Chance stood. "If I leave, then Tammy and the baby will be safe."

"Baby!" Jay had no idea.

"Yes, I'm three months pregnant." Tammy acknowledged.

"All this stress is not good for the baby," Chance paced the room. "I have to leave."

"You cannot leave, Chance." Tammy began to cry. It was evident that she had shed many tears as of late. "We need you."

"Sit down, Chance." Jay was stern, genuinely out of concern. "Let's talk about this."

"There's nothing to talk about. It's my duty to protect my family."

"Yes, it is," Jay agreed. "But it's also your duty to be there for your family, physically and emotionally. Your wife needs you, now more than ever. You cannot just shuck your duties like that!"

"Because of my past, she could die. I'll never forgive myself if something happens to Tammy or the baby." Chance choked back his tears.

"What about moving?" Tammy suggested.

"Running away!" Chanced felt belittled. "I'm not running. I'm not a coward. Besides, they'd find me. These are ruthless people we're dealing with."

"Why do you owe them 5,000?" Jay asked, praying inwardly that it didn't have anything to do with drug money.

"I don't." Chance answered. "They figured that's how much I should pay them since I am not in the gang anymore, a buyout. Either the money or life."

Jay ran his fingers through his hair. *This is way over my head, Lord. I need Your help.* "We'll go to the authorities."

"Snitch! I'm no rat!"

"Whatever you want to call it…anything to keep your family safe and together."

"I won't snitch."

"So, you choose to leave your family before snitching on your old homeboys, who would slit your throat with a knife or shoot your brains out because you don't have the money to pay them."

Chance couldn't believe Jay was talking to him like that. "You don't understand."

"Oh, I understand perfectly. Listen, I fought in a war, where people were dying for their country. My best friend died while using his body as a shield to keep a little girl from being killed. They were sacrificing their lives. Are you not willing to sacrifice your reputation, your pride, and your life for your family?"

"Yes," Chance answered without hesitation.

"Then I think it's time you go to the police. Do whatever you have to keep them, hooligans, from harming your family."

"What about Tammy's parents. I'm tired of fighting with them. It's all the time. They have no respect for me."

"I'll speak with them."

"No!" Tammy interrupted.

"Yes, Tammy," Jay affirmed. "You have to make sacrifices, also. You have to stand up for your husband. You two have become one in God's sight. No one…not even your parents should come between that bond. If they can't accept it, then they must step back."

"You're telling me not to have a relationship with my parents." Tammy couldn't believe her ears. "Pastor James would have never told me such a thing. He'd tell me to live at peace with all men."

"The Bible says, *'If it is possible, as much as depends on you, live peaceable with all men.'* In other words, sometimes peace is not within our control. This is why Paul left the door open. Sometimes, we have to choose not to allow anyone to break up our happy home, even if it's our parents. Then we pray for them that they will come around. However, Tammy, your parents cannot come into your home and disrespect your husband. That's not right. The Word says, '*For this cause shall a man leave his father and mother, and shall cleave to his wife; and the two shall become one flesh.*'"

"Thanks, Pastor Jay." Finally, Chance had someone on his side.

"Listen, if you two love each other, you are going to have to keep the outside...outside. Do you know what causes a boat to sink?"

"Huh?" Chance had no idea where Jay was going with this.

"When water gets on the inside," Tammy answered.

"Absolutely. When the outside elements get on the inside, the boat is weighted down; therefore, it sinks. Same way with life and marriage. When we allow the outside elements... such as family, friends, bills, and our past, to get on the inside of our oneness...we become too weighed down, and we sink. Our marriages dissolve."

"Deep Pastor Jay." Chance appreciated the analogy.

"I don't want to lose Chance. I love him so much."

"And I love you, too," Chance knelt beside her. "You are my world."

"Okay, so there are two things you both have to do. Chance, go to the police. Have you taped any of the calls of them asking you for money to pay your way out of the gang?"

"Yes."

"What about the threatening letters and vandalism to your house?"

"I have pictures and letters as evidence."

"Good. Make copies, give the copies to me for safekeeping and take the originals to the police. I want this done, immediately."

"Done." Chance affirmed.

"And Tammy, talk to your parents. Let them know you love and appreciate all that they have done for you. However, give them an ultimatum. Either they are for you or against you. If they are coming against your marriage, your husband...they are against you. Tell them enough is enough, and you can't condone and accept such behavior anymore. Tell them you love Chance, and you have to stand as one in your marriage, especially now that there is a baby involved."

"I'll try."

"Trying is not good enough," Jay stated firmly. "For when you try, the door is left cracked for failure. Be a doer. Just do it."

Tammy nodded.

"Chance, your past is just that….past! Don't allow any human to make you live in it. Live in the now! God has changed you. Your name says it all. He's given you another chance to be the man of God that He's called you to be."

Chance stood up and shook his hand. "I'm glad you took the time out to see us, Pastor Jay."

"My pleasure. But the most important thing the two of you can do is pray together and pray often. Stand in agreement on what you're asking God to do for you and stand in faith."

After praying with them again, briefly, Jay followed up with one last directive. "I want to see you both as soon as you both have done what I've asked you to do. Call my cell phone, and I'll make time for you immediately."

"Thanks, Pastor Jay." Tammy followed her husband's lead. Obviously, Pastor James and Pastor Jay had different approaches to counseling. Pastor James coddled more while Jay cut straight to the chase. Today they needed a firm *hand*.

Through all the counseling, visiting the sick, and stopping by the elderly home for his father, Jay's thoughts constantly ventured to Isabella. He wondered what she was doing. Did she enroll in college? Did she think about him? If he weren't so busy all week, Jay would have ridden by the motel to see if she was still there. But after leaving the office, Jay was too tired to do anything but sleep and eat.

Besides, it will never work! Look at me. I'm a pastor's son, about to pastor myself. How can I be with a girl like her? Then he was reminded of Tammy and Chance. They were so opposite, and yet their love for each other was intoxicating. Chance was rough, rugged, and had lived a sinful life, but it mattered not to Tammy. She loved him not for the man he was but for the man he was now and the man he was striving to be.

Then he remembered his conversation with his mother. *Dad and mom were as different as night and day. Yet, their love is so deep and passionate.* Just like Chance had changed, so had his mom.

Is it possible for me, Lord? Will I ever know of such love? Is it with Isabella?

Trust Me.

I do.

Share Me with Isabella.

He heard once again. Jay shook it off. He wasn't sure he was ready to step into something he couldn't so easily step out of. Isabella had trust issues with men, while he had trust issues with life!

By Friday night, Jay was dog-tired. Around seven, when he finally got into his car to go home, all he could think of was Isabella. There was a desire to see her. To be near her. There was a longing he couldn't explain or ignore.

Isabella doesn't want to see me. She told me to forget her.

Go!

She told me to stay away.

Go!

I'm tired. Too tired to go running behind a girl who doesn't want to be chased. Jay drove home, ignoring the gentle voice imploring him to go. His heart was torn in two places. On the one hand, Jay ached to see Isabella. On the other hand, he desired to forget her as she requested.

As soon as Jay got home, he went to visit his dad. "I don't know how you do it, Dad." Jay sat beside his dad, who was resting on the bed. "Pastoring is exhausting."

"It's tiring, I'll admit, but it's so rewarding." James smiled. "I can't remember a time when I regretted being a pastor. It's my purpose for living. I find renewed strength from doing it."

Jay looked at his father like he was crazy. "You never regretted it?"

"Never."

"That's almost unbelievable."

"It's not a job for me, Jay; it's my life." Pastor James went on to explain as best he could. "Like Leela's purpose and gifting are dancing. She loves it. Your sister spends many long hours at it, and sometimes her body aches from it. It's not a job teaching others how to become better dancers. It's her life. It is a part of her DNA. She cannot just stop because it's in her," James pointed to his heart. "It's a heart thing. Just as it is not an occupation for Reese, teaching others how to play music, it's his life. It's who we are."

"Then something must be wrong with me."

"Yes, son, it is."

Jay was shocked by his dad's forthrightness. Since he'd come home from the war, his dad mainly had handled him with kid gloves. Presently, the kid gloves were off.

"What's wrong with me?"

"You have not surrendered to purpose." Pastor James assured. "You're still tiptoeing around it. Still doing what you want to do and not what God wants you to do…just enough to get by."

"I'm working at the church…doing pastoral duties."

"Are you preaching Sunday?"

Ouch! He's done it again. He stepped on his toes without even moving an inch from the bed. "I…uh…No."

"Exactly." James closed his eyes. "You can run, Jay, but you cannot hide. God's *got* your number. You better get ready. I have a *funny* feeling that your number is up. He's calling. Will you answer the call?"

"Minister Daniel is going to be back tomorrow. He's preaching Sunday. I talked to him already."

"I know." James opened his eyes and keenly looked at his son. "You better stop running, Jay, and just surrender. Your life sure will be a lot easier and more fulfilling."

"I'm a wreck, Dad! Why can't you see that? I'm not the…"

"Same man I used to be before the war." Pastor James finished the familiar excuse. "Excuses, excuses, excuses! Well, I *got* a revelation for you, son," James scooted up. "None of us are. We've all changed. Life does that to you. The question is will you let life change you for the worse or, the better? Use the war as your footstool to help you reach for higher and better things. Stop allowing it to keep you down. Instead of it stepping all over you, step on it!" James reclined back and closed his eyes. "I'm tired."

Jay got the hint. There was nothing more to say. "Goodnight, Dad."

"Goodnight, Jay," Pastor James uttered. "I love you."
"I love you too, Dad." Jay closed the door.
Harden, not your heart.
I hear You!
But are you listening?

Chapter 19

Saturday, Jay was up early, before the sun showed its glory outside, signaling a new day. He woke up with a feeling of trepidation. It was a heavy sense that something wasn't right, an eerie sensation. A deafening war cry penetrated his being—intense and demanding, beckoning Jay to pay attention to its distressing alarm. Fervently, Jay began to pray in the spirit. Then, he opened his Bible, seeking peace and guidance.

Studying his Bible, Jay found himself enjoying his reading. It was good to feast upon God's Word. Nothing could compare to what God had to say through His Written manual. Everything one needed was found in the Bible. Direction. Guidance. Conversion. Hope. Peace. Joy. Answers. Light. Strength. Love. And so much more.

After spending time in prayer and studying, Jay enjoyed breakfast with his father and mother at the kitchen table. He was feeling better.

"All is well?" It was more of a question than a statement.

"Yes, Dad. All is well." Jay smiled up at his father. "I wanted to ask you a few things about my Bible study this morning. Are you up for it?"

"Always." James transmitted his eagerness to his son. *Lord, I know You're working.*

"Good. I'll go upstairs and get my study notes. Be right back." Jay trotted upstairs. Soon as he got to the door, he heard his cell phone going off.

"Hello."

"Help me." The voice was shaky, almost impossible to hear.

"Isabella!" Still, Jay recognized her voice. He knew it was her. "Where are you?"

"Help me, p-l-e-a-s-e."

The phone went dead.

"Isabella!" Jay felt sick. "Oh God, help her." Frantically, he slipped on his tennis shoes and ran downstairs.

"Sorry, Dad." Jay paused in the doorway, "I have to go!"

"What's wrong?"

"Isabella."

"Isabella?" Pastor James couldn't picture her. "Who is she?"

"Ask mom. I have to go. Just pray for her." Jay dashed out the door like a jackrabbit.

He drove like a madman to her motel, arriving in less than thirty-five minutes, even though it should have been an hour's drive. Once there, Jay bolted through the opened door. There he found a lifeless-looking Isabella, half-dressed. She was a bloody mess. Jay thought he had seen enough blood to last a lifetime. This shouldn't have affected him, but it did in the worse way. This wasn't just any soldier. This was Isabella. Lewis' sister. The young lady who had captured his heart without even knowing it.

"Oh, Isabella. What in the world have you done now?" Jay couldn't stand seeing her like this. Her hair was orange. Her face was painted, black streaks all over. She only had on a ripped T-shirt and undergarments.

Quickly, Jay checked her pulse. She was alive, but barely breathing. Her face was a swollen mess. Someone had beaten her up badly. Speedily, Jay called 911 and explained how he found her. He slipped a pair of jeans on her and gently washed her face. Then he pulled her hair back and put it in a ponytail with a rubber band, which he found on the nightstand. He couldn't let her go to the hospital, looking as if she was some wretched person. Jay didn't want them to treat Isabella differently.

Maybe I shouldn't have done that. Evidence or something, but I don't want them to look down on her!

140

"He took my money," Isabella's eyes opened slightly, tears streaming down her face. "I tried to get it…"

"Shhh, none of that's important right now. Save your strength."

Isabella gave him a feeble smile and whispered, "Thank you."

"I'll do anything for you, Isabella," Jay's heart ripped in two. He felt so helpless to help her. *Lord, she needs You. Save her!*

In no time at all, Jay was following behind an ambulance on the way to the nearest hospital. *Oh God, help Isabella. Save her. She looks like death. I've seen its face, and death is ever so near Isabella. Lord, I can't let Lewis down. I promised him to show her the way. Let Isabella live and not die! I'll preach the Gospel if You do!*

Bargaining with God. Really?

I'm sorry! It's not about me. It's about Isabella!

Share Me with her! Love her to Me. It was the third time Jay had heard this, but this time it was more demanding.

Give me another chance.

Once at the hospital, Jay was told that he had to wait in the emergency waiting area; only family could be with her. He informed them that Isabella had no family but that he had promised Isabella's brother he would look after her. All other relatives were dead, except one who was incarcerated. The nurse said she'd come to get him as soon as it was possible.

Jay waited for several hours before a doctor came outside to let him know what was going on.

"She has a dangerous concussion. She's been beaten pretty badly. Her lung collapsed. Her ribs are crushed. Her ankle is very badly sprained; initially, we thought it was broken. Internally, she was bleeding, but we've stopped the bleeding. We're taking her up to ICU momentarily."

"Thanks, doctor." Jay nervously shook his hand, so glad that Isabella was alive. "Can I see her?"

"Since you're her only family, I'll let you see her in about ten minutes, and then you will be able to see her about two hours later. She's out of the woods for now, but she's still sick."

On that note, two officers came over to speak with Jay. Jay briefly explained what he saw when he entered the motel room, which wasn't much.

"Do you have any idea who did this to her?" one officer asked.

"No."

"No idea at all?"

Immediately Jay thought of the big guy who had beat her up before. But he didn't remember the man's name, nor could he accurately give a description, nothing to tell the officers. It could have been anyone of her male callers. "I'm sorry, but no."

When Jay was finally allowed to see Isabella, he wasn't prepared for what he saw. The sight of her swollen face and all the tubes protruding from her body gripped his heart as if a noose was tied tightly, suffocating him. Isabella's face was so large, double in size, since coming to the hospital. Her eyes were swollen, black and blue. Her mouth was stitched up and still purplish. Her head was bandaged. According to the doctor, other than being beaten and struck in the head, Isabella apparently hit her head on something sharp, for it sliced the back of her head pretty good. Thus she had many stitches. Isabella was seriously ill. Tubes everywhere. She looked ghostly close to death.

Oh God, give me another chance with Isabella.

Tears roll down his cheeks as Jay gazed at her. "Oh, Isabella, I'm here for you." Jay leaned down and whispered in her ear. "I'll never leave you." Softly, Jay kissed her cheek. "You rest and get better."

"We're taking her to ICU." The nurse came over and informed him. "You can come back around noon."

Jay watched them take Isabella away from him. He felt so helpless and guilty. Jay felt as if he let his friend down. He should have been there to protect her. Obviously, this happened last night. He had thought to go see her but chickened out. He was too tired! Why had he not listened to his spirit tugging at him to GO see her?

Jay went home with guilt, riding securely in his car and in his heart. After explaining to his parents Isabella's condition, everyone joined hands and prayed for the patient who needed more than physical attention. Isabella needed God's loving balm to heal her battered heart.

"Are you sure about this girl, son?" Pastor James' fatherly hat was on. "She seems like a lot of trouble."

"No more than I was when you first met me." Esther came and stood by her husband. "I was a handful."

"You sure were," Pastor James laughed. "Sure made my life adventurous."

"I added spice to your life," Esther quoted her husband's favorite saying.

"Seasoned it very well, I might add." Pastor James squeezed her gentle hand, which rested on his shoulder. "My life sure would have been dull without you. I am who I am because of you. Couldn't have pastored without your help."

"Likewise, Darling." Esther gazed at her husband with such deep love. "You calmed me and added structure to my life without stifling my free spirit."

Jay admired the love that flowed between his parents. He never knew just how opposite they were, and yet, they complimented each other so well.

"Back to Jay," Pastor James turned to his son. "Your mom was a handful, but we were meant to be. God orchestrated our paths to connect for life."

"I'm not sure where God is leading me with Isabella. All I know is that I sense His involvement. His approval, somehow. I know foremost, I must share Jesus with her. Isabella is lost, but God wants her to come into the family."

"Your father showed me, Christ, by the way, he lived. You can't preach to her son. You have to be her light in the midst of darkness. You have to live it." Esther spoke from experience. "From what you've told us, she's really out there. More than I was and for more atrocious reasons than I had. You have to love her through this pain of hers. Stand by her when all others are gone. Find your way to seeing the good in her despite the bad that's showing up on the surface. Dig deeper."

"You're asking me to look beyond her faults and see her need for a Savior?"

"Yes," Esther answered. "And see her need to be loved. That's all she wants is to be loved. She's never really had it, has she?"

"Only from Lewis."

"But even Lewis wasn't really there because his father stood between them, and then she was ripped away from him."

"Yes."

"Be patient with her," Esther added.

"Be patient with yourself," Pastor James further suggested. "Don't be too hard on her or yourself. Pray about everything. Let God guide you through the Holy Spirit."

"Yes." Jay embraced both parents. He needed their hugs and supported more than ever.

"I'm going to pray before going back over," Jay said before leaving the room.

"Our son has found the love of his life." Esther surmised.

"Do you really think so?" Pastor James wasn't convinced just yet.

"I know so," Esther spoke softly. "A mother knows her son. Besides, Jay's eyes declare it."

Chapter 20

Jay returned to the hospital eager but cautiously to see Isabella. He had to wait another twenty minutes before he was allowed back in the ICU room to see her. Quietly, he ebbed his way to Isabella's bedside. A coddled sigh escaped his lips as he stood over her. The color nearly drained his face as he beheld her pale face. He had seen that deathly color so many times, usually signifying death with the wounded soldiers. He had seen it in Lewis. Was he now seeing it in Isabella. Jay's knees weakened.

Right on time, a nurse came over and touched his shoulder as if to bring him back from his state of panic.

"She'll be alright."

It was as if an angel had touched him. Jay turned to see the sweet face to match the sweet voice, which had instantly calmed his fears.

"She's a fighter," the nurse went on. "I can tell these things. All she needs is a little rest. Rest from everything."

Jay remained silent.

"God can talk to her now. She'll listen." The nurse patted him on the shoulder. "Just share your love with her, and she'll feel His love." She winked and, just like that, left the room.

Jay was too stunned to follow her. *Thank You, God!*

Jay stayed and prayed, talking to Isabella and encouraging her in the Word of God. He was working on God's time clock, and it felt good. He was sharing Jesus with her, loving her to Him. Jay stayed until another nurse came to inform him that he had to leave. Walking outside, Jay questioned the young nurse about the older nurse who had just left the room.

"She had shiny white hair, blue eyes, slightly tall and slender." Jay racked his brain to describe her.

"We don't have a nurse with white or gray hair on this shift." The nurse quickly replied.

"But she was just here," Jay scratched his head, running his fingers through his hair.

"I'm sorry, sir. There is not a nurse here with white hair. On this floor, we have Nurse Bryant, Nurse Temp…" She named them all from memory.

Jay was stunned. *I know she had white hair.* Jay walked past the nurses' station and looked all the nurses over. She wasn't there. *What does this all mean? Perhaps, she really was an angel. Nah!*

Why not?

Jay's feet came to a complete halt.

Why not?

But…

Share Me with her. Love her to Me!

I hear You, Father

Be a doer of my Word, not just a hearer!

Jay went home and went straight into his room. It would be another four hours before he would be allowed to see her again. Jay needed help. He needed spiritual guidance and direction with Isabella and with his life.

Oh, God! I'm so confused. I know you've called me to follow in my father's footsteps, but I'm not ready. It's too much. And now you're asking me to love Isabella back to you. How can I love her? Look at her? She's lying in the hospital, probably from being beaten by one of her male clients. She's a prostitute. How can I follow in my dad's footsteps and be a minister of God's Word with someone like Isabella by my side? Why can't You just help me to love Janice? She's more acceptable as a minister's wife. But Isabella?

Wasn't I the One who sent Hosea to Gomer?

But…

Can the clay tell the Potter what to do?

No, but…

Wasn't I the One who sent My Son to the Gentiles, a people who knew Me not?

Yes, but…

Didn't He come to the lost sheep to save them…to be their Shepherd?

Yes.

Well, so have I come for Isabella. As I said to Hosea, I say to you…'Go again, love a woman who is loved by a lover and is committing adultery, just like the love of the Lord for the children of Joseph, who look to other gods and love the raisin cakes of the pagans.'

Jay wept.

Love her to Me and preach My Word, for I have much to say through you.

While still on his knees, his dad knocked on the door.

"Son, are you alright?" Pastor James stood at the door.

"I will be, Dad." By faith, Jay responded.

James hesitated, silently searching his spirit to see if words of encouragement were needed. "Minister Daniel just called; he's in town. He'll preach tomorrow, unless…"

"He'll preach," Jay reacted quickly, not giving his father a chance to assert his desire for Jay to preach.

"He'll be tired," James stated, "but the work of the Lord must go on."

Jay looked at his dad's poker face, wishing that his father would let up some.

"Stay on your knees in prayer," Pastor James grabbed the doorknob, "seems like you need it."

Jay lowered his head. Stormy emotions flooded him. Partly, he wanted to surrender to the call, but how? He just wasn't ready. He was still…still…

Bitter!

The truth startled Jay.

Yes, bitter.

Did Jay suppress bitterness in his heart for the war tragedies which damaged him? Did he still blame God for what had happened

147

in Iraq? Was he holding onto grudges at the *Iraq soldiers* for killing his friends? Babies? Innocent mothers and fathers…entire families?

In the crevices of his heart, the truth reigned.

Yes! Yes! Yes!

Jay knew in his heart that his Supreme God wasn't the One who caused bad things to happen. The fact that He was an All-powerful, All-knowing, and All-present God who could stop the unstoppable caused Jay to question his beliefs.

Until Jay could settle his heart's issues, there was no way he was fit to step on the pulpit. There was no way he was going to be a hypocrite. Sure, he believed in God. Sure, he loved God. Sure, he would never curse God and wish to die. And sure, though his faith was shaken, faith resided – may be small like a mustard seed, but that was all that God needed to work with. A little faith was better than no faith at all.

Before Jay knew it, hours had passed, and it was time to see Isabella again. Jay rose from his knees perplexed but optimistic. His life's story wasn't over. God wasn't finished with him yet.

On the way to the hospital, Jay silently prayed for Isabella and God's direction. He was torn, *split smack in the middle*, with his feelings for her. Was he going because of his obligation and promise to Lewis? Was he rushing to her side because God was sending him like Hosea to Gomer? Or was it something privately hidden in his soul? Jay was going because he cared for Isabella more than he cared to admit.

The almost hour drive seemed so long at present. Jay needed to be there for her, and although she was unconscious, Jay wanted to be there for her. He couldn't explain it. All he knew is that the tables had turned. Even though she was the sick patient needing to be revived, they were both sick. Only Jay wasn't hospitalized for his injuries. His injuries were concealed. Notwithstanding, Jay had the emotional scars to prove that he had been injured; the unseen disease plaguing his heart, perhaps, made him even sicker than Isabella. Bitterness had defiled him, slowly killing him inside, out.

He arrived at the hospital just in time for ICU to open up for visitors again.

"Isabella," he held her hand in his. Jay's heart was heavy, a load of burdens he carried inside. "I know you can hear me. I need to talk to you." He spoke softly, needing to release his troubled soul. "I can't talk to my father because he expects so much from me. Not even my mother can understand my inner struggle. You see, I've been called to preach God's Word. To follow in my dad's footsteps. My brother Reese and sister Leela have struggled all their lives, trying not to stand in my dad's shadow. Not to be a typical PK, pastor's kid. But for me, I cherished the fact that I was a PK. I wanted to be just like my dad, until recently. The truth is…, and nobody knows this but me and God…is that I joined the army to run away from preaching. I wasn't ready, then. Everything was happening so fast. Expectations were high, and I was scared," Jay wiped his brow, all of a sudden perspiring. "I didn't think I could measure up to my dad. And in all that running, look what happened? I saw too much tragedy. And…" he abruptly came to a halt, "I can't believe I'm unloading on you when you're fighting for your life. Please forgive me."

He just gazed hungrily at Isabella, as she was the food his soul yearned for. Her face wasn't as swollen, but the aftermath of someone using her face as a punching bag was still evident. It hurt him deeply.

"Oh, Isabella, it's been hard to believe anymore." Jay began again, his heart in complete anguish. "Hard to believe in myself. I feel like I have let so many people down. I let Lewis down. He died, and I lived." The verity of his guilt inwardly plagued him. "I even let you down. I should have been there for you.

"Just like me, Isabella—you *got* to believe. You *got* to hold on, even if you don't feel like it. You're needed. God needs you. Others need you. I need you.

"Fight to live, Isabella. I made a promise to Lewis that I would not give up on you. That I would stand by your side and guide you to Christ. I'm going to keep that promise, Isabella. Not just for Lewis, but for me," Jay was near tears but kept them at bay. "I promise you that when you awaken from your needed rest, I will be here. I promise I will always be here for you."

"You're such a sweet young man," someone touched his shoulder.

Jay didn't hear anyone tiptoe in the room. Thus, he nearly jumped out of his skin. "It's y-o-u!" He pointed, shocked to see the nurse with the white hair and deep blue eyes."

"You remember me?"

"Of course! The problem is no one else remembers you."

"Oh, that's funny," she giggled. "See, I told you she was a fighter. Her vital signs and heart rate are strong…just like her."

Jay looked over at Isabella. She did appear to be peaceful.

"You're a good man," the woman dressed like a nurse, but Jay wasn't convinced she actually was, touch his hand. Instantly, Jay felt the heat, which went through his entire being. There were no words to describe the sensation, and yet, it was just what Jay needed.

"Destiny awaits you," she smiled. "Don't fight it. Just surrender to it. Many are called, but few are chosen. You're chosen."

"Who are you?"

She grinned, not answering. "She's a sweet, young lady. Been through a lot. Her heart suffers. But love will conquer the pain. Love covers a multitude of sins." She checked the machines and tubes connected to Isabella. "She'll be just fine." She walked to the door. "And so will you. Love her to Jesus."

Before Jay could say something, the nurse was gone. His feet seemed glued to the floor. His instincts shouted, "go after her," but his body wouldn't cooperate with his mind. When at last he could move, he bolted to the door, but there was no one. He walked the floor, looking around, but there was no sight of her. She had disappeared.

Was she an…angel?

He sighed, feeling foolish.

Do not neglect to show hospitality to strangers, for thereby, some have entertained angels unawares.

Chapter 21

Another restless night for Jay. The war invaded his sleep. Reliving the deaths of his fellow soldiers was harrowing. To behold the eyes of his friend, Lewis looking up at him and the flickering indicating that the light of life was quickly vanishing as a vapor pierced him with ongoing agony. Will his friend's eyes forever haunt him? When will it all end? Jay was home for the war; still, it raged within him. It was never-ending. Jay went to bed with it and awakened with it.

Jay was at a major crossroad in his life. Why was he living like this? Why did the war entrap him? Why was fear walking in his shoes, taking him to places that he did not want to go? Something had to give and give soon.

Even if Jay wasn't preaching today, Jay felt trepid about going to church. It was a potent reminder that he wasn't doing what he was supposed to do. Another indication that bitterness had taken root in his heart, keeping him from moving forward into his destiny.

That's what the nurse said.

Destiny awaits you. Don't fight it. Surrender to it.

Sluggishly, Jay dressed for church, offering a quick prayer of thanks while adding a petition for Isabella's complete healing, body, soul, mind, and spirit.

With his mother on his right side, Reese, Rose, Leela, and Nicolas on his left, Jay was sandwiched in between, closed in, unable to escape the powerful, convicting message of Minister Daniel.

"We all know the story of Jonah. In short, Jonah was running from purpose. He was running from destiny."

Jay squirmed. *There it goes again – destiny!*

"The Bible clearly says, *'the harvest is plentiful, but the laborers are few,'*" Minister Daniel preached. "Pastor James has labored for this church, this community, this town for many years. I've seen him come and go, early mornings and leave late nights...never complaining and always smiling. Always eager to help and to give of himself. Yet, Pastor James was overworking himself. He was trying to fill the holes in the church where others should have been occupying."

Jay wriggled in his seat, feeling as if Minister Daniel was speaking only to him, pointing an invisible finger that pierced him to the core.

"He's only one man, and yet, Pastor James worked like ten or more men. He was wearing too many hats, and his body got tired. Still, he knew that many lives were depending on him. God called Jonah to go to a wicked city, where evil prevailed, and people were doing all kinds of things. Nevertheless, God loved Nineveh, and He wanted the people to change.

"Jonah, for whatever reason, didn't want to go, refusing to go. His spirit was stubborn. Jonah wanted to do what he wanted to do and not what God wanted him to do. So, what did he do? Jonah ran." Minister Daniel looked into the audience. Complete silence filled the sanctuary. It was apparent that the minister had knocked on the door of many hearts. "What are you running from today, my brother, my sister? Are you sitting on the sidelines of life, doing nothing while the clock is ticking by? The game of life is steadily playing. The score is increasing for the opponent team, the enemy. Meanwhile, the believers' team, team Jesus, is stagnant, lying dormant, quiet, not saying, or doing anything.

"The game of winning souls for the kingdom of God is serious. Whether you are called to sing, usher, preach, work in the mission field, or help ministry, and the list goes on, God has a purpose for you. He wants you in the game, not sitting on the sidelines, warming the bench. There are too many benchwarmers. All dressed up, looking good, but doing nothing." Minister Daniel paused, allowing his words to soak in. "I know I won't get a lot of *amens* today. I know it's tight, but it's right.

"It's time to play ball. Pastor James cannot and shouldn't have to do it all. I cannot do it all. You cannot do it all. But together we can form a winning team. A team that works hard for the kingdom of God. A team that doesn't run from our opponents but runs to them. A team with individuals who realize that others are depending on them. You see, God gifted each of us with a talent or calling not for ourselves…but for others. Remember, Jonah was sent to help others. Jesus was sent for you and me.

"Jonah ran from his purpose…his destiny. God could have said…forget Jonah. I don't need him. I'll get somebody else. Yet, God allowed Jonah to be swallowed by a large fish. For three days and three nights, Jonah was stuck. No place to go and no place to run. He was trapped. He was in a place where he knew that he needed help. Jonah needed God.

"Do you feel trapped? Have you not realized yet that there is no place for you to run and hide from God? Do you feel as if you are going in circles, going round and round, accomplishing nothing, ending right back at the same place you started? Perhaps you should do what Jonah did? Surrender."

Oh, my goodness. There it goes again. Surrender to it. Jay twisted uncomfortably in his chair, wanting just to disappear. His family members sensed his struggle. Reese even elbowed him.

"Get a grip," Reese mumbled under his breath.

Jay's face turned to beat red.

"God didn't give up on Jonah. Jonah was created for the purpose of going to Nineveh to share God with the people. God doesn't want any of us to perish. Whether you win a soul through singing, mopping the floor, picking up paper, or preaching…the goal is to win souls to the kingdom of God. You win them by showing love. You win them by getting in the game and actually playing.

"Stop running. Get in the game. The score is increasing on the other side, and many lives are depending on you. Don't sit on the sidelines warming the bench. Get up. Get in the game and play ball!"

Minister Daniel concluded. Reese got up and sang an altar song. Many came to the altar, convicted by the message. Others remained seated and prayed. Jay observed Leela and Nicolas kneeling at the altar.

Jay closed his eyes while listening to Reese's solacing sound playing his guitar to the tune of "I Surrender All." His tender heart cried out to the Father.

At the close of the service, Jay's legs felt like lead. He still hadn't laid it all at the altar. He hadn't surrendered to the call of his life. What was it going to take for Jay to submit fully?

"Here," Reese held up a pair of shoes, standing barefoot with his socks on but wearing no shoes. "You need these more than I do," he said thoughtfully.

"Shut up, Reese!" Jay barked.

"Man, how could you just sit by and do nothing after such a powerful message like that? Even I repented from running."

"You?" Jay was surprised.

"Sure. I'm going to step up to my calling in the music ministry. I am willfully going to be the Minister of Music. There's work to do. Minister Daniel is right; dad can't do it all." Reese acknowledged. "The clock is ticking. Time is running out. I am ready to play ball and win some souls for Jesus. It's about time you quit being so bitter. Stop trying to figure everything out. The war was tragic. Stuff happened! But you're home now. Life didn't stop. You survived. Jesus was beaten, bruised, and hung on a cross. Yet, He wasn't bitter. He was still playing the game of life on the cross. Even on the cross, Jesus won another soul into the Kingdom of God." Reese slipped his shoes back on. "Second thought. These shoes won't fit you. Wear your own." Reese put his shoes on and walked away.

Jay stood incapacitated. He had no more excuses. His baby brother seemed to have matured in the faith. Reese had endured much, as well. His wife left him for another man. Financially, he struggled taking care of Sandy and Randy while in debt *up to his ears*. For years Reese carried a secret, thinking his twins weren't his, only to find out later that they were. His lunatic wife tried to kill him. Yet, look at Reese! It didn't make him bitter – simply better!

Instead of going home to enjoy dinner with his family, Jay drove straight to the hospital. He just didn't want to face his family and endure the stares and their wondering minds.

Jay sat with Isabella briefly, saying little, only staring at her. His heart was too full after the message. Beyond the bruising, Isabella was beautiful. The swelling had gone down in her face. Though her hair was a grotesque orange color, she had lovely, long hair. Tenderly, Jay combed it with his fingers, relishing its softness.

The doctor had decreased the medication, perceiving that Isabella was out of danger and her brain was healing properly. He longed for her to awaken so that he could see her eyes. To hear her voice, even if she yelled at him to go away. Jay was becoming attached to her, and she didn't even know it, or did she?

After leaving the hospital, he drove back to Lincoln and stopped at the gravesite to visit Lewis. He stood over the grave, saying nothing but thinking a great deal.

As he was about to get into his car, he heard his name being called.

"Wait up!" Minister Daniel jogged toward him.

Not now! Jay forced a smile. "Hi, Minister Daniel. I didn't expect you to be here."

"My dad would have been seventy-five today," Minister Daniel peered back at the graves. "Hard to believe he's been gone five years."

"He was a great man."

"How is your father?" Minister Daniel asked. "I was just about to go visit him. Of course, your mother invited me for dinner, but I told her I would stop by later."

"Dad is much better. You know, dad, he can't stay still. He says he's coming to church next Sunday."

"Great." Minister Daniel was like family. He and Pastor James had been friends for a long time.

"I guess your dad told you about me pastoring my own church."

Jay felt like he had just been struck by lightning. His tongue was glued to the walls of his mouth. He couldn't speak at first.

"Oh, he didn't," astutely Minister Daniel reasoned. "Yes. Well, I've been filling in for my hometown church for the past three months on and off until they could hire another preacher. Well, they hired me."

"Con---grat---lations." Jay finally spoke. "Your own church. That's wonderful." *Oh my...now what? Dad's not ready to preach again, and the other ministers...Lord, this is too much!*

"So, I guess you'll be preaching next Sunday."

"I can't." Promptly the refusal rolled off his lips.

Minister Daniel was balled over by his response, especially after the sermon God had placed on his heart to preach. He knew that not only was God talking to several others, but He was talking specifically to Jay. "You can, and you should. It's your destiny. Your dad needs you."

"There are other ministers. I'm not ready."

"None of us are ready at first, but the Holy Spirit will help you. He'll teach you." No was unacceptable for Minister Daniel.

"You don't understand."

"Help me to understand, then."

"I can't do it."

"You can," his voice was firm.

"I won't." Jay glared at his minister friend of ages. "I won't be a hypocrite."

Minister Daniel truly didn't understand. "You, a hypocrite. That's crazy. You're a sure-enough Believer. Always there for the people. I heard about what you did for Tammy and Chance."

"How?"

"Chance's mother called my mother."

"Of course." Jay smiled, knowing the gossip chain existed in the church, big-time!

"Chance went straight to the police. Tammy confronted her parents and gave them an ultimatum. They didn't like it, but they respected their daughter's commitment to her husband."

"That's good." It thrilled Jay to hear the news. "Chance has truly turned his life around. All he needed was a chance and for someone to believe in him. My dad believed in him."

"Chance believes in you." Minister Daniel looked Jay straight in the eye. "Don't let him down. Don't let yourself down, and don't let others down. Most important, don't let God down."

He had said a mouthful.

"Okay, enough of the second sermon. Let's go eat." Minister Daniel hugged Jay. "I'm starving."

"Me too."

"Meet you at the house."

Jay watched Minister Daniel walk to his car. This had been a long day, and it wasn't even two o'clock. Jay was at a crucial crossroad. He could either take the road to destiny or the road to destruction. The choice was totally up to him.

If you are willing and obedient; you shall eat the good of the land; but if you refuse and rebel, you shall be devoured by the sword; for the mouth for the Lord has spoken.

Chapter 22

Before going to bed, Jay called Tammy and Chance to check on them. Both seemed relieved and freed from their previous stressful circumstances. It was so good to know that somehow, he was used as an instrument to bring peace into the young couple's home.

Resting, Jay's mind mirrored on the loving couple. Tammy and Chance were so opposite. She was so proper, raised in a loving home with two Christian parents. Tammy graduated from a prestigious college and just earned her undergraduate degree in Education. She was incredibly soft-spoken and kindhearted. Chance, on the other hand, being a former gang banger, was anything but soft-spoken. Chance had a rap sheet as long as his arm. He was a bully. His outer appearance would frighten the average person. He was bulky and had tattoos everywhere. Very rugged looking, his voice matched his persona – deep, strong, and demanding attention.

Opposites attract. He thought of the familiar cliché. Perhaps there was validity to it. After all, though he fought to deny it, Jay was attracted to Isabella, the pink-haired, blue-haired, orange-haired young lady with *black-owl-lined* eyes.

Then suddenly, it hit him like a flash of lightning. *Perhaps, I genuinely do care about her. Maybe I even love her! Perhaps that's why my heart flips when I'm around. Why can't I get her out of my mind and keep her from invading my sleep? Yet, look at her. We're as different as night is to day.*

Don't see as man sees. See as I see. Man looks on the outside, but I look within. That's where the beauty lies.

Jay pondered the profound yet straightforward revelation in his heart and finally fell asleep.

Monday morning, before going to church, Jay took his usual long drive to the hospital to see Isabella. To his surprise, as Jay entered Isabella's section ICU, there stood the white-haired woman with crystal blue eyes.

"Hi!" she greeted Jay, smiling wide.

"I've been asking about you," Jay immediately chimed in. "No one seems to know you."

"Oh, you worry too much about things that don't even matter. What matters is this beautiful lady here." The nurse turned and looked at Isabella, love permeating her entire countenance. She practically glowed.

"She's a fighter." Then, with all seriousness, she looked to Jay. "But I'm afraid she's not sure if she wants to fight anymore."

"Huh?" Jay rushed to Isabella's other side. His heart nearly flattened like a pancake about what the nurse just said. "Why do you say that? She looks fine. The doctor even said she was getting better."

"She's sleeping too long. She's hardly medicated anymore. She should have awakened from the induced coma by now."

"She'll wake up," Jay's voice cracked, unsure if he was trying to convince the nurse or himself. "She'll wake up." *She has to.*

The nurse walked over to him. "Love is the only thing that will pull her through. Love covers a multitude of sins. The Agape kind of love loves others through their hurts and pains, tragic pasts, and horrific sins. That's the kind of love that will pull this sweet, precious lady through."

She touched his arm. Once again, Jay felt a tender warmness flow through him as he looked intently at the woman. It was heavenly, something spiritual, for sure.

Her eyes were blazing now, not with fire, but with such warmness, magnetizing Jay. "Love will also pull you through the war that is raging within. Though you are here, a million miles away from war, the war is still with you. You must let it go."

A teardrop escaped his eyes. How did she know he was in the war? How did she perceive that war was taking over his life, even though he was no longer overseas? "How?"

"Love and surrender." She continued holding his arm. "God's love will see you through this, and her love," she pointed to Isabella, "will pull you through. You both need healing, and Love is the only cure. Plus, surrendering to your purpose."

For no reason, Jay fell into her arms. He had never felt such comfort as the nurse wrapped her arms around him. It was like a soft blanket sent from heaven, shielding, and soothing him with such peace, Jay didn't want to let go. "I don't know who you are, but I know God sent you to me and Isabella."

"Fear not. God is with you. Trust Him, and He will guide you. The attack is not unto death but life. Death is swallowed up. Eternal life is in Jesus, not just here, but beyond here. Stand guard. Be her watchman. Be ye prepared to fight for her, for she cannot fight alone. Heaven awaits."

"Huh? Jay feared Isabella was about to die." Jay pulled back, confused. "What attack? Do you mean what Isabella is going through now? Is she about to die?"

"No, young man. The attack that is about to come. Stand guard. God's purpose is beyond what you see. There will be no more running. As far as Isabella is concerned, be prepared to fight for her, for she cannot fight alone." The nurse said again and squeezed his hand. Then she took one last glance at Isabella, smiled, and departed.

For some time, Jay stood over Isabella and held her hand in his. With such tenderness, Jay caressed her hand. She seemed to be sleeping so peacefully. He vehemently pushed back his emotions, struggling to keep his composure. What did the nurse mean with her strange saying: *The attack is not unto death but life. Death is swallowed up. Eternal life is in Jesus, not just here, but beyond here stand guard. Be her watchman. Be ye prepared to fight for her, for she cannot fight alone. Heaven awaits. Who is heaven waiting for?*

"Isabella, please wake up." Jay beseeched, wanting her to open her eyes and see him. "Please wake up for me. You are so needed in this world. I need you!"

Is she getting better? The nurse said she was sleeping too long. Is she? Oh God, help her. Save her. Heal her for Your glory and for me!

Fight the good fight of faith.

Before going to church to work, Jay made a stop at Heaven's Soldiers, an elderly home his father visited every Monday afternoon. Jay's dad told him they usually sang and prayed together, nothing else. So, Jay figured he could walk in his father's shoes for this. After all, it was just a group of elderly people getting together in the facility's chapel. When Jay entered, they were already having church. One man was playing the organ. About 30 women and 16 men were singing a familiar hymn upfront. The pews were filled with about eighty people.

Wow! Dad didn't tell me about this…on purpose. Jay was just about to sit on the front row when a frail-looking man came over and touched him on the shoulder.

"Pastor Jay Cannon," he acknowledged, "you can come and sit where your father sat."

Jay almost fainted. The man practically had to drag him upfront to the small podium.

I can't believe dad tricked me. I have nothing to say. I can't preach. I'm not ready.

After two more selections, Jay was motioned to the microphone. His body felt like it was cemented to the chair. He couldn't get up.

"Come on *ya'll,* let's make Pastor James' son feel welcomed." The man started clapping. Soon everybody was clapping.

Oh God, I need You.

I'm here.

What am I going to say to these people?

Open your mouth, and I'll give you the words to say.

Slowly, Jay got up and stood next to the man who had the biggest smile he'd ever seen.

"Your dad would be so proud." The man said before returning to his seat.

"Good afternoon," Jay cleared his throat several times before finding his voice.

"First, I like to send my dad's well wishes to you all. He's doing great. He's getting a lot of much-needed rest. He's moving around just fine and healing rapidly."

The group cheered and clapped as if their team had just scored the winning touchdown.

Jay was overwhelmed by their response. They truly loved his dad.

After praying, Jay randomly opened his Bible and was dumbfounded by the scripture passage that caught his eyes, highlighted in his Bible.

This can't be what You want me to preach about. This could be misconstrued.

Read it.

"If you will please turn your Bibles to Isaiah 57:1-2," Jay paused, giving the congregation a moment to find it. "***The righteous perishes, and no one takes it to heart; Merciful men are taken away, while no one considers that the righteous is taken away from evil. He shall enter into peace; they shall rest in their beds, each one walking in his uprightness.***" Jay looked out and observed the faces of those to who his father had ministered to countless times.

Oh God, are You sure? Jay questioned, watching how blank their faces appeared. They looked confused. Almost as if he was reading something foreign, a language they did not understand. Words that were more fitting for a funeral than a regular service. *What am I to say about this?*

Open your mouth, and I speak through you. By Faith, speak.

Clearing his throat, Jay began, "When death knocks on our loved one's doors, it causes us great pain. Some of us cry. Some grieve silently. Many become despondent and discouraged. While others secretly question God's purpose for death. Why did our loved ones die so soon? Why didn't God spare him/her from death? Why didn't He just heal them?" Jay cleared his throat again, looking at their blank faces.

"Truly, we should grieve for our loved ones. However, the Bible tells us that we do not grieve as others who do not have hope. It's all right to cry. Jesus did. The most powerful story in the Bible is when Lazarus, Jesus' friend had died. It revealed to me that Jesus, though He was the Son of God, He was still human, having feelings, human emotions. Often people see tears as a sign of weakness, and yet Jesus wept. The strongest man to ever walk this earth wept for His friend and humanity. His compassion for his friends and the world moved Him to tears. We all grieve in different ways. And like Mary, we too may question why God didn't come to save our loved ones from death. Mary said to Jesus, *'If You had been here, my brother would not have died.'*

"Mary recognized that Jesus had the power to keep her brother from dying. But, later on, the story tells us that Jesus raised Lazarus from the dead. Why didn't Jesus show up before Lazarus died? The answer is so that the Son of God could be glorified through Lazarus' death and resurrection.

"The main purpose for anything in our lives is for God to be glorified. It may be hard to understand it at first, but later, when the dust settles, we'll see the footprints of Jesus going before us as we follow Him until our purpose is fulfilled. Ultimately, He is leading us to eternal life, where there will be no sorrow, no tears, no hurts, and no more suffering.

"Death will come to all of us. As long as we are on this earth, we will lose loved ones. Some will suffer tragically, while others will sleep peacefully. Yet, through it all, God has a purpose." As he noticed a woman on the second row covering her face with a cloth and crying, Jay paused. Another woman hugged her, and she also was crying.

What in the world? Maybe this is too sad for these older people. Lord, I'm not preaching a funeral message.
Keep going.
"In Isaiah, it says, **'the righteous is taken away from evil. He shall enter peace. They shall rest in their beds.'** When the righteous die, perhaps the main purpose is that God wants to spare them from evil. Spare them from more pain. Spare them from the destruction that is ahead of them. God sees what we don't see. He is taking them from evil so that they can enter a peaceful place and rest

from all their toils in life." Again, Jay paused as the information became true revelatory to him. In a flash, Lewis came to mind.

With deep emotions, Jay began to talk about his dear friend Lewis and his salvation. "After being born again, my friend Lewis was so happy. Life was finally good. He enjoyed his new relationship with the Lord so much that he was willing to die for a child he did not know. Isn't that what Jesus did? His purpose was to come and show us the way to God and then die so that He could return to His father.

"God had spared Lewis from any more bad things in life by using him to spare this child's life. Lewis' purpose on earth was fulfilled." Jay swallowed, his throat parched, as he concluded his sermon.

"When a righteous man or righteous woman dies, God has spared them from any more bad times. No more heartaches. No more sickness and pain. The righteous one has fulfilled his God-given assignment on earth, and the Father wants him to return to Him. A place where there is complete rest and peace. What a place it must be. Though we may cry about it for a while, we must allow God to heal our grieving hearts so that we can go on and fulfill our purpose. For one day, after we have completed our assignments on earth, we will see all those who have gone before us. What a glorious thought. For this is not our home. We are strangers here. We are heaven-bound, heading to a place where we will be with Jesus forever. He's taking the righteous away, sparing them from any more pain and giving them infinite peace. Let us pray." Jay closed his eyes.

"Dear Father God, thank You for loving us so much that You sent Jesus, Your precious Son Jesus Christ, to die for us. Thank You for loving me so much that You allowed me to befriend Lewis, who has gone before me and is now sitting with You. Father, thank You for this congregation. May they, too, understand that their loved ones are with You, at peace and resting in the arms of Jesus. I pray for peace now, for all of them. I pray for healing and comfort, in Jesus' name, amen."

Still perplexed about the strange message, Jay gave the benediction and closed his Bible. No sooner had he stepped off the pulpit, than the woman who had been crying during his sermon approached him.

"My sister died a month ago," she began. "We were twins and had shared a room here."

Jay was speechless as he listened.

"She suddenly became ill, but we both believed God for her healing. The day before she died, she had shown Travis," she pointed to the guy who had helped him to the pulpit and caused the congregation to clap, "the way back to the Lord. Travis used to be a deacon, but when his family died in a fire, he became bitter toward God. Look at him now! He's excited and happy all the time. Leslie, that's my sister's name, finished her assignment on earth, and now she's gone before me to prepare the way."

"Yes." Jay nodded, now understanding that God wanted to reach his precious daughter today – and him.

"God used you to help me see that I had to let go and stop questioning God. I miss her so much. She was all I had left, as far as family goes. But God knows best."

"Yes, He does. Do you mind if I pray with you?"

"Of course not," she closed her eyes and let him hold her hands.

"What's your name?"

"Laura."

"Father, I thank you for my sister, Laura. I ask Father that You give Laura peace that surpasses all understanding. Father, comfort her right now and continue to use her so that You may be glorified. Renew her strength. Restore her joy. Revive her spirit and rekindled a flame of love in her like never before. Help her to continue to help others find their way to you, until that blessed day when she is reunited with Leslie and with You, in Jesus' name, amen."

"Amen." Laura looked up at him with glistening eyes. "I thought God had forgotten all about me, and then He sent you here just to speak a word to me. He loves me so much."

"Yes, He does."

"Keep on preaching. For God has much to say through you. You are your father's son, that's for sure. But more importantly, you are God's son, and He has work that only you can do. The Almighty has unveiled your assignment on earth. Walk ye in it." She reached up and patted his cheeks with her frail hands. "Your dad would have been proud of you today."

166

Jay watched as Laura walked away. Everyone greeted her with love. She was surrounded by those who loved her – her family in Christ Jesus.

Chapter 23

That evening when Jay returned home, he felt something he hadn't felt in a long time – contentment. Today's message ministered to his soul as well as the heavenly soldier's residents. For just once, Jay didn't question Lewis' or the other soldiers' death. The realization that Lewis had fulfilled his purpose and wouldn't suffer anymore overshadowed the hurt of losing him. Jay would forever miss Lewis, but the memories of his friendship would somehow from now on bring consolation and not trepidation.

No longer angry or upset with his dad for pulling a fast one on him, sending him to preach, and not even telling him, Jay was now grateful. He went into his father's study, where he figured Pastor James would be and hugged him.

"Thanks, Dad," Jay uttered.

"Well, that's unexpected. I thought I was going to have to lock the door and keep you from coming in." James chuckled, looking closely at his son.

"Me too." Jay laughed and sat down on the couch. "I couldn't believe you tricked me, Dad."

"I didn't trick you."

"Oh yes, you did," Jay disagreed. "You knew if you would have told me that I had to give a message, there was no way I would have done it. You would have had to send Nicolas or Minister Daniel."

"Neither could make it."

"I figured," Jay said. "Why didn't you tell me?"

"It's time to stop running."

"Oh, Dad," Jay took a deep, deep breath.

"You have to stop running," Pastor James said more firmly.

"I'm tired of running, Dad."

"Then stop."

"But…"

"Stop there." Pastor James held up his hand. "Minister Daniel will not be here Sunday. You have to minister on Sunday. Nicolas is ministering to the youth, and Minister Thomas is still sick. The others in leadership…well, let's not go there," Pastor James sounded frustrated.

Jay swallowed hard. Suddenly, fright was replaced with contentment, and panic was replaced with peace. *But*… "I'll do it."

"Good! God is about to set fire to you, and it will consume you like all the trees, both green and dry. The blazing fire will not be quenched, for God has kindled it. It will be to you as a fire shut up in your bones as it was to Jeremiah. You will not be able to keep the Word to yourself. You will speak so that others may hear and be saved. God is molding you into a minister, a flame of fire!

"Remember this son – desperation leads to inspiration. Everything big starts small. Take one small step at a time, and soon you will understand that the shoes you're walking in are not your own…they belong to God. Your shoes are fitting into His."

Pastor James got up and stood toe to toe with Jay. "You continue talking to God. He'll give you a message straight from His heart for His people. They are His, just as you are His." Pastor James embraced Jay, long and hard, his heart so full.

Little did Jay know that the commitment he had made that night to his earthly father was the supercharge he would need in the days to come. With his faith being anchored solely on God, Jay found himself sailing on the winds of peace, hope, and joy…for a moment. For just like that, in a moment, in the twinkling of an eye, everything that could go wrong went wrong.

Between the long hours, he was spending time at the church and running back and forth to the hospital to see Isabella, Jay should have been exhausted. However, God supernaturally strengthened Jay through the power of the Holy Spirit to do what he had to do. He now understood the Source of his father's ability to do so much with so little time. Jay was feeling enthusiastic about Isabella. It appeared that she was getting better. Then, suddenly everything changed.

Thursday, when Jay was about to wrap everything up for the day at the office, a sense of foreboding arrested him. He was having a lot of this lately. His spirit seemed to be extra sensitive. He stood up, almost gasping for air. *What is it?*

Pray!

Obediently, Jay sat back down, clasped his hands together, and fervently prayed. While praying, the phone rang. His faith was about to be tested once again. Listening intently, Jay didn't say one word. The one-sided conversation was over in a few minutes. Without even hanging up the phone, Jay dashed out of the church office, bolted to his car, and drove like a madman to the hospital.

Isabella has Pneumonia.

The doctor's words played back in his mind repeatedly, like a tape recorder being rewound.

When Jay finally arrived at the hospital, he rushed to ICU. The doctor assigned to Isabella's care was waiting on him.

"Her lungs are filled with fluid. We've given her antibiotics and…" the doctor went on to explain Isabella's health crisis

"In layman's terms, is Isabella going to survive this?" Jay nervously ran his hand through his hair.

"We'll do all we can to bring her back to health, but really it's up to Isabella."

"When can I see her?"

"Wait here, and I'll have a nurse come get you when she's ready. It may be a little while."

"I'll wait." Jay paced the waiting area before finally sitting. As he sat, Jay immediately thought of the *angelic* nurse and the various words she had spoken to him about Isabella.

"*She's a fighter…but I'm afraid…she's not sure if she wants to fight anymore. Fear not. God is with you. Trust Him, and He will guide you. The attack is not unto death but life. Stand guard. Be her watchman. Be ye prepared to fight for her, for she cannot fight alone."*

"This is the attack she was talking about."

Then Jay thought of her command to Love. *"God's love will see you through this, and her love will pull you through. You both need healing, and Love is the only cure."*

What will Isabella pull me through? Jay thought it odd that he hadn't caught that before.

Jay waited thirty minutes before the nurse had escorted him to see Isabella. He had hoped that it was the nurse with the white hair, but it was a much younger nurse.

Jay leaned over Isabella and whispered for only her ears. "I need you."

'Desperation leads to inspiration. Everything big starts small.' His father's words came to mind.

"I am desperate, Isabella. It started out as a promise to Lewis. To look after you. To make sure you knew about Jesus. I didn't want to let him down. But now...now it's more, Isabella. There is something about you that is spellbinding. It's like I'm under this spell that only you have the remedy for. Oh, Isabella fight. Fight for your life. Please fight. I really do need you. For you see, while you're sleeping, I have fallen in love with you." Speaking out loud, what his heart felt, invigorated Jay.

"I have fallen in love with you," he repeated with more confidence.

For three days, Isabella's survival seemed destined for demise. Her fever remained high. Her blood pressure continued to be elevated. It hurt Jay to behold her misery. Pneumonia seemed to have set in and didn't want to release its potent power.

By Saturday, Jay wondered if Isabella would ever open those beautiful eyes of hers again. Day and night, Jay was at her side. He was running himself ragged, going from place to place, spending long hours at the church, and studying for his first sermon Sunday, then back and forth to the hospital. Jay was tired. He didn't want to let God down, nor his dad, and definitely Isabella. Soon, his dad would relieve him of some of the church's responsibilities, which Jay was looking forward to.

Sunday morning, Jay awakened nervous but prepared to do what God had called him to do. After praise and worship services, Jay stood at the podium, with his father sitting behind him. Pastor James was not about to miss his son's first sermon.

"Today, my brothers and sisters, I have come to share my life with you," Jay began. "I stand before you, a wounded soldier, with many battle scars. Some of my scars are visible, like the scar on my right ear because of my hearing loss and the scar on my arm," he rolled up his sleeve, revealing a long black line where stitches used to be. "And the slight limp I have in my right leg when it throbs. Not to mention the horrific headaches that are debilitating at times. However, I have scars that you cannot see. For you see, my heart was diseased and left with the silent bullets of fear and bitterness.

"In war, I saw so many people dying around me. I held soldiers' hands while they were speaking their last words. I saw atrocious acts of violence. Evil lurked like a shadow behind me everywhere I went. I was always watching my back. There were times that darkness hid the light that was supposed to be in me. It was hard to sleep. And with everything I had experienced and witnessed with my eyes, I found it harder and harder to keep the faith. I prayed for people, and they still died. I sought relief, and destruction came. I looked for a way out, but I remained in the thick of violence. Then it was my time to return home. I thought that I had escaped the war when so many of my friends died.

"However, when I returned home, my dreams were haunted by the war and the tragic deaths I beheld. When the phone rang, I jumped. If someone came upon me, my stance became defensive, and I was ready to attack. If something dropped or crashed, I would hit the floor, looking for cover. Even at home, I couldn't escape the war.

"I questioned my faith on foreign land, and here, in my hometown. I questioned everything I believed in. And most importantly, I questioned my purpose in life. I found it hard to pray. Hard to read my Bible. Hard to hold on. I felt like such a hypocrite! I believed, and yet, God helped my unbelief.

"While in combat, even though I was in spiritual warfare, I pressed on. I continued, through my weakness. God's strength sustained me. I remember one night, it was so dark outside, and I couldn't see anything. We had just been ambushed, we were all hiding in the forest, and trees were everywhere. It was so dark. I couldn't see anything. I was so scared. I couldn't even pray. A song arose in my heart, and I began to sing silently. For hours, I sang quietly to the Lord. Only His ears could hear my voice. While I was singing, I heard gunshots all around me, voices shouting, 'Here is another one, the enemy said,'" Jay paused, pushing by emotions that desired to surface. He needed to stand like a soldier and finish what he started. "One by one, my fellow soldiers were being captured or shot point-blank. I continued to sing in my heart. I don't know why they didn't capture me. I don't understand why they didn't find me. The other men died, but God kept me. It reminds me of Paul and Silas in prison. They were bound and in chains, and yet they praised God and sang.

"That's what God wants from each one of us. The Bible says that God seeks true worshipers. Those who will worship Him in truth and in spirit. While I was hiding in the dark, my spirit was worshiping God, praising Him for Who He is – not just for what He was capable of doing, which was to deliver me...which He did. I couldn't even pray, but my spirit praised God. Inside, of each one of us, is *a praise* in the midst of pain.

"My brothers and sisters, will you still worship God in the midst of what you are going through? The Bible says in Job 2:10: ***'Shall we accept good from God and not trouble?'*** When things are *honkey-dory* we are happy, but the minute trouble comes, our countenance changes. We become joyless instead of joyful, powerless instead of powerful. ***Many are the afflictions of the righteous, but God delivers us out of them all***. Meanwhile, while we're experiencing tough times, we must continue to worship God. Worship is an expression of our love for God."

Jay continued for another ten minutes or so. The sermon was short but sweet. Pastor James had never felt prouder of his namesake than at that moment. Jay was surrendering to his calling.

He's walking in Your shoes, God. Not mine. Not even his but Yours!!!!! Pastor James smiled, winking at his wife, whose eyes glistened with fresh tears of joy.

At the end of service, seemingly, the entire congregation greeted Jay with gratitude, support, joy, and pure love. Even Janice approached him. She hadn't left the church completely.

"Wonderful message," sincerely Janice spoke. "I'm proud of you."

"Thanks. That means a great deal to me."

An awkward silence followed before Janice spoke again. "How are your headaches?"

"Less intense." Strange, Jay hadn't been plagued by the headaches since he said yes to God's will. Usually, the headaches awoke with him, stalked him throughout the day, and went to bed with him at night. However, today, at this very moment, there wasn't even a hint of a headache coming on.

"That's good. I keep praying that you'll be free of them."

"Thank you for your prayers, Janice." Jay touched her hand and then pulled away, realizing that they were surrounded by people who would take something as small as a touch and make it into a mountain of matrimony. "Thank you for always being there and for helping me to keep going even when I didn't feel like I could."

"You're welcome," Janice lowered her head. "Maybe we can go out to dinner one day next week."

Jay didn't know what to say. Did she still want to be friends, or was she still hoping for more?

"As friends," she felt his uneasiness.

"I'd like that very much."

"Call me tomorrow."

"Sure."

"See you later," Janice walked away.

"What was that all about?" Always on cue, Reese came over being nosy.

"Oh, don't give me that look." Jay walked to the door with his brother. "We're friends."

"I was just wondering." Reese laughed. "Well, I guess you won't be needing these anymore." Reese pointed to his shoes. "I must say, the ones you are wearing today fit pretty good." That was Reese's way of saying he was proud of his brother.

"Looks like you need to get yourself a new pair." Jay retorted. "When are you going to take over the Music of Ministry duties?"

"Soon. Dad and I have already discussed it. Janice is meeting with him one day this week. I think Wednesday."

"Sounds good."

"Coming home for dinner?"

"After I go visit with Isabella." Jay couldn't wait to share his incredible experience of ministering God's word today.

"Mom's not going to like you ditching family dinner."

"I won't be long. Please tell her."

"I will." Reese looked at his brother. "She's the one, isn't she?"

"She's like no other," Jay promptly answered.

"Beautiful. Bright. Business-minded." Reese assumed, knowing his brother's taste in women.

"Yes and no," Jay snickered at the description. "Remember, Lewis was her brother. Before he got saved, remember how he was? Let's just say the apple *didn't* fall far from the tree."

"Oh my! So she's not the pastor's wife type."

"Not to the natural eye, but neither was our mother."

"What?" Reese felt like his brother just popped him on the head. "What do you mean by that?"

"Ask mom," Jay opened his car door. "I have to go. Don't forget to tell mom I'll be a little late."

"More like a lot late."

Chapter 24

Jay walked to the ICU feeling a little lighter. He was still nervous about accepting his call as a minister of God's word, but he could no longer run away. He understood that he was not in this alone, which renewed his confidence. Not in himself, but in the One who had chosen him.

Jay pulled the chair closer to Isabella's bedside and sat. Momentarily, Jay just stared at the sleeping beauty. Despite her rugged outer appearance, Jay saw her beauty. Watching her gave him a chance to admire her flawless honey-brown skin tone. Jay couldn't resist touching her face. Her skin was so soft to touch, just like it looked – smooth, soft, and silky – like baby skin rubbed in oil.

With jubilancy, Jay painted the picture of today's service to Isabella.

"I wish you were there. I think you would have been pleased. I know Lewis would have been. Oh, Isabella, when I first stood at the pulpit, my legs were knocking so hard together, I thought for sure the congregation could hear me," Jay chuckled. "I sounded like a frog at first, but then I just felt empowered to speak. Empowered to go on. Half the words I was speaking weren't even on paper. It was like I was making them up as I was going, only it wasn't me. It was the Holy Spirit. I tell you, it was unbelievable."

As he was talking, Jay almost didn't even recognize her eyes flickering. Was Isabella regaining consciousness? Her eyes batted back and forth before they just sprang open. Like a child, Isabella gazed at him, seemingly unaware of where she was, what was going on, or who he was.

"Isabella!"

The way Jay said her name caused her blood to run warm through her veins, pumping new life into them. She felt alive for the first time in what seemed like an eternity.

"Isabella!" his eyes watered. "I knew you would come back to me. I knew it."

She seemed confused as she watched him. Isabella was like a deer in headlights.

Oh God, she doesn't remember me. Oh no. It can't be.

"Isabella, it's me, Jay. Jay Cannon. Lewis' friend. Remember?"

Her forehead creased with wrinkles, signifying her discombobulation.

His heart dropped. Jay never expected that Isabella would awaken and not remember him. Never!

Her eyes closed. Isabella went back to sleep.

Was he dreaming? Did she really awaken? Jay's joy suddenly turned into sorrow. *She didn't know me!* Following, Jay spoke briefly with the doctor, who had cautioned Jay that this would be a long road to Isabella's recovery. Still, he was optimistic about her recovering from any memory loss. Only if Jay could be hopeful about Isabella remembering who he was.

Have faith!

When Jay returned home, the family had finished dinner and were in the den watching a movie. Jay peeped in and then went to the kitchen. His mother was wiping down the counter.

Jay stood in the doorway, watching her for a moment. He couldn't imagine his mother being any other way than the sweet, loving, faithful, giving, dutiful wife and mother he had known all his life. To think that she had a wild side before seemed ludicrous.

"Oh, you're back." Esther turned toward him. "How is Isabella?" Before he even answered, Esther sensed that something was terribly wrong.

"She opened her eyes today."

"Wonderful!" Esther clapped her hands. "We all prayed, and God answered. Then why the long face?"

"She didn't recognize me."

Esther sighed. "How do you know? It could be the medication."

"Could be," Jay sat at the table. "It could be that she's not the same, Isabella. She's been through so much. Head injury can be tricky. Plus, the other internal injuries. Coma. Pneumonia. Who knows what she'll be like?"

"Hush up!" Esther swatted the dishcloth on the table, emphasizing her statement. "God knows what she will be like. He is not going to bring Isabella back damaged. No way! He's going to heal her completely. She's healed already in Jesus' name. Where is your faith?"

"I do have faith, Mom."

"Then act like it! Talk like it!" Esther fixed his dinner. "You have to fight for her! She can't fight herself. Fight the good fight of faith."

There it was again. *Fight for her! Love her through it.*

"Mom," Jay beckoned her.

Once again, Esther turned and looked at him.

"I love her."

"I know." Esther put the plate down in front of him. Then, with a mother's love, she embraced Jay for a long time. "Love will see you both through. Now, eat before your food gets cold again." Esther poured him a glass of lemon tea. Then she sat and talked while he ate. "It takes a good, strong man to love someone who has not had an easy life. Isabella has lived a life that's foreign to you, son. She's done things that you can't even imagine. Things that will disgust you and even make you feel she's not worthy of you. But you must remember, she's important to God. You have to forgive her for her past and never hold it against her. Love does that – it covers – and hovers over the one it loves. Like your dad did for me. If you cannot accept and forgive her past, then you'll never be able to handle a future with her in it."

"What if Isabella's past catches up with her…with us? What if members of the church discover what she's done? She's lived a sinful life, Mom."

Esther digested the information before speaking again. "They will love her, just like they loved me."

"But Isabella has done worse than you can imagine, Mom. She's prostituted her body."

"She was paid for her sins; I wasn't," Esther confessed. "God forgives all sins. He cleared and cleaned my record and gave me a clean slate. My past is over! Old things have passed away. All things have become new. Isabella isn't new yet, but I know she will be."

"Thanks, Mom." Jay felt better.

Monday morning and every morning after that, Jay returned to the hospital, determined to fight for the one he loved. He had every intention of wooing Isabella until he won her over. He might die trying, but he surely was going to try. Even if she couldn't remember him, Jay purposed to create new memories with her. Jay wanted to be her Rock of Gibraltar, giving Isabella support and love during this time of uncertainty.

As she went in and out of consciousness, Jay felt more hopeful. Initially, Isabella's motor skills weren't all there. She still had a slight fever, and her blood pressure was slightly higher than the doctor wanted. She was unable to speak. She seemed confused. One side of her face was somewhat drooping; a possible mini-stroke was suspected.

A few days later, one evening once again, Isabella opened her eyes and stared at Jay. Only, this time, she didn't go back to sleep. She was wide awake and very alert. Tenderly, Jay caressed her face and ran his fingers through her hair. Very few words he spoke at first, as his eyes captured hers. In silence, Jay allowed his eyes to tell the story of his feelings for her.

Pain framed her countenance as Isabella tried to push herself upward. Her head throbbed. Though she was recovering, Isabella was still in pain and very weak. It confounded the doctors that Isabella hadn't spoken. There appeared to be no medical reason for her muteness.

"You need to rest," Jay gently nudged her to lie back down.

Isabella looked up at him and was fearful of the attraction she felt for him, which seemed mutual. *It can't be.* There was an obvious connection, which didn't make sense at all. Unbeknown to Jay, Isabella very much recognized him, and it worried her. She needed time, more time to process his genuine concern and his attentiveness toward her. *Why in the world would he be attracted to someone like me?*

Both had endured personal battles, but now there was an unwritten, unseen treaty to end the wars of their hearts – Love. Would they allow love to smother the past and uncover the love in their hearts?

Being near death makes one appreciate life, be it good or bad. In fact, the bad doesn't seem as bad when good shows up. And Jay was good.

The longer he stayed, the more she appeared less scared and more comfortable. When it was time for him to leave, Jay hated to leave her.

"I have to go minister at Heaven's Soldiers, the elderly home I told you about." Jay hesitated, sensing her fears. "I'll be back, I promise." Standing, Jay held her right hand in his, squeezing it slightly. "I promise I'll be back. If you want me to come back, squeeze my hand." It was the first time he had asked anything of her. "Squeeze my hand if you want to see me again," his voice pleaded for assurance. Not just from her, but for him.

His eyes held hers for a long time.

Isabella felt a stirring in her deep down inside, and with struggle, she squeezed his hand.

Thank You, God. Jay squeezed back. "Do you know who I am? If so, squeeze."

Once again, Isabella squeezed his hand.

His eyes watered. "Welcome back, Isabella. Welcome back!"

Her lips fashioned a smile that lit up the room. A smile that Jay would forever carry in his heart.

After briefly visiting Heaven's Soldiers Elderly Home, Jay went to the office to pick up mail, make a few phone calls, and go over some things with the church secretary. As he was about to leave and head back to the hospital, his father called.

"Chance is missing."

"What?" Jay shouted. "What happened?"

"He went to find the guys," James began to unravel the details. "They broke into his home, and…and …uh hurt Tammy pretty badly. She's in the hospital."

"The baby…" Jay panicked.

"I'm not sure. Tammy's parents are with her now at the hospital."

"Where should I go first – the hospital or looking for Chance?"

"You go look for Chance. Esther and I will go to the hospital."

"Are you up for it, Dad?"

"Yes. I'm still the pastor, and I need to go pray with my members. Enough of this just sitting around doing nothing."

"I'll come over after I find Chance."

"Okay. And son, remember, this is not your fault."

"I know, Dad, but it sure feels like it."

"Remember, you're not God. Never try to play God or be God. Remember, walk in His shoes, and don't try to wear them. They are way too big."

"I don't understand what you're saying, Dad."

"Remember when you were little, and you used to put on my big shoes. You would walk around all day in my shoes. They would fall off because they were too big. You were walking in my shoes, not yours. Remember, they are God's shoes. You're only putting your feet into them to do what He wants you to do, to lead you where He wants you to go. The minute you start wearing the shoes and not walking in them is the minute you're trying to be God and not be like Him, and they will fall off. Do your part, but let God do His, leading you and guiding you every step of the way."

"Thanks, Dad."

"Let's stay in prayer. I'll see you soon."

Jay rode around in Chance's old neighborhood for what seemed like hours. He made several stops, asking people had they seen Chance, but no one had seen Chance in a long time. Indeed, Chance had fought to leave his old life behind. As the daytime bowed to the nighttime, Jay realized that it was no use to drive around in the dark any longer.

Please, Father God, protect Chance. Don't let him do anything stupid. He's worked so hard to change his ways. Vengeance is not the way.

"How is she?" Jay asked his father, who was sitting with Tammy's family in the hospital's waiting room.

"She's going to be just fine."

"And the baby?"

Pastor James shook his head.

"Oh my," Jay felt sick. "Does Tammy know?"

"She knows." Pastor James regretfully admitted. "But her main concern is her husband."

"I looked everywhere, Dad, but there is no sight of him. No one has seen him. What about the cops? Have they arrested anybody?"

"They are looking for the guys. Thank God, Tammy knew their names."

"Can I go see, Tammy?"

"We just left her. She was asleep. But you can go in."

Jay tiptoed in the room, not wanting to awaken the traumatized woman.

Tammy sensed his presence in the room. "Did you find Chance?"

"No," sullenly, he replied.

"Oh no." Tammy's hand was over her heart. She was anxious with worry about Chance's whereabouts. "Where could he be? He's going to do something awful. I know Chance. He was so angry."

"God will protect him and keep him from doing something stupid."

"I hope so."

"How are you? I'm truly sorry about your loss."

"It hurts really bad," Tammy sniffed. "I wanted this baby girl so bad. Our baby made Chance want to be the best man he could be. Why couldn't they just leave us alone?" Tammy closed her eyes and allowed the tears to fall freely. "Why?"

"I wish I had answers for you, Tammy. But all I know is that God is with you, and He's with Chance." Jay's heart ached for them.

"Would you mind praying, Pastor Jay?"

Without hesitation, Jay grabbed her hand and began, "God, you know the hurt that Tammy feels right now. I ask that you comfort her through this grieving time. Give her supernatural strength to endure this. Holy Spirit counsel, help, intercede, standby, and stand with her during this hurtful season. Protect Chance. Calm his spirit. Keep him from doing something that he will regret forever. Angels surround him, keeping him from harm. Lord, either bring him back to us or show us where to find Chance. And even though we may not understand why this precious baby didn't live, we still trust You, in Jesus' name, amen."

"Amen."

Jay left the room, feeling somewhat responsible for Chance and Tammy's mishap. Maybe he counseled them wrong. Perhaps he should have waited for his dad to help them. After all, it was his fault that Chance had snitched on the guys, which caused them to retaliate. *Oh God, did I do the right thing?*

Evil plans are in the heart of fools. Yet, wise counsel comes from Me. All is well! There is now no condemnation for those who are in Christ Jesus.

Meanwhile, Isabella stayed awake, hoping to see Jay again. *He promised!* Every time a nurse walked into the room, her disappointment showed that it was not Jay. *I should have known. He's like every man I know – full of empty promises!*

She had just dozed off when Jay returned around eleven that night. He had to beg the night nurse to allow him just to peep in on her.

Jay ever so carefully touched her hand. The simple touch was electrifying, as Isabella's eyes popped wide open, fearful at first. Softness followed as she looked at him with dreamy eyes. Isabella studied his manly profile as he stood over her. Tall. Handsome. Strong. Masculine. Her eyes glistened with tears, ready to spill over. *He came back!*

"Don't cry," Jay leaned over and gently wiped her tears away.

Her bottom lip quivered as she opened her mouth to say something but couldn't get the words out.

"I'm sorry it took me so long to get back. One of our church members is in trouble, and I went looking for him. I couldn't find him," Jay sighed. "But you were in my thoughts and my heart."

"I'm…I'm…glad you came back," the heartfelt words spilled out. Isabella had finally spoken aloud.

Hearing her voice made his heart leap. "I promised, and I keep my promises." Peace blanketed Jay, which soothed him in a way he couldn't explain. His conscience was clear. His vision was unclouded. He had a purpose. And part of that purpose was to share God with Isabella. To love her back to Him.

Isabella held out her hand to Jay, turning her palm upward. Jay gladly clasped it in his. It fitted so right, so perfectly. The warmth of her hand tranquilized his entire being. Jay was intoxicated by her warmth – her closeness. It was more than just holding hands. Isabella trusted him enough to allow such a connection. This was monumental.

Chapter 25

Chance had been missing now for two days. Angry and armed, Chance ignored the inner voice whispering in his heart, *Vengeance is Mine, saith the Lord!*

"But God, I can't go out like that!"

The battle is not yours...it's the Lord's.

"But God, they hurt Tammy. They came into my home and beat up my pregnant wife. I want to kill every one of them."

Vengeance is Mine. Walk in love and not hate. My Son Jesus did nothing wrong, and they killed Him, yet He loved them and died for them.

Chance remained silent, pondering the words.

Trust Me!

"I can't run from them, God. I'm tired of running."

Submit to Me. Resist the devil. Resist hatred. The enemy will do the running and not you. He will not hurt you nor harm you, for I have given you authority over all the power of the enemy. Walk ye in it.

"I don't know what to do. I miss Tammy. I know she's worried. I'm lost."

Stand still, and see the salvation of the Lord, which He will accomplish for you today. For the Egyptians whom you see today,

*you shall see again no more forever. **The Lord will fight for you,
and you shall hold your peace.***

Lord, I need You to part this Red Sea I'm about to walk into.
Go! I am with you. I will do it!

Chance lowered his head and prayed, seeking strength from
God to stand up against those who persecuted his family.

Leaving his gun behind, Chance prepared himself for the
battle of his life. Only, this time, the Lord would fight for him. First,
with trembling, Chance walked the long alley, which led to his old
gang hideout. He knew the gang would be there. Usually, after a
victory, they would stay away for a day or two and then return to
their home away from home.

With each step, his legs became heavier. His throat felt dry.
His chest was constricting. Chance was petrified. He knew the
destructive forces that were ahead of him. After all, this was his old
gang. He had betrayed them, which usually meant death to the
traitor. Today it surely might be his own.

*I go in the name of the Lord. The Lord is with me. He has
gone before me, and He has hedged me behind and in front. His
hands are upon me. I am not alone. God will never leave me or
forsake me. In You Lord, I put my trust.*

Just like that, Chance went from trembling to trusting.

Boldly, approaching the club area, straight away, at least
forty gang members emerged, guns aimed and ready for combat.

"Well, if it *ain't* the Rat!" one member shouted.

Chance halted, taking a good look at all the members he once
ran with.

"I want to talk to Vix!"

"Talk to this, you punk!" a member cocked his gun.

"I came in peace!" Chance lifted his arms, showing that he
didn't have a weapon. Several guys came over and patted Chance
down without delay, making sure he wasn't wired or hiding a
weapon. "All I want is to talk to Vix."

Momentarily, several guys came over and began shoving
and mocking Chance. "You sure got a lot of nerve, you punk! Two
of our brothers are in jail right now because of your sorry self!"

Lord, don't let Tammy become a widower today.
There is more with you than against you.

Chance took it like a man as the guys continued to bully him. One guy slapped him in the face, and another spat on him. Then another punched him in the stomach, nearly knocking the wind out of him. Chance let out a groan, trying to brave it out.

"Let's kill this sorry punk!" Someone shouted, and the others all agreed, shouting all at the same time.

"Wait!" A voice of authority thundered behind them. Everything stilled. Silence became a deafening noise.

Chance watched as Vix appeared before him. Every bit of a 6'4" tall, bulky giant, with a scar on the left side of his face, brought terror everywhere he went, including now. Vix could whip anybody, fair and square. He was strong, lifting weights day and night. To his credit, Vix was no dummy. He was street smart and book smart. He believed that knowledge was power, and it showed how he ran the gang and those around him.

The Lord is my light and my salvation, of whom shall I fear. **Trust Me.**

"Well, if it *ain't* my cuz turned snitch!" Vix and Chance were true blood. They grew up together, running the streets, getting into trouble, and staying out all the time. Vix was grooming Chance to be second-in-command before he got locked up.

"Vix!" Chance's voice quaked.

"Why are you here, and what do you want?"

"I want you to leave my family alone."

"You *got* nerve coming on my turf giving demands? You must *got* the cops with you." Vix stood before him, getting all up in Chance's face. "You're one of us, and you'll die one of us! So, just accept it."

"I can't accept it, Vix. I've changed, and I don't run like that *no* more."

"You got two choices," Vix viciously eyed him, without mercy. "Either get beat out of the gang or pay your way out. Now the payment is $50,000 since you snitched on your *brothers*."

"You know I don't have that kind of money." Chance responded. "And even if I did, I wouldn't give it to you. I have a family to support."

Wham! Vix slapped Chance on his left cheek, sending him to the ground. Slowly, Chance got up, holding his face, shaking off the feeling of defeat. *Help me, Lord!*

I'm here!

"Don't you get tired of looking over your shoulders and running all the time? Don't you get tired of hurting and killing people, Victor?" Chance called him by his birth name.

"Vix!" he roared. "You're pushing it! You know not to call me by that slave name!

"It's me, Chance. Remember? We were born and raised together. You had my back, and I had yours, until the day I got locked up. No one had my back then, not even you," Chance stated the *elephant in the room* that constantly plagued them. "Nevertheless, we're flesh and blood. I don't want to be enemies. That's why I beg you to stop doing what you're doing. There is a better life for you. I know because I found it. Taking a life is not freedom. But giving your life to Jesus is truly living…and freedom!"

"Look at you!" Vix scoffed. "You *ain't* got *nothing*. But I live in a mansion. I have two Mercedes Benz, Cadillac, a Hummer EV, and more. I have more money than you can even count. I have women, not tied down with just one babe! That's stupid! I never wear the same clothes twice. I got everything, and you got nothing but some fake religion! Please, don't come preaching to me. I'm living the life."

"Living it without peace because you can't trust anyone. Everyone is out to get you. You can't even trust those in the gang completely, and you know it. Vix, you know I know the real deal. You're constantly looking over your shoulders, hiding and going from place to place when the heat is turned up, cops always looking for evidence to convict you. Come on, that's not life! That's bondage."

"Enough!" Vix shouted. Instantly, the members aimed their guns at Chance. "What are you going to do? Pay or get beat to death!"

"Well, I see you are not going to change, but just accept the fact that I've changed, and I don't want any part of this anymore." Chance took a deep breath. "And by the way, though you hurt my wife, I still love you, man. I'll see you around."

"What makes you think that you are going to walk out of here alive?" Vix demanded.

"My trust is not in man but in God."

There is more with you than against you!

Please open my eyes so that I can see, Chance prayed as he put one foot in front of the other. True enough, there was the brightest light he could imagine. No washing machine could produce such whiteness. The image of what had to be angels was in front and all around. Chance walked through with confidence. God had shown Him the truth. He was never, ever alone.

"Where is your God now?" Vix caught up to him and put a gun to Chance's head.

Lord, have mercy on Vix. He knows not what he's doing. Chance looked at him, turned, and walked away, silently praying. If they shot him in the back, so be it. He would never surrender to any of them. *Yea, though I walk through the shadows of death, I will fear no evil, for You are with me.*

With their guns aimed and ready to shoot at any second Vix gave the command, they were prepared to kill the enemy. Chance was not with them but against them. Then, without understanding, without any power of his own, Vix's hand dropped, becoming dead and paralyzed. He opened his mouth to tell them to shoot, but nothing came out. His voice was gone. At the dropping of his hand, it signified for the others not to shoot. Vix tried to move his arm and the other one, but neither wouldn't move. Shaking his head, Vix just watched as his cousin, one whom he had loved and trusted since childhood, strolled down the dark alley. He appeared alone, and yet, Vix sensed that a Higher Power was with him, for him to boldly come in and walk out alive. Only something more powerful than he could make his arms unmovable and his mouth mute!

"You just *gonna* let him walk! He ratted on our brothers!" one of the members dared to question his leader. The others thought it but had the sense not to speak it aloud.

Vix turned and looked at the weak soldier that dared to rebuke him. Suddenly, his arms were raised. **Bang!** Instead of Chance dying, another member died in his place. Vix had to show that he was still the boss, and nobody would just get up in his face with disrespect. Though deep down, he knew by letting Chance live made him look soft. Though he had planned to kill Chance, deep down, Vix was grateful for whatever it was that had prevented him from doing so. He would have always regretted killing his flesh and blood, especially since Chance had saved him so many times in the past.

We're even now! Chance won't get another chance.

After visiting Isabella that morning, Jay was on his knees, interceding and fervently praying for Chance. Instead of worry, there was such peace in his heart. Jay knew that somehow everything was going to work out for Chance. His prayer was interrupted by the phone.

"Hi, Tammy!" Jay answered. "How are you?"

"I'm not doing so well today, Pastor Jay. I can't believe I haven't heard from Chance all this time. I have this awful feeling that something is not right. Maybe something awful has happened to him. The gang probably found him first. He's probably dead!" she sobbed.

"Don't say that," Jay resisted the temptation to allow negative pragmatic thoughts to dictate his faith.

"Then, where is he? He would have called me by now if he were okay. I know my Chance. He's either in big trouble or...or..."

"God is with Chance wherever he is." Jay interrupted. "I'm going out looking again after I leave here in about an hour." Jay had been out almost every day, following up on leads, praying he'd find him.

"I appreciate your help, Pastor Jay. I'm trying to keep the faith, but it's hard."

"A little faith is better than no faith. Remember the mustard seed. It's little, but a big tree comes forth once the seed is watered and cared for."

"Thanks, Pastor Jay."

Jay prayed with the worried wife, briefly. "I'll call you, later on, to check on you." He replaced the receiver.

Running his hands through his once jet-black hair, now showing more grey strands on the sides, Jay closed his eyes and whispered a prayer for the Holy Spirit to lead and guide him to Chance. Though he had counseled several other couples since coming to work at the church, Chance and Tammy were special to him. His thoughts were always on them. Essentially, the situation with Chance was not just spiritual; it was personal. Jay had to practice what he preached and turn the matter over to God. He had to let go and allow God to do what He did best! Work it all out for their good!

"Pastor Jay," Chance called him first.

"Chance!" Jay was about to leave his office. "Where are you?"

"I'm nowhere." Chance was calling from a phone booth. "How is Tammy?"

"She's in the hospital," Jay prayed for the right words, "but she's doing fine."

"And the baby?"

Jay hesitated for some time before answering. "You can see for yourself soon. Where are you?"

"Okay," Chance quickly gave him directions.

"I'm on my way," Jay hung up the phone.
In less than thirty minutes, Jay spotted a scruffy-looking Chance. Looked like he hadn't seen soap and water for days, and when he jumped in the car, Chance also smelled like he hadn't seen soap and water for days.

"Man, you need a shower before going to see your wife," Jay stated.

"It's good to see you too, Pastor Jay," Chance chuckled. "Tammy doesn't care about that."

"Well, you should. I'm taking you to the church so that you can shower there. It's on the way anyway."

On the way, Chance told Jay how God had delivered him from Vix and the others. "It was like a real-life David and Goliath. Only, I didn't have a slingshot, but I had the Lord. I saw Him, Jay. I saw angels all around me. I saw this bright, bright light. I felt His Presence. It was amazing. I just walked out of the alley with guns pointing at me, and not one of them went off! Only God could do that. I don't know how, but I know He saved my life today."

"God is so faithful! Praise Him! Hallelujah!" Jay gave God all the glory. "When God is for you, who dare come against you!"

"Amen!"

"I was so angry, Pastor Jay! I wanted to kill them all!"

"I *bet*." Jay understood. He'd been there himself, during the war.

"And yet, I told Vix, after all that he had done to my family, that I loved him."

"I am proud of you, Chance." Jay reached over and patted him on the shoulder. "You have truly grown, my brother. No longer the angry man."

"I can't say that I'm fully there yet, but I'm learning through the process."

Jay chuckled and said, "Me too. It's definitely a process."

As they arrived at the church and went inside, heading toward the back where the men's room had a shower, Chance stopped walking. "I know...you're withholding something from me," Chance perceived rightly. "Just tell me."

"Your baby...she's with the Lord."

The most dreadful scream arose from the very depths of Chance's soul. He dropped to his knees, covered his hands over his eyes, and wept aloud. Pain like no other choked his lungs almost to asphyxiation. Today was the worst day of his life. He didn't even get a chance to hold her, to kiss her, to tell his baby girl that he loved her.

Jay's heart broke over Chance's grief. All he could do was kneel beside him and wrap him in his arms, praying silently. Jay hurt because Chance was hurting. He felt his pain, which pierced his very being. Yet, neither was alone. For the God of All Comfort was with them.

"I don't understand, Pastor Jay. I prayed. I prayed hard. I tried to do the right thing, and still, my baby died."

"I know," Jay sympathized, "but God had other plans. It's not easy to accept that or understand it right now. This is the time when we must trust God despite our feelings and our circumstances. We must lean on Him and allow His love to comfort us. It's okay to grieve and cry. You have to feel what you feel so that God can heal. You and Tammy will get through. She's worried sick over you. She needs you more than ever."

Wiping his eyes, Chance said with confidence, "God was with me when I confronted Vix and the others. Therefore, I know He'll be with Tammy and me through our sorrow. I don't understand it, but yet will I trust Him."

"Yes, He will." Jay was proud of Chance as if he was his own brother. He'd come a long way.

Getting up, Chance slowly walked away to take a quick shower, his head down and heartbroken. *My baby is gone! Help me, Lord. Help me!*
   I'm here!

Chapter 26

Wednesday afternoon, while at the church, Janice visited Jay.

"Hi, stranger," merrily she greeted.

"Oh, hi, Janice." Jay was surprised.

"I waited on your call, and well…since you didn't, I figured while I was here I'd stop by."

"I apologize." Jay had forgotten he was supposed to call her. "It's been so hectic with Chance and Tammy, not to mention the countless other things…"

"I understand," Janice sat. "I've been praying for Chance and Tammy fervently. It's so sad that they lost their first child."

"Yes it is," frown lines creased his forehead, "but their love for each other is stronger."

"I know you're busy, but how about we go have lunch together."

"Well, Ummm…." Jay had made plans to work straight through so he could be with Isabella sooner.

"You need to eat." Janice felt a no coming on.

"Sure." Jay felt obligated. After all, he had hurt her before, and now Janice was offering him an olive branch, willing to befriend him. "Let me go tell dad, and I'll meet you at my car."

"Good." Janice hurried to the car.

"Hey, Dad," Jay peeped into his father's office. "I'm going to lunch with Janice. I'll be right back. Do you want me to bring you something?

"No, thanks. Be careful," Pastor James cautioned his son. "She's not over you."

"We're friends, Dad." Jay asserted. "I've already made myself clear on the matter. Besides, we've always been friends. There is nothing wrong with two friends having lunch together.'

"What about Isabella?"

"Dad," Jay was frustrated. "You know how I feel about Isabella. I care for her very much."

"I just don't want anybody to get hurt. You're a pastor now. You have to be careful. Avoid the appearances of evil."

"Pastor!" Jay repeated. "I am not a pastor, Dad. You're the pastor, and I…"

"Soon to be the Assistant Pastor," James completed his sentence. "Have a good lunch, Jay."

"We're not through with this discussion, Dad," Jay warned. "Let's take things slow."

Pastor James smiled, with a light in his eyes as if he knew some grand secret. "Tell Janice hi for me," Pastor James went back to reading his study notes.

"This is my favorite restaurant," Janice commented as Jay pushed her chair in. Jay and Janice had enjoyed many meals at Rizzio's Italian Restaurant.

"I know," he smiled—a smile which still caused her heart to somersault.

After ordering, Jay started talking about Chance and Tammy. His thoughts were ever on them.

"They are such an odd couple. Tammy is so prim and proper while Chance is so rough and rugged."

"Opposites attract," Jay looked at her as Isabella came to mind. "I mean, wouldn't it be dull if two people had to live together all of their lives, thinking the same things, doing the same things with no spontaneity."

"I'd rather have stability than spontaneity," Janice spoke with sureness. "I mean, love is great, and I can tell that Chance and Tammy deeply love each other, but look at where they are now. Tammy lost her baby because some thugs broke into their home and roughed her up because of Chance's past."

Immediately, Jay dropped his fork noisily. "You can't be serious."

"I am." Janice squirmed in her chair, now realizing she and Jay didn't see things the same way this time. She had said the wrong thing. "I mean, if Tammy would have married someone who wasn't so…so different, for sure no one would have broken into her home and beat her so bad, she had to be hospitalized."

"Wow! I'm so glad God doesn't see *like* man," Jay was ruffled and frustrated. "God is merciful. Tammy and Chance love each other! It's real. It's genuine. I admire them and respect the love I've witnessed between them. It's rare, and it's beautiful," Jay spoke with passion. "I dare not judge them but pray for them."

Janice felt slapped in the face. "I'm not judging them." The luncheon wasn't going as she had hoped it would. "Can we talk about something else?"

"Let me just say this," Jay was still miffed. "You can't always judge a book by its cover, Janice. There are some exceptional people in Word Alive Fellowship. Members who have lived horrible lives before God took them in, cleaned them up, and used them for His glory," Jay thought of his mother. "What Tammy and Chance have is what I desire to have."

Janice nodded, feeling very uncomfortable.

"I've met someone," Jay spilled the beans. "And as my friend, I think you should know that she's an extraordinary woman who has been through a lot. We're opposites, like Tammy and Chance."

His words were more than just a slap. This time Janice felt like Jay had punched her in the gut, knocking all the wind out of her sail and leaving a sharp pain in her heart.

"Who is she?" Janice managed to ask, looking ill at ease.

"Her name is Isabella. She's Lewis' sister."

"Oh," she said pompously, remembering the rugged man and their conversation about Isabella.

Jay caught her arrogant tone. "I think I love her," he said impulsively.

"Love!" Janice nearly shouted. "Ah, come on, Jay. Wake up! You have too much at stake here. You're the next in line at church. We have a thriving church, steadily growing in membership. You can't just go hooking up with any *old* body. Your reputation should matter…if not to you, then to your family."

"My family will love her."

"How can you be so sure?" Janice sat on the edge of her seat. She hadn't expected any of this. Especially not from Jay, the one who had been running all his life from everything and everyone, afraid of commitment.

"Because they love me." Jay asserted. "All my family ever wanted for me is to be happy."

"Didn't I make you happy?" Janice couldn't help herself. "We had good times together. Then you went off to war, and it changed everything. It changed you."

"Yes, the war changed me," Jay paused, witnessing the hurt in her eyes. He never wanted to hurt Janice. They had always been upfront with each other. "I cannot help what my heart feels."

"Thanks a lot." Janice bit her lip, her eyes downcast.

"I'm sorry." Observing the wetness of her eyes nearly broke down Jay's resolve to be honest with Janice, even if it hurt her momentarily. "When we were friends, we talked about everything. Everything got complicated when we tried to make a relationship. You shouldn't have to make a relationship. It just happens."

"Like with Isabella?"

"Yes. I wasn't looking for her. She just fell into my life, and well…we fit."

"Where is she?"

"She's in the Bayview Hospital, in Williamsburg," Jay answered. "She's recovering from Pneumonia." He didn't see the need to tell her about the other afflictions. "She's better."

"Good," Janice forced her lips to smile. "What does she do?"

"Nothing right now." Jay honestly replied.

Janice's eyebrows arched in curiosity. "Is she a Christian?"

"Not yet."

"My goodness! You know better than being unequally yoked with anyone! Well…go ahead and tell me the rest."

"She's lived a hard life, Janice. She's been through so much. She was living on the streets…"

"What?" Janice couldn't believe it. "On the streets. Probably was into drugs, sex, and God knows what else."

"You're judging!"

"I apologize. But this is just a lot to take in," Janice was sick at heart. There was no way she could eat another thing.

"As I said, Isabella has lived a hard life, but she's not that way anymore," Jay hoped.

"It doesn't matter. Can you imagine preaching to thousands of people, and her past comes back to haunt you? Your name becomes defamed and smeared all over the headline news."

"You and your farfetched imagination!" Jay snickered. "I could care less about stuff like that. You know that part of me."

"That's the problem," Janice said softly. "Jay, I'm not going to lie to you. I still love you. I always have and always will. I still think that we have a chance to make a happy marriage. I've been with you through thick and thin. I've loved you, even when you behaved unlovable at times. I understand that you have changed and so have I. Watching you minister made me realize that we will make a great team together. Jay, my love for you will fill our home with joy and peace. And one day, you'll grow to love me the same."

"Janice, we've discussed this before. My feelings haven't changed. However, I do love you," Jay admitted, "but I'm just not in love with you. I've tried, but it's not there. I don't want to hurt you or keep hurting you. You shouldn't settle for less than God's best."

Janice's eyes watered at the truth. "I don't care. I will support and love you with all my heart. I will make the perfect pastor's wife, and you know it."

"You will," he spoke tenderly, "but just not with me."

Unable to accept the fate that fronted her, Janice decided she had to see the woman to whom Jay confessed his love. Instead of going back to work, Janice took a detour to Bayview hospital in Williamsburg county.

Upon entering Isabella's room, she was horrified by the patient's fading orange hair. "Opposites for sure!" Janice mumbled under her breath, jarring Isabella to open her eyes. Disappointed, Isabella was expecting to see Jay for lunch. *Who is this pompous woman?*

"Hi." Janice came over and extended a cordial handshake to Isabella. "I'm Janice, a VERY close friend of Jay."

"Hello," resignedly Isabella greeted. "Is Jay alright?"

"Oh sure," Janice waved, sliding the chair closer to the bed. "We just enjoyed a delightful lunch together at our favorite restaurant, Rizzio's." This was so out of Janice's character. Rejection had a way of bringing out the worst of a scorned woman.

"I don't know if you know much about the Cannon family, but I felt the need to share a little history with you. The Cannons are well-respected citizens in our community. They are practically famous. Everyone knows the family in the community and outside of the community. Pastor James Cannon's church, Word Alive Fellowship is very important in Lincoln. When Pastor James Cannon retires, Jay will take his place. Therefore, Jay's name and reputation must remain above reproach, and honorable. It must not be tainted in any way," Janice paused. "Do you understand what I am saying?"

Oh, Isabella understood perfectly well. "You're saying I'm not good enough for Jay." Isabella's reply was laced with resentment.

"I have loved Jay all my life. Everyone expects us to be married. Then, someone like you comes along," Janice stared at her orange hair, "and practically steals him from me without any effort. Even though I know that this is just a phase for Jay."

Isabella eyed her with contempt before finally speaking. She had met people like Janice all her life, snobbish people who look down their noses at her as if she was trash from the gutter. "If Jay was really yours, no one should be able to steal him from you."

"Listen up, you homewrecker!"

"Homewrecker! There has to be a home to wreck, first."

"And you're assuming there isn't?" Janice contended.

"So, you're telling me, Jay is married...to you?"

"Not yet."

Isabella grinned. *This woman must really be desperate!*

"My Jay is not your type!"

"And you are?" Isabella's head began to bang as if cymbals were crashing together when she attempted to sit up.

"Well, look at you! You have orange hair, *for Pete's sake*! Jay couldn't possibly be seen with you!"

"Don't you dare judge me! You don't even know me."

"I know that you'd lived a street life; Jay told me so. And I know that you don't deserve Jay. Most definitely, you hardly fit the mold of a pastor's wife."

Isabella wanted to knock Miss High and Mighty right off her high horse that she rode in on. But containing her anger, Isabella couldn't argue with the truth. No, she didn't fit the pastor's mold. She never would. "Please leave. My head is hurting," Isabella closed her eyes, trying to shut out the destructive force in the room.

"Forgive me for causing you distress," Janice stood up. "It wasn't my intention."

"Then what were your intentions?" Isabella opened her eyes again. "It seemed that you came for just that purpose. Now, please leave."

Janice felt as if God Himself was frowning down on her. "I'm sorry."

"That you are." Isabella tried to regain her calm demeanor, not wanting her foe to see her sweat one iota.

Janice waited, feeling berated by a young lady who didn't deserve her judgmental attitude. "I do apologize." Here she was condemning another when God hadn't condemned her.

Isabella refused to acknowledge her.

Janice left.

Isabella shuddered the moment the door closed. The truth hurt. Janice was right; she didn't fit the pastor's wife mold. She wasn't good enough for someone like Jay. On the other hand, Janice and Jay matched perfectly – two peas in a pod. She wouldn't be an embarrassment to Jay or his family. Her past wouldn't infringe on their present or future. Most importantly, Janice loved Jay. That was obvious!

He deserves better than me! He deserves Janice!

Chapter 27

Pronto, Jay knew something was wrong when he entered Isabella's hospital room that evening.

With arms folded, making her stance against the man who had her swooning over him effortlessly, Isabella was prepared and ready to put a stop to all this nonsense. It was for the best! No need to linger or prolong what was staring them both in the face. They weren't meant to be together!

"What's wrong?"

"Nothing." Isabella pouted like a ten-year-old.

"Something is wrong," Jay reached for her hand. Isabella snatched it away.

Jay was perplexed. "I'm sorry I couldn't make it for lunch. I had an unexpected appointment…"

"Yeah, right! Your appointment came right over after her luncheon with you."

"Janice!" Jay gulped. *Why in the world…*

"She wanted to mark her territory!" Isabella blurted. "Like a dog, relieving itself in one place!"

"I'm sorry. Did she upset you?" Jay was floored. He couldn't believe that Janice would do such a thing. It was so unlike her.

"Do I look upset!?"

"Yes."

"Well, Sherlock, I guess you solved the case."

"I had lunch with Janice today to tell her about you."

"Yeah, right! Why in the world would you talk about me to her?"

"Because I care about you," with tenderness, he expressed. "So much so that I wanted to tell MY FRIEND, Janice, about you. We've been friends for a long time."

"She wants more than friendship," Isabella watched him to read his emotions.

"I know, but I feel nothing for her but friendship."

"Did you and Janice date before? Was marriage in the plans?"

"Well, I..." Jay hemmed and hawed before finally answering. "We dated on and off for a couple of years. I never asked her to marry me."

"But she assumed you would?"

"Yes."

"I think you two make a good couple. She's all uptight, and so are you." Isabella avoided making eye contact with him. She was upset. Her raw feelings were all mixed up. Partly, she wanted him to leave, fearing that she would find herself hurt by this man just like all the other men in her life. Yet deep down, Isabella wanted Jay to stay and never leave her.

Her remark hurt Jay deeply. "So, you think I am uptight?"

"You are!" Isabella replied, a slight tremor in her voice. She understood that she was hurting him, but her heart had hardened again. "Look at you. Navy pinstripe suit, plain light blue tie, white shirt, and black designer shoes. Pretty uptight to me."

She popped his ballooned heart with her knifelike words. Jay sat down. Suddenly, he felt like a weak man. Defenseless. An unarmed man, pierced by a venomous arrow straight to his heart.

"Perhaps, I am uptight," Jay swallowed the lump lodged in his throat, "but...but...I care not just about you...I really do care FOR you, Isabella."

Momentarily, Isabella was speechless. No words would come out. Her heart was torn with conflicting emotions. Jay was too good for her. She was a *bad* person, living a *bad* life. *Why can't I be worthy of him?* Tears began to trickle down her face. Her physical scars were healing, but inwardly she needed more than man's medicine. She needed God.

"You lied to me," she sniffed. "You said you would be here for lunch, but instead, you had lunch with Janice. You chose her. And then you came here and said an appointment like it was a business meeting."

"I apologize," Jay stood now, bending over her. "I didn't think it mattered." His eyes begged for sympathy, for forgiveness.

"I can't stand a liar!"

"I promise to be truthful to you from now on," Jay looked at her, hopeful, "but I'm not perfect, Isabella."

"Preacher man, you're the closest to perfect that I have ever seen." Yes, she was becoming too attached to this man, and it scared her stiff.

"Do you really think I'm uptight?"

She laughed. "Just a little."

"I'll have to work on that," Jay aimed to please her, swiftly removing his suit jacket.

"Don't change." Isabella was serious. "Be yourself. I like you the way you are," Isabella's cheeks reddened as her resolve to stop whatever this was, dissolved.

"You're looking so much better today," Jay commented, more at ease. "You had me worried before. Especially when you developed pneumonia."

"I didn't mean to make you worry," she spoke shyly.

"Of course, you didn't." An awkward silence followed before he spoke again. "I spoke with Dr. Young, and he said you could go home in a couple of days. However, he also mentioned that you're going to need someone to look after you."

I have no one. "I can take care of myself. Been doing it all my life."

"I know you have," Jay stroked her hand, "but you're not physically able to care for yourself. Besides, you can't go back to where you used to stay. It's not safe."

She appreciated his concern, but Isabella had to do what she had to do. "I'll be fine."

She didn't sound so convincing. After all, Isabella was moneyless since that creep Big Tim stole all her brother had left her, and she'd probably never get it back. *I wish I would have put it in the bank and not under the mattress.* In her condition, Isabella couldn't go back and earn it on the streets. Her options were – oops, there were no options.

"You can come home with me…" timidly Jay suggested.

"With you!" Isabella jumped to conclusions; her countenance became ghastly looking. *I knew Jay wanted more from me. He's just like all the rest…up to no good…with one thing on his mind.*

"It's not like that. I live with my parents right now," Jay grinned sheepishly. "My mother loves taking care of people. She misses the nesting stage of taking care of family."

"You're too old to be living at home."

"You're right," again he laughed, "After my war injuries, I came home to heal and to help out. With dad recovering from the heart attack…my family needed me."

"Oh," she felt embarrassed.

He nodded.

She was quiet, deep in thought.

"So, what do you say?"

"I'll think on it."

"You do that," Jay cherished seeing this innocent side of her. Isabella was timid and vulnerable. He would never take advantage of her. Never! All Jay wanted to do was protect Isabella. Take her in and love her back to health.

I love you, my sweet Isabella!

The love for her brother had brought them together. However, it would take much more to keep them together.

Esther waved off her son's concern! "I've lived too long to worry about what people are going to say. Now you, on the other hand, might need to think about it. Your reputation and integrity may be questioned. When people start seeing Isabella here, there is going to be gossip. Are you ready for that?"

"*Let'em* talk!" Jay affirmed after asking his mother to help with Isabella. "Isabella needs a family's love more now than ever before. I can't abandon her. I promised Lewis. Besides, it is the Christian thing to do."

"It is," Esther smiled. "Have you spoken with your dad?"

"I wanted to speak with you first. I'm not sure how dad is going to feel about this?"

"He may have a few words of caution, but he'll never turn a lost sheep outside the pasture to fend for itself. Look at me!"

"Thanks, Mom, for your support," Jay embraced her. "Isabella needs smothering, and I know you're just the one to do it."

Chapter 28

Jay scooped Isabella into his arms and carefully carried her into the house and up the stairs. Though Isabella protested that she was capable of walking, her ankle was still healing from the lousy sprain she received from the altercation. Moreover, Jay wanted to carry her in his arms. Isabella was as light as a feather and frail as a toothpick, easily broken. Isabella felt safe, sheltered, and with such unexplainable warmth all over in the strength of his arms. As if she was a priceless china heirloom, Jay laid her in the middle of the king-size bed, which his mother had set up just for her.

Isabella felt so out of place as she looked around the room, all wide-eyed and wondering. Esther spared no expense in making this room elegant. Crisp, clean satin purple curtains hang from the large windows. Fresh flowers were on the nightstand and the dresser. Two candles were lit, sending off a violent fragrance. The artistic drawings of angels were a perfect addition to the room, which Esther purchased just yesterday for their special guest. Isabella did not know the paintings' value, but clearly, they held sentimental value to the mother. Everything was so pristine, making Isabella feel so unworthy. She'd never known such beauty, let alone slept in such luxury.

"Are you comfortable?" Jay helped position the pillow just right behind her head. Then, he pulled the soft lavender blanket over her, tucking her snuggly in.

"Yes," she felt shy again.

"My mom will be here soon. She wanted to make sure you know that she's happy you're here. Rest assured, when she comes, she will tell you herself. She loves to smother, so be prepared."

"I can't believe your parents are so nice to me. They must not know about me," Isabella toyed with her orange hair, wishing she could wash it out while staying with the Cannon family.

"They know all they need to know," Jay playfully touched her nose with his index finger. "They'll love you, orange hair and all."

"I don't deserve their love."

"Neither do I." Jay never put himself above Isabella or anyone else. "I was just born with such loving parents."

"You are blessed."

"I am." Jay leaned over and kissed her forehead. "And so are we…because you are here."

Tears blurred her vision as wetness ran down her cheeks. Honestly, at this very moment, Isabella felt more than blessed.

I don't deserve it!

Sure enough, as soon as Esther returned home, she went straight to Isabella.

"Welcome!" she embraced Isabella with a motherly hug, warm and cuddly. "We're so happy to have you here, Isabella. You rest and don't worry about anything. You're not a guest in our home; you're family. Your brother was here for only a few days, but he was family. We loved Lewis, and we love you."

Isabella couldn't suppress the sob in her throat. She had never felt such genuine caring. She opened her mouth to say something, but she was just too choked up to speak.

"Shhhh," Esther patted her hand, "I understand. You rest, and I'll be back in about an hour or so to bring you some homemade chicken soup." Esther stood. "Do you need anything for now? Some water, tea, or I have some diet sprite."

"No, thank you."

"Well, you rest," she insisted.

Isabella nodded.

Closing the door, Esther stood and allowed the teardrops to fall. *Father God, she needs you! She's been through so much. Heal her body, mind, soul, and spirit. My heart aches for her. She needs a mother's love right now. I love her already. Help me to help her."*

In the following days, both Esther and James hovered over Isabella. Jay found little time to be alone with Isabella because one or both of his parents were always near her, doting over her, smothering her with affection and attention. It did his heart good to see Isabella's eyes light up. To hear the joyous laughter bubbling from the inside of the one who had stolen his heart, without even knowing it.

Life around the Cannons' home was filled with joy and much nurturing for the young lady whose heart had never really known such a treasure. Isabella felt so at home with the Cannons. She expected the family to treat her with a long-handle spoon, but it was the exact opposite. No one interrogated her or put her on trial for her past life of sin. No one made her feel like she was at the bottom of the totem pole. Instead, they treated her equally, like she was a Cannon.

Jay enjoyed watching the camaraderie between Isabella and his mother. It was evident that Esther was quite smitten with her patient. The truth is Esther felt needed again. She loved being a mother, and since Isabella had no one, it was such a pleasant task of hovering over her, as if she were her baby chick.

Leela and Reese's family seemed to visit more since Isabella's arrival. Isabella adored little Sara and the five-year-old twins, Sandy and Randy, who loved Isabella and she, them. Leela felt an instantaneous connection to Isabella, just as she felt for Reese's wife, Rose. Isabella reminded her of Leela's wild days when all she wanted to do was fit in. Yet, Isabella lived the street life because it was her only way of survival.

One evening, Jay walked in on Isabella and Leela dancing to some old-school song. Isabella's ankle was better but not completely healed. Though she was moving in the bed, Isabella was having a *ball* with Leela, adjusting her temporary handicap. The sound of Isabella melted Jay's heart. For fear that Isabella was overdoing it, Jay started to interrupt their dancing. However, seeing the joy in her eyes, Jay didn't have the heart. Jay tiptoed out of the room, not wanting to interfere with their special time together.

The only sadness came when Isabella was alone. Often during the nighttime, her tears reached the ears of those surrounding her. Isabella cried all the time. In her sleep, she mourned and moaned. During the day, when no one was looking, Isabella boohooed. She was letting her guard down, which brought about tears and fears. All the pint-up tears from old were coming forth, bringing about a needed cleansing. The fears of loving and losing – all this unconditional love – consumed her.

Likewise, Jay was going through a transformation on the inside. He began opening up to his father more about the aftermath of being a veteran of war. Through remembrance, traveling down enemy lines, regularly tears sprang forward like a mighty rushing river. Indescribable agony shot through him like lightning. All of the hidden feelings were being released, purging the poison within and without. Jay had to confront the pain in order to conquer the past so that healing could come.

Likewise, so must Isabella. In the wee hours of the morning, Isabella's heartrending tears reached the ears of Esther, which this time Esther couldn't ignore. The Spirit was leading her. Draping on her robe, Esther rushed to Isabella's bedside. Curled up in the fetal position, Isabella wept in her sleep as her body shook.

"Shhhh," Esther gathered the sleeping beauty into her arms.

Slowly her eyelids opened, faced with the warmest eyes she had ever seen. Esther, too, was crying. "It's okay, Isabella. Everything is going to be alright."

"When?" her voice held a hinge of shame.

"Soon," she soothed.

"I'm a big water bucket." Isabella nestled closer in the mother-like arms, something she had been missing for such a long time. "I never used to cry. I don't understand why I'm crying now." All the painful memories of old were resurfacing. Being in a pleasant environment only reminded her of the environment she had come from and the one Isabella would soon return to. It reminded her of the tragic life she had chosen to live on the streets, resulting from her horrible childhood.

"Keep crying. Let it all out. It cleanses the soul." Esther coaxed, holding and rocking her gently. Momentarily, Esther released Isabella, retrieving a Bible from the nightstand. "This will also help cleanse your soul. You will find healing in the Word."

Cautiously Isabella received the gift.

"If you like, we can read together," unflinchingly Esther asked.

"Sure."

From that morning on, Isabella and Esther started their own private Bible Study every morning after breakfast. During lunch, Esther prayed with her, and at night, they both were on their knees praying together.

In private, Isabella began reading Lewis' Bible. Reading it made her feel connected to Lewis, although he was no longer physically with her. *His* God was becoming more than a mystery but a quest.

At times Isabella found herself flustered in Jay's presence. She endeavored to ignore him but couldn't. He had a foot in her heart, and she wanted to take it out...somewhat. Family mealtime was occasionally uncomfortable because Jay made it perfectly clear that he wanted more from Isabella than she could give. His eyes were transfixed upon Isabella at the table, and everyone was aware of this. Often, when she looked up, Jay would be staring at her. He'd wink, and she would lower her head. It was those sweet, intimate moments that planted seeds of love into their barren hearts. Yet, those same moments made Isabella want to run away because this was too good to last. Nothing good lasted in her life. Nothing!

Staying with the family for over a week now, helplessly, Isabella fell in love with all of them. Her guard was mainly down now. Isabella yearned, all her life, to be loved without reservation or hesitation. All of the Cannons were extending her the olive branch of love, but how could she reciprocate? How could they love someone like her? She feared her past would show its ugly face and make them see the real Isabella. When that happened, they would be gone! Vanish like the dew in the morning. This she feared and expected on a regular basis.

One night, Jay couldn't sleep, so he went downstairs into the den and turned on the television. He stopped flipping the channel when he came to his old favorite reruns of *Sanford and Son*. It was a marathon of funny family reruns. He watched television for an hour, not the slightest bit sleepy.

Isabella, restless and weary, came down to the den with the same thing in mind to watch television. She started to turn away, but her feet wouldn't move. "Couldn't sleep either," she stood at the door admiring Jay. There he sat in his matching blue pajamas, *of course, he appeared fashionable even in his sleepwear,* with his feet propped on the coffee table, hands behind his head, totally relaxed, not a care in the world!

"Nope," he smiled, trying to calm his anxious heart. "Come, join me."

"That's probably not the proper thing to do. A single man and a single woman sitting in the den, void of a chaperon in your parents' home." Isabella reasoned, feeling somewhat exposed in her t-shirt and shorts. Isabella lowered her eyes for a moment.

"You're right, but we're two grown adults, with nothing on our minds but watching television. You sit over there," Jay pointed to the couch to his right, and I'll remain here. Scouts honor!" He crossed his heart and raised his right hand.

She chuckled. Timidly, Isabella complied, glad for the distance between them. It wasn't that she didn't trust Jay; she didn't trust herself.

They watched rerun after rerun. It did them both good, as they constantly laughed at the funny sitcom. All too soon, the television watched them as the laughter turned serious and they began to open up to each other.

"Tell me about yourself, Isabella," Jay probed, his eyes off the television and now solely onto her. He leaned back in the recliner and closed his eyes. Yes, life was good again.

"You already know about me," Isabella lowered her head, embarrassment clouding her face.

How often had Jay watched her lower her face as if to cover her shame? It hurt him to see that. Jay wanted to get up and lift her head and tell Isabella that she was beautiful and never to be ashamed of who she was, for God wasn't finished with her. He didn't want her to feel lesser to him or any other human being.

"I want to know things about you that others wouldn't know by just looking at you."

"I like to dance."

He grinned, remembering seeing how freely she danced with his sister. A scene he would treasure forever. "I like to dance, too." He confessed. Not a soul in the house knew that because he never did it around them. Secretly, he enjoyed the freedom to let loose and let his feet do the moving and the frolicking.

"You're kidding," Isabella relaxed a little.

"No, I'm not. You see, Reese was the singer and musician. Leela was a professional dancer; no one could hold a candle to her. And well, I was the brainy one, no rhythm and no tune." Jay chuckled. "But in my younger days, when I was alone, I would turn on the music and just dance. I'm not saying that I was good at it, but I did alright. It was so freeing! No thinking about anything. Lewis taught me a few steps, as well."

"He did." Her eyes glowed in the dark at that tad bid of information. "He was a great dancer."

"That he was," Jay thought back to the time Lewis taught him how to do the *electric slide*. It took some time, but after repetitiously doing it, Jay was soon a natural pro at it, adding his individual style.

"When I was younger, still living with my family, I would put my feet on Lewis's shoes, and he would waltz me around the room. He made me feel so special."

"You are special, Isabella," Jay couldn't help it.

Once again, she looked down to avoid eye contact.

"Tell me something else."

"I'm shy."

"That I already know."

"I have nothing else to tell you." Isabella was uncomfortable talking about herself. "What about you?"

He rubbed his hand on his chin, "The only reason I joined the army was to forestall following in my father's footsteps as a pastor. I've never told anyone that, not even Lewis."

"Were you afraid?"

"Very!" Jay admitted. "I didn't think I could measure up to my dad. He's an awesome pastor. I mean, he has such depth, such knowledge of the Word of God. There is such a passion and zeal about my dad that I cannot explain with words. It's like he's Moses on earth, walking and talking with God regularly. Sometimes, I see the glory of God just shining on his face, and it's hard looking at him directly. Though I wanted to be like him, when it seemed that he was pushing me into preaching so early, it was overwhelming. So, I ran."

"Like Jonah?"

"You know about Jonah?" Jay was pleasantly surprised she knew of the familiar bible story.

"I've been reading Lewis' Bible," reluctantly she admitted.

"Wow! I'm glad, Isabella."

"Anyhow," she cleared her throat. "How do you feel about preaching or pastoring now?"

"I'm learning to stop comparing myself to dad. I'm just me. I'll never be him…"

"And he'll never be you," Isabella swiftly completed his sentence for him.

"Thank you," he was touched. "Tell me about your life with your foster parents."

"They were awful people!" Isabella snapped, tensing up immediately. "They abused me just like my father."

"I'm sorry," Jay regretted asking.

"No need to be sorry. It wasn't your fault."

"What age were you when you ran away?"

"Sixteen."

"Weren't you afraid of being out there on the streets all alone?"

"At first. But, I had no other choice. The streets were better than my foster parents. It was tough, though. I had to constantly watch my back. I had to learn to adjust and make the best of it. I had to learn to fend for myself."

"And…" it was like pulling teeth trying to get her to talk about herself.

"And…that's it. I lived on the streets and did whatever necessary to survive."

"You graduated High School; how?"

"I still went to school. The same school. I'd wash in the gas stations. Find clothes at Salvation Army or Goodwill and go to school like nothing was wrong. No one knew where I lived. I used my last foster parents' address. Mail kept coming to them, and so did the checks. So, they didn't say anything. They were too afraid...afraid I'd..." Isabella cut her statement short.

"Afraid you'd do what?"

"Tell that Mr. Perry raped me." Of this, Isabella admitted to no one before, which shocked her. Hearing it aloud made it seem surreal. Surely, now Jay would see her as soiled, damaged goods. He would want nothing to do with her!

Jay swallowed hard. Things were getting intense now. Hearing that someone physically abused Isabella at such a young age angered him more than he could show. They were supposed to protect her, not harm her. *Lord, take away this anger in me! I want to find the nasty scoundrel and beat him to a pulp!*

Vengeance belongs to Me. I will repay.

Jay did his best to gather himself. Desperately, he yearned to go to her and just hold Isabella and never let her go. "Please go on..."

"There's nothing else to say...You know the rest. No need in dredging up my dirty past." It hurt too much to talk about it. Isabella didn't want him to see her cry as she remembered her physical, mental, and sexual abuse, which drove her to the streets, doing the same thing and experiencing more abuse. It was best to leave the past in the past.

"Isabella," helplessly, Jay was drawn to her like a magnet as he came over and sat next to her. "I'm learning the hard way that if we don't confront our past, we will never be free to enjoy the present. Talking about it helps," Jay took her hand in his. "Let's confront it together, and then there will be no hidden skeletons in the closet for us to deal with later. I'm a big boy, Isabella. I can handle it. I'm not going to run away. I'm here to stay. Trust me. Trust me with the information, and I promise I won't abuse your trust."

Her eyes filled with pain.

He caressed her cheek with his thumb. The gentle touch thrilled her more than she cared to admit.

She cleared her throat nervously. She was a ball of nerves and *mixed-up* feelings. So many emotions were going through Isabella. She didn't know what to say, how to handle it, or what to do at this point.

"How old were you when your dad...first..."

"Lewis told you!" Isabella pulled away, humiliated that Jay knew her deepest, darkest secret.

"Yes."

"He shouldn't have! Lewis had no right!"

"He loved you and wanted me to help you."

"You can't help me!" She exclaimed, totally flustered by the conversation. "No one can."

"I beg to differ!"

"I'm not salvageable." A sob broke through her lips while her fierce, strong armor was coming apart.

"If I am salvageable, then so are you."

"You!" Isabella scoffed. "Mr. Preacher Man, with a lily-white slate, a lily-white home, a lily-white family...you have nothing to be salvaged for."

"I'm a murderer," Jay spoke grimly. "These hands have killed people."

"It's not the same."

"Taking a life is taking a life, whether it be in war or on the streets. Thou shall not kill is a commandment, without exceptions. You can't imagine the guilt I have felt and still do feel."

"How many?" timidly, she asked.

"One is too many."

"I'm a fornicator. I've slept with many men for money."

"How many?" Jay turned the tables.

"One is too many."

"I was mad at God," he confessed.

"I'm still mad at God...sometimes," she consented.

"Why?"

"Because?

"Because what?" Jay probed, trying to extract the teeth that were infected, and he continued to pull.

"Because...who else can I blame? I didn't ask to be born into a life of abuse and misery. I didn't ask to be molested by my father. I had to live on the streets or stay in a foster home and be raped by a sick man. He took my mom from me, a Christian woman who was abused. My brothers, all of them, turned out bad, except Lewis. All of them are dead except Damien, a murderer, and only God knows what else. This world is one big mess. Who else should I blame?"

"What about the devil?"

"He's not more powerful than God. At least that is what my momma told me and what the Bible says."

"No, he's not, but he is the ruler of this world for now, although God is still all-powerful. The devil is bad, and God is good. The devil blinds the eyes, wreaks havoc, steals, kills, and destroys people's lives. However, forget all that. Even in the bad times, in all the tragic, haven't you seen some of God's goodness?"

"No!"

"Come on."

"I don't want to talk about this anymore," Isabella stood. How quickly the joy of being in his company had turned sour, like sour milk. *Yuk!* She hated the taste it left in her mouth. "I'm going back to bed."

"The only way to conquer the past is to confront it."

"Then you confront it!" Isabella's hot anger aroused from within the secret closets of her heart. "You killed men because you had to. I slept with men because I had to…to survive, to eat, to have shelter. Okay, is that confrontation enough?" Isabella nearly ran upstairs, being chased by the ghosts of her past.

Jay wanted to go after her, but it wouldn't do any good. Isabella was too upset now – hurt – broken – ashamed – mad. Mad at her life, the circumstances surrounding her life, and probably angry at Jay for pushing her buttons.

Closing her door, Isabella plopped on the bed and cried herself to sleep.

Father God, comfort Isabella, as only You know how.

Chapter 29

Isabella often dreamed of finding a man like Jay to come in and sweep her off her feet. Someone to love her past her pain. To take care of her. To hold her in the night, when she couldn't sleep because of the nightmares of her past. To love her and not just lust after her. She fantasized about someone believing in her and seeing her potential to be somebody. It was only a dream. For to love someone and be loved by someone would require Isabella to be vulnerable. Never again! She didn't trust anyone. She trusted her father, and look what happened. She trusted her foster parents and look at what happened. She trusted her brother Lewis and look at what happened – Lewis died on her. Alright, the latter one wasn't his fault.

Uncontrollably, the seeds of love were blossoming in both their hearts. Seeds tilled and toiled through hard times, which caused appreciation and deep affection to burst forth and grow supernaturally as if overnight. Yet fear wanted to stunt the growth in Isabella's lonely heart.

Those who sow in tears will reap with songs of joy. He who goes out weeping, carrying seed to sow, will return with songs of joy, carrying sheaves with him.

Isabella awakened not from a bad dream but a sleepless night, tossing and turning, trying to shut down the visions of Jay and her past all mingled together. She had to get away from here. The Cannon's home was only prolonging the inevitable – rejection and dejection. But how was she going to leave? She had no money – no place to live – nowhere to go. Still, Isabella resolved to do something – and soon! She was a survivor!

While at work, Jay couldn't help but reminisce about their private time in the family den. It was beautiful before it turned bitter. However, it was necessary. Isabella needed someone to talk to, and Jay was all too willing to listen. Despite the outcome, Isabella's openness to him renewed Jay's hope for a future with her. Though Jay desired to reveal his feelings to Isabella, he feared she would run away—like she did when the conversation got heated.

He was captivated by the endearing young lady. She was so different from any other woman he had known, which intrigued him even more so. But it was more than that. Isabella was special. She had a big, big heart, but it had been filled with so much pain and abuse, that she didn't allow others to see her goodness. But it was there. No doubt it was there. Jay saw it, and it enamored him. Isabella added spice to his dull life. She was good for him. He couldn't remember ever laughing so and ever being so contented just to sit and talk with someone.

Then doubt quickly obtruded upon his trip down memory lane. *How in the world is this unorthodox union ever going to work? Perhaps Janice was right. Was it worth it all? Isabella was a loose woman, one who had been around. Shouldn't that scare me witless?* Yet, all Jay could see when he thought of Isabella was how youthful and tender her heart was, despite the outward façade she put up of being hard and tough. Isabella was a diamond in the rough, needing someone to uncover her hidden treasures. Jay knew the truth. Isabella was sweet, loving, gentle, compassionate, and so beautiful. Her outer appearance only reflected the barrier Isabella erected to protect the one thing her father and others abused – her heart.

Everyone was already at the supper table when Jay finally arrived home. Even Reese had joined the family tonight. Reese, Rose, and the twins were visiting with Rose's best friend, Natalya.

"Everything alright, son?" Pastor James noticed the tired look on Jay's face, and so did Isabella.

"Yes, I'm fine." Jay hardly said two words after that. Only he kept looking at Isabella, faking a smile. She smiled back but wanted desperately to discern what was bothering him—was it her?

"You *got* it bad," Reese leaned over, whispering in his brother's ear.

"What in the world are you talking about?" Jay played dumb.

"I see how you are staring at Isabella," he began, "everyone sees it. You couldn't even eat your food from gawking at her."

"You're crazy."

"You're crazy in love with Isabella."

"I'm just keeping a promise to my friend Lewis."

"Yeah, keep telling yourself that. You and I both know better. You're in love."

"Mind your own business."

"This is my business," Reese argued. "If my big brother is about to add to our family, I need to make sure that she's the right fit for the Cannon clan. And well, I say she's perfect."

Jay looked up, trying to see if his brother was pulling his leg or being truthful. His eyes spoke sincerity. Jay smiled.

After dinner, Jay and Isabella volunteered to do the dishes. After convincing Esther that she wouldn't overdo it, Jay and Isabella stood side by side at the kitchen sink, washing and drying the dishes together. It felt so right. Several times their hands brushed against the other, sending all kinds of signals within. It was exciting and alarming all at once.

When they finished, facing each other, Jay grabbed both her hands and passionately eyed her, and said, "Isabella, you are the most beautiful woman I have ever seen."

The way he said her name sounded so pure, not tainted like other men who called her. She turned beet-red and lowered her face.

"I can't tell you how badly I want to kiss you...right now...but I don't want to frighten you." Jay was very straightforward, making no bones about his desire to step over their peculiar friendship boundaries.

"You can't," Isabella looked up. "Someone may walk in the room, and I...I don't want them to think...evil of me."

Feelings burned like glowing embers between them. Gently, Jay tilted her chin upward and replied, "No one in this family will ever think evil of you. They love you. *I love you!* Can't you tell?"

"Yes," she lowered her head again. "The Cannons are special people," Isabella uttered quietly. "They took me in, loved me back to health, without hesitation. But…"

"But nothing," his voice cut into her thoughts, then tilted her chin upward again. "Nevertheless, to calm your fears, I'm not going to kiss you right now…but I want to *soooooooo* badly. I'll wait."

Partly, Isabella felt disappointed that he didn't even try to persuade her to kiss him. Isabella smiled anyhow and let his hands go. She turned to leave, but he grabbed her hands.

"Not so fast," Jay wrapped his arms around her. "I will not kiss you tonight, but tomorrow I'm taking you out on a date, and before the night ends, I am going to kiss you, and I'm not going to let anything or anyone stand in the way of me kissing you. Do you understand?"

"Are you asking me out on a date?" Isabella felt dizzy. Her heart was pounding wildly. No man had ever made her feel this way before. So vulnerable, yet so alive!

"No," he stated. "I'm telling you for fear that you might say no."

They laughed together—what a glorious sound to his ears. Isabella was laughing.

"So Isabella, I guess until tomorrow…let's say around 7:00. You better pucker up and be ready to give me what I want," Jay winked. "I'll just settle for this tonight." Jay planted a soft kiss on her forehead. The sweet gesture sent Isabella's heart racing uncontrollably.

"Goodnight, Isabella."

Isabella watched the kitchen door close. Her insides were churning. She certainly felt as if she was going to faint. Then a dull ache settled in the pit of her soul. *This will never work! We're from two different worlds.*

I am with you.

Isabella nearly stopped in her tracks. It was the Scripture she had read from Lewis' Bible.

Fear not, for I am with you always.

Back in her room, hidden from everybody, Isabella dropped to her knees, and for the first time, she prayed for herself. She prayed for Jay. She prayed for Chance and Tammy. And she prayed for Pastor James, Esther, and the entire Cannon family, including

Natalya and Otis, Reese's friend. They were family. Isabella's heart yielded to the One who could wash away her pain and cleanse her filthy heart.

Lord, Jesus, I want You to live in my heart. Come and stay!
I am here. I'll never leave you or forsake you!

As she rested in her bed that night, she thought about how her life had changed so drastically. She always felt that she was a strong woman. She had to be! Life had beaten her down to a pulp. It took strength and determination to pull herself up from the trenches of defeat. *And* here it was, this preacher man was coming into her life, making her weak. She couldn't just say no to him. She couldn't just ignore him. Though her mind said pack your things and leave, the heart yearned to stay. Isabella found herself swooning over him like a love-sick puppy. Now she promised him a kiss.

Despite Isabella's promiscuous lifestyle, kissing was off-limits. It seemed strange with her extracurricular occupation, but kissing meant she cared, of which she didn't. Kissing on the lips signified intimacy. It was the one thing...no man...not even her monstrous daddy, could ever force her to do. To this date, surprisingly but profoundly true, Isabella had never kissed a man. It got her slapped, punched in the mouth, lip busted too many times to count, tossed around like a rag doll, but somehow Isabella maintained her golden rule of not kissing one of her *johns*. It was the only sacred thing she had left, and Isabella wouldn't allow any man to take that from her. That's why Big Tim beat her up. Isabella bit his lip when he tried to force her to kiss him. Now, here she was, considering an intimate kiss with Jay. Though Jay had previously pecked her on the lips and forehead, neither was reciprocated by Isabella.

What in the world was she thinking?

Chapter 30

Isabella was already awake when Esther entered her room Friday morning. She couldn't sleep a wink, anticipating her date with Jay.

"You're up early." Esther came and sat by her.

"I was hoping to help you with breakfast this morning."

"How sweet," Esther patted her hand, "but I have something else in mind. How about we go out for breakfast. James is going to the office with Jay, and that leaves us, two girls. We can go shopping, that's if you feel like it."

"Shopping?" her nose wrinkled. "Are you sure you want to go with me?" It was one thing being together in the home, but going out in public with someone like her, could prove to be embarrassing to Jay's mother.

"Of course?" Esther smiled with reassurance. "Jay told me not to cook too much tonight because he was taking you out."

Isabella lowered her eyes, afraid of what truth would be revealed in Esther's telling eyes. "Are you and Pastor James alright with it?"

"Of course! We love you."

Isabella felt warmth all over. "Can I get some dye for my hair?"

"Better yet, how about we go to the hairdresser and get our hair and nails done." Esther blithely suggested.

"I don't have any money."

"My treat." Esther sensed her pride. "We're going to have a good day. I promise not to tire you out. We don't want you overdoing it."

"Can we still have our Bible Study and then go?" Isabella looked forward to their studies. It soothed her and gave her hope that she never thought possible.

"Yes," Esther's eyes misted.

"How do I get what you have?" Isabella boldly asked. *"What you* and the family have? The peace and love that resides in this home are like nothing I have ever experienced before."

"Only through Jesus." Esther grabbed her hands. "You can have it if you want it."

"How?"

"Just by asking Jesus to come into your heart." Esther opened her Bible to Romans 10 and began to read the life-changing Scriptures.

"If you confess with your mouth the Lord Jesus and believe in your heart that God has raised Him from the dead, you will be saved. For with the heart, one believes unto righteousness, and with the mouth, confession is made unto salvation. For the Scripture says, *'Whoever believes on Him will not be put to shame.' For there is no distinction between Jew and Greek, for the same Lord over all is rich to all who call upon Him. For whoever calls on the name of the LORD shall be saved."*

"I asked Him last night, but can you make sure that I did it right and pray with me." Isabella was all choked up, feeling that her life was changing for the better and that she would be a new person, a better person.

With hopeful tears in her eyes, and a burning desire to have what all the Cannons had, Isabella allowed Esther to lead her into a salvation prayer. "Lord, Jesus, come into my heart. I confess with my mouth the Lord Jesus and believe that God raised Him from the dead. I make You Jesus the Lord and Savior of my life, and I will follow You. Please fill me with the Holy Spirit to lead and guide me throughout the rest of my days. Thank You for living in me and making me a new creation in Jesus' name, amen."

As Isabella spoke the words from her heart, something amazing happened. Nothing changed on the outside, but inside, peace inundated her soul.

"From this point on, you are a new creature in Christ Jesus. The old things have passed away; all things have become new. God has forgotten all about your past, and now you must do the same. It will not be easy at first. But with each passing day, it will get easier. As love grows, the pain will go. As your relationship with the Lord increases, the painful nightmares will decrease and cease." Esther held out her hands to Isabella and embraced her. "Now you are truly a family member. Welcome."

For some time, the two women held onto each other. Esther cherished the fact that God used her to bring Isabella into the family. Isabella felt overwhelmingly blessed to be adopted into God's family – despite her flaws, past, and sins, God accepted her as His own.

Leela met Esther and Isabella at the local diner for breakfast. Then they went to the mall. The threesome shopped until Isabella showed signs of fatigue. Being so well known, Esther and Leela often had people stopping them to chat. Isabella felt conscious of their stares at her orange hair. Fortunately, she had on Leela's clothes so that they couldn't be appalled at her typical attire.

Being pampered at the hair salon was a treasure for Isabella. Not only did she get her hair and nails done, but a facial, which gave her a natural glow. When Isabella finally looked at herself in the mirror, her hands covered her mouth. She gasped in disbelief. Her eyes swelled up with tears. Her natural chestnut brown hair was trimmed and styled beautifully. Bangs shaped her face as her long, locks cascaded to her waistline, not a kink in sight.

Leela and Esther quickly came to her side.

"You're so beautiful," Leela felt proud of her.

"Gorgeous, and your hair, it's silky and beautiful, just like you are." Esther embraced her.

"I can't believe this is really me," she sniffed. "I feel so...so..."

231

"Beautiful!" Esther knew the word would never come off her lips. "You should, my darling one."

"My brother is going to look like an owl, with his mouth wide opened when he sees you!" Leela chuckled.

Made to rest after their shopping spree, Isabella laid down on the bed, her heart pounding with great anticipation of her date with Jay. She had never gone on a date-date before. Undeniably, Isabella had rendezvous with many male callers, but for immoral reasons. Jay was her first.

Before her date with Jay, Leela came over to help Isabella get dressed and fix her makeup. Leela was the sister Isabella had never had but always wanted. Having five older brothers shepherding Isabella in her younger years provided her with security and safety, but not girly things.

"How do I look?" Isabella shyly asked Esther and Leela.

"Like a princess!" Esther happily clapped her hands.

"Jay is going to flip when he sees you." Leela knew her conservative brother. *Tonight, when he first sees Isabella, all his conservative notions are going to fly straight out the window.*

Isabella beamed with happiness, her face crimson red, as she lowered her eyes. Having someone compliment her was very rare unless there was an ulterior motive. People usually put her down instead of building her up.

"Don't be embarrassed," Esther came and tilted her head upward. "You've changed clothes, your hair, but none of that makes you beautiful. You were already beautiful, Isabella. Now that you have Jesus in your heart, the real beauty shows up. No need to hide your beauty. I see it. Leela sees it. Jay will see it. Everybody will see it. Now, you have to see it."

Esther delicately moved her toward the mirror. "Look, Isabella. See yourself through God's eyes. You're so beautiful."

Beholding her face in the mirror, the mask removed, bright color removed from her hair, Isabella didn't recognize herself. It was surreal to see herself looking normal.

Once again, Isabella became emotional. She had never cried so much in her life as she fought to get her composure. "How can you so easily say that? Aren't you worried about Jay's reputation of being with a girl like me?"

"Jay is blessed to have you," Leela said first. "Like me, you were a little rough around the edges, but Christ smoothed out all the edges and made you over."

"Leela is right," Esther added. "I'm proud of Jay being with such a beautiful girl like you. Remember, you're a new creature in Christ Jesus."

"I can barely remember my mother," Isabella swallowed. "She was a sweet woman but suffered so much from my dad. I ached for her love, but she could only give me what she could, which seemed so little. Still, I know she loved me very much and I, her. Today and every day since I have been here, you have given me so much of a mother's love. I'm grateful. If I could have picked a mother to be in my life, I would have picked you."

Esther swiftly embraced her. "I gladly accept the role."

"Now, I have another sister." Leela threw her arms around both of them. Reese's wife Rose had become her sister the moment she entered their lives.

At seven o'clock sharp, Jay waited downstairs with a dozen red roses and one pink one. His parents were behind him, along with Leela. Everyone was excited for Jay. Finally, he was back to his old self, but just more improved. More relaxed and not so intense. Isabella brought his soft side out, making him alive and free.

Gracefully, Isabella descended the stairs.

Jay's knees shook as he beheld his date. Jay could hardly breathe as he took his first glance at her. She was absolutely breathtaking! No picture could rightly paint her beauty. She was indescribable. She was a picture of perfection as her long chestnut tresses bounced with each step she took. The eloquent black dress revealed her hourglass figure. Jay was blown away by her transformation. He always knew she was beautiful, but this was way over the top. She was stunningly gorgeous. A knockout! He would be the envy of every man tonight, for sure. And yet, there was something else different about Isabella that he couldn't quite label at the moment.

"Close your mouth," Leela whispered in her brother's ear.

"You're gorgeous," Jay complimented as his tongue stuck to the roof of his mouth. "Absolutely breathtaking."

"Thank you," Isabella felt like Cinderella.

"Give her the flowers," Leela whispered again.

Jay couldn't think straight. Her beauty dimmed his thought process. "These…are…for you." He didn't take his eyes off of her.

"They are lovely." She inhaled the sweet aroma.

"The pink signifies the first thing I noticed about you at the bar…your hair was pink." Jay leaned over and whispered in her ear.

Isabella laughed softly.

"I like the natural color better," he couldn't help but touch it. It was so soft…just like her.

"Thanks," her cheeks flamed red.

Jay held out his hand. "Shall we go?"

She nodded, feeling giddy and intoxicated by this handsome, kind gentleman.

"I'll go put the flowers in a vase," Leela suggested.

"I'll keep the pink one," Isabella looked up at Jay, all dreamy-eyed.

James, Esther, and Leela all cheered as the door closed as if Jay had just scored a touchdown! Well, he did…in the game called life!

Jay took Isabella to a very upscale restaurant. Isabella had never been in a place like this. It was so regal. She felt undeserving of being there and of being with Jay.

Jay perceived her uneasiness because she avoided eye contact with him and the waitress and others.

"I'm so glad to be here with you. You are a precious gem."

"Not me," Isabella sipped her raspberry tea and kept her eyes down.

"Yes, you are," Jay reached over and touched her chin. "Look at me."

Timidly, she obliged.

"Did you enjoy your shopping spree with mom and Leela?" She nodded.

"I can't get over your beauty. To think you tried to hide it with all that gothic makeup and multi-color hair. I'm not condemning or saying that you weren't pretty before," Jay felt like he had put his foot in his mouth. "It just seems like a crime to hide such beauty."

Isabella giggled.

"I love hearing you laugh."

"You make me laugh," she said sheepishly.

"As you do me."

"I accepted Jesus into my heart today," she proclaimed, not able to contain her salvation.

That's it! I knew something was different! Jay was too choked up to say anything at first. Without control, his eyes misted. God had answered his prayers. "Lewis is doing cartwheels in heaven, for sure." Jay scooted his chair back and went to her. He hugged her, prouder than ever to be with her. "I'm so happy, Isabella. This is the greatest gift you could ever give me."

"I did it for me," she muttered. "I wanted what you and your family have...peace."

"It's yours," Jay returned to his chair, enamored with Isabella's innocent loveliness. The fact that she was now a member of God's family only enhanced her loveliness.

Well, Lewis, I kept my promise to you. She's one of us! Hallelujah!

While eating, Isabella said, "I was thinking about what you said the other night. Think about the good. There must have been some good happening in my life to prove that God was still with me, still blessing me. I remembered some good times; they were few and far between, but there were some good times.

"Like my mother brushing my hair one hundred strokes each night, when dad wasn't ranting and raving about her being in my room. *I had such long hair,* she would say, just like my great-grandmother. My dad often said I wasn't his child because I looked mixed, white. But my great-grandmother was so light-skin, that people thought she was white. She had long hair, like mine. I was named after her, Isabella. Do you know what Isabella means?"

"No," Jay enjoyed listening to her talk. Her voice was sweet and lyrical.

"The Hebrew meaning is "devoted to God," she acknowledged. "My mom was so proud of my name. She said Biblical names set the tone for a person's life. She believed a child's name prophetically foretold his or her future."

"Isabella, devoted to God," Jay repeated with confidence. "Your mother and grandmother were prophesying your commitment and affection to God before you were even born. Before it ever happened. Now it is happening."

Isabella smiled, not arguing, or agreeing.

"And the wonderful times I had with Lewis. My brother treated me like an angel and always made me feel special. No one called me Izzy but him. He loved me, and I loved him so much." The more she talked, the more comfortable she seemed. Then suddenly, pain filled her eyes, and Jay had to strain to hear her words.

"When momma died, my world fell apart. My dad became a beast. He was awful." One teardrop escaped her eyes. "I often wondered why he hated me so much. I believe it was because he, in his sick mind, thought I wasn't his. I don't know why, because my mother was a true Christian. She dedicated her life to God and her family. Plus, I had his eyes…green…me and Lewis."

"Alcohol distorts one's reasoning capabilities," Jay reached for her hand from across the table, and she freely gave it.

"I hated him. I still do," she confessed. "How can God love me with all this hatred in my heart?"

"He does…but you must forgive your father, just as Christ forgave you."

"I know you're right." She replied but quickly changed the subject. "I thought about something else. God must love me a great deal because He allowed my paths to cross with you and your wonderful family."

Jay couldn't stop gawking at her. She looked so innocent. So pure. So adorable.

"Did you know that Reese came by and brought me some books and music CDs and talked with me for a while? Rose sent me a chocolate cake. Leela calls me every day. It's like, I'm not a foster child, but I'm adopted…I have a family."

"You do," Jay squeezed her hand, his thumb tenderly caressing it.

"I feel so blessed."

"We all are blessed because of you. You have brought sunshine into our home, Isabella."

She blushed, gazing at him with admiration and a little something else. His yellowish-brown eyes shimmered. He was such a handsome man with his pearly white teeth, natural thick arched brows, black, wavy hair with strands of grey on the side, and coffee brown skin. He was built like a model, not a hint of fat anywhere, just complete muscle. Jay was all man, from head to toe.

While she admired his handsome features, Jay scanned her face. She was mind-blowing. Those green crystal eyes sparkled tonight. Isabella sparkled tonight. What a spectacular vision of beauty to bask in.

"Well, I be *doggone!*" Their intimate moment was interrupted by someone boisterous.

Isabella shrieked in fear, the color completely drained from her face. She was too terrified to move. She gripped Jay's hand so tightly that Jay thought it would break if he moved one inch.

Right away, Jay recognized the big fellow. The same one he saw leaving Isabella's hotel room in a hurry. The one who had stolen her money. The one who had beaten her and left her for dead.

"Please leave," Jay said curtly, speaking through clenched teeth. He would have never thought they would have run into this man in such a place like this.

"You don't know who you got here, feller," the big man spoke. Unbeknown to either of them, this big burly man was a married attorney who visited the slums to meet his perverted needs outside of the home. "She may be all dressed up, but she's no good."

Isabella squirmed in her chair, noticing that people were staring at them...mainly her.

"She's no lady...she's a...h..."

"A queen," Jay intervened just in time, "and I'm her king. And as the king, I beseech you to go your merry way and leave us alone, or I will be forced to call the police and tell them I found the culprit who raped and beat up the queen, took her money, and left her for dead."

"You have no proof." The man stumbled over his words

"Please, Jay," Isabella feared he would do just that. "I don't want to do that. I..."

"You're wrong there. DNA never lies," Jay stood up, facing the man head-on. "You may bully women, but you can't bully me," Jay spoke softly yet firmly. "But you will return the money, or I will be forced to do so." Swiftly, Jay took out his phone and snapped the man's picture. "I know people in high places."

Big Tim, better known as Attorney Timothy Gaines in the business world, looked at the man, summing him up to see if he were for real or not. "I am an attorney. I know the law. I know you don't have a case."

Isabella would have never believed in a million years that this man had a decent job, yet all along was an attorney.

"Try me!" Jay didn't flinch, picking up his cell phone, he snapped a picture of the big guy. Then Jay reached into his pocket for his wallet. "Here's my card. Make sure you use that address to return the money to me, or we will pursue the matter at hand."

Big Tim looked over at Isabella, admiring how beautiful she looked, all cleaned up.

"Now the Queen and I are enjoying a scrumptious feast and would like to be alone. Have a good evening, sir." Jay dismissed him, sat back down, and devoted his attention entirely and solely to Isabella.

"You're still a slut!" he sneered at Isabella. Then with his head tucked between his legs, Big Tim quietly backed away, feeling lower than the dirt under his feet.

Isabella let out a big sigh. "I can't believe you did that!" She stargazed at Jay with utmost esteem. She had never had a man defend her honor, except Lewis. At that very moment, Jay had fully and completely captured her heart. The bulky stature of the man didn't rattle him in the slightest. Jay saw him for the big bully he was. On the other hand, Isabella was all tangled up, like yarn unraveling, thread going everywhere.

"Please don't pursue it with Big Tim. I'd rather him keep the money than deal with him. Please promise me, Jay, you won't pursue this."

He sighed loudly, and regrettably, agreed. "You have my word."

"Thank you."

"Now, let's just forget him," Jay took her hand in his again and squeezed it. "Isabella, I have fallen hard for you, and there is no turning back now."

She squeezed back, unable to say anything. If only she could find the strength to tell him to turn around. To forget her and run because there were many more *Big Tim's* that may cross their paths. But Isabella couldn't. Isabella couldn't bear it if Jay left her now. To have tasted the fruit of love and then to lose it would be like death to her.

She smiled, lighting up the room and brightening up Jay's life as he knew it. A sweet quietness descended on them. The two hearts spoke words of adoration without opening their mouths.

Riding home in silence, Isabella pondered the horrible ordeal with Big Tim. She couldn't just shake *him* off! He embarrassed her. How many more men from her past would haunt her in the future? Although Isabella wanted to change, her past life was bound to catch up with her, and she didn't want to hurt Jay in any way. He had been too kind to her. *No matter what I feel for him, I can't risk damaging him or his family! Janice was right!*

Back at his home, Jay escorted Isabella to the front door. Before going in, he forced her to look at him.

She was crying.

He tenderly wiped her eyes, not understanding why all of a sudden, she became so sad. "Don't cry. You're breaking my heart."

"I can't help it," she continued. "My past will always be a part of my future. I can't run from it."

"You don't have to. We'll stand up to it together."

Isabella looked at him with unbelief. "You make it seem so easy. Even possible."

"All things are possible if you believe," he replied. "I believe in us."

"But…"

Her doubts were silenced as he bent down and claimed her lips with his tenderly. He'd waited long enough, and he couldn't bear another single moment of waiting. Jay's heart quickened to a wild rhythm and intensified when he brushed a kiss across her lips.

Isabella slipped her arms around his neck and allowed him to pull her closer. Surely, she felt she would faint while Jay thought he was riding on the clouds of heaven.

"My first real kiss," she said breathlessly.

Jay pulled away and looked her in the eyes, blown out of the water by her admission.

"Don't look so shocked. Kisses are intimate. It was the one thing I was saving…saving…for you."

Jay thought he would just melt right then and there. Instinctively, they both leaned in and kissed the other again. The kiss was filled with passion and fire. It was indescribable! Marvelous! Extraordinary!

"We better go inside," Isabella said nervously, pulling away.

"You're right." Jay didn't take his eyes off of her. Then without control, he leaned over and kissed her again.

She accepted his sweetness. "Stop," she said softly, "I'm feeling lightheaded."

"Me too," he chuckled. "I'm intoxicated."

"Preacher man, you best behave yourself, or I'll tell the church members that you're a drunk."

"Drunk off of you." He held her tighter.

"You're a preacher; I was a prostitute. You're kind and forgiving; my heart is raw with unforgiveness. You're wealthy and going places; I don't have a dime to my name. You may not see it now, but my reputation will come back to haunt you. Look at me. I may be dressed up, but you can never dress up my past. It is what it is. Besides, what do I have to offer you?" her statement ended with a long-suffering sigh, as Isabella related all the reasons why they would never work. Isabella had lost too many and had been poorly treated by so many men that she just couldn't allow herself to become vulnerable to losing again. Therefore, Isabella was ready to put on her running shoes and run…any place, but into Jay Cannon's arms. Fear was hot on her tail!

"You can offer me your love." Jay's heart hoped.

With trembling, Isabella looked at Jay. She wanted to shout it aloud that she loved him, but she couldn't. Their relationship was happening too fast, everything falling into place like popcorn.

"I had a wonderful time tonight, in spite of…"

"Shhhh," he put his index finger over her lips.

"Besides receiving Jesus into my heart, this has been the second-best moment of my life."

"Mine too!"

The couple went inside. Jay escorted Isabella to her bedroom. "Sleep in peace," he kissed her forehead and went back downstairs.

Closing the bedroom door, Isabella put her hands to her lips, still feeling the warmth of his lips upon hers. They still tingled.

My first kiss!

Chapter 31

Jay slept like a peaceful baby. He felt like a big kid who had just won the greatest prize at the fair. Only this wasn't the fair, and he wasn't a kid. This was real life, and he was a grown man with grownup feelings for a beautiful lady.

On the other hand, Isabella found it impossible to get a good night's sleep. She daydreamed about her first and only date. It had started out so good, and then Big Tim showed up and made her see the truth. The truth was that her past would always torment her. There was nothing Isabella could do to erase the memories of the life she had once lived. Though she would never go back to such a lifestyle, Isabella knew that she had slept with dogs, and she still had the flea bites to prove it – big ones like Big Tim.

Though Jay said, it didn't matter, not now. But one day, it would, and Isabella couldn't bear to hurt or embarrass him. She would just have to learn how to be content with life…how it is now, not how it was then. Just enjoy being a Believer. Grow in God's Word. Do good by others, and then maybe one day…one day God will send her another man…someone half as decent as Jay would be better than she deserved.

Saturday morning, Jay went for his usual jog, now more of a walk, with his dad while his mother and Isabella were in the kitchen.

Esther knew something was wrong because Isabella was so standoffish. She had erected her wall again.

Lord, help her to accept our unconditional love, especially from Jay. Heal her wounded heart.

While Esther went back upstairs to assist her husband after returning from their walk, Jay quickly showered and came back downstairs to be alone with Isabella.

He reached for her hand, but she snatched it from him. "Please don't."

"Why?"

"*Cuz* I don't want you to." Isabella refused to look at him.

"Why are you acting like this," he felt rejected. "Something amazing happened to us yesterday."

"We were just caught up in the romance of the evening."

"It was more than that, and you know it."

"I know no such thing, Jay," anxiously, she walked away.

"Well, it did for me," he swiveled her around to look at him.

"You're reading too much into it, Jay. Let's just forget about it."

"I'm reading the truth," his eyes twinkled. "And I can't forget it."

"Try!" Isabella attempted to pull away.

"I don't want to." Jay held her closer, confused by her icy remarks and behavior. "I desire to explore this new territory we both embarked on yesterday."

"It's way too dangerous, preacher man."

"Stop calling me that. You're using it as a crutch to keep you from seeing me as a man."

"A man who happens to preach." Isabella maintained her stance. "Same thing."

"Yes, I preach, but I am still ALL man with manly feelings. Manly desires. Manly wants. Manly needs. And what this man feels, desires, wants, and needs are all of YOU."

"You're crazy." Isabella scoffed, this time wriggling herself free from him. "Excuse me for a moment," she left the room.

Later at breakfast, Isabella cleared her throat and reservedly announced, "I truly thank you all for your hospitality, but since I'm feeling much better, I think that it's time for me to go back to my…"

My what? I don't have anything or anywhere to go, "to live on my own again."

"No!" Esther shouted, dropping her fork on the table. She objected before Jay or anyone else could. "You're still healing. You can't go out there with no one to take care of you."

Isabella was touched but still determined, went on to say, "It's not right...me living here with Jay. It's not proper. It will hurt his reputation. We should avoid the appearances of evil." She recently ran across that Scripture in her treasured Bible.

She's reading the Bible on her own! Esther felt proud. "Under the circumstances, God understands. And well, as for people, they can say what they want, we all know the truth."

"That's right, Isabella." Pastor James agreed. "You're family, and we don't put family out in the streets to fend for themselves when they can't. We take them in, just as God expects us to. Besides, if that's the case, Jay can stay in the back room at the church until further arrangements can be made."

Jay was stunned to silence. Her announcement came as a total shock.

Isabella looked at all of them and then at Jay. "I'm leaving."

Jay slid his chair back, making an awful screeching noise, and practically dragged her out the kitchen, into the den, closing the door behind them. "Please excuse us."

"What are you doing?" Isabella defensively shouted at him.

Jay dragged her into the den and closed the door, and asked, "What was that all about?"

"Jay, I've overstayed my welcome." Her bottom lip was quivering.

"You know that's a cop-out. Is it because of last night? Did I come on too strong? Or what?" Jay's spirit was crushed.

"It has nothing to do with you, Jay. Last night was incredible. I'll never forget it."

"Then why are you doing this? What is going on? I feel like you're about to tell me that you're not just leaving this home, but you're leaving me, as well."

"It's for the best." Isabella mustered up the courage to let him go.

"What?" His joy had been turned into sorrow, just that fast.

"It'll never work, Jay. Last night was just a reminder of what it will be like. You saw the guy. There are many more like him. I will not stand in the way of what God has for you. You're living in a fairytale if you think everybody is like you, Jay. Because they are not! People are mean. Cruel. Vindictive. They will hurt you with my past. I will not allow it. I love you enough to let you go."

"You love me!" Jay caught her words.

She didn't answer.

"You said it, Isabella," Jay's hope was restored. "You can't take it back."

"It doesn't matter," she shrugged.

"It does matter," Jay defended his heart. "It matters more than you know."

"Okay, yes, I love you," Isabella admitted, "but I love you enough to let you go."

"Well, I love you enough to hold onto you as tight as I can." He attempted to embrace her, but she drew back.

"It won't work, Jay! I wish it could," she began to unravel in more than one way. She bit hard on her lips, almost drawing blood, trying not to cry. "But this relationship is not real. We're caught up in our emotions right now. We're not seeing clearly; that's why I must go."

"Please don't leave me," Jay begged without shame. "I need you, Isabella. Please!"

"I can't stay." Isabella pivoted away from him and grabbed the doorknob as if her life depended on escaping him.

"Marry me!" Jay touched her shoulder before she opened the door. Her shoulders slumped and shook. Hesitantly, Isabella turned and looked at him, a flowing stream of tears colliding on both sides of her face. Their eyes locked.

"Marry me?" Jay repeated, desperate for her love. *Desperate to make this work! Desperate to become one with Isabella.* Once again, his father's words came to mind, *'Desperation leads to Inspiration! Truly Isabella was his inspiration.'* Isabella inspired him to be the man God had created him to be.

Isabella reached up and touched his face with her hand, both their eyes glistening with wetness. Then, instead of going out the door, she bolted upstairs.

Thank You, Lord! She didn't leave!

Closing her bedroom door, Isabella crumbled to the floor in a heap, distraught over his half-thought but sweet proposal. She should have been honored that a man like Jay asked a girl like her to marry him. She should be elated, but Isabella felt unworthy of Jay. Being married to a wonderful man like Jay would have offered the three things she had never had: safety, stability, and a bonus – sound love. Emphatically, Isabella felt something for Jay. He had touched her heart in places it had never been touched before. Submissively, without force and without effort, her heart had already surrendered to Jay without permission.

Instead of returning to the kitchen with his folks, Jay went upstairs and sat on the bed in a stupor. His world was crashing before him, and he felt powerless to stop it.

What's wrong with me I'm usually levelheaded, making sound decisions after careful thought and much prayer. Reese is typically the one with cockamamie ideas, running off doing things without thinking...especially in his younger days. What possessed me to ask Isabella to marry me just like that? We hardly even know each other. None of this makes sense. Love, at first sight, is certainly a fairytale, like Isabella said. Something you see at the movies or on TV. This must be infatuation. However, from the first time I saw her with Lewis at the club/bar, she stirred my heart with something unusual...strange...but good. I must be losing my mind!

Not your mind, but your heart.

Even worse.

Much Better! Just as one who loses his life gains his life, one who loses his heart gains his heart.

I can't help it, Father God. I love her!

The man who finds a wife finds a good thing and obtains favor from the Lord. Your steps are ordered by Me. Walk ye in the path which I have ordained. Walk by faith and not by sight.

Moments later, the light bulb clicked on in Jay's head. He knew what he had to do. He packed up some of his clothes and personal things. He went downstairs into the kitchen where his parents were sitting, holding hands, and praying. Jay went to them with a made-up mind.

"Excuse me," Jay cleared his throat, getting their attention.

Both looked at him; their eyes stuck on the suitcase in Jay's hand.

"Dad, I'm going to stay at one of the church apartments." He informed. The church owned three of them. Each apartment had two small bedrooms, a kitchen, a den, and a bathroom. It was nothing fancy, but it was sufficient for Jay's needs. Pastor Cannon had the apartments built behind the church for church guests and families in need.

"I thought they were all occupied," Pastor James stated.

"They were until last week. Mary and her children moved in with her mother to help her out since she fell." Jay responded.

"Okay. Good idea." James stood, proud that his son was doing the responsible thing. People were already talking, but Pastor James just prayed about it.

"I'm leaving this house, but I'm not leaving Isabella." Jay went on to explain. "God sent her to us...to me...and well...well I love her, and I want to marry her." He said in all one breath.

"Praise God!" Esther clapped her hands and came and hugged her son. "We're happy for you both. We're so happy."

"Are you really?" Jay was somewhat surprised. He knew his parents loved Isabella, but things were moving fast, not to mention Isabella's not-so "clean" past. He should have known better.

"It's an honor to be her dad," Pastor James sincerely spoke. "Isabella, a sweet lady, and I love her as a daughter already."

Jay had never been more proud of his parents at that moment. They both looked beyond Isabella's faults and saw her need for their love and his. They saw what he saw...a beautiful soul.

"Now, if I can only convince Isabella to accept my proposal. She thinks she's going to hinder me in the ministry, Dad."

"Sounds familiar." Pastor James looked at his wife and wrapped his arm around her waistline. "Esther fought marriage tooth and nail. She didn't want to hurt me. I had to convince her that I couldn't do it without her. That God had called her to help me to be a pastor."

"How long did it take?"

"Two years!"

"Two years!" Jay glowered. "There is no way I'm waiting two years for Isabella!"

"You really do love her," Esther looked into her son's eyes.

"I really do love her," he said softly. "I need her."

"Then love her through her past. Don't rush it! Just love her."

"Love will conquer, and love will cover up the past. Not to hide it, but to destroy its power over her." James counseled.

"Thanks, Dad. Thanks, Mom. I need to be going. I have to stop by Heaven's Soldiers."

"How about I go with you?" Pastor James suggested. "As a matter of fact, how about I minister today?"

"Sounds good to me, Dad," Jay patted his father on the back. "The troops have truly missed you."

Chapter 32

While Jay and James were at Heaven's Soldiers Elderly Home, Esther conveyed to Isabella that there was no reason to move out because Jay was moving into the church's apartment.

Somewhat, Isabella rejoiced because she didn't want to leave the family that had become so dear to her, and secondly, Isabella had no place to go. Yet, she felt guilty for forcing Jay out of his own home.

"Jay is a grown man," Esther perceived Isabella's concerns, "and he needs to be on his own. If it had not been for his father's heart attack, Jay would have moved out earlier. He stayed for his dad…and well for me." Esther smiled and went on, "I missed him so much. The war took Jay away from us for so long. When he returned, he wasn't the same. With him being home has helped heal him physically, emotionally, and spiritually. It was a pleasure to baby him again."

Isabella squeezed Esther's hand. "Thanks for allowing me to stay."

"We wouldn't have it any other way."

"Now that I am getting better, I was thinking…" Isabella lowered her head, "I need to find myself a job."

"That's a good idea," Esther agreed. "Jay tells me that you went to school for accounting."

Isabella nodded. "But I didn't finish. I was going back with the money Lewis left me, but…well, that's spilled milk."

"You will one day. But in the meantime, I have a good offer!" Esther exclaimed, having a solution to Isabella's problem. "James could sure use someone at the church. His secretary is not good at accounting. Jay helps now, but that's not his forte either. Sometimes I help, but accounting is my least favorite thing to do."

Isabella had mixed feelings. She didn't want to be a charity case. She wanted to stand on her own two feet just in case she found herself back on the streets.

"You pray about it," Esther patted her on the shoulder and kissed her forehead. "For the time being, I will ask James."

Later that evening, Jay didn't come home. He dropped his father off and didn't come in for supper. He wanted to give Isabella space. They both needed time to think things through.

Isabella was quiet during dinner. James and Esther knew she was missing Jay already. Her eyes spoke volumes of loneliness.

Sunday, Isabella arose early for church. However, she was somewhat chickenhearted about stepping foot into a church, something she hadn't done since she was about ten years old. Still, Isabella was excited. Now she belonged to God's family. Hopefully, she would belong to this church family as well.

With each step down the aisle, Isabella felt light-headed. The butterflies in her stomach didn't help matters. She was just about to sit in the back when Jay's mother touched her on the shoulder and beckoned her to come and sit with her on the first row.

Jay was already seated in the pulpit. He flashed her a million-dollar smile, which stirred her heart with delight. Jay was grinning from ear to ear as the praise team began to sing. Everyone in the church had to notice his happiness, including Janice.

The choir came up and rendered an upbeat selection. Try as he may, Jay couldn't keep his eyes off Isabella. Here he was sitting in the pulpit, trying to concentrate on spiritual things, and yet his eyes wandered back and forth to Isabella. Witnessing her blush, the pink coloring rising on her face made her even more appealing.

After Esther gave the morning announcements, Pastor James led the church in the most moving prayer Isabella had ever heard. It aroused something within her. Isabella caught her breath as Pastor James announced that James, Jr. would be preaching today.

As Jay stood so tall, so refined, and so handsome before the congregation, momentarily, his eyes got stuck on Isabella. Immediately color heightened her cheeks when she looked up and caught Jay staring at her. All the while, Reese was bursting inside at his brother's perceived liking of Isabella. Everyone noted his hesitation, including Janice. Immediately she followed his eye movement and couldn't believe her eyes. *It can't be the same girl! She's...she's different!*

God, I need you. Clear my mind, my heart, and my spirit so that You can completely use me. Jay silently prayed.

"We all should be living Epistles read of men. When someone reads your book, what are they reading?" Pastor Jay proposed the question to all. "Sure, they will read your past, but that doesn't matter. It is what's written on the present pages that count. What are you doing with your life **now**? How are you living **now**? You can't change the past. You can't change the things that have been done to you or the things that you have done. All you can change is *your* **now**.

"Many of us have some skeletons in our closets which we don't want anybody to know about. We've done and said things that have caused pain to us and others. But those are chapters that have already been written. Today is a new page. Tomorrow, God willing, is another new page – A do-over, I like to call it.

"There are many examples in the Bible of people who had skeletons hidden in their closets, and God gave them all do-overs. The Samaritan woman had five husbands when Jesus talked with her, and Jesus said, *'the one who you are with now is not one of them.'* And yet, God used an adulterer, a Bigamist *if you will*, to spread the Gospel to her fellow Samaritans who believed and were saved. He gave The Samaritan woman a Do-over.

"We all know the story of the adulterous woman who the Pharisees brought to Jesus to have the woman stoned. Jesus replied, *'He who is without sin among you, let him throw the first stone.'* When Jesus looked up, all that was remaining were he and the woman. Jesus said, *'Woman, where are your accusers? Has no one*

condemned you? Neither do I condemn you; go and sin no more.'
For the spirit convicts, it doesn't condemn. God gave this adulterous woman a Do-over!

"Rahab was a fornicator and look what she did! She protected God's prophets and saved her entire family – A Do-over! Moses was a murderer! God used him to lead his people out of Egypt. Moses got a second chance – do-over! David committed adultery with his trusted friend's wife. Then he set him up to be killed. Yet, David wrote most of the Psalms. He was a man after God's own heart. David got a do-over! Saul was a persecutor of the Christians. God changed his name, and Paul wrote most of the new testament. Another do-over! We all know of people who have lived sinful lives.

"Church, take a good look at me," Jay paused, feeling empowered by the spirit within him. "You're looking at a murderer." The congregation gasped all at once; the loud sound proved that Jay had their undivided attention. "Because of war, these hands have blood upon them," he lifted his hands upward. "And yet here I am today, preaching the Gospel of Jesus Christ. I stand before you a man with clean hands and a pure heart – because the blood of Jesus washes away my sins and purifies my soul. God gave me a Do-over!

"You see, God wants to use you, in spite of the things you have done. Your past is just that…in the past. Now, I'm not going to tell you that you weren't affected by it because you were. Moses had hang-ups about speaking; he didn't have confidence. And yet, listen, your hang-ups can't stop you from possessing what God has for you to possess. From being all that God created you to be. People may try to block you and even stop you, but they cannot thwart your assignment.

"God needs you! I know you have heard people say that God doesn't need you. But that's a lie. He created you for a purpose to glorify Him through your gift, talent, and calling. Whatever He has given you to do so that others may know Him. How will people ever see Jesus unless they see Him in you? We are ambassadors of Christ. We represent Jesus on the earth. He's living on the inside of us so that we can work on the outside for Him. When people see us, they should see Jesus."

Isabella couldn't keep the tears from flowing. Esther handɘ her a hanky and put her arm around Isabella briefly. Jay was speaking directly to her heart and his.

"God needed Rahab the fornicator, Moses the murderer, David the adulterer, the Samaritan woman a sinner, and Paul, the persecutor of the brethren. He needed every one of them just like He needs you – flaws and all. He gave them all Do-overs! To do better! To live better! To be better!

"No one can do what you have been designed to do, the way you do it. Sure, God can put someone else in your place, but rest assured they cannot do what you have been called to do the way you do it. My dad is a great preacher, called to impact the lives of countless people. I'm called to preach. But we're not the same. God called him to preach his way, and He called me to preach my way…and yet it is all God's way.

"With the adulterous woman, God looked beyond her outer apparel, her sinful outer state, and he saw her beauty within. That's how we should be. Instead of judging, and casting the first stone, we should take a step back and just look. And before you know it, we began to see the person through the eyes of love and not through the eyes of condemnation and judgment."

Jay looked at Isabella; his heart melted as he beheld her glistening eyes swelling with fresh tears. Then he scanned the choir stand to the right and glimpsed Janice. She, too, was moved to tears. Today's sermon touched many people. Their faces showed the truth.

"There is nothing that you have done, nothing you are doing presently, and nothing you ever will do that will stop God's love from flowing from His heart to yours. Before you were born, God created you for His purpose and His glory. Discover what He wants you to do and do it. First, maybe with trembling. Then with trust. Finally, with triumphant. Leave the past in the past and live in the present. Remember your purpose for today. Walk in your purpose. Live in the now. Today, God has given us all a Do-over!"

At the closing of the message, Jay led the congregation into a confessional prayer to walk in love, live in the now, and let go of the past.

Pastor James Cannon embraced his son and did an altar call for Self-forgiveness. Many came to the altar that day. Among them were Isabella and Janice.

After services, Isabella was overcome by so many church members embracing her in love. Surrounded by people, Isabella caught Jay's eye from across the room. He winked, bestowing a smile that was big and wide. Isabella's face lit up like the Fourth of July. She looked around to see if anyone caught his affectionate gesture. As she turned, her eyes locked with Janice. Suddenly, Isabella pitied her.

"Forgive me," Janice approached Isabella. "Truly, I am sorry about what I said at the hospital."

"Forgiven," Isabella smiled. Yes, she was slowly changing. The old Isabella would have told her to take a hike!

"You look good," Janice's words were sincere, approving of the outward transformation.

"Thanks." Spontaneously, Isabella embraced Janice, which was out of her character in the past. "So do you. It's more than my clothes and hair that changed; my heart has changed. Jesus is in it."

"I'm so happy for you, Isabella. You're a child of the King. We're family. Jay is a blessed man to have you in his life." Courageously, Janice acknowledged. "Now I see why he is glowing today. You're a treasured jewel."

Isabella didn't know what to say. Janice's kindness was more than she expected. "We're just friends."

"Not for long." Janice touched her hand, smiled, and walked away.

Jay didn't come home directly for Sunday's dinner. Instead, he shared dinner with his friend Herman, who needed a friend. Herman's wife was very ill and needed prayer.

Everyone felt his absence from Sunday dinner – especially Isabella. *Had she run him away for good!*

Chapter 33

Monday morning, Isabella rode with Pastor James to the church office. With pleasure, the pastor was willing to take a chance on Isabella to work as his bookkeeper. Into her hands, he was entrusting the finances of the church and the confidentiality of his members. Pastor James was taking a huge leap of faith, believing that it was God who had sent this sweet, precious young lady into their lives in the first place.

"Good morning, Jay," Pastor Cannon stopped as his son opened the door, with Isabella by his side.

"Hi...Dad..." Jay was pleasantly surprised to see Isabella. She looked beautiful standing there, all timid and shy. Her hair pulled back in a ponytail, dressed professionally in a black skirt, pale blue blouse, and pumps. Isabella looked so young. *She is young! Twenty-two, and I'm thirty-two. Such a big age gap.*

"Meet our new bookkeeper," Pastor James beamed.

"Welcome aboard." Jay remained seated. "Dad's secretary, Ms. Marilyn, is a great teacher; she'll show you the ropes."

Pastor James frowned. He thought for sure Jay would do the honors of training Isabella.

"Well, okay, Isabella, let's go meet my faithful secretary."

Isabella stood still a moment as if she wanted to say something to Jay. A multitude of sensations swirled through her as

Isabella's countenance changed. Her heart was secretly in turmoil. A battle was warring inside of her. Jay seemed distant to her. Why wasn't she more relieved? That's what she asked for. Yet, she feared all too quickly Jay had come to his senses, realizing she wasn't the right one for him. This possibility hurt Isabella more than she could have ever imagined. Foolishness gnawed at her; she couldn't have it both ways. Jay was driving her crazy.

"I'm ready," Isabella lowered her eyes and walked away from Jay.

Watching her go, Jay wondered if he had been too standoffish towards her. If they had to work together, it was going to be hard controlling himself. He loved Isabella, but Jay wouldn't force himself on her. She had to want him, as well. He wouldn't allow himself to lose another person, whom he loved dearly, especially if they had a choice. Losing his soldier friends was out of their hands, but not so with Isabella.

Isabella worked all day without running into Jay. It was evident that he was avoiding her. He even went to lunch and didn't invite her to accompany him. It stung, but Isabella was used to this type of behavior. Men were fickle. They wanted what they wanted, and then when they didn't get it, they quickly vanished into thin air.

Pastor James was impressed with how fast Isabella caught on. Ms. Marilyn was also impressed. She only had to show Isabella something once, and Isabella would write it down and then did it. Maybe not perfect at first, but the apprentice absorbed the training like a sponge, sucking up everything thrown her way. Isabella found it rewarding to be doing something she enjoyed. Math was always her specialty. In the future, Isabella thought of ways she could improve their accounting system, but she'd take things slow, not knowing how long Pastor James would keep her. Would he toss her aside as well? Only time would tell.

When it was time to leave for the day, Jay had already left. Isabella had hoped he would offer her a ride home, but he didn't. Even more disappointing, Jay didn't join the Cannons for dinner that night.

Jay didn't show up at the Cannon's home for the entire week. In his absenteeism, Isabella found herself lonely for Jay. Her soul ached for his presence, his warm smile, his reassurance, and even his simple touch. Though Isabella had practically been alone all her life, she never pitied being alone, for it protected her. If no one was in her inner circle, no one could hurt her again. Yet, now the lonely feeling consumed her gravely.

Nevertheless, Esther wasn't having it. She knew Jay well enough to know that he was distancing himself to protect himself – always running away. After insisting, Jay succumbed to his mother, joining them for family dinner on Friday. She was preparing his favorite, lasagna and a German chocolate cake. It wasn't just the food or his mother drawing Jay in its clutches; it was the beautiful crystal, green-eyed girl who had stolen his heart. Being aloof with her was costing him a lot. Restless nights, loneliness riding his coat tail, irritable mood swings, and cloudy thoughts overshadowed Jay's every move.

"Hi, Jay." During her lunchtime Friday, Isabella purposefully, yet hesitantly, stopped by Jay's office, not knowing of Esther's dinner plans. "I have an extra sandwich. Would you like to have it?"

"Thanks," Jay was about to go get something to eat.

Isabella handed him the sandwich, then turned to leave. She usually sat in the church kitchen area for lunch.

"Why don't you join me?" Jay offered.

"Are you sure?" she asked timidly.

"Of course."

At first, they ate in silence.

"How do you like working for my dad?"

"He's great. He treats me like...like I'm..." Isabella didn't want to jinx it.

"His daughter," Jay completed her sentence. "To dad, you are."

Isabella lowered her head, unable to digest such truth without some strings attached. As of yet, she had found none, which worried her instead of calming her.

"Dad told me that he's never seen the church records so straightened out. He can actually make sense of them."

Isabella blushed at his praise. "I love working with numbers."

"Yeah, Lewis said you were a math whiz." Jay missed being in her presence. It had been so hard keeping his distance from Isabella when she was working two doors down. He'd been struggling with himself, questioning if he was doing the right thing. Whether or not he was giving Isabella too much space. Maybe she did not want him, now. But if he crowded her space too fast, he might run her off for good. Yet deep down, Jay was afraid. His heart was raw from the aftermath of war. Was he fully ready to be vulnerable to someone who could run away at any moment, someone who wasn't committed, someone who could rip his heart into pieces, shatter his world more than anybody ever could?

"I put fresh flowers on Lewis' grave yesterday."

"I saw them."

"You did?"

"Yes, I saw you putting them on the grave."

He followed me. An awkward silence followed. "I best be going." Isabella stood up.

"Wait." Jay went to her. "You've touched all of our lives, Isabella. I'm so proud of you." Tenderly his hands cupped her face in his. "Lewis would be so proud of you."

Isabella reached up and touched his hand, her eyes misty. "Thanks for saying that."

"It's the truth." Instantly, Jay dropped his hands and straightened up. "I guess I'll be seeing you at dinner tonight. Mom is baking me a German chocolate cake."

"I'm glad you're coming," daringly she eyed him, endeavoring to witness whether his affections for her were still there.

He fought to contain himself. The look in her big, beautiful green eyes made him weak in the knees. He just wanted to grab her and kiss her senseless!

"Well, I have a meeting to attend." Jay backed away.

She felt his coldness. "See you later." Isabella exited his office, feeling somewhat sad. She fought back the tears while walking back to the office. *Perhaps his feelings for me have faded. He's so different, so frigid around me...that's when he is actually around me...which is rare. He's avoiding me, like the plague. Whatever! I knew it wouldn't work in the first place. I guess he's finally seen the light. I'm not good enough for him.*

Jay's presence in the home was truly missed. Esther was doing everything to make tonight a special night. Playing the matchmaker, she decided to have a candlelight dinner. She was tired of seeing Isabella mope around. Not to mention that every time Esther talked with Jay, all he did was inquire about Isabella. Those two people were more stubborn than she and James were when they were dating.

At six sharp, Pastor James, Esther and Isabella were seated at the dining room table, awaiting Jay's arrival. Six-thirty rolled around, still no Jay. Seven, still no Jay. Pastor James had called his son's cell phone several times, but all he got was his voicemail.

"Well, let's pray and have dinner. Jay must have an emergency." James suggested, noticing the worried look on the women's faces.

"Dear Lord, we thank You for Your bountiful blessings and this food that we're about to partake of. Bless it and the hands that prepared it," James squeezed his wife's hand, "and Lord watch over Jay. Protect him and keep him safe. Let Your will be done in his life and those at this table," this time James squeezed Isabella's hand, "in Jesus' name, amen."

"Amen." The ladies echoed.

Although it was a delicious dinner, no one had an appetite. They nibbled on the food and ate in silence. All hearts and minds were on the missing member of the family. Esther and James both tried to conceal their concern for Jay. It just wasn't like Jay not to come home for family dinner, especially without calling, especially when he said he would. *Something must have happened.*

Quietly, Isabella blamed herself. It was her fault for the parents' vexation. If she had just left, Jay would be free to come and go as he pleased.

It's time for me to find my own place!

Isabella was over-anxious about his absence. Her heart felt as if a rope was wrapped around it, squeezing it so tightly, that she could barely breathe. *Oh God, where is he?*

On the way to his parents' home, Jay received a call from Chance. Immediately, Jay knew that something was wrong.

"I need your help Pastor Jay," Chance began. "It's Vix!"

"Not again."

"Please meet me at..." Chance rattled off the address. "Hurry, Pastor Jay. There's not much time."

Pulling up to the abandoned home, Jay prayed for God's mercy and protection before getting out of the car. The sky was dark, the atmosphere was gothic, and the creepy sound of a death rattle was preeminent. Jay felt the presence of evil with each step he took toward the abandoned building.

"Chance!" Jay called.

"In here!"

Suspiciously, Jay pushed the door open and went inside. *No evil shall befall me. The blood of Jesus covers me!* Walking toward the back area, he saw Chance holding Vix in his arms.

Unmistakably, Vix had been shot by the bloodstain shirt and was in critical condition, standing at death's doors. Once again, he heard the rattling sound signifying death.

"He's in bad shape," Chance's voice was coarse. By his misty eyes, it was apparent he was trying to contain his emotions.

Jay came and knelt beside them. "Vix," he called his name.

Vix opened his eyes, with a haunted look, he gazed at Jay.

"We need to take you to a hospital," Jay first spoke.

"Won't help," Vix muttered.

"I've been begging him," Chance intervened, "but he knows the cops are looking for him."

"You need to be treated at the hospital." Jay asserted.

"Preacher man," Vix started, "What I need the doctors can't give me."

No one called him preacher man but Isabella. It struck a sensitive chord, for sure.

Jay looked at Chance. "I told him he needed Jesus." Chance stated. "He wanted to make sure that he had everything in order," Chance choked on his words. "He asked for a preacher, so I called you."

Jay understood. "God so loved the world that He sent his only Son Jesus so that whoever believes in Him should not perish but have everlasting life." Jay quoted the life-saving passage of Scripture. "That means God loved you so much Vix that He sent Jesus to die for you. If you believe in your heart that Jesus is the Son of God and rose from the head, and confess with your mouth for

Him to be Lord and Savior of your life, though your human body may die, yet will you live forever with Him."

Vix nodded in understanding.

"Repeat after me," Jay led him into a salvation prayer. "Lord Jesus, come into my heart. I confess with my mouth the Lord Jesus and believe that God raised Him from the dead. Therefore, the Bible says I am saved. Forgive me for my sins and take me as I am now. Thank You, Lord, for saving me and giving me eternal life, in Jesus' name, amen."

"Welcome to God's family." Jay leaned over and hugged him gently. "As Jesus said to the man on the cross, today you will be with Me in paradise."

Jay stood up and watched God finish His amazing work on earth between the two cousins. Two former gang bangers, now two Christians, brothers in Christ Jesus – only God could do such a thing.

Vix turned to Chance. "Now I will see my mother," he smiled. "And I will see you again, my *cuz*."

The tears freely fell now as Chance looked at his cousin. Despite their past lives and the pain that Vix had caused his family, Chance loved him. They grew up together, protected one another, and had each other's backs. They were more than cousins, more than gang bangers; they were brothers – now more than ever!

"Yes," Chance whispered. "I love you, man."

"Love you, man," he choked out his words. "Until we meet again." Vix closed his eyes for the last time.

Love looks beyond sin and always sees the need for a Savior. Although Vix had ordered his gang to brutally attack Chance's wife, which led to their unborn baby girl's death, Chance reacted like a true Christian. He did what Jesus would do…*forgive them, for they know not what they do*. Thus, Vix was now a saved man!

The touching scene brought Jay to tears. God's love was contagious. It spreads to the souls of those lost and saved. *For God loved the world – everybody – so much that He gave us His greatest gift – Jesus! We must share Jesus with everyone!*

Chapter 34

Later that evening, as the family sat in the den watching a movie, Jay finally arrived. Reese had come over as well. His mother had called him asking if he had heard from Jay. Everyone rose at once when Jay stood in the doorway, his white shirt covered in blood.

Isabella gasped, pressing her hand to her heart as she saw his bloody shirt. Her heart sank like the titanic. Her knees shook so badly that she couldn't stand and collapsed on the floor.

Immediately Jay rushed to her side. For a moment, everybody forgot about Jay's shirt and focused on Isabella. Reese ran and got some ammonia, as his mother instructed. Straightaway, the ammonia aroused her. Opening her eyes, Isabella gazed at Jay, somewhat disoriented for several reasons. If she ever had any doubt, Isabella now knew for sure that she had lost her most precious gift to this handsome man – her heart.

Gently, Jay picked Isabella up, and she buried her head in his chest and cried.

"It's alright," he cooed.

Jay sat in the recliner, still holding Isabella.

"What happened to you?" Pastor James was the first to ask.

"Chance…"

"Oh no!" Esther immediately assumed the worse.

"No, mother, Chance is fine." Jay quickly stated. "Chance called me as I was on my way over. He said he needed my help." Jay began as he unraveled the mystery of his bloodstain shirt. "It was amazing, Dad. Who would have ever thought that Vix, the same man who had tortured Chance since he left the gang, would seek Chance out so that he could tell him about Jesus?"

"God never ceases to amaze me." Pastor James praised. "He loves us that much. He desires for none of us to perish, but all to come to repentance."

"Yes," Jay looked at Isabella. "He loves us so much that He sends extraordinary people in our lives to help us become the people God created us to be. Forever, I am indebted to God for sending me you, Izzy." He breathed deeply, using the private nickname that only Lewis had the privilege to use, and went on. "For you saved my life. Now I am living for the first time in my life. Fulfilling my God-given assignment, and it's all because of you, Izzy."

She blinked back the tears and sat up. Her eyes fixed on him.

"We'll leave you two alone," Pastor James ushered them out of the den.

"Next time, text or something!" Reese placed his hand on his brother's shoulder.

Jay nodded in understanding his brother's concern.

"You called me Izzy," she responded the moment they were alone.

"I hope you don't mind, but it just feels appropriate."

She nodded. "Lewis would like it…and…I like it."

"Good!"

"I was afraid…afraid something had happened to you."

"I'm sorry for worrying you." Jay ran his fingers through her hair.

Their eyes locked in silence.

"I have missed you badly." Jay willfully expressed.

"I thought you didn't want to see me again," her eyes welled up with fresh tears. "You've been avoiding me."

"I did," Jay acknowledged, "but only because I thought you needed the space. Time to think. Time to heal. I realized that I was pushing you, and I must admit, I was afraid."

"I missed you, too."

"Never doubt my feelings for you. I love you with all of me, Izzy." He kissed her fingertips, one by one. "I need you."

"All my life, I have had to struggle. I have had to struggle to eat, to live, to survive, to stay alive. It's like I am in the middle of this huge ocean of water. I am swimming and swimming, trying to keep afloat. At a distance, I see God. He seems so far, and yet I can see Him. I keep swimming, my legs are tired, and my arms are tired. It's hard, but I keep swimming, trying to keep my head above water. Still, it is harder and harder, as if I cannot swim anymore, and I'm about to drown."

She lowered her head, tears streaming down her face.

Jay tilted her chin upward and said in an indulgent tone, "Your head is above water. You just keep looking down."

Isabella blinked hard, becoming savvy with the truth of his statement. The light bulb clicked. "That's deep." She whispered in awe of Jay's perception.

"With your eyes down, you can't see Jesus. But if you look up, you'll see that He is right there with you. No longer at a distance but right there with you, holding your hand, and leading you to me." Jay spoke, eying her and noticing the stars shining back at him through her glistening eyes.

Now both of their eyes were filled with tears.

"You saved my life," she inhaled. "And now I am living for the first time in my life."

Tasting each other's tears, they kissed, sealing their love for one another. God had brought them together for His purpose and His glory.

"Do you mind if I stay under the same roof with you tonight," Jay spoke naughtily. "I am exhausted, and I don't feel like driving to the church apartment."

"Sure. As long as you stay in your area," she winked. "I'm feeling a little vulnerable tonight." Isabella stood, kissed him on the cheek, and said, "I'm so grateful for you, Jay. Sleep well. Goodnight."

"Goodnight, Izzy." Watching her walk away, Jay's heart soared with the hopeful thoughts of a blessed future with Isabella. Perhaps soon, he would join his sister and brother in having a helpmate to complete him.

Still sleeping, Jay could subconsciously hear a faint knocking. His body was tired after last night's encounter. Usually an earlier riser, Jay had slept past noon, which concerned his family.

"Jay," his father entered the room. "Jay," Pastor James called again.

"Huh," groggily Jay responded, slowly wiping his eyes.

"We were a little worried about you." Pastor James stood over the sleepy-eyed son.

"What time is it?" Jay opened his eyes.

"12:30."

"What?" Jay bolted upward. "I can't believe I slept that long."

"You're tired." Pastor James patted his son's shoulder. "I wouldn't have bothered you, but I think Isabella is going to worry herself sick."

"Oh no!" Jay tossed his cover off and leaped out of bed. "Please tell her I'm awake, Dad. I'm going to take a quick shower, and I'll be down."

"You're quite smitten with her."

"That I am." Jay beamed proudly. "That I am."

"Like father, like son." Pastor James laughed. "I have another daughter – Leela, Rose, and now Isabella."

Later that day, Jay and Isabella went to the movies and then out for pizza, Isabella's favorite – Meat Lovers Pizza with a thin crust.

"This is good," Isabella said, the cheese dribbling down her chin.

"It is. Almost as good as you," he teased.

"You better watch yourself, preacher man."

Jay frowned.

"I'm sorry."

"When you're nervous, you call me preacher man. Am I making you nervous?"

"It's not that," Isabella lowered her eyes. "I just feel...so unworthy of you. You're a good guy, Jay, and..."

"And so are you," Jay reached for her hand. "I wish you could see through my eyes just how precious you are. You're everything I could want in a companion. I need you, Izzy."

"I'm nobody."

"God didn't create a nobody," Jay said firmly. "Look at me, Isabella," purposely he called her by her birth name.

It took her some time to comply.

Fixing his eyes on her. "Didn't you accept Jesus into your heart?"

"I did."

"Didn't He take you as you were, with no strings attached?"

"Yes."

"You are His, and He is yours. Doesn't that make you somebody?"

"Yes."

"Somebody important to Him?"

"Yes."

"Well, you are worthy and so am I...but only because of Him." Jay prayed that she had the revelation of what he was saying.

"But..."

"No buts! God took nobodies and made them into somebodies – special in His Kingdom. Old things, the old you and the old me have passed away, now all things have become new. We are new creations in Christ Jesus. So, let's move forward. Remember, no more looking down or back. Let's just look up!"

"It's hard, Jay." She honestly acknowledged.

"But we're in it together. I want to spend the rest of my life with you, Izzy."

Her heart stopped. She knew where Jay was going. At least she hoped so and feared so at the same time.

Momentarily, Jay withdrew his hand, reached into his pocket, and retrieved a black jewelry box. "I know this place isn't romantic, and I was going to wait to do this...but I can't. I love you so much, Izzy. I want to spend the rest of my life getting to know you. I would be so honored if you would agree to become my wife." Jay got up, went to her, knelt on one knee, and pronounced his greatest heart's desire, "Isabella Arielle Trevino, will you marry me?"

Silent, joyous tears cascaded down her face. Inwardly it was a warzone. Her mind shouted, 'Don't do it!' While her heart whispered, 'Do it! Say, yes.' Too moved to speak, the heart won as Isabella shook her head.

"Is that a yes?"

"Yes. Yes. Yes." Her voice escalated.

Jay slid the diamond on her ring finger and kissed her hand. Standing, Jay drew Isabella into his arms and kissed her, right in front of the overflowing room of strangers.

"I love you," he whispered in her ears as he regretfully ended their intimate moment.

"I love you," at last, the three powerful words rolled off her lips and into his soul.

"I'm so happy, Isabella…Izzy. You have made me so very happy."

"You better keep holding me because I'm floating on air." She spoke softly. Her eyes were glistening, glowing like a spotlight shining down her fresh happy heart.

Chapter 35

Four months later, hustling and bustling, the Cannon family was busy making plans for Jay's wedding and Jay's ordination service for the pastorate, officially Assistant Pastor. Things were happening so quickly because Jay didn't want to wait on marrying the love of his life, nor did James wish to wait in ordaining his son to be second-in-command in the church.

Less than a week away, the wedding was scheduled for Saturday, and the Ordination service was scheduled two weeks later.

While Isabella, Leela, Rose, and Esther were busy with last-minute wedding plans, Jay and James had their plates full of church responsibilities. Reese did what he could to help the family. With the church's rapid growth steadily increasing, which meant more obligations to the members. Three faithful members had died within four months, and several members were hospitalized with serious illnesses. Father and son were counseling several parishioners regarding marital problems, children's issues, and so forth. Being a pastor was twenty-four hours, seven days of the week was an arduous job, yet both found it so rewarding and fulfilling.

Isabella was still enjoying working at the church while attending night classes to obtain an accounting degree. Jay was so proud of her. She fitted so perfectly into his life and his family. It seemed as if she had been a part of their family all along.

However, everything wasn't perfect. Nothing ever is. Isabella still had her moments of insecurity, especially with church folk.

The Sunday before their wedding, Jay and Isabella arrived at church together.

"Next Sunday, you will be Isabella Cannon, my lovely wife," Jay said as he opened her door.

"I can't wait."

"That makes you and me both." Jay stood at the church's entrance, stopped, and just gazed at her. "You are so beautiful."

Her face colored. "And you, handsome," she reached up and gently touched the side of his face.

"We better go in." Jay grabbed her hand and escorted her down the aisle to his mother. Tenderly, he bent over and kissed Isabella on the cheek and then went to sit on the pulpit with his father and other ministerial staff. He looked back once and smiled.

Isabella's heart soared. *Thank You, God, for Jay! Why You chose me for him, I'll never know. But I thank You all the same!*

As always, Pastor James preached a powerful sermon. Although he was pretty much back to his old self, he still felt threadbare at the end of his sermons, at times. Still, he persevered.

"As you all know," Pastor James cleared his throat and motioned for Jay to come forward at the close of his message, "Jay's special day is next Saturday, and he would like to say a few words to all of you." Pastor James stepped aside and allowed his son to stand behind the podium.

"Yes, Saturday is going to be a special day," Jay looked into the audience, his eyes fixated on one particular lady, and continued. "As you all know, I am marrying the lady of my dreams," he beamed, "Isabella Trevano. As my church family, all of you are invited. I grew up with most of you in this church. You've seen me take my first steps. You've witnessed my toddler years, when I wanted to stand beside my father on the pulpit while he preached," Jay looked over at his proud father. "And my dad would say to my mom, let him come…he's following in the steps of a pastor. Little did I know then that he was speaking literally," the audience laughed with him. "Anyhow, when I went to war, many of you sent me cards, letters, and encouraging words to help me make it through the roughest part of my adulthood. Now God has called me into the ministry and has blessed me with a helpmate to support me, as he did for my father." Jay looked at his mother, whose eyes had fresh tears in them. "Isabella, would you please stand."

Timidly, she stood, keeping her eyes on Jay.

"See how blessed I am," Jay spoke with love. "She's a sweet woman, with a sweet spirit, and I know that you all will grow to love her as I do. Please come to our wedding next Saturday." His invitation ended. The audience clapped. Following, Pastor James gave the benediction.

Quickly, Isabella was surrounded by members, wishing them well and asking if they could do anything to help her with the wedding. She felt so welcomed and loved by the Word Alive Fellowship members. This was the first time she allowed herself to be free to receive all the love from a group of practical strangers and yet family.

Tammy, her matron of honor, was right by her side. The two had quickly become friends. Tammy didn't judge her. Instead, she accepted her without reservation. Often, Jay and Isabella double-dated with Tammy and Chance. The couples had a lot in common and enjoyed the camaraderie with each other.

Several times, Isabella looked up and found the guy in the choir staring at her. Something about him made her uneasy. Shaking it off, Isabella walked outside with Tammy.

"Excuse me," the guy approached them.

"Hi, Johnny." Tammy knew him. Johnny grew up in the church but had gone astray for a while. Recently, he returned and recommitted his life to Christ Jesus.

"Hi Tammy," he greeted. "Congratulations, Miss Trevino. Pastor Jay truly is blessed." His eyes spoke something else.

"Thank you," nervously Isabella replied.

"I'm sure we have met before. Your face is so familiar."

"I don't think so." *Oh God, who is this man? Why is he looking at me like that? I hope Tammy doesn't think anything about it. Please, Lord, I'm feeling dirty again. Is it because he was one of my male callers?*

"Oh, Johnny, just because you get around, you think you know everybody." Tammy jibed. "Isabella is taken. So, stop gawking at her like that!"

Busted!

"You're crazy, Tammy." Johnny tried to play it off. "I never forget a face, and I'm sure I've seen you before."

"I don't think…"

"Hey, Baby," Jay came from behind and wrapped his arms around her petite waist. "I thought you had snuck out on me. Not getting cold feet, are you?"

"Never." Isabella was so grateful that Jay was beside her, holding her. She needed him.

"Oh, hi Johnny." Jay shook his hand, brotherly. "You're not trying to steal my bride-to-be right from under me, are you?" Jay was full of teasing today, feeling so happy.

"I don't think that's possible." Johnny chuckled. "I was just saying to your wife-to-be that she looks so familiar."

"Oh hush, Johnny!" Tammy shoved her. "Chance is getting the car. We're going out for dinner. Do you two want to join us?"

"Thanks for the invite, but mom wants us home. She and Isabella have a few wedding things to discuss with Leela and Rose." Jay answered.

"Do you need me to come over and help, Isabella?" Tammy asked.

"Oh no. It's just a few things with the reception. Nothing much."

"Okay, I better go. I see Chance." Tammy left.

"Well, I'll see you two next Saturday," Johnny eyed Isabella. She squirmed, snuggling closer to Jay. Jay sensed her uneasiness.

"Great." Jay patted him on the shoulder, watching him walk away.

"If I didn't know any better, I think Johnny has a crush on you." Jay looked at Isabella. "Can't blame him. Who wouldn't be enamored by you? Every time I look at you, you take my breath away."

"Oh, Jay." Isabella rested her head on his chest. "I wish we could stay like this forever."

"We will."

I hope so!

Tuesday, Isabella was working in her office, typing at her computer, when in walked her worst nightmare.

"You clean up well." Johnny stood at the door with a noticeable smirk on his face.

Isabella looked up into his naughty eyes. "Excuse me," she gulped.

"It came to me last night...the place where I remembered you from. It was at the bar; you worked there. I think you had purple hair, or was it blue, or pink..." he laughed, taking a seat.

Isabella was speechless. Her past had met her present – and in the church, no doubt.

"You were one hot chick," Johnny continued. "We had several drinks together. We danced, and then we were about to go back to the hotel, but some big guy broke up our plans."

"I'm busy," Isabella tried to get her fingers to type, but all they did was shake.

"I bet you are," Johnny remained seated.

"Please leave," Isabella mustered the courage to look at him.

"I was hoping that we could get reacquainted." Johnny stared back. "After all, we never finished what we started that night."

"I'm not that girl anymore."

"Oh, you may have changed outwardly. As I said, you clean up well. But you and I both know that you're still that wild, sexy girl at the bar. A leopard doesn't change its spots."

"No, but God can change a human heart," Isabella spoke through tightened lips. "Isn't that what He did for you?" She turned the tables on him.

"Touché!" Johnny secretly admired her spunk. "I bet Pastor Jay doesn't have a clue about your good old days." He felt smug. "I wondered what he would say if he knew who you really were back then."

"He knows, and he believes that God forgives and forgets. Jay doesn't judge me by my past. He loves me for who I am now." Isabella knocked the self-righteous chip off his shoulders. "Now, I really must finish this report for Pastor James."

"Pastor Jay may know, but I'm sure the church family doesn't. How will they react knowing that Pastor Jay is marrying a lady of pleasure if you will...and flaunting her in the church as a first or second lady of the church?"

"Get out!" Isabella hollered.

"Calm down." Johnny stood up. "Don't worry, I won't tell. This will be our dirty little secret," he winked. "We'll talk later. Remember, we never finished what we started before."

Isabella's shoulders slumped as she watched him close the door. Her joy had vanished. Her buried emotions plummeted out as she lowered her head on the desk. Johnny's insinuation of the church finding out about her past life scathed her emotional state of mind. She couldn't think straight!

There's always a devil, or two, or more, in the church! Wolves in sheep clothing, singing in the choir, ushering, and even in the pulpit.

Oh, God! What now? I'm trying to move on, and yet...yet I can't!

The enemy comes to steal, kill, and destroy. Steal your joy and take the Word. Kill your dreams. And destroy your faith and your life. But I came that you might have life and have it more abundantly.

How do I have this abundant life? I keep trying. Keep believing. How many more Johnnys are going to come at me? Reminding me of the woman I used to be? And Jay...oh Jay is going to be hurt. I cannot embarrass him with this.

Stand still!

I can't just keep fighting this same old fight.

This battle is not yours to fight. I will fight for you. Stand still and see the salvation of the Lord.

Without thought, Isabella grabbed her purse and ran out the door. Her legs were rubbery, her mind in a haze, but she walked on. Not knowing where she was going, she walked some ways, ending at the military cemetery not too far from the church, where her brother's remains rested. Plopped down on the ground, Isabella sobbed at her brother's tombstone.

"Lewis," she drooled, "I've made a mess of my life. I don't deserve Jay. But I love him so. I'm going to ruin his life. I can't do that to him! He deserves better. And that snake Johnny. He's in the choir and still lusting after me. Oh, Lewis, I don't know what to do! If I love him, I ought to let him go before I bring down his family's name. Pastor James has been so kind to me. Lady Esther wants me to call her mom. And now, I have sisters, Leela and Rose, and even Cassi. Brother, I have a family. How do I let them all go?

"No matter how hard I try, Lewis, I still struggle to stay above water. Jay says I'm looking down, but life keeps pushing my head down.

Keep looking up!

Looking around, Isabella thought she heard an audible voice.

Lift your eyes to the Hills from where your help comes from!

After crying her eyes out, Isabella couldn't find the strength to go back to the office. She just had to get away. Indecisively, Isabella took the bus and rode into town. She needed to breathe and time to think!

When Jay returned to take her to lunch, he was surprised that she wasn't there. He asked Ms. Marilyn, but she hadn't seen her.

"She didn't say anything?"

"No," the secretary answered. "After Johnny left…"

"Johnny," Jay repeated, confused. "Johnny, who sings in the choir?"

"Yes. He came about ten o'clock, asking to see Isabella. About thirty minutes or so, he left. I thought Isabella was still in her office."

"Soon as Isabella returns, please let me know." Jay requested and then went back to his office. Several hours later, Isabella still hadn't returned. Jay was worried. He called home several times, asking his mother if Isabella was there, but Esther hadn't seen or heard from her. Now, his mother was worried as well. It wasn't like Isabella, at least not the new-believer Isabella.

What in the world did Johnny say to her? Why was he here?

Jay searched for Johnny's number in the church's directory; it wasn't listed. Neither was his number in the phone book.

"Dad," Jay stood at his father's door. "What do you know about Johnny Finn?"

"On the choir?"

"Yes." Jay impatiently answered.

"Well, you remember his parents both died in a car accident, and Deacon Gregg and his wife took him in when he was twelve. He's always been in the church, it seems. He's quiet and stays to himself. Reese says he has a great voice. He's very bright." James racked his brain to come up with details about him. "Deacon Gregg was worried about him one time, said that he was clubbing and staying out all night. But, slowly, Johnny changed and got on the choir."

Jay ran his fingers through his hair. "Something is strange about him, Dad. He was acting kind of weird on Sunday with Isabella. Then, today he just comes here to see Isabella, and then she disappears. Something is not right. I don't know where Isabella is or where to look for her."

"I'm sure she'll return." Pastor James went to his son. "I'll call Deacon Gregg and get Johnny's number."

"You do that, Dad. In the meantime, I'm going to ride around. Oh, I'll call Tammy!" Jay took out his cell and dialed the familiar number.

After speaking briefly with Tammy, once again, Jay was stupefied with his missing bride-to-be.

Jay drove around for a while. When dusk revealed itself, Jay was panicky. *Oh God, where is she?*

Around nine o'clock, defeated, Jay finally drove to his parents' home. They, too, fretted over Isabella's whereabouts.

"I finally spoke with Deacon Gregg," Pastor James informed. "Here's Johnny's number."

Snatching it from his father, Jay immediately called him. Frustrated, he left a message on the voice mail.

"Johnny, this is Pastor Jay. Please call me as soon as you get this message. I need to talk with you."

"Something is not right, Dad!"

"Let's just pray." The threesome joined hands and prayed for Isabella.

Before going to bed, Jay and his parents called all the hospitals and even the jailhouse. Isabella was nowhere to be found.

Not a soul slept in the house that night. All of their thoughts and prayers were on Isabella.

Be with Isabella! Esther fretted.

No evil shall befall Isabella, or no plague come near here! Angels encamp all around our daughter! Pastor James prayed.

Hear my prayer, Oh Lord, and hear my cry for help! Isabella is in trouble, don't turn away from her. Don't turn away from me. Answer me quickly, as I call to You. Save and protect, Isabella. Bring her home! Lord, bring her home! Jay fervently begged.

Izzy, where are you?????

Chapter 36

ay awakened after only sleeping for about two hours. He felt exhausted and emotionally drained as he got up. The silence of the morning was deafening. He had no peace, no quietness, no rest, but only turmoil. He sought to trust, but worry crept in.

Where is she, Lord?

Trust Me.

In You Oh, Lord do I put my trust – no matter what! Just send Izzy back home to me – to us.

After dressing, Jay went downstairs and joined his family for breakfast. He couldn't eat. He had no appetite. Food didn't appeal to him at all. Looking at his parents, he knew that they hadn't slept either.

"Leela and Reese are on the way over," Esther stated.

Jay nodded, his heart heavy.

"Did Johnny call you back?" Pastor James asked.

"No, which is strange. Are they both missing, and if so, what's going on?"

"Don't let your mind play tricks on you, son," Esther advised. "I'm sure Isabella isn't with him."

"Your mother is right," Pastor James assured. "God's *got* Isabella. He's brought her too far to leave her now."

"Thanks, Mom and Dad," Jay scooted his chair back. "I'm going to look for her!"

"Lord, guide him to her." Esther prayed aloud.

"You'll find her." Pastor James assured. "God will help you."

"If either of you hears anything, please call me!"

Starting his car, Jay silently prayed. "Father, You know all things. You know Isabella's whereabouts. Holy Spirit, lead and guide my steps. Please take me to her." At first, Jay backed up out of the driveway, not knowing where to go – right or left. He turned right. Driving in presumably circles, for a while, his thoughts went back to the place he met Isabella and then the hotel.

That's it!

Driving over the speed limit, Jay drove out of town to Isabella's former residence…the shady hotel.

After parking, he remembered the old room she had and thought it crazy, but Jay decided he would try. Timidly, he knocked on the door. No one answered. He knocked again. No one answered. Jay could hear the television on, so he knocked harder.

"What do…" Isabella jerked open the door, "you want?"

"You," his heart ached. Her eyes were bloodshot red. Isabella must have cried all night.

Fresh tears came to the surface. Isabella's heart was pounding, strength gone, eyes burning, and she was heartbroken. "You shouldn't be here."

"Neither should you,"

"I belong here." Isabella held onto the door.

"You belong with me." Jay inched his way near her.

She held up her hand. "Please don't."

"What's wrong, Izzy?" Jay knew not to push her. "What did Johnny say to you?"

Her eyes stretched with fear. "How do you know about Johnny?"

"Ms. Marilyn told me he came by to see you. What did he say to you to make you run away from me?"

"I'm not running away from you."

"Sure seems like it. You left without saying one word. I worried all day and all night about you. And so did mom and dad, Leela, Rose, Cassi, Reese, and even Nicolas – the whole family."

"I'm sorry, I didn't mean to worry all of you. I just thought...thought it would be better this way."

"Izzy, please let me come in."

"No."

"Please, Izzy. I don't want to stand out here talking."

Isabella thought about it, looking into his concerned eyes. Halfheartedly, she opened the door wider for him to enter.

Not able to help himself, instantly Jay grabbed her hand and wouldn't let it go. "What happened between you and Johnny?"

"He remembered me from...the bar...my past."

"And..."

"He wanted to finish off where we left off," she felt embarrassed.

"That scumbag!" Jay's nostril's flared. He was angry beyond measure. "How dare he make a pass at you in the church! I'll...clobber him!"

"See, that's not you, Jay! You're not a fighter! You can't go around beating up everybody from my past."

Her words calmed him slightly. "He had no right! He's supposed to be a believer!"

It's not just that Jay," she hesitated, before going on, "...he sort of threatened to tell everybody in the church."

"Let him!" Jay declared, trying to keep his anger in check. *Help me, God!* "Your past is the past, Isabella! You *got* to stop letting the enemy jerk your chains! Stop running scared of people like Johnny!"

"You don't get it!" she snatched her hand away. "I don't want to hurt you or taint the family's name! Everyone thinks so highly of the Cannon family...but with me attached, I will only tarnish the family's name. I can't do that to you. I won't humiliate you."

"Stop that!" Jay wrapped his hands around her upper arms, keeping her from moving. "I thought we were past this, Izzy. I thought you said you love me."

"I do. I love you enough to let you go." Her voice was unsteady. "I'll never love another man...but I just can't hurt you."

"If you leave me, I'll hurt more than a bullet piercing my heart...more than the war...more than losing my best friend, Lewis, more than anything! I need you, Isabella. I don't care what people

281

say about you. I know the real you, and I love you desperately. Please don't let the enemy kill, steal and destroy our relationship all at once."

Isabella sighed at his words. Weren't they the exact words she heard at the gravesite?

"If you love me, then stand up for us, Izzy. I believe in you, and I believe in us, don't you?"

She blinked back the tears, shaking her head. "I just don't want to hurt you, Jay. I can't erase my past. There are many more Johnny's out there. Many more Big Tim's, and the church doesn't shield us from that. Johnny is in the church."

"I don't care. All I care about is you. I told you before that we will confront your past together every time it lifts its ugly head. As long as we're honest and upfront, we'll get through this. And as long as you never leave me, again."

"I love you so much, Jay."

"Enough to marry me?"

"Enough to spend the rest of my life with you?" Isabella intertwined her arms around his neck. "I'm sorry for worrying you."

"Promise me that you'll never run away from me again." Jay needed her assurance more than ever before. The thought of never seeing her again nearly sent him back to where he started – guarded and mistrustful.

"Promise." A feeble smile was all she could muster.

"Don't allow the enemy to use people to put fear into your heart. Fear is simply False Evidence Appearing Real. You've got to walk in Faith – Full Assurance in Trusting Him."

"Be patient with me."

"I will." His brow slightly rose as Jay held her closer. "I wish I could package what I feel for you into little tablets so that the world could sample the divine pleasure I find in you. On second thought, that might not be a good idea because you would become too addictive, and everyone would want one of those tablets."

His sweet words played on the strings of her heart. Impromptu, Isabella pecked his lips, melting like butter in his arms.

"Not good enough," Jay suppressed an amused look.

Boldly, he captured his lips with hers and sealed the promise of her love.

Johnny was shocked when he opened the door and found Pastor Jay standing on his doorstep.

"Um…hi Pastor Jay."

"Johnny," Jay spoke with a hint of edginess. "May I come in?"

"I was just about to leave. I have…have a date."

"It won't take long." The challenge in his voice was unmistakable.

"I don't have the time." Johnny was nervous.

"Make the time!" Jay's temper flared.

"Well…uh…"

Jay squared his shoulders and practically pushed his way inside. He was on a mission, and he wouldn't leave this place without accomplishing the task at hand.

"Isabella tells me that you knew her from her past life." Jay jumped right on in, not beating around the bush. "She tells me that you seem to think that there is some unfinished business between the two of you."

"Unfinished business," Johnny coughed, choking on his words. "We don't have any unfinished business."

"I didn't think so." Jay eyed him closely as he sat on the edge of the couch. "Let me make myself perfectly clear. I may be a pastor, but I am also a man. A man who loves his fiancée, wholeheartedly and I will let nothing or no one hurt her. Isabella has nothing to be ashamed of and no one she has to answer to but God. You know nothing of her past, so you wouldn't understand why she chose to do some of the things she did, but that's none of your business! If you ever threaten to harm her or to expose her or make innuendos about inappropriate propositions ever again, I'll remove the pastoral robe and beat you to a pulp!" Jay stood up.

Johnny did, likewise, stunned by Jay's warnings.

"Do we have an understanding?" Jay stood toe-to-toe with him.

"I didn't…"

"Do we have an understanding?" Jay asked again.

"Yes." Johnny felt like a worm buried in muddy soil.

"Good!" Jay went to the door. "I suggest that you get things right with God before you return to the choir. We all make mistakes." Jay suddenly spoke with gentleness. "I forgive you, and I love you, brother Johnny. We'll be waiting for you with open arms…all of us. We will be praying for you." Jay produced a smile that didn't quite touch his eyes, but the gesture was adequate enough, and then left.

Closing the door behind him, Jay let out a painful sigh. *Thank You, God! I wanted to destroy him, but instead, I offered mercy, as You have done for me, time and time again.*

Chapter 37

What a glorious day that awaited Jay and Isabella. It was a wedding day filled with promises as bright as the sunshine emitting light from the heavens to the earth. Love had led Jay and Isabella with bowstrings of kindness, intertwined with love, which lifted the yoke of anger, bitterness, abuse, pain, and death from their necks. Love had bowed down and cared for them – selflessly – generously – endlessly.

Jay was wide awake when his alarm went off. Stretching, he leaped out of bed with childlike excitement! Today Jay was marrying the most beautiful woman on the face of the earth, inside and outside! He couldn't wait to see her. Today would mark the beginning of a lifetime of memories to be made with the love of his life.

He had a lot to do before the wedding. He wanted to make this day memorable for Isabella. She deserved to be pampered, and it was his pleasure to make that happen.

Quickly, he wrote out a to-do list in preparation for his special day. Afterward, he showered and slipped on a pair of jeans and a sweatshirt. He had already enlisted Reese's help for his morning errands. Reese was picking him up.

Meanwhile, Isabella rested in her bed, thinking about her glorious day. Her heart would not calm down while butterflies floated in her stomach. She sighed with the joy of the likelihood of spending the rest of her life with the man of her dreams. The reality of it all was about to happen.

A knocking at her door chiseled in on her daydreaming.

"Good morning, sleepyhead," Esther entered, bringing in a breakfast tray with a pink rose on the side.

"Oh, how beautiful," Isabella immediately sniffed the rose.

"Jay stopped by early this morning and made me promise to bring this tray and rose to you. He prepared your breakfast."

Isabella's eyes filled with moisture at his thoughtfulness. "Did Jay tell you the significance of pink?"

"No."

"I had pink hair the first time we met."

Esther chuckled.

"He never tried to change me," Isabella spoke through dreamy eyes. "He accepted me as I was and gave me room to become who God wanted me to be."

"Just like his daddy."

"I am so in love with Jay," she beamed. "I want to make him happy."

"Just be yourself." Esther sat down beside her. "Remember, he fell in love with you before your outer appearance changed. He fell in love with you, regardless of your past. I've never seen my son this happy before. Jay was always so serious, never saying much, hardly showing outer emotions. But now I get to hear him laugh and see his eyes light up and witness him ministering God's Word. My cup *runneth* over with joy because God has blessed us with three children who have found helpmates who all love God."

"Oh, Mom, my cup *runneth* over too!" Isabella hugged her, using the endearment of Mom, as Esther encouraged her to do so. "I don't think I can eat a thing. I'm too full already!"

"You must eat. I promised Jay I would make sure that you ate so that when you walked down the aisle, you won't faint before you get a chance to say, 'I do.'" Esther laughed again. "He's so concerned about you."

"He's so thoughtful."

"Just like his daddy."

In her dressing room at the church, Isabella walked in and took a deep breath as she beheld the sight of pink roses everywhere. Jay had filled the room with flowers to remind him of the first time he saw her. Her pink hair would always be their alliance of attraction. Yes, Jay was attracted to Isabella then, even with her pink hair – even the more now in the purity of her loveliness.

"I'm marrying a romantic, for sure!" she covered her mouth.

"My son is just like his daddy." Esther felt proud. "He left a present for you."

"He's spoiling me." Impatiently, Isabella opened the big box. Inside was a note. She read it aloud, "Something old, my mother's heirloom necklace. It signifies every female's tradition of walking down the aisle wearing my mother's great, great, great grandmother's necklace given to her by her husband on her wedding day.

"Something new," she sighed at the little box containing an exquisite diamond bracelet. "May it shine as much as my heart shines for you?

"Something blue. Wear this garter, knowing that I will take pleasure in removing it from your *sexy* legs." Her cheeks burned with a pinkish color matching her flowers.

"Something borrowed." The last box was a laced handkerchief she had often witnessed Esther clutching tightly in her hands every Sunday. "I know you will probably shed happy tears, so mom thought this would be best for you to have near to you.

"Today, my life will never be the same again. We will grow in love, grow in marriage, grow in family, and grow in our hearts. Make room for me, sweetheart, because your heart is where my home will be forever. I love you. See you soon. I can't wait."

Her eyes glistened with fresh tears. "I'm messing up my makeup that Leela worked so hard on."

"You look beautiful," Esther kissed her cheek, "but I'll go get Leela anyhow."

At four o'clock, promptly the wedding began. Cassi, Rose, and Tammy were bridesmaids; Leela was the Maid of Honor. Karl, Chance, and Nicolas were the groomsmen, and Reese was the Best Man.

Mariah, Cassi, and Nicolas' soon-to-be 12-year-old daughter walked down the aisle carrying a lighted candle in Lewis's memory.

Sara, Leela's just-turned two-year-old girl, and Karlton, Cassi's two-year-old boy, came down the aisle ringing the bells. Reese's twins Sandy and Randy walked down, Sandy putting out petals and Randy carrying the Bible.

It was indeed a family affair.

In the vestibule, Pastor James lifted Isabella's veil and said, "Today I am gaining a daughter, of whom I love dearly. From this day forward, it would honor me greatly if you would call me dad, as you already call Esther, mom."

Isabella couldn't speak. She swallowed hard, trying not to cry, and yet her eyes misty with joyful moisture. Allowing his heartfelt words to sink deep, she squeezed his hand.

"My biological father gave me my existence, but you, Dad," she emphasized, "gave me love. I've lost so much, but I have gained the one thing I wanted more than anything," she wiped her eyes, "a family."

Pastor James kissed her on the cheek, used his hanky to dab away her tears, then lowered her veil. "Shall we?" he extended his elbow toward her.

"We shall?" Isabella smiled, slipping her arms in his.

At the sound of the wedding march, Pastor James proudly stepped through the church doors. All eyes turned in their direction.

There Isabella stood so lovely and so pure!

"Wow!" Jay mumbled under his breath as he drank in the sight of her standing at the entrance. So angelic Isabella appeared in her white gown with pink beads on the bodice, which fitted snuggly at the top and flowed outwardly at the bottom. Instead of a large bouquet, she carried the single pink rose Jay had placed on her breakfast tray. With her curly hair up due, she was flawless. Isabella was a princess. It was like a fairytale. She was amazingly gorgeous – a work of art – a masterpiece of beauty.

Isabella bit her lips as her eyes beheld her handsome husband-to-be. Dressed in an all-white tuxedo, with a pink rose in his upper pocket, Jay stood tall and regal! Her Prince Charming. Her betrothed. It couldn't get any better than this.

With each step she took toward him, peace like a river, like a flooding stream, engulfed Jay. He was grinning from ear to ear.

Love radiated in his face, shimmered in his eyes, and burned in his heart.

"Today, we are here to join together James Cannon, Jr. to Isabella Arielle Trevano. Who giveth this bride away?" Joseph Cannon asked, officiating the wedding. Once again, Pastor James wanted to play the father role and not the pastor role.

"Her mother and I do?" Again, Pastor James squeezed her hand and whispered for her ears only. "We love you, daughter."

"I love you, Dad," Isabella whispered back. "I love you, Mom," she mouthed to Esther.

The touching words didn't escape Jay's ears as he witnessed the sincere family connection.

Promptly, Jay took Isabella's hand and lifted it to his lips. His eyes were lost in her beauty. All the love of his heart was shining brightly through. Ignoring protocol, Jay lifted his bride's veil.

"Not now." Pastor Joseph Cannon whispered.

"I can't help it," Jay said, not taking his eyes off of Isabella, "I just want to look at her."

The audience snickered.

"You are so gorgeous," Jay spoke for her ears only.

"And you're so handsome."

Their hearts had synchronizing heartbeats, beating to the tune of true love. Their hearts were already one; the ceremony was just a formality of what God had already joined together.

Esther wiped her eyes as her husband held her tightly. This was their last child to be married, yet it felt no different from the first. Each child had found their soul mates, specifically chosen, and set apart by God for each of them.

Jay's gaze was unyielding. The intensity of his look stirred something deep within her. Today, Isabella felt special. God was shining down on her now, through this man He had given to her to love freely.

A teardrop escaped Jay's eyes. Tears of bliss! "I love you so much."

"I love you, Jay." Her eyes matched his.

Joseph had to fight hard to keep his emotions in check. With all the love surrounding him, he couldn't help but be moved. For truly love had filled the room like a soft blanket, resting on everyone present.

Clearing his throat, Pastor Joseph began, "Today is an exceptional day. When a man and a woman become one in the sight of God, friends, and family." Pastor Joseph proudly conducted the spirit-filled ceremony.

The wedding ceremony was so heartfelt and touching. Reese sang a particular song he wrote just for the couple. Mariah held the lighted candle as Isabella recited a poem she wrote in memory of her brother. Following this, Cassi, Leela, and Mariah dedicated a special dance to the bride and groom. Pastor James Cannon prayed over the couple as they knelt at the altar.

The heartfelt vows, written by the couple, were spoken with love through misty eyes. The two gazed at each other as if they were the only ones in the room. Their personal vows left the congregation overcome with emotions.

In closing, Pastor Joseph gave the decree, "James Cannon, Jr., you may now salute your bride."

With both hands, Jay cupped Isabella's face and tenderly kissed her. Their lips had barely touched, but the surcharge was powerful.

Isabella encircled her arms around his neck and placed a wet kiss upon his lips. She responded to him as a man, not a preacher man.

The audience oohed and awed.

Pulling away, Jay felt a surge of pride that this beautiful woman was now his wife. "Now my life is complete." Jay's love was deep and abiding, constant and tender.

God had removed his heart of stone and gave him a heart of flesh, sprinkled clean and washed in the blood of the Lamb. Now, Jay was free to love and be loved.

Isabella leaned closer and whispered in his ear, "Now we are one." Her index finger brushed his lips tenderly. Jay's whole body lit up like fire.

"Can we skip the reception and go home?" Jay winked.

"Our parents will kill us!"

"You're right." He laced his fingers with hers.

"And now I present to you, Mr. and Mrs. James Cannon." Pastor Joseph announced loudly.

Hand-in-hand they walked down the aisle, each looking intently at the other, oblivious of those around them. This was the beginning of their Hallmark of love.

Chapter 38

Two weeks later, family and friends gathered at the Cannons' home to commemorate Jay's ordination as Assistant Pastor. The mini family reunion consisted of Joseph, Sabrina, Cassi, Karl, and their children, Mariah and Karlton; Reese, Rose, Sandy, and Randy; Leela, Nicolas and their baby Sara, and Bruce Hendrick; Otis and Natalya Mickens, Herman, and his family; Tammy and Chance, Ms. Marilyn, Minister Daniel, Evangelist Browne, Minister Thomas, and a few more close church members.

Esther had the enormous feast catered. The outside closed-in patio was set up with three tables so that everyone could sit together. The area was filled with food, fellowship, and an abundance of love. At the head of one of the tables, James sat with his wife to the right and his immediate family. Everyone else sat at the two adjoining tables. James looked around, basking in the joy of being surrounded by those he loved. He was proud to be a pastor, a husband, a father, a grandfather, a brother, and a friend. God had indeed been good to him.

"You blessed my soul today," Pastor James looked to his left, speaking to Jay. "The message 'Look Up' inspired all of us – Looking to the Hills from where our help comes from. Not looking down at the situation, but up at the One who can solve the situation.

Not looking down at the problem but looking up to the One who can solve every problem."

"I had a little help with that message, Dad." Jay looked to his wife. "Isabella was struggling to keep her head above waters, and God reminded her that she was just looking down, not up."

The newlywed, blissful bride, looked at her husband.

"Everyone here today must remember to keep our eyes focused on Jesus. No matter what happens, God is in control. The water may be deep; the tides may be strong; the shore may seem a long way off, but keep your eyes on Jesus. He won't let you sink. He won't let you drown. He won't let you fall. He's right there with you to hold you, to catch you, and to lift you out of the miry waters of life."

Pastor James paused, carefully choosing his words. "I feel so blessed." He squeezed his wife's hand, tears stinging his eyes, and continued. "My family has expanded. My heart is overjoyed. Today my son has completed the circle. My great grandfather, grandfather, and father preached and then passed the mantel onto Joseph and me. Now, my son, Jay, has joined the lineage of pastors within the Cannon family.

"Son, I am pouring out my life, my calling, and my anointing to you like a drink offering so that when I leave this earth, you will pastor our church."

"Thank God that won't be anytime soon," Jay chimed in. "I have a lot to learn."

"God will teach you." Pastor James grew serious. "He will use you more than He has used me. Today I pass the mantle onto you, as Elijah did to Elisha."

"Dad," Jay felt something in his stomach he couldn't explain.

"It's all well, son. Walk in your purpose," Pastor James smiled and looked at his wife to assure her that all was well.

"Reese is working as Minister of Music in the church, soon to be full-time." Pastor James broke, looking proudly at his middle child. "I've never heard a voice that could match yours, nor have I found anyone who could play the guitar with such an anointing; you make the strings sing. May the sounds of heaven always be in your ears and your heart.

"And Leela, my baby girl, is all grown up," Pastor James adored her. "She has her dance studio but still finds time to direct the lyrical praise dancers at the church. Praise is always in your heart, for it exhibits as you dance before the Lord. Like David, you dance with all your might, with all your soul, forgetting about others…it's just you and Him; and Him and you. How awesome it is to express yourself so uniquely to God in praise. May joy always be in your soul and your life be abundantly blessed."

"Thank you, Daddy," Leela slid her chair back and went to her father. She placed a gentle kiss on his cheek.

"I think this is a good time to share our news." Leela looked at Nicolas. "Our family is going to be getting a new member in seven months."

"Congratulations!" echoed everyone.

"Bless this baby," James laid his hand on Leela's tiny tummy. "May he spread the gospel of Jesus Christ everywhere he goes. And may he be blessed in every area of his life."

"He?" she quested her father, returning to her seat.

"Yes, he," Pastor James didn't waver. "I dreamed of him several weeks ago. I just didn't know which family member would have him.

"Rose and Isabella, you're my daughters. I'm proud of you and grateful for the love you have given to my sons and our family."

Both Rose and Isabella got up and hugged their earthly father.

"My brother, Joseph…"

"Okay, let's not get too mushy," Joseph interceded.

"I just want to say that you're the best brother and my best friend. I love you more than words can say."

"Love you, James."

"I love you, Sabrina, Cassi, Dr. Karl…my wonderful grandchildren, and all my family and friends, ministers…" James was overwhelmed with emotions.

"For 35 years, I have been blessed to have a devoted companion in my life. My lovely wife, Queen Esther," Pastor James affectionately called her, "means the world to me." Pastor James gave Esther a long, stargazing look. "You're more beautiful now than ever. My heart still somersaults when you enter a room."

Esther felt impassioned by his words. His love smothered her with warmth like a hot blazing fire. Her eyes glistened with joy as she went to him. "I love you, James."

"My love for you will never die." He held her hand affectionately, gazing into her eyes as if they were the only ones in the room. "Nothing can ever separate us…our love will remain forever, even through death." James leaned over and kissed her on the cheek and pecked her lips.

"Break it up!" Reese blurted while the twins laughed. "Save all that mushy stuff for later."

"Don't be jealous." Pastor James gladly took the bait. "Just be happy."

"I am." Reese grabbed Rose's hand. "The apple doesn't fall far from the tree."

"That's right, Dad." Jay chimed in. "Leela has a good man, Reese has a good wife, and well…I think I have the best of them all," Jay beamed at his blushing wife.

"Oh hush." Leela shoved him.

"Let's not go there!" Cassi chimed in, "I think God smiled on me extra when he made sure Leela hit Karl."

"I know you didn't!" Leela stood up, smiling. She and Cassi always had a way of muddying the waters, in love and fun.

"We've done well." James broke it up, looking at Esther. "Joseph's family is happy. All our children are happy. Like arrows in the hand of a warrior, so *are* the children of one's youth. Happy *is* the man who has his quiver full of them." Pastor James quoted the passage of Psalms.

Esther looked at her husband, feeling happy and yet uneasy. Everything in their lives seemed to be perfect – too perfect. Was this the calm before the storm? *Lord, prepare our hearts for whatever comes.*

"A family that prays together stays together," Pastor James spoke again. "Let's end this night with family prayer."

Everyone bowed their heads as the patriarch of the family led them in prayer. At the closing of the prayer, they sang the familiar family song written by Reese when he was eight years old.

> *"A family that prays together*
> *Will always Stay together*
> *Love has united our hearts*

Nothing can keep us apart
We are One...We are One!"

Early the following day, just before dawn, Jay was awakened out of his sleep. He awakened to a sound...an unusual sound. *Is that a bell?* He listened carefully. Nothing. And then again, he heard a soft bell. Still, staying in one of the church's apartments, Jay and Isabella hadn't found a house to call home yet.

Jay!

He looked over at Isabella; she was sound asleep.

Jay!

He slid the covers off, slipped out of bed, and went into the living room.

Jay!

"Yeah, Lord."

Do You truly love Me more than anything?

"Yes, Lord," Jay said, "You know that I love You."

Feed my lambs.

Jay paced the room, feeling the presence of the Lord with him.

Jay, do you truly love Me?"

"Yes, Lord, You know that I love You."

Take care of My sheep.

"I will, Lord."

"Do you love Me?"

Jay was hurt like the Apostle Peter because the Lord asked him the third time. "Lord, You know all things; You know that I love You."

Feed my sheep.

Jay dropped to his knees, surrendering to the call on his life. "Lord God, I will do whatever You want me to do. I will say whatever You want me to say. I'll go wherever You want me to go. I am Yours! I belong, completely and totally to You. Here I am, Lord, use me!"

Jay was a changed man. God had destroyed the yoke from his neck and broken the shackles of his heart so that he could serve Him freely. Jay was a broken man when he returned home from the war in need of the Potter to remold His clay. For only He could put the broken pieces of Jay's life back together again, making him over and making him whole again.

Many are called, but few are chosen.

When Isabella awakened to an empty bed, she found Jay sleeping on the couch with his Bible in his hands.

"Hey sleepyhead," she gently shoved him.

"Hey, Baby," Jay forced himself up. "What time is it?"

"Seven," she answered. "You're supposed to go to Heaven's Soldiers…remember for Monday morning service?"

"Yeah," Jay yawned.

"Tired of me already?" she placed her hands on her hips. "Sleeping on the couch. What's that all about?"

"Oh, I'll never get tired of you," Jay pulled her down to himself. "Just felt the urge to pray and spend time with the Lord. Must have fallen asleep."

"I better get used to this," she smiled, attempting to get up.

"Oh no, you don't," he snuggled her closer to him.

"Jay, you have to get ready," she playfully swatted at him. "Your coffee is ready. Do you want me to bring you a cup now, or do you want to shower first?"

"I'll shower first," he pecked her on the cheek.

"I made some waffles. Do you think we have time to eat breakfast together?"

"We'll make time." Jay winked. "Dad always sat with us for breakfast before starting his day. Even when we were grown and out of the house, mom and dad never stop enjoying breakfast together. That's a family tradition I always want to keep."

"Me too."

The phone rang.

"I bet that's dad." Jay hurried to the kitchen phone. "He probably thinks I forgot about the elderly home, even though he mentioned it three times last night." Jay chuckled.

Isabella watched her husband while he answered the phone. Instantly she knew something was wrong, as Jay turned ghostly pale. Isabella rushed to his side, allowing her small frame to support his rigid body. She thought Jay was about to collapse for sure.

"I'll be right over." Jay slammed the phone down.

"What's wrong, Honey?"

He couldn't speak. Tears collided down the sides of his face without ending.

He slumped to the floor, and Isabella followed him. Now she was crying and didn't even know why.

"What is it, Jay? You're scaring me."

"Dad...dad..." he choked, "he's...gone..."

She shrieked. "Gone?"

"In his sleep," Jay wept. "Mom turned over; he looked so peacefully she said," Jay gulped, swallowing hard. "He had fallen asleep with the Bible in his hands...just like me."

Death came like a thief in the night, unexpected and quiet. Surely, Pastor James knew that his time was nigh. For last night his dad had passed the mantle onto him and blessed his siblings with words of prosperity and encouragement.

Jay rested his head upon his wife's bosom and cried. Today his pastor, mentor, friend, and earthly father, all rolled up into one, had gone home to be with the Lord. He had gone to sleep reading his Word and awaken in the arms of the Living Word, Jesus Christ. What a way to go!

Life is like the morning mist, like the early dew that disappears without a trace. Here one minute and gone the next. Pastor James Cannon's home-going service was a celebration of the life he had lived and now his eternal new life. The patriarch of the family had gone before them...always leading the way to something greater.

Though the family mourned, Esther brokenhearted, they also rejoiced in hope, knowing, and believing that they would see Pastor James again. Suddenly, in the night, he was taken from them, but God had blessed them with so many memories that would somehow soothe and comfort them in days, months, and years ahead.

There was no standing room in the church, as people from miles and miles came to pay respect to a mighty man of God. Outside, people waited, hoping to get one last glimpse of his body.

Songs of jubilee filled the atmosphere. Words of honor and praise came from the lips of men and women, young and old, whose lives had been genuinely touched by Pastor James.

Reese saluted his father with a song he had written just for this occasion. Through tears, he sang, and yet, he rejoiced! His father had taught them that this life here on earth was just a dress-rehearsal of what was yet to come!

After rendering the eulogy for his father, Jay laid down his Bible and looked at the congregation. Collecting his thoughts and stabilizing his composure, he smiled.

He felt as if he had finally fit into his dad's shoes. Not too snug. Not too big. But just right. He knew his dad was smiling down on him at that very moment. He didn't know whether to laugh or cry – he ended up doing both.

"Though we all will greatly miss my father, the backbone of this church, life will go on. Dad wouldn't want us to grieve long but to rejoice that His name is written in the Book of Life. In time, we all will find hope again. And once again, the sounds of joy will be heard in this church and in our family. My father lived what he preached. He was a faithful follower of Jesus Christ. Today, we celebrate his life, the man who followed in the steps of Jesus. Steps that took him back to the One he was following. He followed the footprints as long as he could on earth, which led to his ultimate destination – Jesus Christ! Remember, for Believers, death is not an ending. It's just the beginning of eternal life with our Savior.

"May God keep you. Bless you. Be gracious to you. Shine His light upon you, and hold you in the very palms of His hands," Jay quoted his father's familiar benediction. "May His peace guide you and may His joy strengthen you and May His love overflow in your life to others. Until we meet again, God bless you."

At the end of the day, Jay, Leela, Reese, and Cassie shared their feelings of loss and happiness.

"I remember when being a 'PK' or pastor's daughter was the most horrible thing," Leela stated.

"It was like being a known criminal with a record. Everyone was always watching you, waiting for you to slip up," Cassi interjected, "which I did so many times."

"Dad was such an honorable man. Everybody knew him, so we had to be on our P's and Q's at all times." Reese stated. "But I wouldn't trade being a pastor's son for anything in the world."

"Now all I can say," Jay began, "it's a privilege to be following in the footsteps of my dad. Now I am a Pastor, but even greater than that…I'm a *pastor's son too!*

Epilogue

Where do I fit in, Lord? Esther sat on the front row of the empty church, in the dark, which is how she felt – in the dark. Esther knew she had to find her way back to the light of joy, but her heart was raw. Thirty-five years of marriage to a wonderful man, and now she had to adjust to life without her beloved James.

It had been six months since her husband had passed. Phone calls, family and friends' visitations, cards, and well-wishes had all decreased. Esther felt so alone, even though her immediate family and James' brother Joseph and family were faithfully by her side.

Life, as she knew before, had forever changed. She wasn't even the First Lady anymore. Isabella held that position. At times, even that was hard. Stepping aside, allowing Isabella to grow and flourish as the First Lady of the church, nicked at her heart. Feeling unneeded in the church was difficult. She went from being so busy helping James run the church to feeling as if she was walking on eggshells, in helping now.

Of course, Isabella did everything possible to keep Esther involved, still feeling uncertain of herself and her role in the church. However, Esther felt like a third wheel. Nobody said it or even thought it. Yet, Esther owned it.

Even her home wasn't her home anymore since Jay and Isabella moved in, not wanting her to be alone. Yet, even with them all living together in the home her husband labored hard to give her,

Esther felt homeless and helpless. She didn't even fit in the place that once meant so much to her.

How do I move on? Perhaps, my time is over as well. Maybe, I shall soon join my James, and we both will walk around heaven all day together. No more tears. No more toils. No more pains. No more brokenness. No more...death. I miss him so much. They say time heals all wounds, but I don't think there is any amount of time that can heal my broken heart. We were one – till death do us part – and death has parted us. Now, I'm half of a woman. Lord, here I am. Take me, too!

For everything, there is a season, and a time for every matter under heaven: a time to be born, a time to die; a time to plant, and a time to pluck up what is planted; a time to kill, and a time to heal; a time to break down, and a time to build up; a time to weep, and a time to laugh; a time to mourn, and a time to dance.

You will heal. I will build you up. You will laugh more than you cry. And you will dance again!

Not without my James!

Dear Reader,

The life of Jay and Isabella parallels so many of our lives. Jay struggled with the aftermath of war and to surrender to the call of God upon his life. Isabella suffered from an abusive past and the choices she made resulting from her past. Sure our struggles may have a different name from theirs, but we struggle with issues and consequences, which can either take us over or under. If we follow the analogy of not looking down – recognizing that our heads are above water, but we keep looking down. We just need to put our eyes on the right thing. Look up! Look to Jesus Christ – the Author and Finisher of our faith.

As I was writing the conclusion novel in Pastor Cannon's Series, I had no idea that death would knock on Pastor James Cannon's doors, the patriarch of the family. It seemed sad to me. I said to God, "I don't want this series to end sadly," and He assured me that death doesn't have to end in sadness but in joy. Celebration! Celebrate the life of a man who followed in the steps of Jesus...steps that took him back to the one he was following. James followed long, hard, doing what he was called to do. He followed the steps as far as he could go on earth, leading to his ultimate destination – Jesus Christ. Isn't that the goal? Ultimately to be with Jesus. This is not our eternal home. God wants us not to see death as a tragic event but as a triumphant destination. Not as an ending but as a new beginning. When we cross over from this earthly life to our everlasting life, we truly began to live! No more pain. No more sorrows. No more hurt! No more death! Death is inevitable for all, but eternal life is not. Choose life here, and then you will have a better life there – with Jesus!!!!!

We may weep and cry for those whom we loved, but joy will come in the morning. It will come into your heart. God said so. Believe it!

Live a full life! Laugh often! Love all the time! Then when your name is called in heaven, you will have no regrets!

Rai Lindsay-Wallace

P.S. Writing the Pastor Cannon Series has been so exciting and encouraging for me. However, the Pastor Love Series will continue the journey, expanding the family. In the first book of the series, Esther Cannon will discover that her life is not over. Although she is a widower, losing her first and only love, God still had work for her to do. Esther will have the doors of joy, healing, forgiveness, and living opened to her. However, the choice is up to Esther whether she walks in or stays on the outside looking in.